THE
KING'S
CHOSEN

BLOOD TIES

THE
KING'S
CHOSEN

BOOK I

BLOOD TIES

L. WAITHMAN

GREENLEAF
BOOK GROUP PRESS

Published by Greenleaf Book Group Press
Austin, Texas
www.gbgpress.com

Distributed by Greenleaf Book Group

For ordering information or special discounts for bulk purchases, please contact Greenleaf Book Group at PO Box 91869, Austin, TX 78709, 512.891.6100.

Design and composition by Greenleaf Book Group
Cover design by Greenleaf Book Group
Cover images used under license from ©Shutterstock.com/owpower225
Cover illustration by Carrie-Sue Kay
Map design by Carrie-Sue Kay

Publisher's Cataloging-in-Publication data is available.

Print ISBN: 978-1-62634-922-3

eBook ISBN: 978-1-62634-923-0

Part of the Tree Neutral® program, which offsets the number of trees consumed in the production and printing of this book by taking proactive steps, such as planting trees in direct proportion to the number of trees used: www.treeneutral.com

Printed in the United States of America on acid-free paper

21 22 23 24 25 26   10 9 8 7 6 5 4 3 2 1

First Edition

To my dad. For telling me stories as
a child and inspiring me to do the same.

AUTHOR'S NOTE

It was when I let my mind wander some years ago that I met Lucas. He walked in front of me behind a circus wagon on a sandy road that left the forest. A castle appeared in the distance. I cannot remember what it was that caught my attention. What made this image different from all the others I have had? Maybe it was Lucas's young age, the circus wagon, the castle, or the sizeable white goat he was leading into the high grass? Perhaps, it was a combination of all four? I watched Lucas as he allowed the goat to nibble on the wildflowers while more circus wagons were passing him on their way to the castle. Then I heard his name called, and he looked up. I knew that he was no ordinary boy at that moment. His life was a mystery, his journey unknown, and I had only seen a glimpse of it. Intrigued by what I saw and wanting to know more, I set out to write his story. For that, I had to go to the beginning, to when it all began . . .

LORD HAMMOND'S CASTLE

BLACK LOG INN

KING ITAN'S CASTLE

LORD ARON'S CASTLE

MONASTERY

BLACKSMITH'S FORGE

KILLEAND'S CASTLE

MELOC'S CASTLE

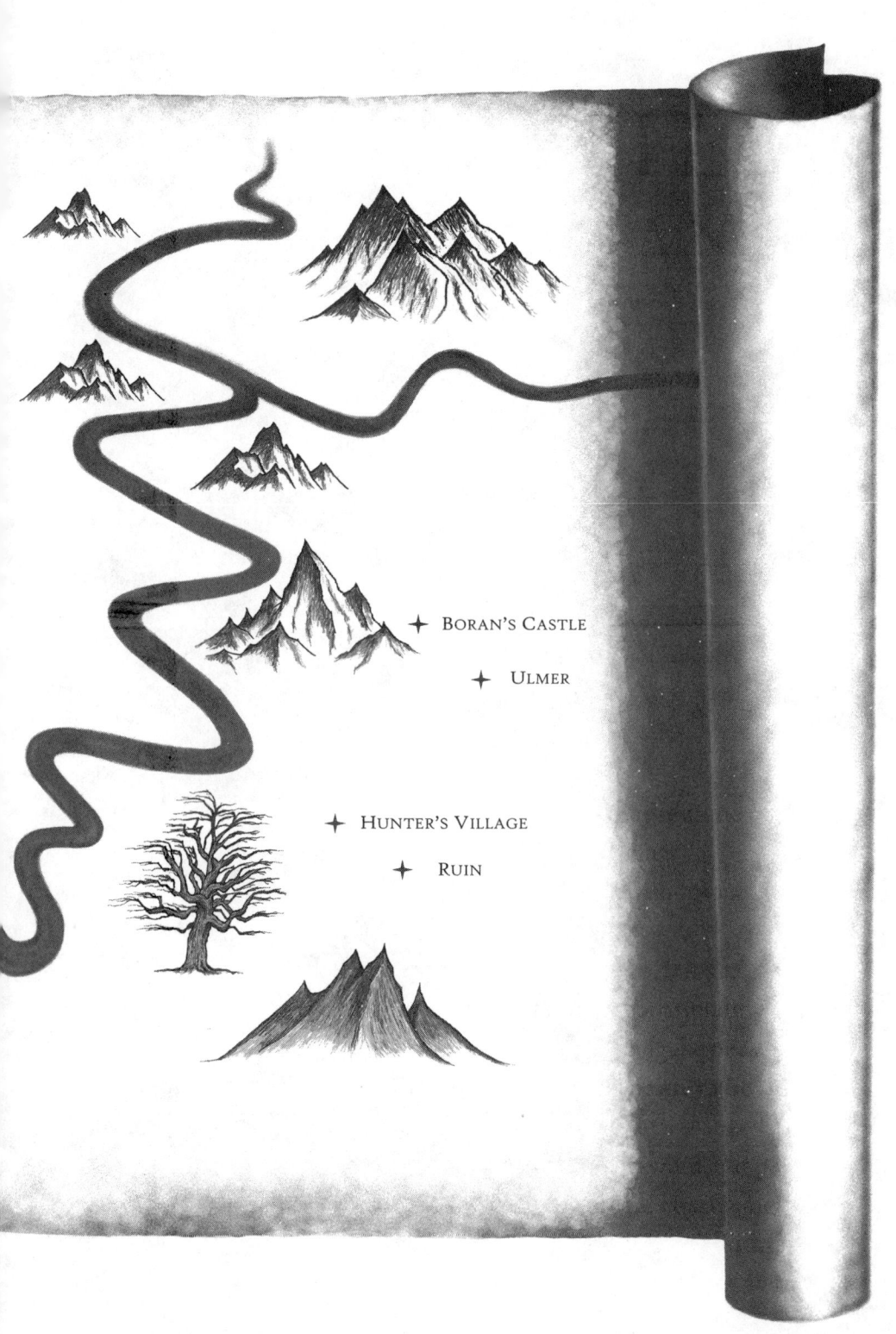

BORAN'S CASTLE

ULMER

HUNTER'S VILLAGE

RUIN

CHAPTER 1

Lucas sat with his feet dangling off the table, watching as his father pulled a piece of glowing-hot steel from the fire and placed it on the anvil. His eyes followed the orange sparks that were flying off with every hit of the hammer and disappearing just as quickly, as if into thin air. It was hard to imagine that the length of steel, still thick and rough, would become a gleaming sword once it was finished. He held his own sword in his hands, one that his father had crafted for Lucas's ninth birthday. He waved it through the air. It was half the size of a real sword, but perfect in weight for him, and he enjoyed fending off the seemingly endless supply of invisible villains.

His father plunged the steel in a barrel of water to cool it off and smiled. "Who are you fighting this time?" he asked, wiping the sweat off his face with a cloth.

"Hunters," answered Lucas, stabbing another enemy. "They come from across the wild river and are big and strong. Like bears! Did you know they can remove a man's head from his body with only their hands?"

"Hunters, eh?" mumbled his father. "Where did you learn about them?"

"The village elder told me," said Lucas, standing up on the table to strike one last time. "He said that it's King Itan's responsibility to keep the hunters from coming and raiding the land, and that there are boys in the king's army who are just like me—he thinks I should report to the king when I turn ten."

His father frowned. "What made him say that you are like those boys?" he asked. "Did you get into another fight with the village kids?"

"No, Father," answered Lucas. "They avoid me now." The blacksmith's forge, where he lived, stood two miles outside the village along the main road, and Lucas had never felt accepted by the village kids. His father had moved to the village after Lucas's mother died when he was born. With no family in the area, they were treated as outsiders. A group of older kids had liked to remind him of this whenever they saw him by himself. Most of the time he had ignored their taunts. He preferred to walk away, as his father had instructed him to do. Except, the last time, one of the boys had picked up a stone and thrown it after him.

Lucas had no idea how he had been able to avoid it. It happened so fast. A surge of energy had come over him when he had heard the whizzing sound behind him—he reacted by turning instantly on his heels. In the same movement, he had raised his hand and caught the stone. He remembered a fury welling up deep inside of him and the instinctive desire to throw it back. It wasn't a feeling he had ever felt before. He had stood still, with stone in hand, unsure of what to do. If he threw it, he knew he would not miss. The boys had stared at him—their eyes wide, and mouths dropped open. Then they had slowly backed away from him. As he watched them leave, so did every bit of energy in his body, and he had collapsed on the ground.

His father picked up the piece of steel from the barrel again and put it back in the fire for a while before letting the hammer loose on it a second time. His face looked worried—a look Lucas had noticed more and more since that day with the village boys. Whenever Lucas

2

returned from his adventures in the countryside, his father questioned him as to where he had been.

His father let out a deep sigh before putting the hammer down and walking over to a different table. His long, quick strides told Lucas he was not pleased with him.

"I have told you to stay away from the village," his father said, picking up the sword he had finished the day before and wrapping it in cloth. "It only leads to trouble, and it's clear the village elder is putting wild ideas into your head. Hunters may be feared because of their appearance and how they can sneak up on a man without making a sound. Their muscular bodies and fur clothing make them look like something untamed and wild, but they are normal people like you and me. As for those boys he speaks of . . . they are specially selected at a young age because of their heritage, their ability to fight, and the special bond they have with each other."

"But I *can* fight!" cried Lucas.

His father walked over to him and lifted him high up into the air before placing him back on the ground. Even though he was getting a little big, it was still one of the many things his father did that Lucas always very much enjoyed. "Yes," he said with a proud smile on his face. "I know you can fight, but trust me when I say you are not like those boys. You do not carry their bloodline, but there is good in that. Maybe you will choose to join the king when you are older or perhaps you will stay here with me and become the best bladesmith ever. That way, you can make swords for the king, instead of having to use them against real people."

Lucas shook his head. He admired his father and enjoyed watching him forge steel into things of magic, but it was not something he felt he wanted to do when he grew up.

"Come now," coaxed his father, staring into his eyes with a look that always softened Lucas. "You have a job to do." He strapped a leather belt around the wrapped sword and fastened it to Lucas's back. "Time for you to deliver this to the monastery. And play it safe, please. No exploring today or leaving the path. It worries me that the village elder has already started taking notice of you and soon, the wrong sort of people may do as well."

"Yes, Father," Lucas managed to muster, and he stood straight as an arrow, waiting for his father to check that the sword was secure. "But what do you mean? What kind of people?"

"Just do as I say, son," his father told him, and gave his hair one quick ruffle before letting him dart out the back door.

Loose rock rolling under his heels, Lucas ran up the winding path towards the whitewashed stone monastery that resided on the cliff above his house. If he ran all the way, he could make it in twenty minutes or less, but often he took his time to stop whenever he saw something interesting. He could never get enough of watching a dung beetle roll a large ball of animal dung in a straight line, regardless of any obstacles put in its way. This time, however, he skipped over any beetles on his path and kept running—his father's words still occupying his mind. There had to be something his father was not telling him.

He was exhausted when he finally made it to the monastery, but marched right up to the large wooden door, knocked, and waited.

As he steadied his breath, he could hear the shuffling of footsteps behind the door, and a monk peeked at him through the little hatch high above him. Lucas listened to the clunky turning of a key and, eventually, the door swung open. When the monk bent down to unstrap the sword from his back, Lucas noticed movement inside and strained his neck to see. There, in the somewhat dim light, a man stood in the shadows. He wore a red satin robe with gold trim, and his head was shaved. His eyes were different, and his brown skin had a glow to it. He looked nothing like the monks Lucas had seen walking in the village, or the ones who always opened the door at the monastery. Lucas watched this strange monk step forward and take possession of the sword after it was removed from his back. He then disappeared into the shadows soon after.

"Who was that?" Lucas asked the monk who stood near the door. Lucas had taken a step forward to see more, but he was gently pushed back, and without a word, the door was quickly shut before him. For a moment, he stood staring at the closed door, but then turned abruptly and ran alongside the wall.

During the times he had played in the area, he had often heard noises coming from inside, and he wondered if the swords he delivered had anything to do with that. He ran around the outside of the monastery until he came to a part of the back wall where vines had started to grow recently. They had not quite reached the top of the wall yet, but Lucas started to climb anyway.

When he ran out of vines, he reached for the top and, digging toes and fingers into crevices in the rock, pulled himself up the rest of the way. From where he was positioned, he looked over an open courtyard, which was empty aside from a few wooden benches and some crates stacked neatly beside a stone wall. Lying as still as he could on the flat top of the wall, he listened to the noises coming from farther away. He then stood and began to run along the top of the wall, making his way past two other courtyards until he came to the one where the noises had come from—there he saw a large group of monks, all in gold-colored robes. They stood in rows with their backs to him, and each man was holding a longsword. When he saw the monk whom he had seen standing in the shadows by the door enter, Lucas crouched down in order to better hide himself.

He knew it was wrong to be spying like he was, and wondered what would happen if they saw him. He shivered at the thought that they might hurt him, or tell his father. Then he would have to face the consequences at home. He didn't know which would be worse, a clout on his ear or his father's deep disappointment. Lucas hoped that the wall was high enough that he couldn't be seen—he was intrigued by what he saw below him and wanted to know who they were and what they were doing.

The strange monk holding Lucas's father's sword took his place in front of the group with his back towards them, and began demonstrating a series of unusual moves. He made a slow step forwards, backwards, to the side, and let the sword follow in sweeping motions. He was much older than the group of monks behind him who diligently copied his every movement. Lucas stood in awe as he watched the group moving their swords through the air and taking up one stance after another. He watched until he was afraid he would be discovered and quickly went back the way he came.

Unable to shake what he had seen from his thoughts, and even his dreams that night, he chose to return the following day around the same time. His heart pounded in his chest as he climbed the wall, and he could already hear faint noises coming from the courtyard. The same group of monks had gathered, and the same mysterious man was leading them. Lucas lay flat on the wall and watched them closely, studying their every move. He left again before they finished but knew he would have to come back. Every fiber of his being told him so.

Lucas was reaching for the latch on the back door a few days later when he heard his father's voice behind him, stopping him in his tracks.

"Where are you off to?" asked his father.

Lucas turned around and looked up into his father's face. "Nowhere," he answered.

"There is no such thing as 'nowhere'," said his father, "and you have been leaving the house at the same time for the past four days."

Thinking quick on his feet, Lucas tried to come up with an innocent explanation for his regular departures. "I found a fox den," he said. "Just off the path that leads to the monastery. The little ones come out to play in the afternoon and I go to watch them."

His father narrowed his eyes as he stared down at him, but then nodded and reached for the door to open it. "Just be careful," he said. "Don't get too close. Even small cubs can leave a nasty bite."

"I will, Father," said Lucas as he darted out the door. He would have to leave at different times from now on if he didn't want to rouse further suspicion.

The more Lucas watched the monks, the more he felt that he wanted to move along with them when they did and, after two weeks, he couldn't help standing up on the wall behind them and mimicking their elaborate routine. When it dawned upon him that he was able to keep up, to move the way they did, he felt a warm glow spread through his body. He had to remind himself that he was not one of them, and should not get caught. There was a sense of ritual in all that Lucas observed, and he imagined that what the monks did, they did in secret. He did his best not to be seen and always left before they finished. He began practicing at home, behind the woodshed of his house. He should have known, however, that his father would take notice that he was taking his sword outside and come to see what he was up to.

Late one morning, he had just performed the first sequence of moves and was taking a break when he noticed his father leaning against the corner of the shed—arms folded in front of his chest, a stern look on his face. Lucas's heart started beating faster.

"Nice moves," his father commented. "Anyone been teaching you?"

"Thank you," answered Lucas. "I am just perfecting what you taught me." He hated lying.

"Hm," mumbled his father. "It has been a while since I taught you, but I don't think we had gotten that far yet." There was a moment of silence before he continued. "You have not been going back to the village, have you?"

Lucas shook his head. "You told me not to."

"Have you been anywhere else I should be aware of, apart from that fox den you told me about?"

"No," answered Lucas. He knew he had responded too quickly when his father's eyes narrowed. He looked away briefly to stop his face from reddening and pretended to be interested in the chatter from the chickens in their coop.

His father seemed to think for a moment, then nodded and pushed himself away from the shed. "Here," he said, stepping behind him. "I noticed you were bending your wrist slightly." Lucas could feel his father's warm breath on his neck when he leaned over to put Lucas's arm in the right position. "Keep your wrist in line with your forearm and let your shoulder take the weight," his father directed. "Now, when you are ready . . . cut down and forward."

"Did your father teach you how to fight?" asked Lucas, making several cuts through the air with his sword.

"He did, yes."

"Was he a blacksmith, like you?"

"No, he wasn't," answered his father. "And I only became one when I got you to look after."

"Was he a warrior?" asked Lucas. He couldn't think of any other profession requiring the need of a sword. No farmers, or tradespeople he had ever seen carried swords, and he never saw any children in the village being taught how to fight.

"Something like that," answered his father.

Lucas looked up into his father's face. There had been a hint of sadness in his voice, and he could see the same reflecting in his eyes. He realized his father had never talked about his past before and now understood why. "Did your father die fighting for the king?" he asked.

"Not everyone dies fighting *for* a king, Lucas," answered his father. "Sometimes, people die *because* of a king."

"Did King Itan kill him?" asked Lucas. He had only heard good things about King Itan from the people in the village, and his father had never given the impression he felt any differently when they had talked about him wanting to join the king's army. It was hard to believe that King Itan had been responsible for his grandfather's death. He was therefore pleased when he saw his father shake his head. Lucas wanted to ask which king he was referring to then, but his father had stepped back and started to walk away.

"I have work to finish," his father called back, half looking over his shoulder, "and you should go and tend to the chickens. By the noise they are making, it doesn't sound like you fed them this morning."

Lucas looked towards the chicken coop where the chickens were aimlessly wandering up and down behind the cane fence and sighed. Feeding them wasn't the only chore he had skipped that morning in favor of wanting to practice. With the sun already high in the sky, he'd better hurry. He didn't want to miss the monk's afternoon practice session.

Out of breath from doing his chores in record time and running up the path, Lucas stared at the back wall of the monastery in disbelief. The wall was bare, the vines that he had used to climb up no longer there. Perhaps, he thought, the monks knew he had been watching them. But did that matter enough to deter him? He looked around to see if there was something else he could use to get himself up on the wall. He found some sturdy fallen branches in the forest nearby and started dragging them, one by one, towards the wall. One of his favorite things to do at home was to build hideouts behind his house, and his father had shown him how to use branches to make strong walls.

He leaned three of the strongest and longest branches against the stone wall and intertwined others in between, until he had built steps that could hold his weight. He had soon built a structure high enough to climb.

Once he had reached the courtyard, Lucas thought he saw the leading monk glance upwards in his direction and remained flattened against the top of the wall until he determined he had imagined it, since practice continued without pause. But when he returned the next day, the branches were nowhere to be found.

Staring at the empty space where his structure had been, he let out a deep sigh and then remembered the rope ladder his father kept in their shed. It had a large iron hook at the end that he could swing over the wall, and he could take it back home with him each day.

He was pleased that he'd finally found a way to easily scale the wall and smiled as he climbed the ladder.

His joy, however, was short lived. Upon his return from watching the monks, the rope ladder had disappeared. He had a very risky and tedious climb down off the wall before he could start making his way home. But this gave him an idea for how he could make his way up the wall without any assistance from ladders or stacked branches. Determined not to be defeated, Lucas studied the walls the next day until he eventually found holes big enough to get some grip for climbing.

He felt more comfortable than ever climbing with his hands, rather than relying on something that could snap or fray.

He knew the monks were aware of his presence, but since they did not outwardly look at him or chase him off, he kept attending the sessions. After a full month of observing and practicing, he became more confident in his moves. What drove him was his desire to be as skilled as the monks in the courtyard below him.

He decided it was time to bring along his own sword, but performing the right moves with a sword in his hand while balancing on the wall was more difficult than he thought it would be, and he nearly lost his footing. He wobbled backwards, catching himself at the last moment, with his heart feeling as if it was lodged in his throat. The unexpected movement, and the way his feet had to scuffle to steady his body, caused little stones to crumble off the wall, which made noise as they tumbled onto the ground below. He froze when he saw the monks stop and turn to look at him, the leader of the group giving him an intense stare. When Lucas saw that the older monk was motioning for him to climb down the wall and come to him, he began to tremble.

Fearing a good beating, he was hesitant and considered disobeying. He turned and examined his escape route down the wall, but decided he would rather take his punishment here than have the monks arrive at his house and tell his father what he'd been up to. He took a deep breath and lowered himself onto his stomach. The older monk was standing at the base of the wall when Lucas jumped the last bit down, landing in a crouched position, and it wasn't long before he felt himself being pulled up by the collar of his shirt.

Lucas shuddered and braced himself for punishment when he looked up into the monk's face. Without a word, he was swiftly taken past the group of men, all the way to the front, where he was turned to face the same direction as everyone else. A monk sidestepped to make space for him. Lucas was shown how to grip his sword correctly with two hands. How to hold it away from his body with the pommel right above his belly button and his left foot behind his right foot. When the monk was finally satisfied with Lucas's stance, he stepped back.

"You have been watching us for a while now," the monk said in a stern voice. "Show us what you can do."

Still shaken from having been caught, Lucas stood frozen with his hands around the pommel of the sword. He felt the eyes of the other monks on him. Afraid to disobey, he closed his eyes and pretended to be at his father's house, where he felt safe, and no one was watching. He then took a deep breath and slowly started to go through the stances as he had memorized them. When he finished, the monk gave him a satisfactory nod and took his place back in front of the group again. Lucas looked around him. The other monks had taken up their positions as well. Confused, but happy to finally be standing among them, Lucas followed their moves when they continued their practice. They behaved as if he wasn't even there, and nothing could have made him happier, for it meant he was one of them at last.

He stayed until practice was over, then waited patiently while the other monks filed out, staying in one place until the leader came up to him and then guided him through the monastery, towards the exit.

"I am known as Father Ansan here," the monk told him. He motioned to the front door, where they now stood, and added, with a wink, "And up until recently, this was our only entrance to the monastery!"

"I'm sorry," said Lucas. "I promise to never climb the wall again. But can I come another time, Father?" asked Lucas, when the door was opened for him to leave.

"I admire your ambition and determination," said Father Ansan kindly, "but I am afraid this is not a place for a young boy. Now that I have shown you exactly what to do, you can continue practicing at home."

Lucas hung his head and stared at the patterned tile below his feet. "I understand."

He felt Ansan's hand on his shoulder and the weight of the monk's eyes as he stared down at him. "I need to talk to Einar, your father," he said. "Can you ask him to come and see me tomorrow?"

His father never questioned Lucas as to how he'd come by the message that the monks wished to speak to him the following afternoon. Lucas guessed that his father assumed it was for a new order of swords, perhaps one that they would have to describe to him in person or draw up, and they went together up the path the following day.

They were escorted in and left to wait by the entrance. Before long, Father Ansan came to meet them.

"Thank you for coming," said Father Ansan, and held his hand out to greet his father.

His father returned the greeting and asked if his latest sword had met their expectations.

"Your swords come from true craftsmanship and never disappoint," answered Father Ansan, "but I have not asked you here today to talk about your work. There is something else we need to discuss. Privately."

The monk's eyes fell briefly on Lucas and Lucas felt his body tense up. Father Ansan directed his father to a room where they could speak in private, and Lucas was instructed to wait outside. Lucas avoided his father's eye by quickly doing as he was asked and sat down on the floor outside the room. He suspected his father would be informed about his visits, and he was not looking forward to having to face him when he came out! He tried to see if he could hear anything and put his ear against the door. The two men were speaking quietly at first, their words muffled, but then his father raised his voice slightly. "I understand," Lucas heard him say, "but I was told that this is where he belongs. Only the order of warrior monks can prepare him for what he is to become. It's why we came here, and why we have stayed all these years. He has been accelerating in his ability to grasp all of the concepts and skills taught to him, far beyond that of any normal boy in the last year, and his senses are heightening. Surely that must be a sign that they were right and that he is the one the people will come to follow?"

Father Ansan replied, but Lucas could not hear him clearly, and his father had lowered his voice again as well.

Lucas sighed and pulled his legs up in order to rest his head on his knees. His father's words were confusing. He closed his eyes and focused on his breathing. A moment later, the door opened, and he jumped up when his father stepped out.

"They tell me you've been sneaking over here for weeks!" scolded his father. "Climbing the walls and nearly killing yourself yesterday?"

Lucas lowered his head in shame. "I'm sorry," he said softly when he saw Father Ansan standing in the door opening watching him. "I won't do it again."

His father pulled him to the side and bent down, bringing himself to Lucas's level.

"You should be in so much trouble over this," he said quietly, "but it appears you have impressed Father Ansan. He has invited you to come and practice every afternoon from here on out."

Lucas's eyes lit up and he looked into his father's face to see if he was serious.

"Is this really what you want?" his father continued. "It will mean hard work and no play. You will have to follow all their rules—Father Ansan has made it quite clear that if you can't, you'll be asked to leave and not invited back."

Lucas nodded. He felt a little bit dizzy. It was hard to believe that what his father was saying was real. "I understand. I will listen and do everything they tell me to do."

His father raised himself up and looked down at Lucas. "I still expect that you get all your chores done in the morning. And I need you home before dark every day. No exceptions," his father said firmly, before surprising Lucas by heading to the door. Was he going to leave him here, to begin right away?

Lucas nodded eagerly, but as he watched his father go, he felt un uneasy twinge of doubt. He took a step forward, but Father Ansan had walked up behind him and gently put his hands on his shoulders to hold him back. "It is time!" he said in a soft voice. "Come—we have much work to do."

From that day forward, Lucas would knock on the door of the monastery every afternoon and slip inside as soon as it was opened to make his way down the long hallway to the inner courtyard. Occasionally, he would get angry looks or a *shh* when he passed, for making too much noise, and he would slow down, only to speed up again when they were out of sight. He didn't want to be late or miss anything, and he took his spot at the front row with pride. He marveled at the columns of the cloister that connected the courtyard to the main building and felt safe with the solid wall behind him.

The courtyard where they practiced was the only one with a sandy floor in the middle. There were others with cobbled stoning, and one had a garden with paths between flower beds and a cherry tree that stood in the center. Father Ansan could tell when he put his feet in the wrong position by the impressions his footsteps left in the sand. As soon as they finished for the day, a monk would come in to rake the sand and make their footsteps disappear.

He could no longer behave as a child would, as he was treated like everyone else. "You are a fast learner," Father Ansan would tell him. "You have shown us that you have self-control, determination and natural talent."

Even the other monks gave him approving nods from time to time. It felt good to be all grown up, at the monastery and at home. Father Ansan, he learned, was a master warrior. That was why his robe was a different color and the sash around his waist had a black tip at the end. There were other master warriors, but most were still in the process of learning the art of sword fighting.

Just as he had promised his father, he did his chores before going to the monastery and came home in time for dinner every night.

One night, after his lessons, when he was making his way to exit the monastery, he heard whispering voices coming from a dark corridor he had not noticed before. He stopped and looked behind him to see the warrior monks all still in the courtyard and then peered down the empty corridor again. The voices were whispering, but the words did not sound like the prayers he heard in the rest of the monastery. Again, he looked to the courtyard to see if anyone was watching him and, when he determined that they were not, he slowly walked down the dark corridor until he came to another inner courtyard he had not known existed. He stopped at the edge of the cloister surrounding it and carefully looked to see if he could see whose voices had caused his curiosity, but no one was there. He could see no other entrance other than the one he had just walked through and wondered where they could have gone.

With the sun setting and the evening sky getting darker, he knew he was already going to be late in getting home, but was intrigued by what he saw in the middle of the courtyard—a small pond with an island in the middle that had a large black stone on it. It was blacker than black and the size of a farmer's wagon. He stepped forward and walked onto the grass surrounding the pond to get a little closer, but then stopped when he heard his name spoken behind him. Father Ansan grabbed him by the shoulder, preventing him from going any farther.

"You are not supposed to be here," he said angrily. "Why are you not on your way home?"

"I'm sorry, Father," Lucas apologized. "I wanted to see the people who were talking."

"People?" asked Father Ansan. "No one comes here, Lucas, except for on special occasions. You could not have heard people talking here." He paused and gave Lucas a silent stare that seemed to last forever. "You need to go home now. It is late and your father will be worried."

Lucas glanced at the giant stone one more time and quickly made his way back down the corridor. It was totally dark when he finally stepped outside.

Fearing his father would be angry, he made his way down the path as fast as he could. Small rocks rolled underneath his feet and he had to be careful not to slip and fall, but he did not slow down. The path zigzagged down the mountain and came out at the back of his father's house. He was about to burst through the back door of the workshop when a large black-and-white bird swooped down from a tree right in front of him and made him stop in his tracks. He paused, looking around to see where the bird had gone and, at that moment, he heard the snorting of horses nearby and talking inside the house. His father was always wary of visitors on horseback and would never allow them to come inside. Stepping slowly and carefully, Lucas quietly made his way to the door. All his senses told him to be cautious. Nothing about this felt right to him.

He gently put his hand on the door to push it open just a crack, but stopped. Instinct told Lucas to go to the window first. He went to it and stood up on his toes in order to peer inside. His father was kneeling on the ground with his hands tied behind him, looking up at a large man who had a sword pointed at his chest. The man was dressed in all black—his shirt, pants, leather vest, and even his boots. Four other men, dressed the same, were posted by the front door. The dust on their clothing told Lucas they had ridden here with urgency. With their arms crossed over their chests and their faces grim and serious, Lucas knew they were dangerous. They, too, had swords, but had not pulled them out and were watching his father closely.

The large man spoke and his father replied, but Lucas could not make out their words. He wanted to go to his father and help him, and made his way back to the door. Lucas started pushing it open, slowly so it would not creak, but stopped when his father noticed the slight movement and gave Lucas a look of alarm. It was an expression he had never seen on his father's face. The look was warning Lucas—no, commanding him—to run.

One of the other men had also noticed the door moving and said something that made all of them turn their heads in Lucas's direction. Still hidden by the shadows, Lucas watched in horror when his father suddenly raised himself to his feet and stepped forward into the sword that was pointed at his chest. The large man stepped back in surprise and withdrew his sword, but it was too late. Lucas's father dropped to his knees and turned his head towards the door. Lucas gasped for air when he read the words from his father's dying lips. "Run, Lucas! Run," he mouthed, before collapsing to the floor, right in front of the stone furnace where Lucas had watched his father create his magical swords. But he knew this was no time for memories, or time to cry. He had to follow his father's orders. He had to unfreeze himself, make himself move.

Without further thinking, Lucas turned around and disappeared into the night. He ran until he found the familiar fallen tree that lay some distance from the house. It had been rotting away for some time and had a hollow center perfect for hiding. As he worked his way inside of the tree, he heard the back door of his house slam open, followed by some noise and a muffled shout. Tears were running down his face and he buried his head in his hands. Realizing he might not be safe where he was, he crawled out of his hiding spot in the tree trunk and started to run once more. He ran towards the only place he knew he would be protected, hesitating only when he reached the top of the path. He wanted to knock on the door, scream for help, but he was afraid the men had followed him and would get to him before the door could be opened. Instead, he ran around towards the back of the monastery, to the very spot where he had climbed the wall time and time again. Using small crevices between the stone for his fingers, he managed to scramble over it without losing his grip and balance.

The evening prayer echoed from the chapel as he made his way along the walls to the inner courtyard, where he jumped down. He huddled in a corner with his arms wrapped around his legs, rocking back and forth. Was what he had just seen real, or had he imagined it? He did not know what to do. The image of his father stepping into the sword flashed through his mind, over and over again, until he was exhausted and collapsed in a heap.

A pair of monks discovered him the following morning. His eyes were swollen from the many tears he had shed, and he could not say a word. Father Ansan was called and gently scooped him up in his arms to take him to the infirmary.

"What is it, child?" Father Ansan coaxed. "What has happened that has brought you here?"

Still, Lucas could not bring himself to speak, but allowed himself to be brought to a room where a few empty beds lined the walls, with nightstands between them. He was laid down and, shaking the vision of his own bed at home from his head, he buried himself underneath the blanket.

"We must go to his house right away," Lucas heard Father Ansan say to someone at the door. "I fear something dreadful may have happened."

Lucas dropped a clump of earth on his father's coffin as it was lowered down into the ground of the monastery's cemetery, in an area reserved for common people. Father Ansan stood by his side, his large hand resting on Lucas's shoulder. Lucas liked the way the weight of the monk's hand steadied him, but it was cold comfort—his father was dead and seeing him lowered into the ground made that all too real.

"Can I stay here with you now?" he asked when they walked away. Another monk had already told him that he would not be able to live at the forge by himself. Now that he was an orphan, he needed someone to look after him.

"For now, yes," answered Father Ansan. "But your future is not up to me. I have sent word about the death of your father to those who need to know. We have to wait and see what will be decided."

Lucas wondered who those people could be, but he had seen and heard so much in just one day that he did not want to question anything. He wanted to forget all that he had observed, and was ready to join the warrior monks in practice as soon as he could.

He spent most of his days out in the courtyard, even on his own. His tenth birthday passed by without anyone knowing, and he kept quiet about it. He settled into life at the monastery and asked again if he could stay some days later. "I am waiting for someone to arrive," Father Ansan told him. "Someone who is to make that decision."

It wasn't until several weeks later that this happened. Father Ansan was late for practice one day, and all the monks were waiting for him when he eventually entered with a man by his side. Lucas had been sitting on the ground, drawing pictures in the sand to deal with the boredom of waiting, and only briefly looked up at them, but he noticed the stranger to be tall and maybe in his late twenties. He had short brown hair and a fine beard that looked like it had started to grow recently, possibly because he had been on the road.

Lucas finished his picture of a king on a horse and stood up to join in the practice. The man was watching him closely, and he started to wonder if he was the one who would decide if he was to stay or not. He focused on each stance during practice and made sure he made not a single mistake. He followed the group when they stepped to the right, and he lost sight of the visitor by the entrance for just a moment. When he turned back around, the man was nowhere to be seen. Wondering where he could have gone, Lucas continued his movements and was lifting his sword overhead when he suddenly became aware of a presence close behind him. Instinctively, he spun around on his heels, and a strong hand grabbed his wrist to prevent him from bringing down the sword.

"Careful now," the man scolded.

Lucas raised his head and caught the look of surprise on the man's face when he realized there was no sword in Lucas's hand. At the last second, Lucas had switched hands and was holding the sword concealed behind his back.

"Smart move!" the man remarked. "What made you do it?"

"You were going to take my sword from me."

"Was I?"

"Yes," answered Lucas resolutely. He followed the man's questioning eyes to the hand that was still holding his wrist. "With your other hand," Lucas clarified. "You were going to take my sword with your other hand."

"And you did not want that to happen?"

Lucas shook his head. "Father Ansan always says, if you lose your sword, you are going to be a dead man."

His wrist was starting to hurt from the firm grip, and he was relieved when he was finally let go. He watched the man take a step back and eye him from head to toe. Placing his hands behind his back, he told Lucas to continue with the practice and walked away.

When the session came to an end, Father Ansan told Lucas to wait and went to talk to the man. Lucas sat himself down on the ground nearby and pretended to be busy drawing pictures again, paying close attention to whatever words he could hear being spoken.

"The boy finding his way to you, as well as the timing of Einar's death, cannot be a coincidence," he heard the man say. "We believe it to be a sign, and the boy needs to be taught in the ways of your order."

"He is too young," said Father Ansan. "Yes, he wants to learn to fight, but there is so much more he needs to know that he is not yet ready for. I agreed when Einar asked me to teach him for a short period of time. It was not supposed to be indefinite. Why not take him and bring him back in a few years when he is older?"

Lucas couldn't help but look up in alarm. He didn't want to leave. He wanted to stay. The stranger caught his eye but turned back to Father Ansan and shook his head.

"I wish I could," he said, "but we are under constant threat and not in a position to keep him safe."

Lucas had no idea what any of it meant. All he cared about was staying at the monastery and learning how to fight with the sword. Father Ansan waved Lucas over, and Lucas reluctantly obeyed. "Do you want to stay here?" asked Father Ansan when he stood before him.

"Yes, Father. I will be good and cause no trouble for anyone. I promise."

Father Ansan put a finger under Lucas's chin and lifted his head to look him firmly in the eye. "I have been asked to take you on as my student," he said. "That means hard work and no more play, as your father already told you, before you came to train here."

"I can do that," replied Lucas happily. "I don't play much anyway."

"We will see," sighed Father Ansan, and let go of him.

Soon after, the stranger left, and Lucas found himself seated on a stool staring at a sharp razor. A monk he knew by the name of Father John was holding it in his hand. He was not a warrior, and wore a plain brown habit, but had been tasked with looking after him. Lucas shuddered when he realized Father John was going to shave his hair off, and put his hands on his head to prevent that from happening.

"It has to be done," said Father Ansan firmly, when he saw Lucas objecting. "If I'm to take you on as my student, you'd better look like one."

"But I like my hair," said Lucas, hoping to persuade his teacher to change his mind.

"Did you not just promise to cause no trouble?" asked Father Ansan.

Lucas quickly averted his eyes and lowered his head.

"Proceed, Father John," he continued.

Father Ansan left without saying another word, and it was at that moment Lucas knew his life at the monastery had changed.

"Sit very still," Father John told him, taking his chin in his hand. "If you move, the razor might cut your scalp. We do not want that to happen, do we?"

"No," answered Lucas, subdued. When he saw the razor being dipped in a bowl of warm soapy water, he gripped the stool with both hands and braced himself.

With one hand, Father John held the top of Lucas's head, and with the other, he let the razor find its way over his scalp as he carefully and methodically started to shave Lucas's head.

Lucas saw the first few blond locks fall to the floor where he sat and then closed his eyes so he did not have to watch it—the crunching sound of the razor cutting through his hair was enough to remind him that he would soon look like a miniature version of every warrior monk there.

Afterwards, Lucas was fitted in a white robe with gold trim.

"Why do I not get a golden robe like everyone else?" he asked Father John, who had dressed him.

"You are to be Father Ansan's apprentice now," Father John answered.

Lucas shook his head. "I don't want to be different from everyone else," he said, holding his arms out and looking down at the robe he was wearing. He had been made to put on a matching pair of white trousers, which he wore underneath the robe, and had been fitted with a stiff pair of leather sandals that he would take off as soon as he got a chance, as he preferred to go barefoot.

Father John frowned at him. "It is a great honor to be Father Ansan's student. He has not accepted a new student in a long time, and never one as young as you," he continued when Lucas did not respond. "He must have seen your potential and you should be proud of yourself. And grateful."

When Father John was happy with the way Lucas now looked, he led him out into the hallway, where Father Ansan approached them. He looked Lucas over from top to bottom and then, as if contemplating his verdict, rubbed his hand over his bald head. "Much better," he said, and motioned for Lucas to follow him. They walked down the hallway to the corridor that had previously been forbidden to him. He stopped when Father Ansan walked onto the grass and sat down close to the water that surrounded the island with the stone. He remembered the voices he had heard that caused him to be late getting home. Memories that he had tried so hard to push away now flooded his mind, and his breath came heavily.

Father Ansan followed his gaze to the stone. "It is impressive, isn't it?"

"Why is it here?" asked Lucas.

"It is sacred and used as part of the final initiation into the order, at the time when a warrior monk is thought to be ready."

"Does it do anything?" asked Lucas. He was still standing and didn't want to get any closer.

"The stone speaks to those it chooses to be worthy," answered Father Ansan. "Warrior monks vow to protect the stone with their lives when they become masters against those who might oppose the gods and seek to destroy it. Monks who have been taught all the skills to be the best sword fighters will take their place on the stone during a final ceremony. To some, the stone will reveal its powers and make them stronger. To others, it remains silent. After the stone releases a warrior deemed worthy, he then must fight against multiple opponents, in a final test. If he can do that—and he usually can, because the stone has empowered him to do so—he will be initiated into the order as a master. It will take some monks years before they accomplish that, and some never make it."

Lucas still had his eyes on the stone when he sat down next to Father Ansan in the grass. "You are a master warrior, so you must have sat on it?" he asked.

Father Ansan nodded. "I did," he answered. "A long time ago."

"I will never sit on it," remarked Lucas.

"You don't know that. If you work hard, and you have grown older and more experienced, you may. It is a great honor to be chosen by the stone."

"I will not be chosen," said Lucas resolutely. "I don't like the stone. It gives me nightmares and it's surrounded by water. I don't go near water."

"The stone has given you nightmares?" asked Father Ansan, raising his eyebrows. "And why do you not go near water?"

"You can drown in water."

"Only if you do not know how to swim. Your father did not teach you?"

"He tried," answered Lucas, "but then I got nightmares about drowning in a wild river and he stopped. The stone made the nightmares come back."

"I see," responded Father Ansan. "We might have to deal with your fear of water, then. Now, follow what I do," he said.

He started by showing Lucas how to sit in a pose for meditation. Father Ansan then crossed his legs and placed his hands, palms up, on his knees. He closed his eyes and demonstrated how to breathe in and out. Lucas sat there and observed, feeling a bit uncomfortable, until Father Ansan finally leaned over and adjusted his legs for him so he too sat in a cross-legged position. He arranged Lucas's hands on his knees, turning his palms up. When he looked satisfied, he sat up straight again, only to sigh when Lucas moved his hands off his lap. "Why are you not doing as I tell you?"

"I thought, now that I am your student, you would teach me how to fight as a master warrior?"

"I am and I will," Father Ansan replied. "This is part of it. You need to learn how to meditate, how to calm your soul and body. I know right now you may feel confused, but to be the best warrior entails more than knowing how to wield a sword. When the mind is ready first, the body will follow."

Father Ansan closed his eyes again. "Concentrate on your breathing," he said. "Feel how your body reacts to every breath you take in and breathe out."

Lucas did as he was told and, before long, the position and the way he was breathing began to feel more natural. It felt . . . good. They sat silently for a while until Father Ansan stood up and told him it was enough.

"We will practice again tomorrow. I want you to come to this place every day when the sun rises," he said sternly and left.

Lucas arrived at the courtyard with the stone the following morning to see that Father Ansan was already sitting and meditating. "I don't want to do this again," he said. "I just want to learn how to fight, like we did before, with the group."

"And I told you, you will again," answered Father Ansan, keeping his eyes closed. "When you are ready."

"I don't want to do this stupid meditating," he shouted. "It's boring. I hate it!" He stomped his feet and ran out of the courtyard.

For several days after, Lucas avoided Father Ansan. He was expecting him to chase him down, to make him listen, but he didn't. No one did—no one even seemed to care. They ignored him and let him do what he wanted to do. He began to wonder if they had simply had enough of him. Would the stranger now come back and take him away? Perhaps that had been Father Ansan's plan all along. Lucas knew that he hadn't wanted to take him on as a student, and if he could prove he was not listening . . .

He spent a lot of his time climbing on the roof, looking at the path that led towards his house and the village in the distance. Away from prying eyes, he let his tears run freely. Most nights, Lucas tossed and turned in his bed and could not sleep because of the many dark thoughts coming into his mind. Other nights, he would fall asleep exhausted only to wake up from a nightmare. Not only was he dreaming that he was drowning in a wild river, but now there were five dark figures on horseback watching him from the forest's edge near the riverbank.

He was certain he cried out during his dreams, but nobody ever came to his bedside.

Tonight, he'd just had another nightmare and woken up in a sweat. He had a deeper sense than ever before that he was all alone, and he felt an emptiness inside his heart as he sighed and pushed back the tears. He missed the way his father's comforting arms wrapped around him whenever he had woken up from his nightmares. He missed the smells and sounds of the forge and the dancing sparks flying from the pieces of steel his father was working on.

He opened his eyes to see the light from the moon shining from the tiny window in his room. Wide awake now, he lay staring at the window for a while and then swung his legs over the side of the bed. He quietly walked to the door to see that the hallways were empty and no sounds were coming from the chapel, which meant it was still too early for morning prayer. He left his room and tiptoed down the hallways, his feet moving as if on their own, playfully stepping on every other floor tile as he went along.

When he got closer to the inner courtyard, he started to hear noises and quickly sidestepped to the wall. Staying in the shadows, he moved closer and hid himself behind a cloister column—from there, he had a clear view of the courtyard and could see several master warriors standing in a circle, each holding a long white wax wood stick. In the middle, stood Father Ansan, who was twirling his pole high up in the air before taking up a defensive position.

One by one, the warriors attacked and Father Ansan defended himself with skill and precision. After they had each taken a turn, multiple warriors attacked him at once and again Father Ansan fended them off. To Lucas, they looked like dancing figures moving gracefully in the moonlight. He let his imagination go, let himself forget that he was a boy hiding behind a column—Father Ansan was the good guy, and he was being attacked by evil villains.

He could not keep his eye off the fighting warrior monks. He watched until the fight was over, and each man bowed to Father Ansan, who bowed to them in return. Lucas had learned enough to understand that this was out of respect. Before they could see him, he retreated and ran back to his room.

Father Ansan smiled a satisfied smile when Lucas showed up at sunrise a few hours later and lowered himself down to sit next to him. The monk, much to Lucas's surprise, seemed not at all shocked by his arrival. Had he noticed, last night, that Lucas was spying on him? Without a word, Father Ansan closed his eyes and continued his meditation.

Lucas followed suit, trying to mimic the precise cross-legged position and to keep his back very straight and still. Afterwards, Lucas quietly followed him to breakfast and then to a study full of books and scrolls, where he was informed he would be taught to read and write. He did as he was told without complaining, even when he felt the urge to run again, and was relieved when they finally went to the inner courtyard late in the afternoon, where Father Ansan started to instruct him in the different ways to fight with the sword.

After dinner, he was led back to the study. They finally finished the day when Lucas fell asleep with his head on a desk.

They kept this routine up for several weeks, until Lucas became too exhausted. He was still not sleeping well and was becoming more and more irritable. He had what Father Ansan called "outbursts," which usually resulted in him being reprimanded or locked up in a room to cool off.

Father Ansan told him one afternoon that there would be no more fighting practice until they had dealt with his sleeping problem. He walked him down several corridors until they came to a thick oak door. Lucas followed him reluctantly, as he already knew what lurked down below, and he had avoided that part of the monastery for that reason. They walked down some steps to an underground room. Light came through openings in the vaulted ceiling and sparkled on the water of the natural spring-fed pool. The bathhouse.

"What are we doing here?" asked Lucas, his voice echoing off the stone walls. "I told you I don't like water."

Father Ansan stepped closer to the pool and turned around. He saw that Lucas was tense and ready to flee. "I know," he said. "I also know you have nightmares that keep you from sleeping at night. This is causing all sorts of problems for you. It is time you learn to swim."

"Swim?" gasped Lucas. "I cannot swim. I'll drown."

Father Ansan stepped farther down the steps into the water and held his hand out to him. "You will not drown. I am here. Come!"

"No," said Lucas, shaking his head and backing up. "I will face other fears. I will let a spider crawl over my hand."

"You are not afraid of spiders. I have seen you play with them," said Father Ansan. Before Lucas could even have time to flinch, Father Ansan reached forward and grabbed him by the arm, and in another swift movement, he pulled him in the water and let go. Lucas panicked. He couldn't breathe, and the bottom of the pool was too deep for him to stand. All he could hear were echoes in the water from his flailing arms and legs and the last bit of air leaving his lungs. Then two strong hands grabbed him under his arms and pulled him to the surface. He coughed and sputtered and was about to complain when he saw Father Ansan's red face. He had never seen him angry before and he had not expected to in this moment.

"I have been very patient with you," he said when he put Lucas back on the side of the pool. "You have the ability to become the greatest, but it will not happen if you do not reach inside yourself and try to heal. I am only here to guide you, but if you do not trust me, then I cannot help you." He continued to stare at him, as if waiting for a response, but Lucas could not find the right words. "Now, are we going to try this again, or are we finished here?"

Lucas wanted to be done, but he didn't want Father Ansan to be mad at him either, so he slowly nodded his head. Father Ansan reached out to help him slide back into the water. "Now lie back and relax—I will keep holding you."

He did as he was told and could feel the water cover his ears and gently touch half his face.

"Make yourself lighter than air by filling your lungs as deeply as you can. Spread your arms and legs. Keep your head back, stomach up, like a star floating in the sky," said Father Ansan, now more gently.

Lucas listened to the sound of his own breathing and felt a calmness wash over him, until the images of wild water and the feeling of not being able to breathe returned. He could see foaming white water rushing towards him, and the helpless feeling of not being able to keep his head above water overcame him. The vision of raging current could not be a memory of his own. He had never been near a wild river, yet these images had plagued him in his dreams ever since he could remember and had become more frequent since his father's death. He struggled against the water, feeling the weight of his own body, and knew in that moment that floating was not going to happen.

Father Ansan pushed him to the side so he could sit on the steps. "Same time tomorrow," he said as he climbed out of the water and headed towards the door.

Lucas sat on the side, cold and still dazed. "I saw how my father was killed," he blurted out, before Father Ansan had walked out of the bathhouse. He had not planned on telling anyone, but it suddenly felt like something heavy had been lifted from his chest, something he had been carrying around for a long time. "He sacrificed his life so I could get away. If I had not been late, maybe it would not have happened?"

Father Ansan paused. "I am sorry that you had to see that. I know it was a sacrifice he did not hesitate to make, but it was not your fault that it happened." He waited for Lucas to say anything else, then continued on his way, leaving him alone by the pool.

With his feet in the water, Lucas stared at the pool in front of him. The water was still and clear. The walls of the bathhouse had a green glow to them, caused by the moss that was able to grow on the stones in the damp, underground environment. The only sound he heard was from water dripping off the walls into the pool. He sat motionless for a while and then lowered himself down the steps. Water reached past his hips; he paused, then went down another step and moved his hands over the surface, causing ripples in the water. Standing on the last step, with water coming up to his waist, he waited until the ripples were gone, then did it again and again.

After a while, he closed his eyes and let the nightmare enter his mind. The images slowly formed and took control. When sleeping, he would normally startle awake when the water covered his entire body and he felt like he was drowning, but he stayed with it this time and let the dream continue. He was awake, so he could control it now. The water washed over him and, as he was sinking, he felt he was held and pushed back up to the surface. He took a deep breath, and the sound of tumultuous water began to fade into the distance and disappear.

Lucas opened his eyes. He was still moving the water around in front of him. He stopped and climbed back up the steps. He sat for a long time beside the pool, until the light through the ceiling started to fade and he began to drift into sleep, right there on the smooth slate tiles, with his head resting on his arms.

CHAPTER 2

Lucas never again resisted any teachings Father Ansan put him through. The nightmare about drowning never returned, and he eventually mastered the art of swimming that had formerly eluded him. He learned to meditate properly, to balance on a beam suspended high up in the air. He jogged on the forest paths and swam in the pool. He worked on focus and self-control. Learning these things came naturally to him and when his eleventh birthday passed, he excelled in his fighting skills and, despite his young age, had quickly absorbed all the monks were able to teach him. They worked him hard, with little time to relax, but once he could read, he enjoyed the time in the evenings when he was allowed to sit by the dim candlelight, devouring book after book. Father Ansan would sometimes write on scrolls or read as well.

There was one book in particular that Lucas enjoyed reading. Father Ansan had handed it to him one day when he was tired and not in the mood for reading. It was a story about the great battle between the kings that had taken place a long time ago.

It told the story of the time when there was only one king who ruled the lands on either side of the great river and high mountains. The gods chose this first king and made sure he was honest and just to the people. Life was prosperous for everyone. There was peace and order, and each king who succeeded the last upheld the laws as they were written, in their pure form. That was until King Rodin came to power. He succeeded his father after his death, at a young age, and before he was truly ready.

Rodin did not understand what it meant to be a good king. He was spoiled and selfish and lusted for expensive things. He ordered a throne to be cut from white marble and desired that it be inlaid with precious gems. It took months to make and required many of the townspeople to mine the stones in various locations all over the country. When the throne was finally revealed, Rodin was far from pleased. He wanted more gems to be set into it. His advisors argued that they had exhausted all the mines and they did not have enough men to keep sending them away. All this mining was keeping them from the much more important task of farming the lands.

King Rodin heard none of it. He ordered all men over the age of fourteen to come and work in the mines. Soon there were not enough people working the fields. Food became scarce. More often than not, children were going to bed hungry. Several lords rode up to the king's castle to ask for a meeting, but the guards would not allow them to pass through the gates and they returned home without being heard. One of those lords was Linus, who ruled land across the river. After being turned away at the castle, he removed his men from the mines and put them back to farming. The people across the river appointed Lord Linus to be their new king and refused to follow orders from King Rodin after that.

With his people and lands divided, King Rodin marched a great army through the mountains and the two kings came face to face at the entrance of the mountain pass. King Rodin's army was ravenous and poorly equipped, but they outnumbered King Linus's army ten to one. With those odds, King Linus knew that defeat was imminent, yet he stood his ground and refused to surrender. He felt the earth trembling under his horse's feet before he could even make out the first soldiers. He strained his eyes and recognized the warriors to be from a tribe that dated all the way back to the first king. Their superior fighting skills and devotion to the king were passed down through their bloodlines and conquering them would be near impossible. Each warrior had a column of horse soldiers behind him. Linus was able to identify the warrior in the first group—it was Toroun, leader of the warrior people and right-hand man to King Rodin.

Linus knew Toroun would be coming straight for him, and that his brief rule as king would soon be over. Even his horse seemed to sense the danger and was prancing impatiently as Toroun's group got closer. Linus raised his arm to start the counterattack. But Toroun, oddly enough, was turning his horse around. In fact, all of Toroun's men slowed down and simultaneously turned their horses around. They rode back the way they came, attacking their own approaching army. King Linus lowered his arm, signaling his army forward to join Toroun's rebellious warriors.

Blood was spilled on both sides in the mighty battle that followed, but eventually King Rodin was pushed back, retreating with what little remained of his army into the mountains to save himself. King Linus met with the warrior leaders and offered them land and title in return for their loyalty.

Lucas looked up from his book. "Is Toroun still alive?" he asked.

Father Ansan dipped his pen in the inkwell and answered him while he continued to write. "No, the battle took place a long time ago. Long before our time."

"Why did he betray his king?"

Father Ansan put his pen down and moved closer to where Lucas was sitting. "Toroun was a warrior, chosen with the gods' blessing to be a protector to the king. He was given special powers to protect and serve the people, like other warriors before him. He could, however, only serve one king and when there were two, the gods chose who should be the true king. That day on the battlefield, they spoke to Toroun, and he followed their orders to serve the king the gods had chosen."

"How did the other men know to follow him?" asked Lucas.

"It is said that Toroun could speak to horses and, in that way, control them. It was a gift that could only have been given to him by the gods. Others claim that he could also speak directly to his men with his mind, and that this was how they knew to follow him."

Lucas frowned. "Is that true?"

"Some believe so," said Father Ansan. "In any case, King Linus asked Toroun to stay, but Toroun had left a wife and young son behind. He feared King Rodin would take revenge and kill his family. Leaving his warriors behind, he decided to go back alone, but never made it. He was captured and found guilty of treason. When his executioner stood next to him, Toroun spoke his final words. He said that he had failed the gods when in a moment of weakness, he had spared Rodin's life, but that he was still under their protection. If he was to die at the hands of others, he foretold that another would be sent to finish what he could not and those responsible for his death would suffer the same fate. That evening his executioner died while choking on a chicken bone. Several officers responsible for his capture died in accidents or from unexpected illness in the days following, and King Rodin himself became ill as well. On his deathbed, he told his son that he had been wrong to take Toroun's life and was sorry for the curse he had unleashed."

Lucas had rested his head on his arms to listen and drifted off to sleep as Father Ansan finished the story. He woke when he felt himself being carried to his bed by Father John. He opened his eyes slightly as his head hit the pillow and saw Father Ansan look at him from the door. "Are you not working him too hard?" asked Father John, pulling the blanket over Lucas.

Father Ansan shook his head in disagreement.

"And you still want to go through with it tomorrow night?"

"Yes," answered Father Ansan. "He has been taught all we can teach him. The rest is not up to us."

"But he is just a child. He has not yet vowed to devote his life to the protection of the stone. The stone only speaks to those who have."

"That has not always been so," answered Father Ansan quietly, "and besides, the stone already spoke to him once."

"You do not believe it was a coincidence he discovered the stone the night Einar was killed?"

"No," replied Father Ansan. "I know it wasn't."

Father Ansan backed away from the door when Father John blew the candle out and made his way out of the room, closing the door behind him.

The warrior monks stood assembled in a circle around the pond, where a wooden plank had been laid across it. Moonlight shone on the water and torches lit the path where Lucas stood with Father Ansan.

"What if I'm not ready?" Lucas whispered, examining the dark stone in front of him. "What if the stone does not want me?"

"Then you will remain the same and there is nothing wrong with that." Father Ansan placed his hand on Lucas's back and Lucas welcomed the comfort of the gesture. "You have to go now," he said. "It is time."

Slowly, Lucas walked across the plank and heard them remove it when he set foot on the island. He touched the stone and looked behind him. He saw Father Ansan nod to encourage him, so he took a deep breath and climbed to the top of the stone. It was flat, with carvings on the edge that you could only see from above. He sat down in a meditation pose, just like he had been told to do, and watched as the warrior monks moved closer to the water's edge and sat down as well. He knew they would eventually disappear and leave him alone as he had seen them do before, but they would wait until he was no longer aware of their presence, as he tried to connect with the stone through meditation. For some master warriors, he had been told, it could take a whole day—for others, only a few hours.

Lucas took a deep breath and closed his eyes. He didn't know what to expect, but was disappointed when nothing happened. He heard the call of birds overhead and the sound the water made, lapping the island—it all felt very ordinary. Discouraged, he opened his eyes and looked down at the stone's surface. It was so black and smooth, like it had been touched by a thousand hands that had stroked the roughness away. He placed both hands flat on the stone. It was still warm from the sun beating down on it all day and he could feel that warmth beginning to flow through his body. He shifted around a bit and closed his eyes again.

All he saw was darkness. Nothing was happening. He sat still for a long time, not wanting to disappoint Father Ansan, but when he could stand it no longer, he opened his eyes again. It was daylight and all the monks were gone. He had the impression that many days had passed, though he knew that could not be the case.

When it was apparent that no one was coming for him, he decided to take it upon himself to climb back down. The plank had not been put back, but since the water wasn't too deep and he didn't want to wait for it, he just waded across. When he reached the other side, he saw Father Ansan walk into the courtyard. He ignored Lucas and stood at the water's edge, staring at the stone. He looked pleased and not disappointed or angry that he had left, but why was he smiling?

Lucas walked towards him and followed his gaze to the stone. He was shocked when he realized what it was that he was looking at. He was still there, still on the stone, sitting cross-legged with his eyes closed as if in a deep sleep. He looked down to his feet and saw they were dry. Before he could question anything, the world around him started to spin and bright lights forced his eyes to close. When he opened them again, he was standing on top of the stone, looking through the eyes of a magpie. Oddly enough, the stone was no longer on top of the mountain, at the center of the monastery pond, but positioned in the middle of a deep crater. Vegetation all around, once lush and green, had been burned by fire from the stone's impact on the ground when it had fallen to the earth. Somehow, Lucas knew and understood this. He saw people stand along the crater's edge, and watched a warrior approach him on the stone.

The warrior treaded carefully until he was close enough and turned to the people, a smile of relief on his face. "It's just a stone," he called. "Just a stupid stone and a bird," he muttered under his breath. "And not a sign from the gods that I angered them." He faced the stone again and walked forward. "I will have to destroy you to make the people believe the same," he said. "I did not kill my brother to become leader and have *you* take it all away from me." His eyes turned dark when he raised his sword. Lucas looked up and spread his wings. When he took to the sky the stone burst into flames, and with it, the warrior who had wanted to kill him. He flew high and higher as the world underneath him started to change. Grass started growing and different seasons passed beneath him and turned the vegetation inside the crater lush and green again.

Lucas landed back on the stone and folded his wings when a warrior approached the crater, a different one this time, barely out of his teens. Fog rose from the ground, and the wind picked up to deter the warrior from approaching him, but he pushed on until he stood before Lucas. The warrior stared at him with kindness, even though he was wet through and shivering with cold. Exhausted from his travels and too tired to continue on, he lay down at the base of the stone and fell asleep. The rain stopped and the fog slowly cleared. When morning came, the warrior rose and touched the stone gently with his hand. Lucas took to the sky once more and flew again. He watched the land being built up with villages and towns and saw how the young warrior, who was now an old man, supervised the stone being moved up the mountain and the monastery built around it to protect it.

When he landed back on the stone, images of what he imagined were other monumental events flashed in front of his eyes before all went dark again.

He woke up with his body stiff and cold. A blanket was wrapped around him and he was carried off the stone. He felt something had changed inside him that he would need time to understand, and he was pleased when he was not asked to take the final test that day so that he could recover.

He avoided all contact with people over the next few days and aimlessly wandered through the corridors alone or sat watching the fish in the pond. He had to make sense of what had been shown to him, accept what was given to him, and learn how to use it.

One morning, as he wandered into the courtyard, he found a cat and stopped to stroke it. The fur felt soft on his skin and the cat purred as it rubbed its head around his legs. He sat down and let the cat settle on his lap. Lucas could sense Father Ansan behind him silently entering the courtyard with seven master warriors. They stood in a semicircle around him and waited, not making a sound. Lucas lowered his head so that he could rub it against the cat's head and closed his eyes.

"Why have you not come alone to see me?" he asked.

"How many did I bring?" asked Father Ansan.

"Seven!"

"What do they hold?"

"Four are holding swords, two have wax wood sticks, and the last one has a spear."

"And are you ready?"

Lucas gave the cat one last stroke and lifted it off his lap. He stood up without turning around and answered. "I am."

Father Ansan approached him and tied a blindfold over his eyes. Then he gave Lucas a stick and stepped to the side. The courtyard filled with the rest of the warrior monks, who had come to witness the final test.

Father John entered and took his place next to Father Ansan.

"His time with us is coming to an end," said Father Ansan quietly as they waited for the fight to start. Lucas could hear their conversation clearly, though they spoke in whispers.

"Yes," said Father John. "He already possessed the ability of speed and accelerated learning. Now the stone unlocked the rare ability to see with his mind, which means they were right. He is the one we have been waiting for."

Lucas took a stance. He still had his back to his opponents, but when he focused, he could see them around him as if he was watching from above. He waited patiently until the attack began and then defended himself with ease. His moves were swift and precise. He took out one opponent after another and the fight was over before the time was up.

That night, Lucas walked hesitantly towards Father Ansan, who stood waiting in between two flaming torches by the water's edge in front of the stone. He knelt before his teacher and felt the weight of two hands placed on top of his head. A calmness came over him, pushing out the nerves he had felt only moments before. Darkness engulfed the courtyard when clouds moved in front of the moon, making the torches that had been placed in the water reflect even more brightly on the stone. Lucas closed his eyes and listened to the words Father Ansan recited over and over from an ancient script. Words that were asking the gods to empower the new chosen warrior, to guide and protect him. When Father Ansan stopped, the warrior monks continued in a chant and Lucas was asked to rise. Father Ansan removed the sash around his waist and replaced it with a black-tipped one. This new belt reflected his status as master, and Lucas noticed Father Ansan's hands tremble a bit as he secured it.

After his initiation into the warrior monk order, his lessons with Father Ansan became less frequent. He spent more time training with the other monks and on his own. He gained more freedom to do what he wanted.

He loved to go for a run outside the walls by himself. With the wind rushing past his face, he challenged himself to go faster as he leaped over rocks and fallen logs. He was content with the way things had come to be, and thoughts of leaving the monastery rarely entered his head. When they did, he took care to chase them away, and told himself to be grateful.

One day, when he was out running, the clanging sound of iron pots banging into each other and the snorting of a horse caught his attention. He stopped and saw six colorfully painted wagons, through the trees, on the road below him. The wagons creaked with the burden of their weight. He could read the words "Cirque Royale" painted on the side of the first wagon. Intrigued by the name and wondering if the traveling circus had any association with the king, he followed the wagons until just outside the village, where they stopped to make camp.

That night, as he sat reading across from Father Ansan, he told him what he had seen that day.

"They probably travel from village to village, performing and earning a living that way," answered Father Ansan when Lucas asked why their wagons were painted in bright colors. "The wagons draw attention, so the people grow curious and will come to watch them."

"Just as it got my attention."

"Just like that, yes."

Father Ansan looked up when Lucas didn't say anything else. Lucas kept his head down, and his eyes on the pages of his book, but he felt like he was already somewhere else, and he couldn't help asking another question.

"Do you think they have been to the king's castle?"

Father Ansan frowned. "Maybe they have," he answered.

"I wonder what it is like."

"What?"

"The king's castle."

"When I first met you, you talked about joining the king's army when you were older. You have not mentioned it for a long time. Is it still what you want to do?"

"I have not thought about it," said Lucas honestly. "Now that I am with the order, am I not to stay here to protect the stone?"

Father Ansan shook his head. "You were not accepted into the order to commit your life to the monastery, and you are too young to give your vow. There is another path for you to follow before you can make that choice."

"Is that what you did," asked Lucas, "choose when you were older?"

"For me, it was more like answering a calling," answered Father Ansan. "I followed in the footsteps of my uncle. As every first son of the second son in my family has done for generations."

Lucas pondered over Father Ansan's words until he fell asleep. When he woke up the next day, he couldn't wait to get through the morning routine and head to the village right afterwards.

He found a good rock to sit on, from which he could observe the circus camp below. The wagons were arranged in a semicircle, with a campfire in the center. A lady with long black hair was stirring something in the pot above the fire and she called to someone to bring her more herbs. Another lady appeared, identical to the first one, and walked over to the pot with herbs in her hand. He saw another lady hanging wet clothes on a line between the wagons. She had short, blond curly hair and was much younger. Lucas thought she looked pretty. There was a small girl sitting in the sand nearby, who he assumed belonged to the lady, since she also had blonde hair and curls. Farther along, a stocky man sat on a chair in the shade of the wagon that had the words "Cirque Royale" written on it, and not far from him sat a long-limbed, skinny boy of maybe fifteen.

Lucas counted seven horses and a baby goat grazing nearby. He sat watching them for a while and was thinking it was probably time to go when he heard voices and saw three men entering the camp carrying firewood. The first man who came into view was very short—the height of a child—but had the features of a grown man. He was chatty and did most of the talking. The next man was of average size and the last one was tall, big and strong. He reminded Lucas somewhat of his own father. His upper arms were so muscular that they strained the seams of the short-sleeve shirt he was wearing.

The small man dropped his firewood next to the fire. He was still talking as he stretched his arms and—turning this way and that to do so—he spotted Lucas sitting on a rock above their camp.

"Hello, there!" he called out and waved.

Lucas wasn't sure what to do, but finally waved back.

"We'll be performing in the village tomorrow at noon," the small man called out to him. "Spread the word and come and watch!"

Lucas raised his hand as if to say "all right" and then left quickly.

He really wanted to go and see the circus performance the following day and anxiously waited for the right time to sneak away.

Because he was distracted and rushed his lessons in the study that morning, Father Ansan had him stay longer and made him redo some of his work. It was well after the midday hour when he finally saw a chance to get away, and he rushed down to the village square as quickly as he could. He hoped that he would still be able to see at least some of it, but just as soon as he arrived, he saw that people were already leaving.

Disappointed that he had missed everything, he leaned against the wall of a house and watched the circus group pack up. He saw the lady with the blonde hair taking a sign down close to him. It was a sign with a picture of the people in the group with the words "Cirque Royale" written on the top and "Today at Noon" on the bottom. She noticed him standing there and smiled.

"Why, hello!" she called out. "You're the boy that was sitting on the rocks yesterday, spying on us! What's your name?"

"Lucas, ma'am," he answered softly.

"I'm glad you came, Lucas," said the lady with a smile. "Did you enjoy the performance?"

"I was too late," he answered. "I missed it."

"That's a shame," she said, approaching him. "Your parents keep you too busy with chores?"

Lucas shook his head. "I had practice and my studies."

"Practice?" he heard someone else say. He looked over his shoulder and noticed the small man walking over. "What sort of practice do you do?"

"Sword fighting, mostly," Lucas answered.

"I didn't think you were just any *regular* kid," chuckled the small man, motioning at Lucas's clothing. "You come from the monastery up there?"

Lucas nodded.

"Hey," said the lady. "Why don't you come to our camp this afternoon and watch us practice? Maybe you can show us what you can do?"

"I'm . . ." stammered Lucas, not sure what to say.

"I think you are moving a bit too fast for him, Nadia," said the small man, smiling sympathetically at Lucas. "You know where our camp is, and you are more than welcome to just watch. Even if it is just from the rocks." He followed the last sentence up with a wink.

"Maybe we'll see you again?" he added. "We're staying here a few days, and we practice every morning and afternoon. But, for now, we must pack up."

Nadia and the small man stepped away from him to begin gathering up the materials and props they had used in their performance.

Lucas didn't know why, but he waited around unseen while they finished packing their things—an elaborate and time-consuming process. When the last wagon door had slammed shut, instead of going back to the monastery, Lucas followed them back to their camp. He was curious. How carefree and happy they appeared together! Nadia had slowed down when she noticed he was following them and waited until he caught up with her. She immediately started talking to him, as if they were old friends and it was always the plan that he follow them back. Lucas couldn't help but like her.

As they neared camp, she put an arm around his shoulders and led him inside the circle of wagons to the middle.

"Everyone," she called out loudly to get everyone's attention. "This here's Lucas. He's from the monastery above the village and I've invited him to watch us practice this afternoon, as he missed our performance. He's a sword fighter," she continued happily.

"Really?" asked the young boy he had seen sitting by the wagon the day before. He put some crates down and turned around to face him. "This scrawny little kid?"

"Be nice now, Rowan," said Nadia. "I am sure he'll be more than happy to show you what he can do."

The rest of the circus group gathered around them, and Nadia started to introduce them to him. She first pointed out the two older ladies, Rosa and Lisette. They were twins and did a dancing and tight-rope act together. Then there was Ned, Nadia's husband, who was holding Ana, their four-year-old daughter. Ned was a knife juggler and Nadia was his assistant. The stubby man was Stan. He was the circus boss and organized all the performances. The largest man in the group, Bernt, looked even bigger up close, his arms and legs as thick as logs. It came as no surprise to Lucas that he did a strongman act, lifting heavy objects up in the air and generally just impressing people.

Rowan was Stan's son and didn't have an act of his own but helped out wherever he was needed. Rowan eyed Lucas from head to toe and smirked. Finally, Nadia introduced the small man as the dwarf, Everett, who served as the announcer, the storyteller and jester. After introductions, they all went separate ways to finish chores and left Lucas alone to look around. Nadia, who had made Lucas feel so comfortable, went inside her wagon with little Ana to change her clothes.

Lucas walked over to the baby goat that was tied up near a patch of grass. He dropped to his knees and started petting it, admiring its spots and downy ears.

"He's called Tiny," one of the twin ladies told him. How she had come up right behind him without him noticing, he had no idea. "He will be a big goat one day and hopefully we can use him in an act."

"What will he do?"

"We don't know yet. Stand on a barrel and roll it around? Maybe even walk over a tightrope."

"Really?"

"Yes, goats are very good at balancing. But come," Rosa said. "You must be hungry. We are about to sit down and have something to eat."

"Oh, I can't," answered Lucas.

"Of course you can—we have plenty. Come, don't be shy."

Lucas stood up and followed Rosa to the campfire, where Lisette was handing everyone a bowl of soup. They were all friendly and talking to him, except Stan and his son. They seemed to be different. Stan seemed stern and serious—all business. He didn't want them to waste too much time chatting and urged them to start practicing right after lunch. Rowan was very quiet. Lucas glanced over to him a few times and was met with a glare each time.

Everett took the biggest interest in him and made an effort to come sit next to him when others started to leave.

"So, you're a monk then?" he asked. "If they allow your size, do you think I can become a monk as well?"

"I cannot see you happy as a monk, Everett," said Ned, who was still eating as well. "It would mean no talking, and since when have you ever been able to shut up?"

Lucas could not help but chuckle. "I am not officially a monk," he said. "I'm too young to accept the vows."

"But you will, one day?" asked Everett.

"I don't know. Maybe, maybe not."

Everett went on to ask him a few more questions about his life at the monastery and how he ended up there in the first place. Lucas answered some of them but didn't go into too much detail and avoided answering some questions all together.

He stayed all afternoon, watching Bernt lift logs over his head, and Ned juggling apples up in the air and then chucking knives at a large circular board with an outline of a person on it. That was where Nadia would stand during real performances, but now she was looking after Ana, who had woken up. Lucas was glad. He didn't think he could watch knives being thrown at her, even though they reassured him that Ned had never missed.

Rosa and Lisette walked on a tightrope together. They used long sticks to balance themselves. After starting from opposite ends of the rope and meeting in the middle, they would gracefully climb over one another before making their way to the other side. It was something to see!

Everett did all the announcing in a funny way—with plenty of side comments and jokes—when Lucas least expected it. It made him laugh, something he had not done in a long time, and he was sorry when the time came for him to leave. He said his goodbyes and promised to visit again before the circus moved on, which Nadia told him would be in two days' time.

Father Ansan was standing in the entrance when Lucas came back. They looked at each other but didn't say a word. As Lucas stepped over the threshold and walked past him, he could see that his teacher was frowning, and it made him hurry more than usual to make it to his bed.

CHAPTER 3

Lucas stroked the horse the circus performers called Sable on his cheek and spoke softly to him. He had spent a great deal of time around horses when his father used to shoe them, and he had always liked them. As a young boy, he used to stand in front of a horse and let them ruffle his hair when they lowered their big heads to nuzzle him. Sable did the same, but Lucas was taller now, so the horse didn't have to lean down as far.

"Still playful, I see! But he's getting old," said Ned as he walked by. "I used to ride him and use him in my acts, but I'm afraid he will not hold a grown man's weight anymore. Of course, you are not very heavy, so you could ride him."

"I don't know how to ride," answered Lucas. He had been coming down to the circus camp for the past two days. He had enjoyed the company of the crew and was trying to put the fact that they would be leaving the following day out of his mind. It was no easy task.

"It's child's play," said Ned, smiling. "Do you want to try?"

"Sure . . . I mean, I would love that," answered Lucas. He stepped aside so Ned could untie the horse.

Ned lifted him up and put him on Sable's back.

"How is that?" he asked. "Are you scared?"

Lucas shook his head and stroked Sable's shoulder, noticing the way the bone protruded just slightly.

"Sable is a good horse—he won't buck you off. Here," he said as he handed Lucas the reins. "Let him walk you around a bit. Give him a bit of your heel, right here—a little tap—to get him going. And just relax and stay in the middle of his back so you don't slide off."

Lucas took the reins and then pressed his heels against Sable's flank as Ned had instructed, to make him walk. He followed Ned's direction on how to turn him and walked several circles around the camp. He felt at ease on Sable, as if he'd ridden him countless times before. He noticed a smile creeping over his face.

"A natural," commented Stan. "Are you sure you've never ridden before?"

"Oh, I am sure," answered Lucas. "I would have remembered this!"

Stan walked up and stood next to Ned, and the two men watched him walk Sable around. They exchanged words and Ned seemed to agree with something Stan had said. "Hey, Lucas," he said a moment later. "Are you ever going to show us what kind of sword fighting you do?"

"If you want me to," he answered, somewhat reluctantly.

He did not know if he should show off his skills outside the monastery. Other than the monks, he had not come across anyone else with special abilities, and the village kids had feared him when they became aware of his speed. But these were circus folk. They made a living of impressing crowds with their acts. Maybe it would make them remember him, when they moved on, and have them return one day to come and see him.

"I think it'd be fun. I'm pretty sure we have an old sword laying around somewhere in the equipment wagon."

"It doesn't have to be a sword. I can use a long stick."

"I'll go and look," said Stan, and he disappeared in the wagon. Lucas could hear him digging around in there.

Lucas turned Sable towards Ned and jumped off. "Thank you for that," he said. "I really did enjoy it."

Ned nodded and took Sable from him, and in that moment Stan came over to Lucas and handed him an old sword. "Can you use this?" he asked.

The sword had not been used for a long time. It was rusty in places and Lucas would have liked to have it sharper, but the weight felt all right as he moved it over his head. "I can use it," he said.

"Great," said Stan. He called everyone over and had them sit down. "Lucas is going to show us what he can do with a sword."

With an enthused murmuring, they all sat down and cheered him on. Ana, smiling and rosy cheeked, was sitting on her mother's lap and clapped her little hands together.

He first showed them several practice stances, but then, noticing Rowan's unimpressed look, he asked for an apple and placed it on top of a table. He concentrated for a moment on the round shape of the fruit, finding the center point and blocking everything else out around him. With one swift move he sliced the apple through the middle without touching the table. An almost impossible task, it had required an extreme amount of control and a stable hand. Lucas watched as both halves of the apple fell away and took in the applause he received, shortly after, from the people who had become dear to him.

"Hooray," shouted Lisette and Rosa at the same time.

"Marvelous," commented Ned.

Everett whistled through his fingers and Ned and Bernt stood up to clap. They all smiled or had something positive to say and it made Lucas's cheeks warm. He was still beaming with pride when Rowan, the only one who had not seemed to join in the praise, ruined the moment for him by speaking up.

"That's easy," Rowan said out loud. "Anyone can do that."

Lucas stared at him and then walked over. "All right. Give it a try, then," he said, handing him the sword.

Rowan let out a nervous laugh and anxiously looked around. Everyone was watching to see what he would do. Lucas could see that he didn't have much choice but to take the sword from him and walk over to the table where Everett had already put another apple in place.

He tried to replicate the moves Lucas had made and then brought down the sword. The table rocked as the sword hit it and the apple rolled off, untouched.

"Well," he said in his defense. "It's not exactly a fair contest. I haven't had any practice."

"Don't say that anyone can do it then," said Everett.

"I bet he just got lucky and can't do it again," Rowan went on to defend himself.

Now Everett looked at Lucas and challenged him. "Do you want to do it again?"

"Can I have two apples and a blindfold?" asked Lucas softly.

Everett placed two apples on the table a short distance from each other and Nadia secured the blindfold. "You don't have to do this," she whispered to him sweetly. "You've already impressed us."

"I can do it," he reassured her, though he was not entirely certain he could, and he waited until she sat back down. He had the blindfold over his eyes and purposely did not close them. Before he received his gift from the stone, he had been able to do this trick with his eyes closed. Now, if he closed his eyes there was a chance he could see, and he did not want to feel that he had cheated. He briefly felt where the apples were on the table, concentrated and then sliced one after the other in half without missing or rocking the table.

The group clapped and cheered as he took his blindfold off. He smiled. He felt pleased with himself—he had been able to pull it off without using his gift to see.

"You should join us," said Stan as he came up to him and patted him on the back. "We can use talent like yours."

"Leave him alone, Stan. Don't put ideas into his head. He is going to be a monk one day," said Everett. "That is much more noble."

"I might not be a monk!" objected Lucas. "I want to see if I can become a soldier in the king's army."

"Why is that?" asked Stan.

"When I was younger," Lucas explained, "I used to dream about sitting on a black horse, with the king's banners flapping in the wind around me, an enemy army in the distance. I would pull my sword, raise it in the air and lead the charge into battle. I always woke up after that, but it gave me the feeling that it's what I should be doing one day."

"Wait," said Rowan. "You think you will be leading the king's army into a battle one day?" A smug smile appeared on his face. "You do know that was just a dream, right?"

"It could happen," Lucas said. "If I get a chance to show the king that I can fight."

Rowan's father made a quick motion for Rowan to leave, and he did so still laughing.

"Don't listen to my son," said Stan. "He has no aspirations of his own." He put his arm around Lucas's shoulders and pointed to the name on the side of his wagon. "Cirque Royale, the name says it all. Performances, fit to impress a king. We sometimes perform for the king, and if you want to become a soldier, maybe we can help?"

Everett looked ready to say something, but Stan gave him a warning look and continued. "It would be a good way for you to get noticed by him if you joined."

"So you've met the king?" asked Lucas.

"Well, no . . . I haven't personally talked to him," Stan said, "but I have seen him."

"It is not right to get the boy's hopes up," Everett objected.

Ned quickly interrupted, to stop Everett from saying anything else. "No, but you know how the crowds have dwindled recently. You must agree that having an act with Lucas in it might draw the crowd again. He's a child with an enormous talent and people like to see children perform. He might help us all do better."

"Of course I like the idea of Lucas coming with us," Everett said. "But, Lucas," he added, looking at him, "you must know, we've never really—"

Stan elbowed him before he could finish, towering over the dwarf in a paternal way and wagging a finger at him. Lucas was too preoccupied with the opportunity that had presented itself to linger on the circus men's silly antics or what lay behind them.

"So?" asked Ned. "What do you think? You want to come with us?"

"I will have to talk to Father Ansan, my teacher," Lucas replied. "I don't know yet."

"Well, we are leaving in the morning. If you want to join us, we will see you. If not, then maybe another time," said Stan, and left him standing with Everett and Ned.

"We'd be happy to have you," said Ned. "You could use Sable to perform, if you like."

Lucas tried to digest all that he was hearing. "Really?" he asked.

"Sure! That old horse could do with some more exercise. He would be all yours."

Everett sighed loudly after Ned had walked away. Lucas wondered what was troubling him, and why Stan had quieted him. "Think about this carefully, please," he said while walking Lucas out of their camp. "Life in a circus is not always glamorous. We work hard, for little pay."

"I will," answered Lucas and waved goodbye. "I will think about it the whole way home!"

Lucas did not think Father Ansan would allow him to leave and put off asking until later that night, but the monk's reaction surprised him.

"Do you truly want to go with them?" he asked, when Lucas told him he had been invited to join.

Lucas lowered his head as they walked in the garden near the stone. "I don't know. Should I?"

"What does your heart tell you?"

"That I need to go with them."

Father Ansan nodded. "If that is what you feel you need to do, then you must. Your destiny is not here. It never has been. You were put on our path so we could teach you and guide you. I don't believe your destiny is to be a circus performer either, but it may lead you to other things."

"They may get me closer to the king?"

"I think there are multiple ways for you to get close to the king. This is merely one of them."

Lucas had changed into civilian clothes and folded his rope and sash neatly. He handed it to Father Ansan, who was standing by the door.

"Will you keep it for me, for when I come back?"

Father Ansan took the bundle from him and nodded. "Hopefully, you will have grown too big for these by then. We may have to make you a new one, if and when you return."

"I will miss you, Father," said Lucas. Even though he would never be able to replace the love he still felt for his real father, he had come to see his teacher as a parent.

"I am sure you will for a little while, but you will soon have forgotten me when you meet new people and get to see the world."

Lucas looked up and then suddenly stepped forward to hug him.

Father Ansan wrapped his arms around him and hugged him back. It was the first time they had embraced.

"I hope I am doing the right thing by letting you go," said Father Ansan. "You are still so young. You know, I was once reluctant to teach a young boy who was said to be the one. I kept my distance, but during this past year I have grown fond of that boy. It is with a heavy heart I am now letting him go."

At this, Lucas no longer held back his tears. He had not known how deeply Father Ansan cared for him.

"You possess gifts and abilities that make you special. Accept them, listen to them and use them when you need them," he said, pushing Lucas gently away from him.

"Let the gods guide you, my son, and when they allow it, our paths will cross again. Now, come—you had better go, or you will miss them."

Lucas stepped out of the monastery that had been his home. It was time for him to go. He could feel it and that made him more determined when he walked down the rocky path.

"Are you sure about this?" asked Everett when they met him on the road just past the village.

Nadia had stepped off her wagon and hugged him when he said he would join them. "Come. You can ride with us," she said happily and led him to her wagon.

Wordlessly, Ned held his hand out to pull him up onto the front seat. Lucas sat between Ned and Nadia, with Ana on her mother's lap. They slowly rode away from the village.

They were in the fifth wagon back. Stan was on the first one, the red one with the bold yellow letters on either side. After him, came another red wagon. It was the largest one, because it held all their performance equipment, and it was driven by Rowan, though he slept in his father's wagon. The third was the fanciest wagon of them all, painted with flowers all over and owned by Rosa and Lisette. He soon learned they loved flowers. Every time they would pass a patch, one of them would jump off and pluck a few, sticking them in their long hair. They even had window baskets on the side of their wagon, which they tended to very carefully.

Nadia and Ned's wagon was a bright yellow one with a green roof. It wasn't very big, and it soon proved too small for four people. He stayed with them for a few nights but was then asked politely to sleep in Bernt's wagon, the fourth wagon in line, and painted different shades of blue. He had not gotten to know Bernt yet, because the large man rarely spoke and his size scared Lucas, so he declined and made himself a bed underneath the equipment wagon instead, that is until it rained one night, and water flowed underneath, soaking Lucas's bedding and causing him to wake in a shiver.

It was then that Everett opened the door to his wagon to call him in. Everett's wagon was always the last in line and not very big, but Lucas liked it. It was painted green, with a red roof. Inside was a little stove used for cooking and heating, when the weather outside was cold. The benches on either side were used for sleeping and the cupboards overhead for storing things. The table in the middle could be taken down when not in use and a small lantern hung from the ceiling, giving them light in the evenings. It was cozy and all they needed.

He had been welcomed with open arms the day he decided to join them. They were all friendly and helped him settle in as best as they could. During the first few weeks, they didn't ask much of him and he could tell that they just wanted him to acclimate to circus life. He helped with setup and takedown at each show and he did chores around the camp. He fed the animals and collected firewood and water. He would watch Ana when Nadia and Ned were rehearsing, and he became fond of entertaining her with silly stories and games.

He practiced his sword fighting every day as he had promised Father Ansan he would. He even meditated from time to time. He had cleaned and sharpened the sword and it now sliced the apples even more smoothly. True to his word, Ned gave him Sable as his own. He felt a connection with the horse, who seemed to know what Lucas wanted him to do before he had even signaled it. Rosa and Lisette sometimes watched him on Sable, and they soon began talking to Everett about working on an act for Lucas. They were coming up with different scenarios he could act out while Everett would tell a story about long-forgotten folk heroes fighting battles, or dragons or giants.

Soon everyone got involved in creating a new act for Lucas. Lisette made several costumes for him, and Ned helped him with Sable and with knives and swords. Bernt got him lifting heavy things to build more muscle and Rosa and Nadia worked on agility by teaching him to do flips and turns. He showed very quickly that he could balance, so they had him walk the tightrope one day. It was different from running over the monastery wall, but he did it and they all clapped. Lucas observed Stan watching it all from a distance and always making sure they had all the equipment that was needed.

The only one who seemed left out was Rowan. By the comments he made and the looks he gave, he'd made it clear from the start that he did not want Lucas along for the ride. Lucas could only assume Rowan was jealous of all the attention he was getting and the prospect of him having his own circus act. Rowan had never been given an act—assisting others in their acts was as far as they would involve him.

Apart from setup and takedown, another job they allowed Rowan to do involved going around with a hat after the show and collecting money. It was easy for Lucas to see that this was the only time Rowan could put an act on and squeeze a little more money out of the crowd.

He clearly enjoyed the attention—it was his moment to shine, to feel important when he returned with the hat and the group was eager to find out how much extra they had earned.

A few weeks after Lucas's arrival, Nadia suggested that Lucas should do it with him. Lucas's blond hair was growing back, and she believed people might be more generous in giving money to a sweet young boy than they would a teenager.

She turned out to be right, and Lucas collected more money simply by smiling than Rowan, who went out of his way to try and make the people laugh with silly jokes. They decided to have Lucas do it on his own, despite his objections. Rowan watched him like a hawk as he went around with the hat. As soon as he was done, Rowan would snatch the hat out of his hand and say he would give it to his father. Lucas was certain Rowan was taking coins out when Stan would announce the takings to the group and it was less than Lucas had counted going in, so one day he followed him behind the wagons and watched Rowan grab some coins and put them in his own pocket. He then casually handed the hat to his father and started packing up the equipment.

"You took some," Lucas said, sneaking up on him.

Rowan froze when he heard Lucas behind him and then turned around, his face red with anger. "I did not, you little rat," he said, and he swiped Lucas on the back of his head. He would have done it again if Lucas had not ducked.

"I know you did," said Lucas. "I could have them check your pockets. There are five coins in there."

"You will do no such thing. If you even consider it, you better start watching yourself when you sleep at night," threatened Rowan, making a motion to cut his throat.

Lucas ran off, but every time Rowan caught his eye after that and no one else was looking, he would make the same motion to remind him he was serious.

One day, Lucas was returning to camp with firewood he had collected from the woods, when Rowan purposely bumped into him and knocked it out of his arms.

"Oh, I'm sorry," remarked Rowan. "I guess you'll have to pick it up again."

Before Lucas could say anything in return, Lisette had come around the corner of her wagon with a basket full of laundry and told Rowan to leave.

"I'm sorry he's giving you a hard time," she said, putting the basket down underneath the clothesline that was spun from her wagon to a nearby tree. "He seems to be taking all his anger and frustration out on you."

"He's just mean," responded Lucas. "I don't understand why he hates me so much."

"Probably because you choose to be here and you fit in, while he, like his mother when she was still here, never cared for circus life."

"What happened to her?" asked Lucas while collecting the dropped firewood. "Did she die?"

"No," answered Lisette, picking up the first piece of clothing from the basket and hanging it over the clothesline. "The circus was never her dream. It was Stan's, and she hated everything about it. The constant moving around and cramped living quarters, especially after Rowan was born, and the times when there was barely enough money for food to feed us all. Then, two years ago, she met a man who promised her all the things Stan could not give her and that was it—she was gone. She didn't even try and take Rowan with her; she just left and never returned. Her departure changed him."

"I never knew my mother," said Lucas. "She died shortly after I was born."

Lisette paused for a moment and gave him a sympathetic smile before continuing to hang the washing. "I'm sorry to hear that," she said. "She must have been a lovely lady."

Lucas nodded and picked up the last of the dropped firewood.

Soon, the day came that Lucas was to try out his first act in front of a real audience. He was nervous, but they had rehearsed for so long that he knew he could do it. They were in a small town where they would do two shows over two days. There wasn't a huge crowd, but nonetheless Sable sensed his nervousness as they waited for their act to start and pawed his hooves over the ground.

"Are you ready?" asked Everett, who stood next to him.

"I think so," he answered.

They waited a few more moments while Bernt wrapped up his strongman act, and then Everett walked out to announce him. Because it was his first time, they were just going to let him do a general demonstration of all the things he could do. When he heard his name being called, he rode out on Sable and galloped in a circle around the staging area. They had set up scarecrows and he pierced them effortlessly with his sword. When he had done them all, he did a backflip off the horse and walked over to the table with the apple. The crowd was impressed when he sliced the apple, but they were even more impressed when he did it blindfolded. Lucas enjoyed the excitement of the crowd more than he had expected and didn't want it to end. He was supposed to take off his blindfold, bow and immediately leave the staging area, but he waited too long and the crowd suddenly became quiet. They looked at him when he took his blindfold off and then started chanting that they wanted to see more. He didn't feel he could leave now, and he turned around to call over to Everett. "Everett! Can you throw an apple up in the air?"

"What?" Everett said. "No! We haven't rehearsed that!"

"It's all right," whispered Lucas back. "I can do it."

Everett shrugged and with a nervous smile walked towards him with an apple in his hand. "Tell me when," he said.

Lucas took up position. With his sword pressed upwards against his shoulder, he took a deep breath. "Now!" he said.

Everett threw the apple up into the air towards Lucas. With several rapid moves of his sword, the apple fell onto the ground in four sliced pieces. This time, Lucas took a quick bow while the audience was still cheering and ran backstage.

The following day, there was a noticeably larger audience than before. As Lucas was getting ready to go after Bernt, Stan came up and stopped him.

"You will go last," he said quickly and then told Rowan to get different props ready.

"Why does he get to go last?" asked Rowan. "Ned always goes last. He finishes the show with his knife-throwing act. It's what the people come to see. It makes it so that they stay till the very end."

"Not today!" said Stan hastily, motioning for Ned and Nadia to get on. "Word has spread. Why do you think all the extra people are here? To see Lucas! They have seen grown men with swords before, but never a young boy. Lucas will finish the show and follow it up with the hat straight after."

More comfortable this time, Lucas put on another good act and finished again with Everett throwing an apple up into the air. They took in more money that day than they had in a long time, and Stan had Lucas's name put on posters announcing his act in every town they visited from then on out.

Circus life suited Lucas. He was kept busy and, apart from some trouble with Rowan now and then, which he tried to avoid, he enjoyed being with the others. They were like family to him and treated him well.

He held on to the reason why he had joined the group as they traveled all over the country, but in the three months he'd been with them they never came close enough to the north part of the country, where the king lived.

"When will we be traveling to King Itan's castle to perform for him, like you said you have done before?" asked Lucas of Stan one night, when sitting down by the campfire, where the delicious smell of roasted pig filled the air. They had earned enough money that week to be able to afford meat and it made for a joyous occasion. Everyone had been happy and chatting, but now a silence came over the group.

Lucas was confused by the surprised expression on Rosa's face when she heard his question and looked straight to Stan for clarification. It had been no secret that he wanted to meet the king, but from the look on her face and that of the two other women, something was up.

"Stan?" Rosa asked. "What exactly have you told him?"

Stan avoided answering by sinking his teeth around a rib bone he was holding, and just raised his shoulders. "Ned, Everett, Bernt?" she continued. "You are all very quiet."

"You know anything about this, Ned?" asked Nadia quietly of her husband who was sitting next to her.

Ned gave Nadia a sideways glance and cleared his throat to say something, but Everett spoke before him. "We have never performed for King Itan, Lucas," Everett said with sorrow in his voice. "We've never even laid eyes on him, and it's unlikely we ever will. You were told this with the hope that it would persuade you to come with us, which it clearly did." He paused for a moment and lowered his head. "I'm sorry."

Lucas tried to take in what he had just been told. He looked at the faces of the people he had so blindly trusted and slowly started to back away from the fire. They each stared at him with either sympathy or guilt. Except for Rowan, who smirked, clearly enjoying the moment. Lucas shook his head in disbelief. He turned around and ran into the darkness of the forest, Everett's calls diminishing the farther away he got.

Lucas returned the following morning but was still angry that he had been lied to, and he refused to perform.

Stan saw his profits plummet in the week following and finally told Lucas that, if he wasn't performing, then he wasn't eating either. In the end it was Bernt, who had not spoken more than a handful of words to him before, who told him that, just because he was lied to, it didn't mean he had to give up on the dream.

Lucas felt angry for a couple of more days, but then got hungry. The scraps the others were sneaking him did not suffice. He decided he didn't have a choice but to work for his food and settled back into circus life, until the day would come when he was old enough to make it in the world on his own.

To take his mind off something that suddenly seemed beyond his reach, he helped train Tiny in his own act. He had grown into a big strong goat, and they had taught him to climb onto a table on command. They would put a smaller table onto the first table and have him climb onto that, followed by another smaller one on top of the second one, until it was such a small table that Tiny's hooves had to touch in order for him to not fall off. Once he had steadied himself on top of these four diminutively stacked tables, he would then leap off. Since someone had to guide Tiny through the act and everyone was busy with their existing performances, the act was finally given to Rowan. Having an act of his own—one that the crowd cheered for—combined with the fact that he was the boss's son and could do no wrong, empowered him. He felt he could now order Lucas around, and took every opportunity to do so.

CHAPTER 4

Lucas had taught Sable to hold the hat for him when he went among the crowd to collect money after each show. He would walk along the circle of people with Sable following close behind—the brim of the hat between the horse's teeth—and would carefully watch the money being dropped into the hat. He thanked every person, but very rarely raised his head to look at them. So, when someone reached out to stop him one day, it startled him. He had just given his best performance yet, with Everett telling the story of a mighty battle in which Lucas did several tricks on Sable, including slicing the head off a scarecrow and his apple slicing act. The crowd had cheered vigorously. He was still out of breath when he suddenly felt a hand on his shoulder. The first thing he noticed were the boots the man was wearing and an elaborately decorated sword hanging by his side.

"Your performance was impressive," a deep voice informed him. "I enjoyed it."

Lucas looked up into the face of a man with a mustache so long that it nearly reached his sideburns. He had brown hair and was of average build, and wore the king's crest embroidered on his tunic— a red-and-black shield with two horse heads facing each other, one black and one white, with a sword in the center that divided them. He immediately knew this was an officer of the king's army. Two soldiers were standing behind him watching closely. He had not been aware they had been part of the evening's crowd.

"Thank you, sir," Lucas answered politely.

"Who taught you?" the officer asked him.

"Umm," stammered Lucas. He wanted to answer, but the words didn't come to him. This was the closest he had ever been to anyone associated with the king and his heart began to pound in his chest.

"Are your parents here?"

Again, Lucas wanted to answer, but he heard his name being called by Rowan and took a step back in response. It made the officer lose grip of his shoulder.

"I have to go," Lucas said breathlessly, and hastily ran off without collecting money from the rest of the crowd. He noticed the horses tied up behind the supply wagon and hid himself close by to get a better look at the king's men. Sure enough, a moment later, the officer appeared and mounted his horse, and called a soldier, who obediently pulled his own horse up alongside him.

"Yes, sir?"

"I want you to put a discreet watch on that boy and find out everything you can about him."

"Was he on the list?"

"No, I am fairly sure he is not on any list. I think we would have known if he was, but he may be one that has gone undetected," the officer answered, before they all rode off.

Lucas had a hard time making sense of their conversation. What list were they referring to? Was it a good thing or a bad thing to be on one and what had the officer meant by having gone undetected? He wished he had not panicked and been able to talk with the officer. When he got back behind the stage, Rowan was there waiting for him. He grabbed the hat out of Lucas's hands, knocking him down in the process.

"You were too slow! You let the crowd walk away," he snarled.

Lucas got up from the ground and gave him a hard stare. An officer of the king's army had showed interest in him and he had blown the opportunity, so he was in no mood to be reprimanded by Rowan. Lucas pushed past him and headed off to do his chores.

Everett found him after the sun had set, sitting on a haystack not far from where they camped outside the town. He climbed up and sat down next to him. Together they stared at the clear, starry sky.

"You did well today," he eventually said. "The people love you."

Lucas did not reply but kept looking at the stars.

"I also saw the king's soldiers stop by today," continued Everett. "And that officer talking to you. He have anything interesting to say?"

Lucas sighed. "He asked me questions."

Everett nodded. "About what?"

"Who cares? I missed the opportunity and he left," replied Lucas.

Everett pulled himself into a cross-legged position to get comfortable. "Oh, I think if we run into him again, I am sure he will remember you and then you can still answer his questions. So, come on, tell me?"

"He said that the performance was impressive."

"And what do you think he meant by that?" Everett grinned. "That you were impressive, the show was impressive, or maybe . . . that I was impressive?"

"Does it matter?" asked Lucas.

"Yes, it does. He had you pinned by the shoulder, so I am quite sure he wasn't talking about me or anyone else."

"He asked me who taught me and if my parents were here."

"Well, there you go. You impressed one of the king's trusted staff. I asked around and someone told me that was Officer Verron, a senior officer. We may see him again."

"I wish I hadn't messed that up," responded Lucas. "In all the time I've been with your group, we've never come across any soldiers and, the day we do, I'm too afraid to open my mouth!"

Everett rested his hand on Lucas's shoulder. "These things have a way of working themselves out. If it's meant to be—"

"You sound like Father Ansan," Lucas couldn't help but grumble.

"I'll take that as a compliment," said Everett, but his expression no longer looked playful. "You've always spoken highly of him."

Lucas hoped Everett was right, and that the officer would come back. He was on the lookout for him and for any of his soldiers during the next few shows, but he did not return, and Lucas found himself moping about.

With their acts attracting more people, they started putting on more shows in each town, which meant they traveled less and had more time to relax or pursue their individual interests. As a distraction, Lucas would often wander off to explore, to watch other children play, or he would find a place in town to sit and practice his gift of seeing. He was able to extend the distance he could see around him, and it made for a fun game when he watched people in the street going about their day.

As much as the people enjoyed watching their shows—cheering enthusiastically when they performed—when any member of the group was seen walking among them in the street, their reaction was totally different. They would stare, or even point, as if the circus performers had come from another land. It seemed, to Lucas, that the townspeople hadn't even considered that the performers were just people, not so different from themselves.

Lucas did not mind being stared or pointed at, but he hated it when someone challenged him to a fight and then called him names or chased him off when he refused. It reminded him of the kids from the village he grew up in, and therefore of his father, who he still missed. Nadia noticed his sullen mood one day and tried to explain to him that circus folk were perceived as different, and people did not always like different.

"Maybe they're even jealous of us," Nadia suggested. "Of how we live and of all that we can do. Many of these are simple farm folk, that have never left their towns."

"As long as they pay for what they come to watch, I don't care if they stare at us in the streets," Ned had replied when he overheard them talking. "But if it wasn't so important that we not stir up trouble, I'd tell you, if kids want to fight you, let them fight you. Show them you are better than them!"

Nadia shook her head dismissively. When Ned went on with his business, she turned to Lucas. "Yes, that is one way of handling it," she said. "But that would just give people more reasons to dislike us. Promise me, Lucas, that you will never fight anyone in the street, no matter how they pester you."

Lucas nodded without hesitating—he had little desire to do anything that would jeopardize his chances of one day meeting the king.

Nadia's promise was one Lucas had every intention of keeping until he found himself spending an afternoon in town one day. He'd been sitting on some empty crates that were stacked up just off the sidewalk, watching people as they went by and daydreaming, when he felt something behind him. As he tried to tune in, he immediately felt a threat and jumped to his feet to face it. A group of boys stood behind him with sticks in their hands, and he could tell they were out for a fight.

"Freak!" the boy at the front said to him. He was older than Lucas and clearly the leader. The other boys mumbled in agreement. As he backed up, they continued advancing towards him. In the past, a gang of children or even teenagers might have called him names but, without any reaction from him, they would have lost interest quickly. These boys seemed different. Encouraged by their leader and their sheer number, they kept on coming.

"Not so tough now, are you," said the bigger boy, "now that you're not in your fake act? Let's go! What are you waiting for? Show us what you got!"

"Let's go!" chanted the other boys.

Lucas shook his head and retreated. "You'll get hurt if I fight you. I'm sure that's not what you want."

The boys roared with laughter, and the largest boy poked him hard in the back. "Ha! There are five of us and only one of you."

Lucas hoped that, if he just kept walking, they would soon get bored and leave him alone. They followed him for a few more minutes, but something made them suddenly stop. The boys had redirected their attention and he turned to see Everett leaving one of the stores to his left and walking right towards him. Lucas froze in the middle of the street. He could tell that Everett, who was clutching a bag of groceries and whistling, was not aware of the group of boys, who were now watching him like vultures waiting for a kill, and when he passed, one of them stuck his leg out to trip him up. The boys all laughed when Everett lost his balance and fell flat on his face in the middle of the street, apples and cabbages from the sack he had been carrying rolling in all directions.

Lucas's blood boiled as he watched the boys trample the produce. He was not going to let them get away with this. He started sprinting forward. The boys were still laughing and did not see him coming. When he was close enough, he jumped up with his right foot forward and kicked the boy who had tripped Everett up, landing his heel hard in the boy's chest. The boy went flying backwards, taking one of his friends down with him. Lucas made eye contact with Everett, who was slowly

73

dusting himself off and getting to his feet. Lucas took up a defensive stance—it could all stop if they took notice and let him and Everett be. Except the boys looked furious and were picking up their sticks.

"Lucas!" shouted Everett while he was still on his knees. "Here!" He had found one of the sticks close to him and threw it over.

Lucas caught the stick and began twirling it. He walked in little circles, waiting for the boys to make the first move. All around them, people in the street stopped and watched to see what was going to happen.

"You don't have to do this," he told the boys. "We can all still walk away."

The bigger boy grinned. "Ha! I'll have you down on your knees, begging for mercy sooner than you can cry for your mama to come save you." He signaled to his friends to start the attack.

Lucas fought with all the strength and power he had. At first, he just blocked their attacks, as he was used to doing in practice, but soon enough it dawned on him that this was his first real fight and they were out to hurt him. He saw Everett watching him intently and knew in that instant that, if he lost the fight, they might hurt him too, so he changed his tactics and started taking one boy down after another.

Some he managed to hurt more than others, even though his goal was just to make them stop, but he continued until they were no longer a threat and were either backing away or groaning in pain on the ground.

His muscles relaxed. He took a deep breath and viewed the scene around him. The people standing around had different expressions on their faces. Some seemed happy that those boys finally got what they deserved, but others appeared shocked, seemingly unable to comprehend what they had just witnessed. A mother was covering her child's eyes, and several onlookers stood frozen with their mouths slightly open. Lucas threw the stick on the ground.

"Come on. Best get out of here quick," he heard Everett say, giving his arm a gentle tug.

When they both backed away from the boys, Lucas saw two men in the crowd doing the same. One of them, he knew, had watched the fight with great interest and was smiling when he walked around the corner and mounted his horse.

"Not sure if there are going to be any repercussions," Everett began, when they located Stan back at the camp, "but I feel we aren't safe to stay near the town."

Stan had listened intently to Everett's explanation of events and stared hard at Lucas, who stood with his head down. He couldn't bring himself to look Stan in the eye.

"You fool," Stan scolded him. "You may have just put our livelihood at risk. Do you not understand we are at the mercy of the people in these towns? If you start beating up their kids, we will no longer be welcome anywhere."

"I'm sorry," yammered Lucas. "I tried to walk away—honest."

"Well, you didn't and now we may all pay the consequences for it."

"What's going on?" asked Ned, walking over to them.

Stan turned towards him and let out a deep frustrated sigh. "Lucas here decided to fight some boys in town this afternoon."

Ned started to give Lucas a little smile as if to say "good for you" but stopped when he locked eyes with Stan. "Did anyone get hurt?" he asked.

"I don't know," answered Everett. "We didn't stay around long enough to find out."

"Lucas?" asked Ned. "What do you think?"

Lucas shrugged but didn't say anything. He knew of at least one boy who had broken his arm when he had fallen hard to the ground—the sound, like a twig snapping, was a dead giveaway. The others might have gotten away with bruises, but he knew it could have been much worse.

"Well," said Ned when Lucas remained silent. "I don't think we can wait to find out. They may already be gathering a posse in town to come and visit us. We need to pack up now and leave."

Lucas knew he was to blame. He walked away to get the horses ready and heard Ned ask Everett one last question. "Tell me," he said. "How did he do?"

"He was amazing," answered Everett. "Nothing I have ever seen before. Those boys are lucky to be alive, but I fear their parents will not see it that way."

Once the women were informed of what had happened, the camp was broken down quickly and they were on the road within the hour. They traveled through the night to get as far away as possible. Fearing that some of the townspeople could come looking for Lucas in the nearest towns, they kept on going and didn't stop to perform. Stan was hard on Lucas and made him feel guilty that they were not earning money while on their hasty retreat. Rowan took full advantage of this, and whenever no one was looking, he snatched food from Lucas's plate.

"You don't deserve to eat," he hissed. "It's your fault there's not enough food and I'm going hungry."

Lucas didn't feel like complaining, and since no one seemed to notice or even care what Rowan was doing, he let it go. He was glad when they came to a new area where Everett told him they were not known, and they could finally perform again. The group was now situated farther north than they had ever been, with larger towns and people with money to spend. Being in the north also meant that he was closer to the king. If he was somehow lucky enough to run into Officer Verron once more, he told himself he would find the courage to go and talk to him.

The entire group was keen to get back to work, and Lucas worked hardest of them all. He drew in huge crowds with new sword tricks and by using more agility when riding Sable. He would hang from the side of the saddle to pierce the scarecrow's chest or stand on top of the horse without holding the reins and then jump to slice its cabbage head off in midair. Stan was pleased with all the money that was coming in and praised Lucas for his extra efforts. He became even happier when he was approached by a messenger one day and handed a note with the king's seal. Despite being the circus manager, he couldn't read to save his own life, so he quickly passed the note to Everett.

"Well, what does it say?" said Stan impatiently.

Everett handed the note back with a smile across his face. "The king is holding a birthday celebration for his daughter at the castle and is requesting entertainment groups to perform for the occasion. We are invited!"

Stan's face lit up. "When?" he asked.

Lucas held his breath while looking at Everett with as much anticipation as Stan and the rest of the group. It was the break they had all been waiting for, but it meant so much more to Lucas.

"We are expected to arrive in two weeks."

The road was bumpy, made so by the ruts and trenches formed over time by the many wagons that had traveled there before them. The terrain was difficult to walk over without the risk of twisting an ankle. Lucas finally stepped off the road and into the long grass, leading Tiny on a rope along with him. The goat chomped on a patch of wildflowers while the circus wagons passed them one by one. When the last one went by, Lucas heard his name called and he looked up.

"Coming!" he called out. He let Tiny gather a few more mouthfuls of green before tugging on the rope to get him to move. With his legs coming up as high as Lucas's hip, a plump, round body and a stubborn personality, Tiny was a strong goat. It was with great difficulty that Lucas finally convinced Tiny it was time to go and was able to lead him back onto the road.

"We're almost there," he heard Everett call out from the front of his wagon, where he sat holding the reins of the large cart horse. "You should be able to see King Itan's castle after this last hill."

Lucas quickly tied the rope to the back of the wagon, put his foot on the back step and pulled himself up. He proceeded to scramble up the back corner of the enclosed wagon until he was at the top of it. He brought himself to a dangerous standing position, knees slightly bent to absorb the rocking. Balancing on the sloping roof, he tried to see if he could get a glimpse of the castle he had longed to see for week upon week, but the view was blocked by the many wagons in front of them.

"Get down from there, boy," Everett scolded. "Before you fall and hurt yourself."

"You know I never fall," called Lucas, a grin spreading across his face.

"Nevertheless, you don't want this to be the first time. You've waited too long to get where we are about to arrive."

"Only a few months," said Lucas, climbing down to join Everett where he sat on the front bench of the wagon.

"A lifetime. At least for you." Everett smiled. "Just look at how restless and fidgety you are—you can hardly keep still."

"It's true. I really can't wait a moment longer. Why are we going so slow?" Lucas asked.

"Be patient. It looks like we are not the only group of entertainers who received an invitation to perform during the princess's birthday celebration. It will take a long time to find a place for all these wagons."

Lucas let out a frustrated grunt and jumped off the seat to run to the next wagon, where Sable was tied to the back. He pulled the reins loose and jumped swiftly on his back.

He then rode past the long train of wagons on the road until he finally went over the crest of the hill that had been blocking his view. He could see the castle in the valley below him, surrounded by open fields. All the wagons were being directed to a field on the right side of the castle, where an enormous camp had started to take shape.

At long last, they had secured a place amid the chaos, and all five wagons came to a halt. They were given a relatively generous little plot, not terribly close to the neighboring campers on either side of them.

Some performers were busy setting up, while others were already rehearsing. Most had never performed for the king and an atmosphere of excitement and apprehension hung in the air. Nadia was stressed and shouted at Ned over every little thing, telling him what to do and what not to. Rosa and Lisette talked nonstop about everything they saw around them. Stan was pacing up and down—it was clear he felt the pressure of making sure that everyone was going to give their best performance.

In the end, Lucas tried to make himself scarce but, just as he began to duck away, Stan took him aside.

"Listen," he said. "Word is, the king is going to reward the best performers. Since I'm counting on the fact that there will be no other sword-fighting acts, my bets are on you to impress the king. I want you to act out that scene from the final battle between Toroun and King Rodin. The people have always loved to watch it in the past. To make it more realistic, Rowan will play the role of Rodin."

Lucas felt his face go hot. "Why?" he asked. "I always do it on my own. I don't need Rowan to help me."

Stan shook his head, firm in his decision.

"It's well known that the king is not fond of circus acts," he said. "He's only doing this for the princess, so there's no telling which acts he will favor. Yours needs to stand out. If we can make it more realistic, it will be even better."

Knowing that further arguing was of no use, Lucas decided he would get to work and practice nonstop until the day of their performance. The act included all his skills, from dangerous acrobatics on horseback and balance beams to slicing props with his sword.

Rowan had not been too thrilled either when told he was to play the role of Rodin. Having been told he could take a little time to explore, Lucas was just about to lead Sable past Stan and Rowan's wagon, when he heard Stan's hushed voice.

"Look," he heard Stan say, "I know that Lucas will deliver, but I'm not so sure about you."

"Why not?" answered Rowan. "I've been practicing just as hard as he has."

"Yes, you have, and I appreciate the effort you've been putting in, but I can't say it always went smoothly and without conflict or irritation between the two of you."

"That's because he is a rat," Rowan said with hostility in his voice. "You know I've never liked him."

Stan let out a deep sigh. "You've made that quite clear from the moment he joined," he said. "But you know he's the best thing that could have happened to us. There've not been many days since we came across him that we've struggled to put food on the table. I am pretty sure the king's invitation was because of him, so we have a good chance to bring in the big money with our act. All I need is for you to put any animosity you have for him aside—for once."

Hearing a pause in their conversation and fearing one of them might come his way, Lucas quickly snuck past. He wished he had not eavesdropped on their conversation and was thinking about Stan's words as he led Sable through the camp towards the road. Knowing that Stan expected their act to wow the king and win them the prize money felt like a heavy burden on his shoulders. On top of that, he was dealing with his own nervousness—this had been his dream for so long, and now he was finally here. A warm tingling feeling spread throughout his body when he mounted Sable and stared at the vastness of the castle in front of him. But with the gate closed and the drawbridge up, there was no way for him to get a peek inside yet.

"We'll get to go inside, right?" he had asked Everett when they had pushed their wagon into position.

"Only in the first part of the castle," said Everett. "King Itan's castle was built with an outer bailey, or courtyard, and an inner bailey. Both baileys are separated by yet another gate." Everett smiled at him. "Why don't you take Sable when we're done here and ride around the castle? You'll be able to see it for yourself."

Wagons were still coming in and were lined up on the road, waiting for instructions. He walked Sable past them until it was clear and then started galloping over the open field. He wanted to have a good look at the castle but made sure he kept his distance.

Lucas could see what Everett had meant by saying the castle consisted of separate parts. As he rode past, he could see that the first part of the massive structure, which was the outer bailey, consisted of just four walls around it and turrets on every corner. The second part was set back from the first and separated by a moat. He caught a glimpse of a bigger gatehouse connecting a drawbridge to the outer bailey, which one would have to cross to be able to reach it.

He could see the main living area of the castle at the back, with rounded watchtowers on the corners. He rode all the way around and stopped on a hill on the opposite side of the castle, to let Sable rest. He looked towards the road, and could see one last wagon approaching in the distance. The sun was starting to set and, with darkness coming, he thought it was best to return to camp.

At that moment, something behind the approaching wagon caught his eye. Soldiers on horseback were coming out of the forest into the open ground, carrying the king's banners and riding fast. As they got closer to the castle, they sounded a horn, warning everyone of the king's approach and to make way. Lucas saw that one of the two horses pulling the wagon that was still on the road became startled by the sudden noise and jerked to the side. When the horn sounded again, it broke into a hard gallop, forcing the other horse to follow. The driver manning the horses tried to calm them, but he was panicked in doing so and only made it worse. Both horses reared and took off running.

Lucas heard screaming and realized people were inside the wagon. Instantly, he set Sable into motion and galloped forward to try and cut the runaway horses off. They were running faster and faster, with the wagon bouncing wildly behind them. The driver had lost the reins and was struggling to hold on, but when the horses left the road, he was thrown off. People were running forward to help him, but no one was able to stop the horses, which were now running across the field towards Lucas. He would be trampled if he tried to stop them head-on, so he turned Sable away to get behind them. He made another turn and ran parallel to the wagon. Sable's hooves pounded the earth as he strained to keep up—Lucas had no idea the horse could still run like this. He had never pushed the animal beyond an easy gallop.

Screams were still coming from the wagon, and Lucas could now see a woman and two small children trying to hold on to the window frame. He pushed Sable to go even faster, until he was alongside the two horses. They were foaming from their mouths and their eyes were wild with panic. He saw the reins dangling dangerously between their legs. If they became tangled under their feet, the horses would trip, and overturn the wagon. He tried to reach for the closest horse, but

Sable was getting tired and losing ground. The wagon passed him again and he saw the terrified faces of the woman and her children, pleading for help.

There was no time to consider the danger he was putting himself in. Lucas let go of Sable's reins and took his feet out of the stirrups. He pulled himself up onto the saddle, with his feet underneath him, and got Sable to run as close to the wagon as possible before he jumped. Dangling on the back part of the wagon, he could see that the king's soldiers had set off in pursuit as well, but they were still too far off. Wasting no time, he pulled himself up onto the roof and made his way to the front. The wagon was bouncing up and down over the uneven ground and he had a hard time keeping his balance. He slid off when he reached the front and tried to grab the reins, but they were too far down, and he could not reach them. He then stood up and took two quick steps across the beam and jumped onto one of the horses' backs.

The horse shuddered slightly, but then responded to his presence. He grabbed hold of the reins at the horse's neck and pulled lightly. He spoke with a calm voice and both horses started to slow down, eventually coming to a complete stop. Exhausted and drenched in sweat, they breathed hard through their noses.

"Are you all right?" he shouted over his shoulder to the woman in the wagon.

The children were still crying, but the woman nodded.

Lucas jumped off and stood stroking the horses' necks until the king's soldiers arrived. They carefully helped the woman and her children off the wagon. A man, dressed differently from the other soldiers, remained on his horse and gave the orders. He was tall and muscular with long black hair tied back in a ponytail. He wore a gold-trimmed black vest over a maroon shirt and black leather trousers. There were a few more dressed like him, but he was the only one giving orders and, by the way he carried himself, Lucas could tell he was well respected. When the officer was sure the woman and her children were safe, he walked his horse over to Lucas and sized him up.

"You may have saved that woman and her children, but you could have gotten yourself killed," he said sternly and waited for Lucas's reaction. When Lucas did not answer, he softened and continued in a less harsh tone. "Where are you from?"

"From the camp, sir," said Lucas, pointing. "I was just taking my horse out for a ride."

"You'd best get back, then," said the officer. "It's near dark. We will handle it from here."

Lucas found Sable some distance away. It was dark when he reached the road where the rest of the king's soldiers still stood waiting. All eyes were on the wagon and the woman with her children, who were being brought back, and Lucas passed them like a shadow on the road. He stopped and stood perfectly still when he saw that the king was waiting there for his men to return. The king himself!

"Did you thank the man who stopped that wagon, Egon?" the king asked the officer when he returned.

"Not a man, sire. It was a boy of maybe twelve or thirteen."

"One of ours?"

Egon shook his head. "Never seen him before. He told me he came from the camp."

"Is he a performer?"

"I'm afraid I didn't question him further and let him return to his camp."

The king nodded. "See if you can find him tomorrow and reward him for his bravery."

"I will see to it, sire," Egon answered before they rode into the castle. Lucas wanted so badly to step forward in that moment, to tell them that it was he who had saved the woman and her children, but something held him back.

CHAPTER 5

News of the daring rescue went around the camp quickly in the morning, but no one suspected it had been Lucas. The horse described in the rescue had been fast and the boy much older than him. Everett had seen Lucas come back that night and rub a very sweaty Sable dry with straw, but Ned dismissed the possibility it could have been him. Sable was a cart horse—although fast for his age, he would not be capable of catching a runaway wagon.

Rowan was the only one who seemed to suspect him. He walked straight up to where Lucas was sitting by the campfire and gave him a slap on the back of his head for fun. "Are you ready for today, squirt? You probably like all that soldiering stuff around here."

Lucas didn't answer. He knew Rowan had no interest in what he liked or didn't like.

"I heard a boy on a horse saved a family last night from a runaway wagon. Don't happen to know anything about that, do you?"

Again, Lucas didn't answer.

Rowan paused a moment. "Didn't think so. Sable only knows how to run in circles."

Just then, Everett walked into the camp. "We have a schedule," he announced excitedly. "We're up this afternoon. After a fire-breathing act. Ned and Nadia go first, then Bernt, then Lucas and Rowan, and Rosa and Lisette last. That gives us the morning free. Want to come and watch some performances with me, Lucas?"

"Sure," answered Lucas. He was happy to get away from Rowan and couldn't wait to get closer to the castle. They made their way over the drawbridge to the outer bailey of the castle. General seating had been built up on three sides of the normally empty bailey, with seating closest to the main castle reserved for the king, nobles and castle staff. The drawbridge into the main castle was down, but heavily guarded, and Lucas was disappointed he could barely get a glimpse inside. He followed Everett into the stands and took a seat on the opposite side of where the king was supposed to sit. The queen and his daughter were there, but the king's throne remained empty all morning.

Lucas watched the princess smile and laugh at everything she saw. She seemed to be a carefree girl of perhaps nine years old. Her mother sat in a chair next to her and only smiled from time to time. She looked pained and tired, and Lucas wondered if she was ill.

"What's wrong with the queen?" asked Lucas after observing her for a while.

Everett leaned into him. "Not so loud," he whispered. "No one is to make any comments on her condition."

"Why not? What is wrong with her?"

"No one knows, but I heard she is rarely seen in public."

"She looks tired," said Lucas.

Everett gave him a look and told him they would get thrown out if he did not stop watching the queen or the princess. Lucas tried to watch the performances instead, but his eyes soon drifted to the empty seat next to the princess. "Why is the king not here?" he whispered.

Everett let out a deep sigh before he answered. "It's his daughter who loves this sort of thing and he organized it for her, not for himself. He may come later."

Lucas certainly hoped so. The princess continued to have a good time. She was laughing and clapping and was asked to participate a few times, which she happily did. A lot of other performers sat around them, and they all seemed to know Everett. Lucas started to settle into the festive atmosphere. He smiled and laughed when the crowd did, but his mind was still elsewhere. He looked around at the imposing walls around him, where plenty of soldiers stood watch. A couple of times he saw boys his age and older on the walls. He could not keep his eyes from them, and his heart beat faster every time he looked up, wishing he was one of them. In the king's seating area was a different group of boys, smartly dressed in red shirts and black pants with a red stripe along the side. They were also close to his age.

"Who are those boys?" he asked Everett, nodding at the opposite side of the arena.

Everett looked, but he didn't know.

"They are elite borns," a man behind them explained.

Lucas turned around to face the man. "What are they?"

"Elite borns! Sons of the nobles who carry the bloodline of the officers who helped Toroun defeat King Rodin. They were given lands and titles in return for their loyalty. Their sons get their education and training here from an early age. Then they return home or take up leading positions in the king's army. They are the best of the best!"

"What about those boys?" Lucas pointed to some boys on the walls who were also in uniform, but more plainly clothed in white cotton shirts and black pants.

"Chosen ones. They hunt for them all over the country. They are believed to carry a different bloodline, carried down from Toroun's warriors, in fact—those men who stayed here after the Great Battle. They get trained here as well, but do not enjoy the privileges of the elite borns, since they are not of noble blood. They get treated more like normal soldiers, if you ask me, but I would not like to get in a fight with one. They can be just as fierce as the elite borns. What makes them different is not only their inherent skill to fight, but the connection they have as a group."

"How do they know someone is a chosen one?"

"They test them. I had a friend once who was thought to be a chosen one. He was smart and athletic, and good at fighting. Beat up a much older kid who was pestering me. The village elder put his name on a list, and he was watched closely until he turned ten. He then had to report to the castle, and I never saw him back in the village after that. His parents told me he belonged to the king now and I was to forget about him."

"Do they always report to the castle at the age of ten?" Lucas asked.

The man nodded. "The king has a watch system in the lands he rules, and has people looking out for them. They are hard to find. Only two or three a year show up and sometimes only one turns out to be a true chosen, if any of them do. The king does not allow them to be younger or older than ten when they come here. It has been a tradition like that since his grandfather first discovered the different bloodlines."

Lucas raised his head and looked at the chosen boys on the wall. He remembered the conversation he had with his village elder, suggesting that he should report to the king when he turned ten. His father had been quick to dismiss the thought that he could be one of them. He remembered Officer Verron talking about a list and that perhaps he should have been on one. He lowered his eyes and rested them briefly on the elite borns.

They watched the rest of the morning performances and left when the stands cleared out for a lunch break. The king never made an appearance and Lucas was disappointed that he had not seen him.

Rowan was pacing up and down when they got back and was snapping at everyone.

"Relax, Rowan," said Everett. "The king never showed up this morning and I doubt he will this afternoon. All you have to do is impress a little girl and her mother."

Lucas was preparing Sable for the performance when Ned showed up behind him.

"There were some soldiers here earlier," he said. "They showed an interest in Sable."

Lucas stopped brushing. "Why?" he asked.

"They thought Sable was the horse that ran like the wind after that runaway wagon last night. They were also looking for the boy who rode that horse."

Lucas started to brush again, slowly and carefully. "What did you tell them?" he asked.

"I told them we had a boy, but in no way could Sable run as fast as they described. I told them they had the wrong horse and they left." Ned put his hand on Sable's neck and patted him. "Anyway," he said, "I thought you needed to know, in case they come up to you, so you can say the same."

Lucas waited until Ned had walked away. He watched Ned pick up Ana, who had come running at him, before he returned to brushing Sable again.

When they arrived at the castle later that afternoon, a long line of performers in front of them were waiting for their turn. When they finally made it far enough in, Lucas peeked towards the king's seating area, but it was still empty. Only two more acts were ahead of them, and Lucas was getting anxious. They were now closer to the second drawbridge, and he kept looking towards it.

Everett followed his gaze. "Don't worry," he said. "Even if he is not there, you will still show the audience what you got. Plenty of other people watching."

"Is Lucas the only one who needs words of encouragement here?" asked Rowan. "I have never seen so many people in my life."

"You'll do just fine, Rowan," answered Everett. "You always do."

As Lucas looked around, he recognized the woman from the runaway wagon in a crowd off to the side. She had seen him also and started to point. Several people around her looked in his direction, when at the same time, a commotion came from the drawbridge. Soldiers were coming out to line up and were pushing people back to make a path. A moment later, Lucas caught his second glimpse of the king—a man in his midthirties with short dark brown hair, and a stubbly beard. Dressed in a red leather tunic with a black fur cloak, he looked in good health and stood out as a man of importance.

He was making his way over the bridge towards the stage area with big strides, closely followed by Officer Verron, who he had seen in the village, a general, and the officer Lucas recognized from the night before.

"It's him! I'm sure of it!" he heard the woman shout. Lucas took his eye off the king and saw the woman trying to get closer to him.

He didn't want the attention. Not now, in the midst of the enormous crowd, with the king heading in his general direction. He tried to make small talk with Everett in an effort to look busy. He could see that the woman was getting closer to him, but then the soldiers stopped her from crossing the king's path.

The king had been in deep conversation with his general, but Lucas could see that the commotion nearby had distracted him. For one thrilling moment, the king made eye contact with Lucas, but then kept on walking and climbed onto the stand. A huge cheer rose up from the crowd when the king faced them and raised his hand in greeting. The noise died down when he finally took his seat.

The fire-breathing man had just completed his performance, which meant that their turn had finally come. After Ned and Nadia, Bernt made his appearance, with an assortment of logs that he lifted in the air and threw a distance in front of him. The crowd was impressed, and even the king was absorbed in the act. Lucas saw that the soldiers had finally allowed the woman to pass and she was making her way over to him—just as Everett tugged on his shirt and told him to get ready. Bernt had finished and they were setting up their props, Everett strutting into the arena with a confidence Lucas always admired in him. Rowan, on the other hand, was twitching and pacing behind him. The crowd roared when Everett reached the middle of the arena and climbed on top of a barrel. For a small person, he had a huge personality. His voice was loud and strong, and he could tell stories with an animation that captivated the audience. Lucas glanced over to the king, who seemed to enjoy listening to Everett and even laughed out loud a few times.

Lucas was mounting Sable just as the woman reached his side.

"I want to thank you for saving our lives last night," she said, looking up at him. He heard Everett mention Toroun's name and knew he had to get out there. The woman was holding him by a pant leg, oblivious of the fact he had to enter the arena at any minute.

Everett announced "Toroun!" in a booming voice and Lucas heard the crowd calling for him. He looked toward the king's stand, where the tall dark officer standing behind the king leaned forward to say something. The king immediately looked in his direction and Lucas knew he had been recognized. Now he felt even more pressure and bent down to the woman. "Miss, I have to go and do my act now. I will speak with you when I am done."

The woman looked a bit shocked when she realized all eyes were on them and that she was holding everything up. "I'm so sorry," she said. "I was just so happy that I found you. I did not think. You go quickly!"

Lucas nodded to her as she stepped aside and spurred Sable forward.

"Toroun!" shouted Everett loudly.

The crowd cheered and then laughed when they saw a young boy on a horse posing as Toroun. They assumed it was a joke, but Lucas did not let that deter him, as that was always the case when he was acting this particular story out. Sable moved in a graceful circle around the arena as Lucas attacked each prop with his sword. Some were set up low, so he hung to the side of the saddle with one foot in the stirrup. Others were so high he had to stand on Sable's back, and he always felt a little bit bad for the old horse, even though Ned insisted it wouldn't hurt him. To get at the final few props, which were not accessible by horse, he jumped off doing a forward flip. He then ran across a thin tightrope to pierce the last few dummies. He raised his sword in victory, standing high on several barrels.

From the minute Egon had told him that the performer was the boy from the night before, the king had not let his eyes off Lucas.

"Do you know his name?" he asked, looking up at Egon, but Egon shook his head.

"His name is Lucas, sire," answered Verron, who was standing behind the king's seat, next to Egon.

The king turned to his officer and looked at him questioningly.

"How do you know this?"

"Because I have met him before."

"When?"

"A few months ago, down south. I have had him under watch ever since. I must say I regret I didn't get to witness what he did last night, but I cannot say I am surprised."

"You had him under watch, and you neglected to inform me about this?"

"I needed to be sure."

"But you think he is a chosen one?"

Verron nodded. "I believe him to be, yes, but it has been hard to figure that out. They have been announcing him at shows as having been raised by warrior monks in the far west, taken in as an orphan, after the death of his father. That is where he learned all his sword skills."

"And no mention of a mother?"

"No, none."

"Hmm," muttered the king. "There is something about him that is captivating, and his skill set is more like that of an elite born." Without taking his eyes off the stage area, the king leaned towards the general on his left. "And what is your opinion, Finton? You were with me last night, but you have not said a word."

"To me, he is just a boy, sire. He may have had good training, as Verron just pointed out, but all that he is doing now, is just a rehearsed act. It is not a real fight. Our boys can do what he can. If he is a chosen one," continued Finton, "then we must accept that we are too late. He is past the age of ten, when they traditionally come to us."

The king turned to Verron. "How old is he?"

"Eleven."

"You see—too old," muttered Finton.

The king gave no reply and continued to watch the show before him. The crowd cheered when Lucas had defeated all the soldiers and Everett announced the arrival of King Rodin.

Rowan entered the arena, waving his sword at the crowd. He was tall and lean, but he was wearing a costume with stuffing inside to make him look older and stockier. The people booed, but then immediately cheered again when they saw Lucas whistle for his horse and jump back on. He rode several circles around Rowan, who was trying to act like a raging king by pointing his sword and shouting angry words at him.

The energy of the crowd was flowing through Lucas. He had Sable do a slow canter in front of Rowan, swung his leg over the saddle and gracefully jumped off to land in front of him. He saw a look on Rowan's face that he did not like. He looked very unhappy, and Lucas guessed it was because the positive energy of the crowd was focused on Toroun.

It occurred to Lucas how hard it would be for Rowan to accept his doomed, losing role in front of all these people.

"My turn!" hissed Rowan, and before Lucas was ready and the act was supposed to continue, Rowan leaped forward and with the hilt of the sword, hit Lucas on the side of his face. Lucas instinctively touched the spot where he was hit and wiped away a small trickle of blood from a cut. He was furious, but he wasn't going to let Rowan ruin anything, and instead pretended it was part of the act. Everett picked up on it and quickly included it in his commentating. But when Lucas looked up at the king's platform, he could see whispering between the king and his general. They had most likely understood that this was not an intended part of the act.

Lucas and Rowan had rehearsed the act by counting the steps for the sword duel that followed, and for a while Rowan stuck to the script. When they came to the final part, where Lucas would pretend to give King Rodin a fatal stab to the heart, which was not the original story, but gave a dramatic finish to the show, Rowan suddenly went off script again, stepping to the side. Lucas got caught by surprise and lost his balance in the process. As he started to fall forward, Rowan gave him a hard kick in the ribs and he crumpled to the ground. The crowd gasped, as it was obvious this time it was not part of the act.

Lucas glanced over to where the king was sitting. Their eyes met and he quickly looked away. With the king watching his every move, he had to do something. Rowan was making a fool of him, deliberately, and he had enough. He had taken every slap, every kick and every snide comment because he didn't want to stir up trouble within the group, but this was his time, and he was going to take it.

While Rowan was enjoying having the attention of the crowd, Lucas slowly rose to his feet and picked up his sword. He surveyed the grounds and then started towards Rowan, who had moved away. Rowan had his back to him but spun around quickly when he heard the crowd cheer again. Lucas jumped on the barrel in front of him and pushed off to leap through the air. When he landed on the other side of Rowan, he spun around and kicked the back of Rowan's legs from under him. Rowan dropped forward onto his knees and at that point Lucas stepped in front of him and pretended to inflict a fatal stab wound to the heart, finishing the act as it was supposed to be finished.

Lucas was out of breath and panting. He looked at Everett, who winked and gave him the thumbs-up. He smiled, too, when Everett addressed the crowd and told them Toroun was the victor. He hoped he had done enough to impress the king, but he was also worried that he would not be forgiven for this. Rowan made a big show of getting to his feet, pretending it was all part of the act, and limped to the middle, where all three of them turned to the king and bowed. Everyone in the stand stood up and clapped, including the king. Lucas looked to the commander on the king's right side and saw him nod approvingly. The princess smiled and waved to him, and he made an extra bow just to her.

"That boy is wasting his time pretending to fight in mock performances," said the king when they stood clapping. "I believe you may be right, Verron—we may just have something here. I want to explore this further."

He then looked over his shoulder and gave his orders. "Talk to the group's owner and make it happen," he said to Egon. "Have the boy come to the gates in the morning."

"You want to put him through the chosen's test?" asked General Finton.

"No," answered the king. "I want to know what his true fighting ability is. I will have him fight your son tomorrow."

"Eli will be no match for him, I'm sure. But, even if he beats my son, he cannot be an elite born . . . if that is what you are thinking," argued Finton.

"I don't know what he is," answered the king, "but that boy is driven and has a range of gifts I don't see very often. He is bold. It will not be the first time you and I disagree on something, Finton." He watched Lucas ride out of the arena, and sat back down to take his daughter on his lap. "Let's leave it at that and just see how he does. Unless you do see his potential, but don't welcome the competition for your son?"

Lucas went straight to the task of taking care of Sable when they returned to camp. He had watched Rowan disappear into his wagon to tend to his sore legs. When he had finished rubbing down the horse, he decided to make himself scarce by taking Ana for a walk around the camp, just in case Rowan decided to come out and confront him. They met a group of musicians and sat down to watch them play the rest of the afternoon.

Lucas had left a sleepy Ana with Nadia and went back to get her favorite toy for her from their wagon—a cloth doll Rosa had made for her fifth birthday. He was about to set foot inside when the discussion that was coming from just on the other side of the wagon made him stop in his tracks.

"So, tomorrow, bring him by the first light of morning," he heard an unfamiliar voice say.

"I cannot let him go," Stan said. "He brings in a lot of money. It would be difficult to replace him."

"You cannot refuse the king's orders," the man replied. Lucas recognized it as the voice of Egon, the man the king had tasked with finding Lucas in order to reward him for saving the woman and her children. "You have admitted that no one in the group is the boy's kin, and therefore he is not yours to keep. That said, the king does realize he is a form of income and is willing to pay." Lucas heard the clinking of what he assumed to be a small pouch of coins. "This is just for having him show up in the morning. More will follow if it is decided that he stays."

"This is a considerable amount of coin."

Using his mind to watch the two men on the other side of the wagon, Lucas saw the smile creeping over Stan's face, and he cringed.

"The king is generous. If he is offering this much up front just to see the boy fight, you can only imagine how much he would be willing to pay to keep him."

"I will accept your offer on one condition, that you do not mention our monetary exchange to the other members of my entourage."

"As you wish," Lucas heard the man say, and then he listened to the sound of his horse trotting off.

"Time to go get me a well-deserved drink, I think," he heard Stan grumble merrily, and then he was off, too, leaving Lucas leaning up against his wagon, his heart hammering in his chest. It was almost impossible to believe that, after all these months with the circus, he was being traded for a few coins. Yet, if that was the way for him to be able to join the king, then so be it.

The entire group stayed out until late that night and attended the various parties that were going on, but Lucas was the first to return to tend to all the animals before bed.

He had brought fresh water and hay to all the horses and was feeding Tiny when he heard the door from Stan's wagon open. He knew Rowan had stayed in there this entire time, but he seemed calm enough now, and it appeared that his legs felt just fine. He didn't see Lucas kneeled by Tiny until he was about to walk right past him. The moment their gazes met, Lucas watched anger flash through Rowan's eyes, anger so intense that it frightened him. When Rowan picked up a shovel and swung it above his head, Lucas spun around in an effort to avoid it, but it happened so fast. The shovel hit him on the side of the head and the force threw him against the wagon. He collapsed to the ground, flashes of light blurring his vision and all sensation in his body leaving him. He struggled against the blackness that was clouding his mind, knowing somehow that if he succumbed to it, it would all be over for him.

Stan, Ned and Bernt were marching back into camp. He could vaguely hear their jolly voices and their laughter. Until it stopped abruptly.

"What's wrong, son?" Stan was asking.

"I couldn't help it. I just lost it," stammered Rowan.

Then there was some shuffling and Lucas could see the blurry shapes of men dropping to their knees next to him. At that point, his eyes would not remain open, and he could feel the pool of blood forming underneath his head.

"Go and find the women," Ned was saying. "Don't try to explain what happened, just get them here quick!"

"Is he breathing?" asked Stan.

"He is, but barely," answered Ned. "Bernt, can you lift him up and get him into some light, so we can have a better look?"

"No," said Stan quickly. "Nobody can see him like this. The king wants to see Lucas tomorrow morning at first light."

"For what?"

"To assess his fighting skills. And then... possibly buy him from us."

"Well, that is not going to happen now," Ned growled.

By the time Rowan returned with the women and Everett, they had laid Lucas down in the supply wagon. Ned told Nadia to keep Ana away, and Rosa and Lisette stepped inside.

Everett entered, too, and sounded angry, but Lucas was having trouble sorting through the group's range of emotions. All he knew was that he couldn't allow himself to fall asleep. But he was losing that fight, and before long, he felt himself slipping away.

"He needs to see a doctor," Everett snapped, unable to take his eyes from Lucas. "That son of yours . . . he was an accident waiting to happen. He needs to deal with the consequences."

"It is not just him I'm worried about," said Stan hastily. "And lower your voice, please."

"What do you mean?" Everett growled. If he were of normal size, it was likely he'd be shaking Stan by the shoulders.

"I have already received payment. They are expecting Lucas to show up at the gate, first thing in the morning. Who knows what they will do to Rowan when they don't get what they paid for?"

Everett threw his hands up and shook his head. "Just give the money back! Say you changed your mind!"

"I can't," said Stan. "I spent some of it already and having been paid . . . with the king, that means he basically owns him already. I tried to refuse to give him up in the first place, but by the way this officer was talking . . ."

"You played raffle, didn't you?" asked Everett. "I watched some people gamble at it earlier this afternoon. A game of dice that requires only luck. All you have to do is throw three dice and hope they land on the same number to win the round." He stared at Stan. "How much did you lose?"

"More than I can repay," sighed Stan. "We have no other choice than to say he had an accident. That he tripped and hit his head."

Lisette interrupted their conversation. "They won't buy that," she said, stepping out of the wagon. "He has a huge wound on one side of his head and a lump the size of an apricot on the other. You don't fall on both sides of your head. I need to go and get a needle and thread and try to stitch up the wound."

Nadia boiled some rags to clean up the blood and Everett took them from her, moving quickly. Lisette and Rosa worked carefully to stitch Lucas up. The men sat around the campfire and waited. Rowan had his head in between his legs and was trembling. "They are going to hang me for this," he muttered.

"Don't be so dramatic," said Ned. "It's not like he's a soldier in the king's army. He's a circus boy they happened to take some interest in. It's no big deal. If we scrape all our money together and sell some stuff, we can pay the money back."

Rowan shook his head. "You didn't see how they were watching him. All of them. The king, the senior staff. When I kicked him, that officer who had talked to Lucas a few months ago . . . he looked angry."

Everett stood up and began to pace up and down. "Rowan is right," he said. "They did take great interest in him. They know he's something special." He paused and, when no one else spoke, he continued. "For goodness' sake, we all know that as well. He anticipates things before being able to see them, knows things before being told . . . and the way he gets that old horse to do things. Not to mention his handling of the sword. There's a good possibility Lucas is either a chosen or elite, and those are hard to come by—which means they won't be happy if they don't get him. Given Rowan's behavior during the performance, he is the likely suspect to have hurt him. If he doesn't wake up before first light, we have no choice but to keep him hidden. We'll have to tell everyone he ran off or something."

"That story would be more believable if the horse was gone," said Bernt.

"I can take care of Sable," said Ned. "We will have to hide him, too."

They made a plan that night and agreed on what to do. Everett knew how much it would have meant to Lucas to join the king's army, but with the injuries he had sustained, that more than likely would never be possible. He hated Rowan for what he had done and would love to see him get punished for it, but he could not let anything happen to the circus. It was his life. It was all of their lives. Without it, he would still be begging on the streets.

He watched Ned take Sable away before first light and return without him a short time later. He had sold Sable to some performers who were already moving out, telling them he had to sell the horse to settle a gambling debt.

Everett had a lump in his throat just thinking about how Lucas would take the news that Sable was no longer with them. He had sat by his side all night, but there had been no improvement and the boy never woke up.

Stan woke at first light, and made sure that they all started packing, like everyone else around them. He ordered that all props and other equipment were carefully placed around Lucas and tied down, so nothing would fall on him. They could still get to him from a front window, but from the door he was completely out of sight. Ana had been told that Lucas had gone for a ride when she asked where he was, and they gave a common cold as explanation for Nadia's watery eyes.

Stan knew they were likely to get a visit from soldiers looking for Lucas. He was dreading having to face the tall officer with a lie, so he was relieved to see a different officer, one with a large mustache and sideburns, with the soldiers when they eventually came. He hoped he would be easily convinced of their story.

When they showed up, Stan acted busy and pretended to be surprised. He waited as they took a quick look around camp before approaching them.

"Can I help you, sir?" he asked, walking up to the officer in charge.

"We are here for a boy named Lucas," said the officer.

"He's not already with you?" asked Stan. "I told him last night to report to the castle gate first thing this morning. His horse is gone, so I assumed he went."

"No, he never showed," said the officer.

Stan turned around and called out to the rest of the group. "Anyone seen Lucas this morning? They say he did not show up at the gates."

Most of them shook their heads, but Ned stood up and walked over. "I saw him leave on his horse before the sun was up and he has not come back. I'm sorry," he said to the officer, "but he disappears from time to time without any of us knowing where he goes. Always turns up, though. Can we send him over when he does?"

"Hmm," answered the officer. "Do you mind if we have a look around?"

"Be my guest," said Stan and stepped out of the way.

The officer ordered his soldiers to look in the wagons and he himself walked to the wagon Rowan was sitting in front of. He looked at Rowan suspiciously. He had seen him kick the boy in the show and had not been impressed.

Rowan quickly got out of the way when the officer opened the door to the supply wagon. "What do you keep in here?" he asked.

"All of our equipment, sir," answered Rowan nervously. "We've loaded up, so as to be on our way."

The officer tried to look past all the equipment, but as the wagon appeared full, he shut the door again.

"Where are you headed?" the officer asked Stan after closing the door.

Stan cleared his throat and thought fast. "We're planning to go east from here. We've not been there yet and hope to draw some new crowds."

"To the east?" The officer frowned. "Best be careful out that way. There are quite a lot of raiding parties, on account of hunters crossing the great river at this time of the year."

"Oh, we won't be going that far," Stan quickly added, choosing his words carefully. "I appreciate the warning, though."

The soldiers all reported back to the officer. "No sign of the boy," one of them announced, and the officer had them move out.

The whole way back to the castle, Verron was hoping he would catch a glimpse of the boy somewhere. He dreaded going back empty-handed. He'd already seen how furious the king had been when he found out this morning that the boy had not showed up at the gate. At that point, everyone still held high hopes that his performing group was holding him back and that they would locate him, but he remembered the boy running away from him once before.

Verron crossed the second bridge and saw the king convening with his advisors in the inner bailey. He approached them but waited until the king acknowledged his presence and invited him to speak.

"No sign of the boy, sire. He rode out this morning, and his group assumed he had showed up here."

The king frowned. "You believe that to be true, Verron?"

"I have no reason not to. The horse was not there. They said he often goes off without telling them where."

"Very well," said the king. "Inform all outgoing patrols to be on the lookout for him."

Verron gave a quick bow. "Of course."

"Have you considered the possibility that the boy might have run away because he does not want to join?" asked General Finton.

"Do we give any of our boys that choice?" asked the king sternly.

"No, but we could still be wrong about the boy. What he showed us yesterday was a well-rehearsed act. He could be smart enough to have realized that. He may have been raised by warrior monks, but even they haven't had to fight to kill in a long time."

The king looked at Egon, who had remained quiet. "What do you think, Egon?"

"I don't think the boy is afraid. I remain of the opinion that the message to report to us this morning did not reach him."

The king nodded. Egon had been a trusted member of his staff for a long time and wasn't often wrong. Unlike Finton, who was opinionated and acted out of emotion instead of reason.

"When he is found, which is only a matter of time," continued the king, "I want him handled carefully and I don't want anyone jumping to their own conclusions. Any decisions that need to be made will be made by me and no one else."

The next time Lucas woke up, he could feel the rocking motion of the wagon over the sandy road. He remembered what had happened, at least the part where Rowan had come at him with a shovel. The aftermath was not as clear. His head throbbed, and he felt the bandage around his head, and the lump underneath. A sharp pain on the other side made him realize he had a wound there as well. He drifted in and out of sleep while the wagon rocked all day. By nightfall, they finally stopped, and Nadia came in to help him sit up.

"Happy to see you are awake, sleepyhead," she said, attempting a smile.

"What's happening?" he asked. He drank from the cup she held to his mouth. "Why am I in the equipment wagon?"

Nadia laid him back down and touched the side of his cheek. He felt hot and feverish.

"We had to hide you," she told him. "The king wanted you to come to the castle the morning after the show and test your skills. I believe he wants you to join his army, but we couldn't hand you over like this. They came looking, but Ned told them you'd left and didn't know where you were."

Lucas felt his eyes well, and his throat tightened. Bits of the conversation the group was having immediately after his injury began to float into his head. "You knew it was my dream to join the king's army."

"I know, sweetheart," Nadia said in a soft voice. "As soon as you are back on your feet, I am sure they will let you go back. Right now, you need to rest and get better." She kept gently rubbing his cheek until he closed his eyes and fell into a deep sleep again.

When Nadia emerged from the wagon a moment later, the others all looked at her and watched her sit down by the fire.

"How is he?" asked Stan. He had taken up the unpleasant habit of wringing his hands.

Nadia sighed. "He talked for a bit, but his fever's still very high. The lump has not gone down much."

"We're running out of time," said Ned, taking a deep sigh. "It's been two days. It's just a matter of luck that we haven't had another visit from the soldiers yet."

"That's only because they were told we were heading east and not south," said Bernt.

"I know," answered Ned, "so it won't be long before they figure that out. We can't keep him hidden. If they find out we lied? What then? We'll be finished. We need to get rid of him!"

"What?" asked Everett. He looked angry. "I am not going to have you kill him!"

"That's not what I meant," roared Ned.

"There is no need for that," said Stan, who'd been thinking about this for a while. "My brother runs an inn northeast of here. I'm sure he'd take Lucas in. Rowan knows the way and can take him there. If Lucas recovers, he can work to earn his keep and when things have cooled down, we can take him back. In the meantime, we can cross the border to the south."

"That land is governed by the king's brother, Lord Meloc," commented Ned.

"Yes, but we all know they rarely see or talk to each other," said Stan. He looked around and didn't see much enthusiasm for his plan. "Look, we don't have a choice. Ned is right. If they find Lucas with us, who knows what will happen to him, to us, or to Rowan." With these last words, he looked at Everett and Nadia. It troubled him that the time of decent money was coming to an end, but they had managed before Lucas. They could do it again.

"Are you sure your brother will take good care of him?" asked Everett.

"Absolutely," answered Stan. "He's a good man."

Everett looked at Rowan, who had remained quiet. "And you better look after him when you take him there," he warned. "That's the only part of this plan I do not like."

CHAPTER 6

Lucas's fever finally broke a day later, and he became more conscious of his surroundings. He was aware that he was still in the equipment wagon and that it was moving, but much of its contents had been taken out. He tried to sit up and knocked a metal pail over in the process, and his movement must have alerted whoever was guiding the cart that he was awake, because the wagon came to an abrupt halt.

Within a moment, the back doors swung open and Rowan appeared. "You and I are on a trip," he said as he climbed inside and kneeled next to Lucas. He started to tie his hands and feet together.

"Where are we going?" asked Lucas, too weak to resist him.

"My uncle's inn. You get to stay there until the king stops looking for you and it's safe for us to come and get you again."

"The king is looking for me?"

Rowan tied the end of the rope through a hook on the wall so Lucas couldn't get up. "Yes," he answered. "We think he is, but don't flatter yourself. He will soon forget about you. You are not that special."

"Why are you tying me up?"

"Because I don't trust you," Rowan answered. He finished tying the rope and backed out again.

Lucas knew they had finally arrived at the inn when he heard Rowan talking to his uncle and explaining why they were there. He let his uncle know he had only tied Lucas up for his own good so that he not run off into the wilderness in the midst of recovering from a concussion. Had Lucas not been in such discomfort, he might have laughed at the preposterous statement. A moment later, the door to the wagon opened and a young man with almost white hair entered. He smiled at Lucas as he untied him.

"I'm Lee," he said. "I work here, and I hear you are joining us?"

Lucas didn't say anything and followed Lee out of the wagon. His legs were shaky, and Lee helped steady him. He saw Rowan standing next to a short, round man almost identical to Stan in appearance.

"Take him in, Lee," said Stan's brother.

The inn consisted of a dark two-story wooden building with a front entrance in the middle and a large stable block attached to it. A sign, with a name that fit the appearance of the building, hung from the eaves of the roof and read, "The Black Log Inn." Lee led him through the double stable doors and then through an inner door that connected the stable with the inn.

The interior was dark and gloomy. A low-beamed ceiling with thick pillars holding the second floor up made for a claustrophobic effect, and an excess of tables and chairs added to it. A few rough-looking guests were eating or drinking, and they glanced up at Lucas with disinterest. They were not the kind of people he was used to, and he averted his eyes.

Lee told him to sit down by the large fireplace on the far side of the room. Several cauldrons hung above the fire and a lady was stirring the contents of one of them. Lee told him that Stan's brother's name was Niall, and that the woman by the hearth was Aida, and that she was the innkeeper's wife. She turned around when Lee spoke of her and wiped her hands on her apron before coming over to Lucas and taking a good look at him. She then carefully took the bandage off his head and inspected the wound.

"Took quite a hit there," she said kindly. "How did this happen?"

Lucas wasn't sure what he should say, but before he could say anything, Lee answered for him. "Goat kicked him in the head apparently. It made him fall against a wagon and took him out for several days."

"Really?" asked Aida. "A goat did this?"

Lucas dropped his eyes to the floor and did not contradict the story. He could tell she did not believe the lie Rowan had told, but it would do him no good to tell the truth while Rowan was here.

"Well," said Aida when he did not answer. "Whoever stitched it up did a good job. We will leave the bandage off for now and see how it heals. It should not be visible for long." She took a cloth and cleaned around the wound before handing him a bowl of stew to eat.

Lucas thanked her and gladly took the bowl from her, just as Rowan and his uncle walked in.

"Don't spoil that boy too much, Aida," said Niall. "He is going to have to work to earn his keep."

"Not until he is all healed up," she replied firmly, and gave Lucas a wink. He instantly liked her—she reminded him of Nadia, who he already missed.

His stay at the inn wasn't bad the first few days. Rowan left the morning after they arrived and never spoke another word to him, for which he was grateful. Aida looked after him and let him sleep on a bed in one of the back rooms, until he started to feel stronger and was able to walk without the world spinning around him. Then Niall told him that his lazy days were over, and he had to start working to earn his keep. His job was to look after the travelers' horses and to keep the fireplace stocked with firewood.

He no longer got to sleep in the back room but had to sleep in a corner of the stable block, on a dusty straw mattress. He was only allowed inside the inn to do chores or to get his food. He soon realized why he had to sleep in the stables. The travelers who were frequenting the inn came and went at all hours of the day and night and he had to be at their service at any given moment.

It was exhausting. He took naps wherever and whenever he could, especially when Lee was there to help him, which became less and less as time went on. Niall had assigned Lee to indoor work, and, in the end, Lucas hardly saw him at all. Lucas didn't mind taking care of the horses, and most of the travelers were friendly enough when they handed over their horse or came to pick it up.

He was told to avoid any interactions with the guests when he came inside the inn and he rarely got to speak to Aida, as she was always busy. With people coming and going the way they did, he decided it was best not to get attached and started to distance himself from everyone. He did his chores and kept to himself. He reflected back on his time at the monastery and all that he learned there. He decided he wasn't going to return to circus life, even if they came for him. Instead, he would wait for the right time to leave the inn and find his own way back to the king's castle. If the king did not want him, he would go to the monastery, take the vow to protect the stone and live out his days there.

The inn was situated on a main road that led to a decent-sized town, which he could see in the distance. No other houses or buildings were anywhere near the inn, and this made it the perfect place for travelers who did not want to draw attention to themselves, or for meetings they didn't want anyone to know about. Lucas would often see Niall sit down at a table and talk to the guests. As soon as Lucas was close enough, they would stop talking and only continue after he was some distance away again.

One evening, a different kind of traveler stopped at the inn. It was a cold and wet night when Lucas was told to rush outside to collect a late incoming horse. He threw a rain cloak over his shoulders and opened the stable doors. The wind was howling, and the rain splashed in his face as he struggled to hold the doors open.

"Sir," shouted Lucas, shielding his face from the rain. "Sir, can you lead your horse inside, and I will take over from there?"

He could not hear a reply over the wind, but the rider rode his black horse through the entryway and dismounted. Lucas quickly shut the doors behind him and rushed over to take care of the horse.

"There is a door, sir," he pointed out. "It will take you straight into the inn. It's warm inside, and there is plenty of good food."

The rider took off his cloak, removed his saddle bags, and disappeared through the door without a word or as much as even looking at him.

"You're welcome," Lucas mumbled as he rubbed the horse dry. He was drenched, so after he put the horse in a stall and fed it, he went inside to try and dry up by the fire. It was late and all the guests had gone to bed. He made his way over to the fire and picked up a stool along the way to sit on. He threw an extra log on and sat down with his hands out in front of the flames. His trousers were soaked through and he was shivering.

Creaking sounds coming from the stairway told him someone was descending the stairs, and he watched as the new guest came down and entered the room. He had changed into dry clothes and sat himself down at a table not far from him. Aida came from the back and served the guest a bowl of thick pottage soup and a plate of crusty bread. When she saw Lucas by the fire, she came over to him. "You haven't eaten dinner yet, Lucas. Will you have something?" she asked him.

"Yes, please," answered Lucas, and he turned back to face the fire.

He noticed how the guest had raised his head when he heard Aida say his name and started watching him with interest. He was different from the usual travelers who stopped at the inn. This man was clean-shaven and wearing clothing of good quality—leather trousers, a white laced-up shirt and a suede vest. Lucas thought that he might be a soldier. He looked fit and strong, like someone who would not shy away from a fight, but he didn't carry a sword, only a dagger that hung on a belt around his waist. It was probably the weather that had made him stop for the night instead of riding the rest of the way into town, decided Lucas. He took the bowl of food from Aida and stood up after she left so that he could take it into the stables to eat.

"You don't look very dry yet. Why not eat in front of the fire?" he heard the man say to him.

Lucas tried to answer politely. "I'm not really supposed to be here when guests are present and the innkeeper is not," he said.

The man looked around and indicated to the empty inn around them.

"Just me here," he said. "I won't tell."

Lucas hesitated for a moment. The man seemed nice and kind, but he no longer trusted anyone at this point.

"No, I'd better go, sir. Good night to you," he said, and made his way back to the stables.

The next morning, Lucas grabbed breakfast before any of the guests had come down and started to get the black horse ready. He had assumed the new guest would be leaving first thing, but the request to prepare his horse never came and Lucas put him back in his stall.

Later that afternoon, a large group of six guests arrived. They were more like the travelers he was used to seeing—shady-looking riders with cold expressions who made him feel uneasy the moment he laid eyes on them. All six were dressed in almost identical black clothing and leather boots. They looked like soldiers, but carried daggers and no swords, just like the guest from the night before. One of the men had a black beard with a deep scar across his face and one eye covered up with a patch. Lucas quickly took the horses and avoided eye contact. Staying outside, the men talked quietly among themselves, and he felt their eyes on his back the entire time. He tried to ignore the uneasy feeling these men gave him and continued leading the horses away, when one of them suddenly called out, "Hey, boy!"

Lucas froze and looked over his shoulder. The man with the scar had stepped away from his friends and stood in the barn.

"What's your name?"

"Lucas, sir," he answered.

"How long have you been here?" the man asked. "I've not seen you before."

"Only a few weeks, sir," he replied and led the horses inside their stalls. The man seemed satisfied with his answer and headed inside the inn with the others. Lucas was still busy putting all the horses away when the guest with the black horse showed up behind him and asked him if he could get his horse tacked up.

"You are leaving us, sir?" Lucas asked. The bad feeling about the six new guests had not left him yet, but he somehow felt calmer in the presence of this man and was sorry to see him go.

"I'll return later," the man answered.

Lucas nodded and rushed off. When he returned with the man's horse, he waited for him to mount up and handed him the reins.

"Thank you, Lucas," said the man and gave him a smile before riding off in the direction of the town.

Lucas kept himself busy the rest of the day and, when he finally went in that evening, he noticed the six men sitting at a table close to the fireplace. One of them turned when he came in and followed his every move. He was the one Lucas felt most uneasy about. The man with the scar was the leader, but this other one, with his scraggly blond hair and cold blue eyes, gave him chills. The other five continued their conversation but had their eyes on him as well.

Every muscle in his body felt tense. He sat himself down and took some food, but he felt sick and a strong urge to leave came over him. He quickly forced his food down and stood up. He would have to walk past their table again unless he left through the front door, but Niall was seated at the table next to it and would scold him if he did. He looked toward the kitchen to see if Aida was anywhere nearby, but he could not see her. Some guests at another table were playing a dice game and suddenly laughed loudly, slamming their fists on their table. Everyone in the inn turned their heads to see what they were so enthusiastic about, including the six men, and Lucas took his chance. He was nearly past them when suddenly, the man with the beard and scar grabbed his arm.

"Leaving so soon?" he snarled.

Lucas tried to pull his arm back, but the man had a tight grip on him. He hastily looked around to see if Niall, Lee or any of the other guests saw what was happening, but the guests at the dice table had calmed down again and they had all returned to talking and eating.

He tried to pull away again. "Let go of my arm, sir," he said firmly.

The man smiled. "We know who you really are, and we know *what* you are," hissed the man under his breath, tightening his grip and pulling Lucas even closer.

"I have no idea what you mean, sir," said Lucas. His arm was hurting. He felt the beginnings of an inner energy boiling inside of him and he was about to try and break free when the front door to the inn opened and the guest who owned the black horse stepped inside. He searched around the room until his gaze fell on Lucas.

"Hey, boy!" he shouted. "Come over here and take care of my horse, will you?"

The other guests all stopped talking and looked from the door to Lucas. Niall stood up from the table and started shouting at him. "Go on, boy! What are you waiting for? Go and do as you are told."

Lucas looked down at his arm. Everyone at the table had their heads down, and any who may have witnessed the interaction between him and the man who grabbed his wrist now pretended nothing had happened. As fast as he could—without breaking into an outright run—he made his way for the front door, but he was stopped when he felt a hand on his shoulder.

"Was he giving you trouble?"

"I appreciate your concern, but I can handle it, sir," he answered.

"I know you can," said the guest, but Lucas was already heading out the door.

He found the black horse tied up outside. He stroked the soft nose and allowed himself to think of Sable, which was something he tried not to do very often. The black horse puffed warm air on his face while Lucas stood still, contemplating what had just happened. Something was not right, but he didn't know what. He looked up at the dark clear sky and took a deep breath before leading the horse inside.

When he finished all his chores that night, he walked to his bed in the corner and paused. He looked around and then up towards the hayloft. Perhaps that would be a nicer place to sleep, and safer. He turned away from his bed and made his way halfway up the ladder before pausing a second time. Again, he changed his mind, jumped off and quietly opened the stall door where the black horse stood. The horse nickered softly when he entered, and he pushed some fresh straw underneath the hay feeder. He made a little nest and then crawled in with his back against the wall and his knees tucked up. He was tired, but knew he couldn't sleep, and just rested his head on his knees.

He listened to the horse chewing his hay until another noise soon caught his attention—it was the outside door opening slightly. Soft footsteps made their way inside. He closed his eyes and used his ability to see four of the black riders sneak inside the stables. He had never had such vivid results with his gift before—he could see them perfectly. They were motioning to each other and the man with the scar pointed to the bed in the corner. One of the men walked over and then turned around and shook his head. He then pointed to the hayloft and another made his way up the ladder. When he didn't find what he was looking for, he climbed back down again.

Lucas had no idea why they were after him, but he instinctively knew they should not find him. He held his breath when the men started checking each stall. The stall he was in was the last one. If they looked closely, they would see him. He started to brace himself. He wished he had a sword. Fighting without it would be near impossible, and he was outnumbered.

The black horse had stopped eating and looked down at him. Lucas opened his eyes and stared at the horse while opening up his mind to speak to him. It was something he had discovered he could do with Sable. The black horse snorted and raised his head. His eyes became alert and his body tense. When the man with the blond hair and cold blue eyes stepped closer to his stall, the black horse stepped forward and put his head over the door. He started to stamp his hooves and huffed loudly. Just when the man wanted to look inside his stall, the horse reared up and clattered his front hooves on the door, nearly hitting the man, who only escaped by jumping backwards.

"Wow, that's a wild one," the man spoke, a little too loudly.

"Byram!" hissed the man with the scar. "Be quiet."

Byram shook his head. "Why? He is clearly not here. I thought that kid said the boy would sleep here."

"He did."

116

"Well, he's not here now, is he?"

"We'll get him another time," said the man with the scar. "We better go for now. That horse made enough noise to wake the whole place up."

The black horse nudged Lucas gently after the men left. In return, he touched the horse on his nose to thank him and yawned. It had taken an enormous amount of concentration to watch the men with his mind, and he was tired. Soon the horse focused his attention on eating again. Lucas curled up and the repetitive sound of the horse chewing the hay lulled him to sleep.

His dream that night was of a memory he had tried to forget, and he woke up when he heard the rooster's call in the morning. He stretched his legs and sat quietly, thinking about the dream. It had been the vivid memory of his father dying and of five men dressed in black, whose clothes were similar to the six staying at the inn. He had no idea if there was a connection, or even if they could be the same group. He did not remember seeing one with a scar or cold blue eyes, but as long as these men were at the inn, he did not feel he was safe. If they did not leave this morning . . . he would.

Lucas got up and started to clean out the stalls. He fed the horses and cleaned tack, keeping himself busy. Before he had finished his chores, Niall peeked his head around the corner and called out to him.

"Lucas, we need firewood. Now!"

"All right, sir," answered Lucas, and he put the rake he had been using in the corner. He went outside and walked around the stables. The firewood was kept in a shed behind the inn, and the door was latched by a steel bar that he had to slide. He looked over his shoulder before going in and saw a magpie perched on a fence not far from the shed. Lucas paused. The bird was facing him—its dark eyes fixed as if looking straight into his soul. It sent a shiver through his body and a foreboding feeling came over him. He brushed it off and turned away. It was just a stupid bird and not even a big one at that.

He continued into the dark shed and picked up a basket. Kneeling on the floor, he started loading the logs into it when suddenly his body froze. The air behind him was changing. Someone had come through the doorway and was approaching carefully. Lucas reached for the iron poker on his left and swung it backwards behind him in one swift movement. A gurgling sound confirmed he had hit what he'd aimed for.

He immediately pulled the poker back and swung around to lunge it forward into another target. This time there was no sound when he pierced the second man straight through the heart. With the poker still in his hand, he stood up and looked at the two men dressed in black on the ground before him. He felt nauseous and would have emptied his stomach had anything been in it.

Both men lay on their backs with their eyes wide open, staring up at nothing.

He was shocked by what his own trembling hands had done but felt he had moved without having had any control over it. Just as he began to wonder if the other four men would show up, Lee appeared in the doorway. With his mouth hanging open, he stared wide-eyed at the dead men on the floor before looking to Lucas, who still held the bloody poker in his hand. He ran off, returning in seconds with Niall, whose face looked white. Lucas had made it out of the shed and stood by the door when Niall peered inside and retched at the sight. He then stared at Lucas, whose clothing and face were splattered in blood.

"I don't know what happened," stammered Lucas. "They tried to get to me and—"

"And you decided to kill them?" shouted Niall. He took one last look inside the shed and then grabbed Lucas by the collar.

"I didn't mean to," pleaded Lucas when Niall dragged him to another storage shed and pushed him inside. "I'm sorry!"

"Too late for that, boy!" Niall shouted, slamming the door and locking it. "You are going to hang for this!" More people were coming out of the inn, and he heard Aida sobbing fearfully and asking her husband what was going to happen. He heard the urgent sound of a horse galloping away, and someone was stationed outside the shed door to make sure he would not get out.

It was at least an hour before the shed door opened again and two town guardsmen walked in. They shackled him by his wrists and ankles and took him to a prison wagon that stood waiting on the road. He saw Niall and Lee standing by the inn's door. Lee looked upset, but Niall looked angry. Lucas could sense that he was only thinking of what it would do to his business now that a double murder had taken place. None of the other guests could be seen, nor did he see the other four men dressed in black, whose horses were no longer in the stables.

Lucas sat down on the bench when they closed the door behind him and locked it. He was numb and could feel nothing, though he tried to. The wagon started to move, and he was led away from the inn. He wasn't able to wrap his brain around what had happened, no matter how many times he played the scenario over in his head. One minute he was reaching for firewood and the next minute he was covered in blood with a fire poker in his hand and two dead men at his feet. Could the kid the men had been talking about in the stables last night have been Rowan? Is that what they had meant by saying they knew who and *what* he was?

None of these thoughts were going to help him get out of his current predicament. Lucas leaned back against the iron bars of the prison wagon and tried to clear his mind.

He sat quietly on the way into town and obediently stepped out of the wagon when they arrived at the prison. Because of the shackles on his ankles, he could only shuffle his feet, and thus he followed the guards into the dark prison that reeked of sweat and other bodily fluids. They walked past other prison cells, and grimy-looking prisoners reached their hands through the bars of their cells, trying to touch him. The guards did their best to push them away and to make a clear path. Some prisoners were shouting or making funny noises and the sounds echoed off the walls as they went deeper inside the prison.

They stopped at the far end of the hallway, where a cell door was opened, and he was led inside. He was relieved to see, when he looked around, that there would be no other prisoners in there with him. The guards took his leg shackles off and replaced them with shackles that were attached to the stone wall. When they finished and were backing out, he heard a guard asking what he was in for and another guard answering, "Murder! Killed two guests at the Black Log Inn."

Lucas looked through the bars of his cell when the guards left and saw an older man sitting by his bars in the cell opposite. His clothes were totally worn. He was thin and the long hair and beard gave Lucas the feeling he'd been there for some time. They looked at each other and the man grinned.

"Murder, boy? Is that right? Is that what you're here for?"

Lucas slowly nodded.

"Those two guests . . . they try to hurt you, boy?" he asked, but Lucas did not answer.

"You probably should have let them hurt you," he muttered, crawling back into the shadows. "The judge's not a forgiving man. He'll have you swinging by your neck."

Lucas let the old man's words sink in and found himself surprised that he was not panicking. Something inside of him told him he would be all right, no matter what. Father Ansan had always said that each person had a path to follow. If this was the end of his, then so be it. If not, he would continue to follow it wherever it would lead him. He no longer felt he had control over his life, and he resigned himself to the fact. He was at the mercy of others now who would make decisions for him.

He could still hear other prisoners calling out and he moved as far away from the bars as the chain would allow and put his hands over his ears to distance himself.

The prison stayed noisy most days and nights, echoing with the shouting and screaming of other prisoners. The strong odor of feces, urine and sickness, which he had smelled when first entering the prison, always hung in the air, and the rats that were constantly running across the floor made it difficult to sleep or find any peace. The shackles on his legs had started to rub into his skin and created sores, which attracted one rat who came dangerously close to him. If it bit him, he risked disease and death, which he knew was happening in other cells already.

After he had been there for an entire week—though it felt like a year—he woke up to the sound of cell doors being opened and the clanging of chains. He slowly rose to his feet when the guards arrived at his cell door.

"Judgment day, boy!" he heard the prisoner in the opposite cell say to him.

Lucas was let out of his cell and shackled to a long chain with other prisoners.

"Where are we going?" he asked the prisoner in front of him.

"The courthouse. You get to meet the judge, who will decide your fate today. Some of us will rot in prison a bit longer. Some of us will waste away doing hard labor at the mines. The lucky ones will meet their maker today."

The prisoner half turned to look at him. "Are you the boy who killed two men?"

When Lucas answered that he was, the prisoner shook his head in sympathy. "Then I guess you will be one of the lucky ones today. May the gods have mercy on your soul and the rest of us, who must continue to suffer."

With the last of the prisoners attached to the chain, they moved out. Lucas squinted under the bright sunlight when they were led across a courtyard, where guards were busy setting up the gallows. He watched them test the trapdoors as they walked by. It was a sound he would not soon forget. He looked away and concentrated on keeping up. The chains on his ankles felt heavy and pressed down on his feet every time he fell behind.

Finally, the long chain of prisoners made their way past the gallows and were led into the narrow room of the courthouse. Here they were made to stand and wait, with their backs against a long wall. At the far end, a man was seated behind a high wooden desk. He wore a dark cloak, and Lucas took him to be the judge. Directly in front of the desk was a small stand in which prisoners were placed, one at a time. The rest of the courtroom was full of benches filled with witnesses and spectators. When a prisoner was led before the judge, a statement of the crime committed was swiftly read out by a clerk. The judge then asked the people in the room if anyone had anything to say, either in favor or against the prisoner. The judge barely waited for anyone to speak before he would slam his wooden hammer on the desk and announce the appropriate sentence for the crime.

There were only three different outcomes for each prisoner. Thieves were sent to the mines—domestic violence and disorderly conduct, well that meant more time in prison. Murder and crimes against authority meant the gallows. Everyone was guilty and no one was released. The mood in the courtroom was depressing. Even the prisoners' family members were quiet and already knew the outcome. Some sniffling could be heard from time to time when a prisoner was led away after his sentence, but most of the time there was just silence.

The line of prisoners in front of Lucas was getting shorter and shorter and sentences were being dealt out faster and faster. Soon it was his turn. They removed the shackles from his feet and ushered him onto the stand.

"The case of the boy, Lucas—no surname mentioned here," stated the guard when he announced his case. "Accused of killing two guests at the Black Log Inn, a week ago today!"

The judge, who had hardly looked up all day, raised his head when he heard the word "boy" and stared at him.

"How old are you, boy?"

"If it is the month past the summer, then I am now twelve, sir!" answered Lucas.

The judge raised his eyebrows. "Hmm . . . and already a killer," he muttered. "I am sorry, boy," he said, raising his voice, "but there is only one punishment here for murder. You will be taken to the gallows and hung by the neck until dead."

He raised his hammer and was ready to slam it down when a voice echoed through the room.

"Wait!" someone shouted from the back of the room. "You haven't asked if anyone has anything to say in the boy's defense."

All heads turned, including Lucas's, to see a man make his way down the aisle and stop in front of the banister. It was the guest from the inn, the one with the black horse.

"And?" asked the judge. "Do you have anything to say?"

"I do, Your Honor! The boy acted in self-defense!"

The judge studied the scroll before him. "It says here, there were no witnesses when the crime was committed."

"That's right, and therefore it cannot be determined that it was murder. Yet, I was a guest at the inn and witnessed the two men harassing the boy the night before. I had to intervene myself, for not even the innkeeper would. It is my belief they followed him into the woodshed the next morning, to commit a crime they had every intent on carrying out the night before. Do we not all have a right to defend ourselves in that case?" He turned around to face the audience and several people nodded in agreement.

"You swear this to be the truth, sir?"

"Dastan, Your Honor. My name is Dastan."

"Hmm," said the judge. "If you were a guest at the inn yourself, am I right in concluding you do not reside locally, and therefore have no personal connection to the boy?"

Dastan looked briefly at Lucas and then turned back to the judge. "That's right, Your Honor. I do not have a personal connection to this boy. I never met him until I stayed at the inn. I am only here to see justice done and to inform you that it is my strong belief that no murder was committed."

All eyes were on the judge, who seemed very conflicted. Finally, he looked up and addressed the courtroom. "Two people lost their lives, whether they deserved it or not. I cannot let it go unpunished. I will change his sentence to five years of hard labor," he said and slammed the hammer on the desk.

Two guards stepped forward and grabbed Lucas by the arms to take him away.

Dastan walked past him and whispered, "I am sorry. I tried. But at least I bought you time."

"I am grateful for it, sir," said Lucas before he was taken out of the courtroom and led back to his prison cell.

"So, the gods were with you today," he heard the prisoner from the opposite cell say when he returned. "Someone must be watching over you."

Lucas sat down and listened to the prisoner praying to his savior. Other prisoners were led back to their cells and for the first time the prison became eerily quiet. Then Lucas understood why—the sound of the trapdoors started to make its way deep down into the prison. Lucas put his hands over his ears to block the sound out—he was afraid to close his eyes out of fear that his mind would drift outside and he would see. Only when the sound stopped did he allow himself to lie down. He felt lucky that it had not been him.

Several days went by before the guards came for those who were destined for hard labor in the mines. The sores underneath his shackles had gotten worse and made it hard to walk, but he was relieved to finally leave the prison, where death came knocking every day and he very well could have been next. A dozen other prisoners were loaded up with him and driven out of town. Several guards on horseback rode alongside to make sure no one escaped, but Lucas wondered why. His fellow prisoners were either too sick or too weak to even attempt an escape. They had been living on a watery corn soup with old crusty bread that, more often than not, was stolen by the rats before they could get their hands on it.

A prisoner across from him had been watching him for a while. "I know you," he finally said. "I have seen you before, in an act with a circus down south. You are the boy who can slice apples with a sword . . . blindfolded."

Other prisoners lifted their weary heads and looked at him.

"How did you end up all the way over here?"

"A long story, for another time," was all Lucas could bring himself to say, and turned his back so he could watch the countryside passing as they made their way east.

―――――――

Each evening, the prisoners were taken off the wagon so they could be given food and relieve themselves before being tied down to the trees for the night. When they got close to a tavern one evening, several of the guards disappeared and did not return until after sunrise. The prisoners were waiting in line to finally be loaded up again when the thundering sound of horse hooves made them all lower their heads. It was the sound of something they feared more than prison guards, and Lucas could hear some of them starting to pray. He was the only one who raised his head and watched the group of soldiers as they passed by.

A few months ago, he would have been excited and full of admiration, but now he was too tired and watched them with little emotion. He lowered his head just after he caught the eye of the lead officer, who he recognized as Officer Verron, glancing back over his shoulder. Lucas felt a prison guard nudge his back roughly—it was his turn to get into the wagon and he shuffled forward. He had one foot on the step leading up, when he heard the soldiers and their horses turning around. They were coming back. Officer Verron rode up to the prison wagon and pulled his horse to an abrupt halt. The rest of the soldiers stopped as well and waited behind him.

"Who's in charge here?" he asked sternly.

One of the older prison guards stepped forward. "I am, sir. Can I help you?"

"That boy over there," he said, pointing. "What is his name?"

The prison guard turned and looked at Lucas, who was still standing halfway up the step.

"His name is Lucas, sir."

Officer Verron moved his horse closer to the prison wagon to have a good look at him, but Lucas didn't think he would be recognizable. His hair and skin were dirty from having been on a prison floor for nearly two weeks, he was still wearing the blood-spattered shirt that had turned into a rusty color, and he was close to losing consciousness from sheer exhaustion. He looked down at his hands, and they didn't even look like his own.

"What was his crime?" asked Officer Verron, without taking his eyes off Lucas.

"Murder, sir!"

"Murder?" asked the officer, raising his eyebrows.

"Yes. Single-handedly killed two guests at the inn where he was employed. With an iron spike. A fire poker. Straight through the heart, they say. He was going to be hanged, but someone stepped up to speak for him and claimed the boy was attacked first."

"Who was it that came to his defense? Do you have a name?"

"Someone who was also a guest at the inn. May I ask what this is all about, and who do I have the pleasure of talking to?"

"The name is Verron. Senior Officer in the Army of King Itan. We have been looking for a boy, and I believe this to be him." He moved his horse closer to Lucas and looked down at him. "Your name is Lucas? Did you work in a circus? Maybe perform for the king, a few months ago?"

Before Lucas was able to answer, the guard spoke for him. "Must be a different boy, sir. The owner of the Black Log Inn stated that he'd been working there for two years."

Officer Verron looked towards the guard, an expression of frustration on his face. His eyes examined the rest of the prisoners, who all stood quietly. Some already looked sick with the fever, and others showed signs of weakness and malnutrition. "You can speak the truth, boy," he said firmly. "Were you, or were you not, performing for the king a few months ago on a horse in a sword-fighting act?" Again, the guard wanted to interrupt, but the officer silenced him by raising his hand, so Lucas was finally able to answer.

"Yes, sir!" he said wearily. "On the princess's birthday. My horse's name was Sable, and I met you on one occasion, after a performance."

Verron smiled and turned his horse towards the guard. "Release him!" he ordered.

The guard looked perplexed. "He's a prisoner! He has been sentenced, and I cannot free him."

"I am aware he is a prisoner," said Officer Verron, clearly even more irritated with the guard. "As you know, all prisoners are prisoners of the king. You will release your responsibility for him over to me. I will take him to the king, who will then decide the boy's fate."

The guard still wanted to object, but when he noticed that Officer Verron was motioning a couple of his soldiers to come forward, he seemed to change his mind. "Well, if you put it that way, I guess you can take him," he said, and stepped forward to release Lucas from the chain.

Officer Verron called for a horse to be brought forward while he watched the shackles being taken from Lucas's ankles, but not from his wrists.

"You can take them off as well," he commented. "I don't need him secured while we are riding. He will be surrounded by the king's soldiers and will have nowhere to go."

The guard sighed and removed the last restraints before handing him over to two soldiers, who had to help him on a horse.

"Do you think you can manage?" the officer asked Lucas when he saw the sores on his legs.

"Yes, sir," answered Lucas with determination. He was happy to get out of there and would walk all day and night if he had to.

Officer Verron gave the order to pull out. They rode off in a canter, leaving the prison wagon with its prisoners and guards soon behind them. The stirrup was rubbing on his sores, but he didn't care. He felt luck was on his side again. Or maybe the prisoner had been right, and the gods were with him. He reached forward, placing a hand over the shoulder of the horse. Beneath his hand, he felt the rhythm of forward momentum, which could only lead him somewhere better.

CHAPTER 7

Soon after they left the prison transport, Officer Verron stopped at a clear-running creek and told Lucas he could wash before they would continue on. He sent two chosen, who were a little older than Lucas, along with him. They had been riding in the back of the column and Lucas recognized them by their uniform. To his surprise, he saw that one of them was a girl. She had slender facial features, long dark eyelashes and hazel eyes. Her long black braid rested between her shoulder blades. Like the boy, she looked strong and fit. Lucas became aware he was gawking at her when she glanced over to him, and he quickly looked away.

Both chosen observed him silently as he stepped into the creek and cupped his hands to quench the thirst he had felt for a long time.

The cool water made him feel alive again and he started to wash himself, scrubbing away the prison smell that had seeped into his skin. He took his bloodstained shirt off and dropped it on the bank, since it was beyond washing and he would rather go shirtless than have to wear it again. He noticed the girl walk away, only to return a moment later with a clean shirt for him. As Lucas took it, he couldn't help but let his eyes wander down to the sword that hung from her waist. Instinctively, the girl put her hand on the pommel and backed away. The boy stood up from the rock that he was resting on.

"You fear I might try and make my escape?" They were the first words he had said to them.

"It is our duty to be prepared for that," the girl replied.

Despite his worn-down state, Lucas almost had to suppress a laugh. "If only you knew how little desire I have to leave you! You are my first hope in weeks!"

Both chosen seemed to relax at this, the boy nodding at him. Regardless, he was careful not to make any sudden moves when he put the clean shirt on and finished washing himself.

The boy and girl acted like seasoned soldiers and he watched them obey every command that day without question and with poise and authority, but he would soon discover that when camp was made for the night, they were the ones carrying out most of the chores. He also learned that he had been picked up by a patrol group that was monitoring the illegal crossing of hunters across the great river. Hunters would come across every year in groups to poach deer and other animals when the river was at its lowest. They were also known to raid food storages at farms or villages in the dead of night—taking sacks of grain, dried fruits, sugar, and salt, and on occasion wounding or killing unsuspecting civilians who tried to raise an alarm. It was the patrol group's duty to check up on reports of sightings and deal with them accordingly. They stopped along their way to ask people if they had seen or heard anything. When no sightings were reported, they would move on.

When they set up camp on the first night and the soldiers were all settled, the girl approached Lucas with a bowl of hot water and a cloth. "Here you are," she said. "You need to clean your sores. Otherwise, they can fester, and make you sick."

Lucas thanked her and dipped the cloth into the water. The girl stood over him and watched as he pressed the cloth against one of his wounds. It was painful, and he pulled it away. The girl then dropped to her knees and took the cloth from him. Lucas could only grimace and watch when she took over the task.

"Am I allowed to know your name?" he asked her, in order to distract himself from the pain.

The girl nodded. "My name is Zera and, over there, is Warrick."

Lucas glanced over to where Warrick was playing with an apple. With his back on the ground and knees raised, he kept tossing the apple up in the air and catching it, his wavy blond hair bouncing with every movement. He turned his head when he heard Zera say his name, and Lucas knew straightaway that Warrick was not one to miss anything.

"You are chosen ones," remarked Lucas. "Someone told me about you. But I feel silly for not considering that a girl could wield a sword. I hope I have not offended you."

"Don't worry," responded Warrick before Zera could and without interrupting his play. "She's used to being stared at. You are right. Girls usually don't carry the chosen bloodline. Zera is the exception."

"How so?" asked Lucas.

"Because I'm a twin," explained Zera. "My brother is a chosen as well."

"I see," said Lucas, even though he wasn't sure how that worked. He looked away from her and glanced around the camp. "What about elite borns? I was also told about them, but I don't see any of them here."

"Elite borns don't go on regular patrols," answered Zera. "They ride with the king and the king's guard."

"King's guard?"

"You will have seen them if you've been to the castle. They wear the maroon vests and black trousers. They are always close to the king, to protect him."

Lucas watched Zera pat the wounds dry. He remembered the stern-looking officer who had spoken to him right after he had stopped the wagon and now knew he had been a king's guard. He was glad he was not here now and felt Officer Verron had already shown to be less harsh and kinder in his words.

"I heard the king wants to see how I would fare in a real fight. Is that true?" he asked.

Zera nodded her head. "They will have you fight an elite born. We all did, before we were taken on." Zera put the cloth aside and opened a small pot that Warrick had brought over, with a smelly cream inside it. Two soldiers came up behind Lucas and kneeled on either side of him.

"This is going to hurt," Zera explained, as the soldiers pinned him down. "They have to hold you down for your own protection and for mine."

As soon as the ointment was applied, Lucas knew why he had to be secured. He felt it biting into his skin like a thousand ants. All he wanted to do was kick Zera out of the way to make her stop. Zera waited a moment before applying the cream onto the next wound and smiled empathetically. "I told you it would hurt," she said. "If it makes you feel any better, we've all been there at one point or another."

"What is it?" asked Lucas, biting on his lip while Zera continued.

"Not sure. The king's physician likes to experiment with herbs, and this is his concoction to stop infections in wounds. It burns like hell, but you will see that it really works." Zera reached next to her to hand Lucas a small bottle. "Drink this. It will make you sleepy almost right away, and you'll forget about the pain."

At that moment, Officer Verron came over to observe Zera's work. He stood with his arms folded across his chest, a somber look on his face. Lucas had become accustomed to the sting and was proud to be able to tolerate it, though he flinched every now and then.

"I'm pleased to see that the boy who has impressed the king is finally coming back to life," the officer stated before moving on, and Lucas could not tell if he was being warm or just matter-of-fact. There was distance in his eyes. Or maybe it was distrust. Lucas was certain that the knowledge that he was convicted of killing two people had not slipped the officer's mind.

"That should do it," said Zera when she had sealed the pot back up. "Are you all right?"

Lucas nodded, but felt overcome with exhaustion. The soldiers released him, and he vaguely heard Zera say she was going to bring back some food. Hunger was the furthest thing from his mind as he laid his head down and fell fast asleep.

He woke at dawn, when the first soldiers started to rouse, and noticed his hands and feet had been tied, making it difficult to sit up.

"Officer Verron thought you might try and make a run for it in the night," Warrick said, crouching down to untie him. "With you still being a prisoner and all. At least until the king decides what to do with you."

"I won't run," replied Lucas, rubbing his wrists where the rope had been.

Warrick nodded. "We know," he said, and made a gesture towards Zera, who was walking over.

"Here—you have to eat to get your strength back," she said, handing him a big bowl of porridge. "How are your sores?"

Lucas looked down at his legs and noticed they were no longer oozing yellow pus and fluid. Scabs had started to form already, and his ankles felt less sore and achy. He hadn't expected his wounds to heal so quickly.

"What did I tell you? It's good stuff," said Zera with a smile as she sat down to eat her own food.

"You were right," said Lucas, before digging into the porridge.

They broke camp and Lucas was made to ride up front, close to Officer Verron. Lucas knew they remained wary of him, but when he did what he was told and made no sudden moves during the days that followed, they began to relax a little. They still secured him every night when they laid down to sleep, but the rest of the time he was allowed to walk around and help Zera and Warrick with camp duties.

One day, Officer Verron requested to hear Lucas's account of how he was injured that night after the show. They sat down together by the fire, just the two of them, and the others seemed to understand it was time to make themselves scarce. Lucas had begun to trust the officer and sensed that it was all right to tell the truth at last. He told the story of how Rowan had hit him with the shovel.

"And—let me guess—the circus people hid you?"

Lucas didn't want to cause any trouble for his old friends, even if what they had done had taken him down a painful path. But he also could not lie to an officer of the king.

"Is that what happened?" Verron asked again, more gently.

"Yes, sir," Lucas answered, unable to meet the man's gaze. "There was great fear . . . fear of retaliation, if they were caught and accused of some sort of foul play."

Verron frowned at this. "Had they only done the responsible thing and handed Rowan over, only he would have been arrested. You would have been treated at the castle and not made to fight until you were fully recovered. Hiding you is news that may not sit well with King Itan. There may still be consequences for them. But let's focus on the recent past. You were convicted for killing two guests at the inn you were working in?"

"I was."

"Did you kill them?"

"Yes, sir."

"Why?"

Lucas thought back to the moment he had kneeled down to pick up the firewood and sensed the danger behind him. He had reacted before he himself knew what was happening. The men had held no weapons. Could he have been wrong? He looked over his shoulder and caught Zera and Warrick's gaze from afar, where they were rubbing down their horses. He felt close and at ease in their company. Their presence made him feel safe, like nothing could happen to him. He sighed and turned back around to see Officer Verron look at him directly, waiting for his answer.

"They had their attention on me from the moment they arrived," he answered. "They came in the stables during the night looking for me, but I hid myself and they could not find me. Then they snuck up behind me into the woodshed the following morning and I grabbed an iron poker from the wall. It all happened very quickly, sir."

Officer Verron nodded his head but said nothing.

"Will the king still want me?" he asked reluctantly.

"Sounds to me that those men gave you reason to fear your safety," answered Officer Verron. "If what you tell me is true and you acted in self-defense, the king should still want you, but it will not be up to me to decide. Nor will my say have much influence, I am afraid. I could have left you with the prison transport and simply informed the king of your whereabouts, but it did not look like any attempt was being made by the guards to deliver you or your fellow prisoners to the mines alive. That is why I took you."

The group spent a few more days checking different areas to see if hunters had crossed the river before turning around and heading back in the direction of the king's castle. In the evenings, both Zera and Warrick would sit close to him to eat their dinner, but they became more reserved and didn't talk much. Lucas had the impression that they were instructed to behave that way and let them be. He did find out that both were thirteen, and that Zera's brother's name was Davis.

They had joined the king's army within weeks of Warrick and the three of them were close, as all the chosen ones were.

"We have to stick together," said Zera. "Life at the castle is not always easy. We get fed and are cared for as long as we stay in line and follow orders. The elite borns are higher in rank and have more privileges."

One afternoon, the heavens opened. After hours of riding through heavy rain, they finally found an empty barn to shelter in for the evening. While all the soldiers had been wearing cloaks, Lucas had not, and was soaked. He was shivering from the cold and noticed Officer Verron's worried look. As soon as a fire was built, the officer called him over.

"Here," said Verron, handing him a blanket. "Go and warm yourself up by the fire. There will be no more chores for you tonight."

"Thank you, sir," said Lucas. He was grateful for the officer's kindness but felt something had changed when he was also given extra food that night. This seemed to be confirmed for him when he watched a soldier being dispatched with a message for the king.

"What is going on?" he asked Warrick quietly.

"We will be arriving at the castle tomorrow and Officer Verron is to hand you over," explained Warrick. "He doesn't want you sick, as that will reflect badly on him."

So that was it, thought Lucas. What he mistook for kindness boiled down to the fact that he was an object to be delivered in proper health and adequate form. It was the same with the circus. He was only of worth to them so long as he brought in the money. He pushed the bitter thought out of his head and found a solitary corner to curl up in. That evening, they did not bind him, but he felt the presence of invisible restraints all the same.

As they approached the castle that following day, Lucas began to recognize the road where he had walked Tiny into the field and where he had climbed on the wagon roof. How impatient he had been to get a first glimpse of the king's castle, riding Sable to the front of the wagon train. Now that excitement was replaced by the apprehension of what was to happen to him. Again, Officer Verron had seen to it that he was given extra portions of food that morning and did not make him do chores.

As they neared the castle, four soldiers closed in on him, flanking him on all sides as they made their way through the first gate. His horse had nowhere to go but where the other horses went. They crossed the first bailey, where the arena for the performances had been built, which was now empty, and they rode across the drawbridge through the second gate, entering the inner bailey. Here, Officer Verron and the front riders stopped.

There were buildings on either side, with the main castle centered at the far end. The four soldiers and Lucas kept going, turning through a gate on the right to enter a training ground, and leaving Verron and his men behind. When the four soldiers stopped and dismounted, Lucas looked around and saw guards and various other people, all of them watching from the walls surrounding the area he was now in. The soldiers waited for him to dismount and took him by the arms as soon as he did. They opened an iron-barred door, which was the only thing built into the wall, and revealed the small space behind it. He stepped inside the small prison cell and they closed and locked the door behind him before mounting up and riding away. From the shadows of his new home, he could see the people on the walls walk away, and he was left alone.

Officer Verron climbed the stone steps to the castle and walked the long corridor towards the Great Hall. He waited outside the doors before being let in and heard Egon come down the corridor behind him.

"Have you seen him?" Verron asked, turning towards Egon.

"I watched them put him in the hole, yes," answered Egon. "Let's go in so you can relay your report."

The double doors to the Hall were opened by guards and Verron walked towards the throne on which the king was seated. Egon joined the one general and other officers, who were standing in front, on either side of the pathway.

Officer Verron reported that no hunters had crossed the river and then went on to tell how he had found Lucas and under what circumstances.

The king listened intently before speaking. "I was pleased when your messenger arrived this morning to inform me that the boy was found and on his way. I also understand that he was recovered from a prison transport. Now that I have heard the full story of Lucas's conviction, I would like to know where your discord comes from. I see some of you shaking your heads in disapproval."

"Officer Verron should have left him be," commented General Finton.

The king turned to Verron, ignoring the general's comment. "Do you know who the two men were that he killed?"

"No, sire. Just that they were guests at the inn where he had been working."

"Did he seem to have any regrets, or remorse? Was he emotionally distraught in any way?"

"No," answered Verron. "He was quiet but obeyed when he was told to do something. He gave us no trouble."

General Finton stepped forward. "Sire," he said, and waited for the king to look at him. "I know how impressed you were when you saw the boy last, and you know that I was not in favor of him. He was never selected as a chosen one and now it turns out he is also potentially dangerous. I say we thank Officer Verron for his effort of finding the boy, but we should return him to the mines so he can work out his sentence."

"If I may be so bold as to speak freely, sire?" asked Verron. He waited for the king to give him a nod of approval before he continued. "The boy acted in self-defense. We should applaud the fact that he already has the training to fight and is not afraid to apply his skills. That is what we strive to achieve for all our boys, is it not? He has lived away from our eyes and he could well be a chosen. Since he is in the hole already, I'd say we detain him there, for the time being, and put him through the test. The other chosen will soon be able to let us know if he is one of them or not."

The king had been listening quietly and now turned to Egon. "Egon, what do you have to say?"

Egon cleared his throat and stepped forward. "I believe putting him through the test is the only way to get any indication of what he might be. How he came to kill those two men . . . he could even be an elite born."

"That is outrageous," shouted Finton, rubbing a hand through his brown shoulder-length hair. Verron noticed some gray locks when he did. The general's beard had started to change color some time ago. "First a chosen one, and now this," continued Finton. "You cannot think him to be an elite born."

"There is no reason why he could not be," replied Egon. "Your son and Verron's nephew would not have hesitated to defend themselves either and would have had the exact same outcome."

Finton shook his head wildly. "His father was a swordsmith in a remote village, where he could have barely made a decent living! He is of common blood."

Egon turned to the king. "I suggest we allow him to duel against Finton's son or Verron's nephew. If he is not an elite born, he will not win. If he is not a chosen one, then he will not pass the test and we can still send him to the mines."

The king remained silent for a moment. "You've given me much to consider," he said. "For now, we will continue with the test. I will make further decisions later."

CHAPTER 8

Lucas sat on the cold stone floor. Questions filled his head. Why had he been put in this prison cell, and why had no one come to see him? Sunlight had only come in halfway at midday and for the remainder of the day the cell was in the full shadow of the wall. It was cold and damp inside. He had explored the walls and found water dripping into a small groove of one of the stones that he could reach with his tongue. He was thirsty and hungry, but no one came to give him water or food, and it was the only thing that kept him somewhat hydrated. He sat next to the iron bars of the door all evening, observing the guards patrolling the walls and listening to every new sound. Occasionally, he dozed, leaning up against the bars so that he would not miss anything.

He watched the area in front of his cell come to life the following morning when a large group of chosen ones entered. This was their training ground, and they wasted no time in starting their warm-up session. They split up into small groups, with each group training in different ways. He saw Zera and Warrick next to who he assumed was Zera's twin brother, Davis. They were of similar height and Davis's hair had the same black sheen as hers. He had it cut short all around, except at the top where the longer hair was brushed to one side. Lucas called out to them, but no one looked or paid any attention to him. Even Officer Verron, who was overseeing the training, never looked in his direction. No food or water was delivered to him that day either. It was as if he did not exist.

He paced up and down for hours, but in the end, he sat back down and observed the training. He was starving and his lips were parched with thirst.

The following day was the same. He tried to get their attention as they marched in, but soon decided he might as well use this time in learning their ways.

In the afternoon, he got his first glimpse of the group of elite borns when they joined the training session. He knew he was expected to fight one of them, so he observed them closely. They were fast and strong and were winning every fight, but he felt that at times a chosen one could have easily won as well. The chosen ones were holding back.

There was one elite born in particular who caught Lucas's attention. With his golden hair, he was taller than the others, and his fighting skills were superior, but his facial features did not make him look any older. Lucas noticed that he tolerated no mistakes from any of the other elite borns and would shout at them if it looked like a chosen one was getting the upper hand. He learned that his name was Eli and instantly disliked him.

On the third day, the water that was dripping from the wall wasn't enough anymore to keep him hydrated and his stomach was hurting badly. He stayed out of the sunlight and he slept more in the day to pass time. The following morning, he stayed back more and was less interested in what was happening on the grounds. It occurred to Lucas that, after the king had been informed on the details of his conviction, he may have lost interest in him. Perhaps they were just leaving him to die, as punishment for what he did at the inn.

———

After four full days of Lucas being locked up inside the cell, Officer Verron made his way back to the Great Hall. The king was seated at his large oak desk and finished reading the scroll before him before he let Verron speak.

"Sire, I am here to ask you about the boy, Lucas."

"What about him?" asked the king.

"Sire, it has been four days. I assumed he would take the test two days ago. Everyone had gathered at the training grounds to witness it, but then Egon came and told me there will be no test?"

"That is right. Not yet at least," answered the king casually, while placing the scroll on top of others he had already read.

Verron was confused. "I don't understand. He's gone four days without food and water, sire. We have surpassed the standard amount of time we let pass before pulling them out of the cell and allowing them to prove themselves."

The king pushed his chair back and stood up. He walked over to the window and looked out. "Tell me, Officer Verron," he said, "what *does* usually happen when we lock a new chosen one up in the hole?"

"Well, it depends, but normally the boys call out . . . try to get our attention. They get desperate and pace up and down. When hunger and thirst truly set in, they may clutch their stomachs, roll on the floor and cry out in pain."

The king nodded. "And has he done any of those things?"

Officer Verron shook his head. "He called out some at first, but stopped."

"Precisely. Now what is the purpose of locking them up without nourishment?"

"To weaken their spirit and their body, sire. To see if they can hold up and still fight."

"And do you think this boy's mind and body are weakened?"

Officer Verron did not answer straightaway. He wasn't sure where the king was going with this. "They must be, sire. It's a long time to be without food or water, and he was already quite physically compromised when I found him."

The king turned and faced him. "I can inform you, Officer Verron, that he has not grown weak. This boy is special and nothing like the others. I have been told that he is paying great attention to what is happening on the training grounds and is very alert. He may have stopped trying to win outside attention, but he shows no sign of fatigue or distress. He knows how to kill, and I am afraid he might try to do so again when pushed to defend himself during the test. I want this boy, but I cannot take the risk of letting him out when he is still that strong."

"How much longer are we to leave him then, sire?"

"Until he shows signs of weakening and I am satisfied he will not come out fighting like a cougar," responded the king firmly.

Officer Verron wanted to object, but knew it was not his place and remained silent.

"That said," continued the king, "I will allow you to give him one cup of water a day. Just enough to keep him alive and to stop you from believing I am torturing him."

Displeased with the outcome, but realizing he was not getting anywhere, Verron left straightaway to give the order to send water. He watched from the wall when a guard pushed a cup of water through the bars of the cell door. The boys in the courtyard had paused their training and watched intensely as well. Lucas had not sat at the front all morning and Verron was worried he might be too weak already.

A moment passed, but then he saw Lucas crawl to the front, look at the cup and then retreat deeper into the cell without touching the water. "By gods' bones," cursed Verron and then stormed down the stairs. He wanted to burst back into the king's room to inform the king but halted before entering the castle. It occurred to him that Lucas refusing the water would not be taken as a sign of weakness, but of his strength. He would not be helping him if the king or Finton were made aware of Lucas's refusal of the water, so he turned around and told a junior officer to collect every untouched cup of water given to Lucas before anyone noticed he was not drinking.

Lucas watched the guard come to his door with a cup of water from the darkness of the back of the cell. He was no longer interested in seeing what was going on in the courtyard. When the cup was pushed through the bars, he had instinctively and desperately crawled forward, but then a thought came to his mind. If he was left to die, there was no reason to prolong it. His body was weakening and, to stop his mind from despairing, he had started to meditate. It helped his body and mind to stay connected and stopped him from going insane. The monks often fasted, and meditation helped them get through it. He had decided to do the same. When he was not meditating, he slept. He thought it best to stop paying attention to the outside world entirely and was able to ignore even the sounds drifting through the courtyard.

"They are letting him die," said Zera. She stood in a triangular formation with Davis and Warrick in the corner of the training grounds, kicking a rock between them—something they weren't supposed to be doing, as childish games were strictly prohibited. They had all been watching from a distance for days now. It was not permitted for anyone to speak to Lucas, but a few times, Zera had accidentally made eye contact, and it was painful when she was forced to look away. There were questions written all over Lucas's face, and she was powerless to answer them.

"I don't understand why they are keeping him in there this long. It's not right."

"I agree," said Davis, looking over his shoulder towards the hole. "Even if they let him out soon, there's no way he can fight in the condition he's in."

"He will lose the will to," commented Warrick. "If he hasn't already. The way he has been withdrawing himself towards the back of that horrible place . . ."

The three of them stood in silence and Zera looked at her brother. He did not normally share her concern for anyone who had to endure time in the hole. He was also the most reserved when it came to connecting with new boys, but from the moment Davis laid eyes on Lucas, she knew something was different. "It is not like you to express concern about a new boy," she said.

"That's because I'm never convinced they are a true chosen until they take the test," answered Davis, playing around with the stone under his foot.

"Then you have already made a connection," said Zera, "as Warrick and I did when we met him."

"No," answered Davis. "Not yet."

"But you think it is coming?"

"Maybe," answered Davis before kicking the stone over to Warrick.

Zera followed the stone and watched it roll past Warrick without him making any attempt to stop it. Warrick had given up the game, which was unusual for him, and she saw him staring in the direction of the hole.

"Even Verron is worried," said Warrick, sensing her eyes on him. "He's spending more time standing close to the hole nowadays."

Both Zera and Davis followed his gaze. Indeed, Verron had stopped there and was peering in, genuine concern written on his face.

"If the king saw any potential in Lucas," said Zera, "it will be lost if he does not recognize what this is doing to him. We should ask Verron to talk to the king."

"By the looks of him, I am sure he already has," said Davis, sighing deeply. "The king must have his reasons. We have to trust he is doing the right thing."

When the sun started to set behind the hills on the sixth day, King Itan was walking along the wall with his daughter. She was running up ahead to hide, jumping out and trying to scare him when he passed her. Egon came up the stairs and joined him when he stopped on the wall above the chosen ones' courtyard and looked down towards the hole.

"I know it is not my decision," said Egon. "But I believe it is time to take the boy out."

"You are right," said the king, turning to him. "It is not your decision, but what has changed your mind? You had agreed that this boy needed to be dealt with differently when we learned he had killed."

"Yes," acknowledged Egon, "and I still do. We have never had a boy who has been trained by the warrior monks and I believe this has given him an advantage. It has clearly also made him more dangerous, and so I agreed that he needed to be broken before putting him through the test."

"What makes you think it is time?"

"Officer Verron has expressed grave concerns." Egon stepped closer to the wall before he spoke and lowered his voice. "The boy has not been seen close to the door. He has not moved from where he lies by the back wall."

"Hmm," muttered the king. "Why do you think that is? Verron came to me a few days ago to complain, and I agreed for water to be delivered."

"Which the boy has not been drinking apparently."

The king gave Egon a hard stare. "Since when?"

"Since the day it was given to him. I did not find out until this evening when Verron insisted I had a look at the boy myself."

"Why did he wait to tell you?"

"Verron believed that for the boy to refuse the water he showed himself to be too strong, and he feared we would leave him in the hole even longer."

The king let out a frustrated grunt. "The fool! He may have also signed his death sentence that way. Did you have a look at the boy?"

"I just did, yes," answered Egon.

"And?"

"The boy is strong in mind and certainly not afraid to die. It would be interesting to see how he does in the test, but we may have waited too long. He didn't look so good when I saw him."

"Let's hope it is not too late then," said the king, and turned to watch his daughter come running towards him. She had grown tired of waiting for him to come and find her. He scooped her up in his arms as she came near. "Do you want to watch a fight tomorrow, Amalia?" he asked her.

She nodded happily when he put her back on the ground and he took her hand to walk back to the castle.

Lucas was hardly able to move when he heard the door to his cell door open in the middle of the night. Someone was kneeling next to him and lifting him gently by the shoulders. He felt a cup being put to his lips and a thick, warm substance being poured slowly down his throat.

"They are coming for you in the morning," he heard someone whisper. "You need to be ready to fight."

He was laid back down again after the cup was emptied and he heard the door close. The liquid warmed his body and stopped his stomach from hurting. He fell into a deep sleep shortly after and did not wake again until two soldiers sat by his side, trying to get him up.

"He's too far gone," he heard one of them say. "He's not even moving."

"Let me try one more time," he heard the other one say. "Come on, boy! They're all waiting for you. You have to do this," he urged, pulling at his shoulders.

Lucas heard someone else enter the cell and felt himself being rolled onto his back. An arm supported his upper back as he was pushed up into a half-sitting position. Someone was splashing cold water over his face.

"It's time, Lucas—they want to test you today," a familiar voice whispered. "You have to get up."

Lucas tried to say something, but his tongue was swollen from dehydration and no sound came out. He knew that if he did not give them a sign of life soon, it would all be over. A flask was pressed between his lips and more of the substance he had tasted in the night dribbled down his throat. He coughed but was finally able to open his eyes. Two strong hands lifted him up under his arms and leaned him against the wall.

Officer Verron stood before him and gave him water to drink. "You don't have to speak—just nod," he said while supporting Lucas. "Can you fight?"

Lucas was struggling to regain control over his muscles, but he could feel that whatever the substance was that had been given to him was restoring some strength in his body and the water helped with the dryness in his throat.

"Can you fight, Lucas?" Officer Verron asked again, more urgently this time. Lucas saw that the crowd outside was becoming restless. Finally, when he had summoned every ounce of courage he had left, he gave a nod and Verron took a step back to let him recover. "You'll make it out of here on your own?"

"Yes," managed Lucas, and straightened himself up against the wall.

"There are people out there who do not believe in you," he heard Verron say quietly, "but you need to prove them wrong."

Verron then left his side and went to speak to the stern-looking king's guard. Lucas could see the chosen ones and elite borns, along with senior staff and guards, all waiting for him. The two soldiers took up their places on either side of the door and Lucas started to make his way along the wall. Each step he took was painful, but with each one he also gained more strength. He was determined to get out. He grabbed the iron bars of the door and slowly stepped outside. The sun was too bright, and he shielded his eyes with his arm until he grew somewhat accustomed to it. He saw soldiers and guards lined up on the walls above, watching his every move. The entire castle had gathered in one place to watch the fight.

Lucas took a deep breath and let go of the bars. Slowly he walked towards the gap in the circle of people that had opened up for him. When he had finally made his way into the circle, the gap closed. No one said a word. The only thing he could hear was his own shallow breathing and the shuffling of his feet. He looked around the circle and recognized some of the faces. Zera was standing next to her brother. Then he saw the boy he was supposed to fight and recognized him as well. It was the tall blond elite born they called Eli.

With any other boy he might have been all right, but he had seen Eli fight. Even if he had all his strength, it would be hard to beat him. A smile came over his face as he looked up towards the sky and mumbled, "This must be a joke. I don't stand a chance here."

He then looked at Eli again, before his legs gave away and he dropped to his knees. A sword was thrown towards him, landing in the sand. Somewhere, someone was announcing the rules. "This is not a fight to the death, but to demonstrate skill, will power and endurance! Either party is allowed to forfeit at any time! The only other way the fight will end, is by simulating a final strike resulting in death, or if called by the king!"

"Are you ready?" asked Officer Verron, who stood behind him.

Even though he was still on his knees and had not picked up the sword, Lucas nodded that he was. He closed his eyes, collecting all his inner strength. He was at death's door. He heard the call of a magpie as it flew high above him and he let his hand feel for the sword in the sand. When he touched the cold steel, however, a burst of energy flowed through his veins and his mind became clearer.

The sign for the start was given and Eli rushed forward. He swung his sword overhead just when Lucas gripped the hilt of his own sword. As Eli's sword came down to strike, Lucas lifted his sword up from the ground and blocked the blow. With the two swords locked together, Lucas pushed forward and was able to use the resistance to stand up. For the first time, they came face to face and looked each other in the eye.

Eli had looked surprised that he was blocked, but a smile curled his lip. "I thought this would be over quick," he told Lucas, their swords pressed against each other. "But you still have fight left in you. I'm glad. I don't like easy."

"No, but you do like an audience," Lucas responded, his voice low.

"My only hope now is that you'll stay on your feet long enough to make it worthwhile for them." Eli broke his sword free and stepped back. He circled Lucas a couple of times before striking again.

Lucas followed his move and blocked again. He was staggering on his feet and seemed to have no strength to carry out an attack of his own. All he was able to do was watch his opponent's moves and block them. Their swords clanged together several times before they locked again, and they pushed shoulder to shoulder.

"Are you ready to give up yet?" Eli hissed.

"I've come a long way to get here," Lucas replied through gritted teeth. "What makes you think it's not going to be you, wishing to never have been put forward to fight me? I've watched you, and you're not as good as you think you are."

At those words, Eli pushed Lucas away.

Lucas was thrown backwards and landed in the group of chosen ones, who reached down to help him up. One of them held him by his arm for a moment and whispered into his ear. "You have to win this fight," he said. "There are people who don't want you here."

Lucas weighed up his options. Anger would not win him the fight. Anger blurred the senses and invited mistakes. Eli was a skilled fighter, strong and determined, but he had no control over his emotions. Lucas would have to do something to give himself the advantage. With his body growing weaker by the minute, he was running out of time. As soon as he was pushed back into the circle, Eli attacked again. Instead of blocking, Lucas did a quick sideways step and immediately followed with an attack of his own. The surprise attack made Eli lose his grip on his sword and it dropped to the ground. He quickly looked to see where it was so he could pick it up, but Lucas was already standing on top of it. Without a sword in his hand, he was forced to back up.

Lucas could take him out easily now. He bent down to pick up Eli's sword. A look of defeat filled Eli's eyes, but quickly changed to surprise when Lucas threw the sword towards him. Eli caught it and mimed the word "fool" to him. Again, he charged forward.

An intense sword fight followed, with both boys defending and attacking. With every move, Lucas was paying attention and soon learned that Eli started every attack with his left foot forward. He stepped back two paces and let Eli charge at him. When he was close enough, Lucas lowered himself to the ground and, with his shoulder, pushed against Eli's left leg to take him off-balance. He blocked the sword coming down on him and then pushed forward hard. Eli fell backwards onto the ground and again lost grip of his sword. Lucas had used his full body weight and landed on top of him.

Hate flashed through Eli's eyes when the sword was put on his throat, simulating a strike of instant death. Lucas waited for confirmation that he had won, but the crowd surrounding him remained silent. He was panting, gasping for breath . . . he had spent the last of his energy and could feel himself slipping away. He started to lose grip on the sword that was slowly pressing into Eli's throat, but still no one told him the fight was over. He looked desperately over his shoulder to the blank faces staring at him.

What were they waiting for? Could they not see how he was struggling to remain in control? That if he lost consciousness he would fall on top of Eli and the sword would be pushed deeper into his throat? Had he heard them wrong? Perhaps it was a fight to the death? No, Eli was a general's son, an elite born, privileged in every way, and they had not expected him to lose. Now they did not know what to do, or how to react, but he was running out of time. He felt cold, despite the sun that beamed down upon him. As the seconds of silence passed, Lucas lifted the sword off Eli's throat and threw it to the side.

It was the opportunity Eli had been waiting for, and he grabbed Lucas by the shoulders and threw him off. Lucas landed hard on his back, the last bit of air in his lungs escaping him. Eli scrambled to grab his sword and Lucas knew he needed to roll away, but he had nothing left. He lay helplessly as Eli towered above him, a look of satisfaction on his face as he raised his sword for the final strike. Lucas watched the sword going higher, catching the rays of the sun before it was about to come down, but then it froze.

A booming voice had sounded across the courtyard, diverting all eyes to the king, who now stepped into the circle. "Enough!" he shouted again when Eli remained standing with the sword above his shoulder.

Eli lowered his sword and made a bow when the king walked up to him. "Sire!" he said, and stepped to the side.

The king nodded and looked at Lucas's body, which lay almost lifeless on the ground. He kneeled to touch him, looking with a fierce curiosity into Lucas's half-open eyes, and then quickly motioned for guards to step forward. The men picked him up and carried him out.

For a moment, everyone remained motionless and then the circle dispersed, the soldiers returning to their posts. Eli, winded and suddenly very tired, stood staring at the gate where they had removed his opponent. He was processing the fact that he had almost been beaten by a boy who had been locked in a cell for days and starved to near death. He hardly noticed when his friend Milton walked up to his side, and the tap on his shoulder startled him.

"I thought he had you," said Milton.

Eli shook his head. "No," he said, touching the scratch on his neck where the sword had pressed down. "I was just giving everyone a good show." He glanced over his shoulder at a group of chosen ones who were giving him a dark look and then finally followed Milton out. They rested outside the gates of their own training grounds and looked across to the surgeon's room, where Lucas had been taken, and watched Egon go in.

"Egon the king's guard, and Egon the physician," muttered Eli. "The irony of it—one kills and the other will try to stitch you back up."

"It's not like he has much choice in either," replied Milton. "Having been Garrad's apprentice, he has the skill set to heal, and his natural cold-heartedness makes him a perfect king's guard."

Eli saw Verron approach, just as Egon came back out again. A heated argument unfolded, with Verron storming off and Egon going back inside.

"What was that all about?" said Carleton, strolling up to where Eli and Milton were resting.

"Your uncle's probably upset because he believed that boy to be a chosen, and he was proven wrong," Eli replied. Carleton was his strongest rival—they often did not see eye to eye. Carleton's existence only made bigger the already overwhelming pressure Eli's father put on him to be top dog. It had caused a divide within the elite born group that had become more apparent now that they were getting older. They were both striving to lead, and the only thing working in Eli's favor was that his father was a general while Carleton's father had died of the fever before he was able to become one.

"How?" asked Carleton.

Eli shrugged. "I think I showed everyone that boy is nothing. He's weak—if he's not dead already, he soon will be."

"From where I stood," answered Carleton, "it looked like he was putting you in your place. He had his sword at your throat. He won, even after days of confinement and starvation. My uncle believes he's the strongest chosen yet and I think he's right. What you showed everyone today is that you are nothing."

"You're mistaken," snapped Eli. "The sword never came down that far. I threw him off of me."

"You can lie to yourself, Eli, but I'd have that cut on your neck looked at if I were you," continued Carleton with a smile as he walked off. Other elite boys looked when they heard Carleton's comment and grinned when they walked past. It made Milton turn towards Eli as well and he was shocked to see what everyone had been looking at. "Eli!" he called out. "Your neck!"

"It's just a scratch," Eli responded, irritated.

"Maybe a few minutes ago it was, but not anymore!" urged Milton.

Eli touched his neck and was surprised at the amount of blood that was on his hand when he pulled it back. He strode towards the surgeon's room for help, but the guards blocked his way and would not let him in.

"I need Egon to look at my neck," demanded Eli. He kept his hand over the wound. It felt like his neck was splitting open.

"You'll have to wait," said one of the guards. "He's busy trying to save the new boy's life. King's orders."

"He's not dead then?" asked Eli.

The guard looked over his shoulder into the room and Eli followed his gaze to see Lucas on a table with several people around him. All of them looked defeated.

"He wasn't," answered the guard, "but by the looks of it, that may have changed."

Eli wanted to have another peek, but was pushed aside when Garrad, the king's personal physician, was trying to make his way into the room.

"If Verron sent you," Eli heard Egon tell Garrad, "then you are too late. The boy has just stopped breathing, as I told Verron he would."

"When?" demanded Garrad. "When did he stop breathing?"

"Just now," answered Egon.

Garrad rushed over to where Lucas lay and grabbed his wrist, his eyes scanning the room. "It may not be too late," he said quickly and pointed towards the fireplace with one hand. "Pass me those bellows."

A soldier standing closest to the fireplace reached to pick up the bellows.

"Tilt his head back," Garrad told another soldier. "We need to open up his airway. Egon, close his nose." The doctor then carefully placed the bellows inside Lucas's throat. Eli was curious what he was trying to do with it, but heard his name being called behind him and hastily

157

stepped away from the door to turn towards his father, who was now returning from the castle.

When Lucas opened his eyes again, he was lying on his back in a field of lush green grass. The sky was bright blue, and the sun was finally warming his body. Tall grass swayed in the wind, and he felt his hair being lifted by the breeze. He felt all the strength was back in his body when he pushed himself up on his elbows and sat up. He was on a hill with fields stretching for miles around him. He rose to his feet and looked to where he thought he saw people in the distance. Thirteen warriors stood silently watching him. They were gathered around the black stone, which he recognized from the monastery.

He started walking down the hill. All the warriors stood behind the stone in a semicircle with swords by their sides and hands folded in front of them, all but one. The most impressive warrior stood in front of the stone. Lucas felt he should not approach any farther and stopped. He watched the twelve warriors pull their swords at the same time and insert them into the ground in front of them. They slowly kneeled, their heads bowed, each with both hands on the pommel of his swords. The thirteenth warrior raised his sword and went down on one knee as well, but unlike the others, he did not insert his sword into the ground. Instead, he laid the sword on both his hands and held it out in front of him.

The wind picked up when Lucas walked forward and touched the cold steel of the sword with his hands. It was the prettiest sword he had ever seen, and he was tempted to take it, but didn't. He pulled his hand away and stepped back.

The king's physician counted in between each push of the bellows and watched Lucas's chest go down before doing it again. After a few minutes, he told everyone to stop what they were doing and step back. He felt Lucas's pulse and observed his chest for the slightest movement. Everyone in the room sighed with relief when they heard Lucas take a deep breath and saw his chest rise on his own.

"What just happened?" asked Egon.

"I heard he fell back hard at the end of the fight—probably collapsed his lungs. In his weakened state, he could not get enough air in on his own. That is all I just did. I gave him air."

"Will he be all right now?"

Garrad stepped back and raised his shoulders. He had never performed anything like this before, only read about it as a theory in one of the many books he kept in his room, but he felt pleased. Since he only looked after the royal household and senior members of the staff, he had more time on his hands to read and increase his knowledge of the human body. He had been reading when Verron had burst into his room and insisted he have a look at the boy.

With no obvious signs of a mortal wound, Verron had not accepted Egon's claim that the boy was lost. Garrad, however, knew they had kept Lucas without food and water, two vital things for any human body, which probably had stopped his heart. He had told Verron he would have to agree with Egon that it would be too late to save him. "No one can come out of the hole without food or water for a week and expect to be able to stand up," he had explained, "let alone fight. He has defied all odds already, so you should accept that it was the last thing he was able to do. Let the boy die in peace." He had returned to the book on his desk, but Verron would not leave.

"I gave him some of the concoction you have been brewing for the queen," he had said abruptly. "The one you have been hoping will restore the energy in the queen's weakened muscles?"

Garrad had looked up in surprise. "When?"

"Last night. And again, just before the fight. The king does not know about this, and I would like to keep it that way."

"That was not yours to take. I have been changing the recipe on it, but I've not given it to the queen yet. I don't even know what it would do."

"It appears to have worked on the boy," said Verron. "If you help him live, I can arrange it so you can keep him for a while and continue testing it, before giving it to the queen."

Garrad closed the book in front of him and turned to Verron. "What makes you think my potion helped the boy?" he had asked with more interest.

"He was very weak last night. Immobile. But, this morning, he was able to walk out of the hole, fight an elite born and even win. Unfortunately, he then landed hard on his back—"

"Collapsing his lungs," Garrad had thought out loud and without waiting for Verron, he had left the room and hastily made his way to the surgeon's room.

Garrad now looked at Egon, who was waiting for him to answer. "I don't know if he is going to pull through," he stated, "but I don't think we should give up on him. If he can be brought to my room, I will keep an eye on him."

Egon rubbed the back of his neck. "I'm not sure if this would be feasible. We are well aware that the chosen's rank does not permit them in the castle unless directed by the king."

"The king wants this boy alive, Egon," Verron interjected. "He thinks him to be special, and I believe he is right. After what we put him through, there is no way he should have been able to stand up, let alone fight."

"Very well," said Egon. "I will have him brought over to Garrad's quarters, but as soon as he is fully awake, he will be moved to the infirmary for further recovery."

Verron glanced over to Garrad, who nodded, and they prepared to move the boy.

Eli reluctantly walked away from the surgeon's room when he heard his name called and met his father halfway. He was still holding his neck and wanted someone to look at it.

"Any news?" his father asked while nodding towards the room.

"Garrad is in there now, trying to save his life."

"Garrad?" asked his father, shocked. "He has no business treating him."

"I think Verron may have asked him," said Eli.

"And what were you doing over there? Why are you holding your neck in that foolish manner?"

"My neck is cut. I am waiting for Egon or Garrad to look at it," he explained.

"Let me see!" said his father and pulled his hand away from his neck. Finton shook his head angrily. "It is nothing, Eli! Cover it up with a scarf and it will heal on its own. It is not even bleeding."

"What?" asked Eli. "It's not?"

"No. So do not embarrass yourself any further," he scolded.

Eli put his hand back on his neck and felt that the cut had closed up. He looked up to see Lucas being removed from the surgeon's room and taken towards the castle. He caught Davis smiling at him as he walked past, and it made him furious.

CHAPTER 9

When the doors to the queen's chambers opened, King Itan questioned the scene before him. His wife was sitting in her favorite chair by the window, overlooking the fields and hills beyond the castle. Itan knew very well that the scenic view was but a grim reminder of the happy days before Amalia was born, when the two of them would go for long rides in the countryside. Complications during the birth had left her weak and unable to walk on her own. The handicap had caused her to withdraw inside herself, and she rarely left her room these days. He made the effort to go and see her whenever he could and would sit and talk with her, filling her in on current events, but he prayed for the day she would be strong enough to be by his side again and take more interest in their daughter. As he walked in and hung his cloak over a chair, he saw her drink from a cup Garrad had handed her. The liquid had a strange odor, one he recognized as medicinal.

"I thought you said you had given up on finding a cure," he said.

Garrad raised himself up after the queen handed the cup back. "Yes, but then I changed the formula and discovered it was working on the boy."

"What boy?" asked Itan, sitting down in the chair opposite his wife. He had not seen her since yesterday morning, and noticed her cheeks had more color. She sat more straightly in her chair, and he was pleased when she smiled at him.

"The new boy, sire."

Itan raised his head in surprise. "What about him?"

Garrad shook his head. "I am sorry, I thought you had been told," he said. "He's been in my care these last three days, and I have been giving him my new recipe to help him recover." He stepped towards the queen. "Here, let me show you!" He helped the queen stand and stayed right by her side, allowing her to navigate a few steps alone. It was something she had not been able to do for a long time.

"Sire! I see you are pleased. It is something, no?"

"It certainly is," the king answered, trying to curb his enthusiasm. It was almost too good to be true.

His wife's eyes lit up when she made it to the window. Garrad stepped aside when Itan joined her, and quietly slipped out of the room.

Lucas woke up staring at high-ceiling rafters that supported a pointed roof. There were gaps under the roof tiles, and that was the only source of light coming into the long narrow room he found himself to be in. He was lying on a bed in the middle of a row of beds. Across the room, another row of empty beds lined the walls. He turned his head to the left when he heard someone and saw Zera getting up from a bed at the end of the room. She came over to sit on the bed next to him.

"You are awake," said Zera. "They said you would come around soon."

"Where am I?" asked Lucas.

"Our dorm room," answered Zera. "Congratulations. You're one of us now!"

Lucas smiled and tried to sit up, but Zera put her hand out to stop him.

"You don't have to get up yet. They said you might be too weak to get out of bed and should stay here until you are ready."

Lucas pushed himself up on one elbow. "I think I'm all right," he said. "How long have I been here?"

"You were brought here this morning, but they kept you somewhere else for the last couple of days. They say you died soon after the fight, but that Garrad was able to bring you back. Is that true? Did you walk towards the light?"

"I don't know," answered Lucas. "I don't remember much. Who's Garrad?"

"The king's physician. He made the cream we put on your legs," Zera reminded him. "You were lucky—he doesn't usually treat chosen ones."

Lucas vaguely remembered a man who kept waking him up and making him drink more of the same fluid that was given to him in the hole. He would then ask Lucas funny questions and move Lucas's arms and legs around to test his strength. He had felt drowsy throughout the whole ordeal and never really became fully awake.

He still felt dizzy, but pushed himself up to sit on the edge of the bed. He felt something on his right shoulder and reached to feel for it. Part of his skin was raised and sore.

"They branded you with the mark of a chosen one," explained Zera. "Three circles within a triangle, linked together by a star in the middle."

Lucas was grateful for the explanation since he could not see it. To him, it just felt like a swollen mess on his shoulder.

"I know it hurts," continued Zera. "We all get it when we pass the test."

"They did this to you as well?" asked Lucas. He had still not completely gotten over the fact that the king allowed a girl to become a soldier. Even though he had watched Zera in training and had seen she was very capable—even against an elite born.

Zera nodded. "I am treated no different than the boys," she answered. "Nor would I want to be." She stood up and picked up a uniform from the bottom of Lucas's bed. A white lace shirt, black trousers, leather boots and a belt. "Officer Verron had a feeling you would not stay in bed once you were awake, so I am going to show you around, explain your duties and the rules we have to abide by. They've assigned you to the king's stables."

"Is that where you work?"

"Yes," answered Zera, handing him the clothes. "They should fit. The tailor is good in sizing everyone up and if not, we can ask permission to go see him and get it amended." Zera turned to exit the room. "I'll wait for you downstairs, then."

Lucas stood up and started getting dressed. As he did so, he took the opportunity to look around. The dorm room was on the topmost floor. Twenty beds, in two rows of ten, lined either side of the room, all made up with blankets neatly rolled up at the end. A small trunk was tucked underneath each bed. His bed was halfway down. Lucas made his bed after he put the uniform on and then made his way out of the dormitory. He walked down the wooden stairs, where he found Zera sitting on the bottom step.

"Feeling all right?" asked Zera, standing up to watch him come down.

"I think so. Thank you!" He was a little lightheaded and held on to the railing for support, but was eager to get going.

Zera nodded and then wasted no time in starting to explain things. "As a chosen one," she said, walking into a room underneath the dorm room, "you have to know where you are allowed to go on your own. Many places are off-limits. We have the dorm room above us, our weapons room right here, training grounds, the mess room, infirmary . . . and wherever they put you to work. In our case, it's the stables."

Lucas had followed Zera into the weapons room and looked around. Swords, daggers, and bows hung neatly on hooks along the walls. Next to each one hung a tunic displaying the king's colors of black and red.

"You'll be given your own sword, which you will keep here when it's not in use. We only carry our swords and tunics when we leave the castle or when the king is present. We have different swords and weapons we use in training, and they are kept on the training grounds. It's your responsibility to keep your own weapons clean and in working order."

Zera let Lucas look around a moment longer before leading him out of the building and turning left towards a set of high double doors close to the castle gate. She pulled one of them open and entered.

"These are the king's stables," said Zera, walking them past the horses in their stalls. You will start here first thing in the morning, then again before bedtime and anytime horses come and go. We have the horses that belong to the king and his guard here, as well as the generals', and a few of the senior officers' horses. Some horses at the very back are for us to use when we have orders to go on patrol. I see that interests you! Don't get your hopes up," she said quickly. "It's usually months before they trust anyone to go out."

"How long did you have to wait?"

"More than two years. They don't take anyone until they are at least twelve."

"I just turned twelve," said Lucas, walking up to the stall of a large gray horse.

"Well, yes," said Zera, smiling. "So hopefully you will not have to wait that long."

The horse snorted when Lucas stepped towards the half door and hung his head over so that Lucas could rub his nose.

"That is the king's favorite," said Zera. "He rides him all the time."

"Who does that one belong to?" asked Lucas, pointing to a big black horse who had poked his head out to look.

"That is Egon's horse. He is head of the king's guard. He used to be a chosen one, like us, until he was given the king's mark by the former king."

"What is a king's mark?"

Zera stood next to Lucas and rubbed the gray horse on the neck. "It's a recognition for someone who has proven himself to be exceptionally loyal or brave in serving the king. It is presented in the form of a tattoo on the left shoulder," started Zera. "Only once in his lifetime can a king give someone the mark. It is usually someone of nobility and much older. Carrying the mark raises someone's seniority above anyone else's. From that point on, they only receive orders directly from the king. Egon can do what he likes as long as the king approves."

"But you said Egon was a chosen one, not of noble blood?"

"That's right. He was also barely seventeen at the time. People were not happy when such an honor was bestowed upon him. And this included King Itan."

"Then why did he get it?"

Zera moved away from the horses and showed Lucas the tack room while continuing the story. "When King Itan's father was still king, but had already fallen ill, a fire broke out in one of the stables. The king's youngest son, Meloc, was trapped in it and would have died if not for Egon, who went into the burning stables to get him out. The king was extremely grateful and decided to give Egon the king's mark, but some say he did so when he was not of sane mind. He died soon after. When Itan became king, he could have made the deed invalid or had Egon removed from court, but he decided to grant his father's last wish and keep him. He moved Egon out of the chosen ones' group when he turned eighteen and into the king's guard. Egon excelled there. Itan took note and ultimately put him in charge a few years later. He's now never far from the king's side. Since he was once a chosen, he keeps an eye on us as well and can be strict. You want to keep a low profile and catch his eye only for good reasons. He sees to it that we receive the correct training and makes sure we stay in line. You don't want him to get involved in carrying out discipline, because he'll come down hard. He also takes care of prison interrogations. They say all prisoners end up talking. In any case," said Zera, closing the stable doors behind him, "if you do as you're told, you'll never have to deal with him."

Lucas looked towards the castle gate and the outer bailey beyond.

"That's where we exercise every morning," said Zera, pointing past the gate. "But we're not allowed in there on our own."

They walked back past the chosen ones' barracks and towards the gates of the training grounds next to it. Zera stopped and pointed out where the infirmary was and said that was as far as they were allowed to go. "Beyond it, you have the officers' barracks, the king's guard barracks, then the storeroom with the kitchens, the blacksmith, tailors and carpenter. Those are all connected to the castle at the end."

Lucas looked across to the other side of the bailey and saw an almost identical gate to the one for the chosen training grounds. "What's over there?" he asked.

"Elite born training grounds," answered Zera. "Their barracks are behind that door to the left of it. Totally off-limits for us. They keep us very much separate. They come to us for training, but we're not allowed to go to them."

"Midafternoon, right? That's when they come over?"

"Yes," answered Zera. "How do you know that?"

Lucas shrugged. "I had a whole week to study the schedule."

"Of course you did," said Zera, smiling, giving him a warm look. "Come on. I'll introduce you to everyone."

They continued through the gate into the chosen training grounds and Lucas avoided looking at the iron door of the hole as they made their way past it towards the back. There, the chosen boys had taken shelter under a canopy for their break. The boy with black hair and similar features to Zera stood up and walked towards them.

"This is Davis, my twin brother," confirmed Zera when they met him halfway.

Davis held his hand out and Lucas shook it. He remembered Davis being the one to tell him to win the fight and in training he had noticed him to be a well-respected member of the group.

"Good to see you up and about," said Davis. "We've all been waiting for you."

"Thank you," said Lucas and followed him back to the rest of the boys. Davis relayed their names, pointing as he did so. Some of them stood up and shook his hand, and others nodded in his direction. There were many of them and he knew it would take him a while before he remembered all of their names, but he felt at ease among them.

The boys suddenly all got up and moved over to the different training stations, at which point he heard someone shout that break time was over. Lucas turned and saw an officer begin directing the boys. He waited for his instruction, but then noticed Officer Verron walking onto the grounds and making his way over to him.

"Feeling strong enough to participate?" he asked when he got close.

"Yes, sir," answered Lucas.

"Great," said Officer Verron. "Then you can go and join Davis and Warrick for today." He pointed towards the pells, where both boys now stood, and Lucas walked over to the wooden posts firmly planted into the ground for the intended purpose to practice the striking of a sword. He trained with them the rest of the afternoon through the different stages and was happy to finally be able to join them. It sure beat watching them from the hole.

That evening, inside the stables, when they were mucking stalls, Davis asked Lucas what he thought of his first practice.

"Very good. And it feels like I've known everyone for a long time."

"That happens when you are a chosen," explained Davis. "We are connected to one another and feel a strong bond, like brothers. It's what the king looks for during the test. Some of us will create that bond before the test, some of us during, but if we don't feel a bond at all, we drop our heads and will not look at the boy. That let's the king know that he is not a true chosen one. If only some of us do, then they will look at fighting skills, willpower, strength and base their decision on that. We look out for each other and stick together. If one of us gets disciplined, we all do. The officers know we accept that, and they keep us in line that way. It also means they have us under stricter rules than the elite borns. Since we are more united, they believe it makes us more dangerous."

"How does it make us more dangerous?" asked Lucas.

Davis shrugged and threw some fresh straw down before exiting the stall and moving on to the next one. "I guess, if we were to truly unite as a group in a fight, there would be no stopping us."

"Is that not a good thing?"

"It would depend on who we were fighting and why. They know we will protect each other at any cost, and against anyone."

"Do the elite borns have a bond like we do?" asked Lucas, following him out.

"They do, but it's different. As chosens, we all view each other as equals and don't choose a leader. The elite borns are more individually driven to be the best. It creates rivalry amongst those who are born leaders. Right now, it is Eli who is their leader, but Carleton looks to be a close second."

"What happened during my test?" asked Lucas.

"Yours was very different than the last few we have experienced," Zera chimed in when they met her at the back of the stables to collect hay for feeding. "All the boys felt the connection when you were in the hole. Even my brother here—although he would not like to admit that." She gave Lucas a wink when Davis playfully pushed her and continued. "Warrick and I knew you were a chosen from the moment we saw you at the prison transport."

"I sure did," a voice suddenly said behind them. When all three turned they saw Warrick, joyfully walking up the aisle towards them. "Never thought that would ever happen."

"You're already finished in your stables?" asked Davis.

"Almost," answered Warrick. "Tanner and Archer said they'd finish up for me. You know how they work better together."

"That may be because you talk incessantly and distract them, and then they get into trouble for being too slow," responded Davis.

"That's not my fault. I still get my work done."

"Anyway," said Zera, "we were just answering some of Lucas's questions." She waited until Warrick started helping with the feeding before she continued. "Since we had all connected with you already, the test was more to determine your skills than establishing whether you were chosen or not."

"Why did they keep me in the hole so long, if everyone already knew?"

"I believe you were kept in longer, because some officers, and General Finton in particular, saw most of us connect with you the day of your arrival. They didn't want you to succeed and convinced the king you were too dangerous."

"Why would they not want me to succeed?"

"I overheard some soldiers say that you could be an elite born," said Zera. "Which caused many heated debates on the wall and may have contributed to why you were kept in longer. The king and Egon may have believed this, but Finton was very outspoken against your arrival here. With Eli being his son, and your fighting skills so advanced, he would not have taken the possibility you are elite born lightly. Since

171

not much is known about your parents, they were contemplating that. Eli must have known this, and I believe that explains why it looked like he was going to kill you."

"And he nearly did!" said Davis, throwing fresh hay in a feeder with more force than necessary.

"I heard they were still discussing the possibility after the test," said Warrick. "But Finton put a stop to it by branding you a chosen before a final decision was made."

"I'm glad he did," said Lucas, finishing up his chores. "I feel this is where I belong."

"So do we," said Zera, giving the horse in the last stable a mound of hay.

Lucas soon learned what life as a chosen one was all about. Every morning, before the sun was up, he'd rise and make his way to the king's stables with six other boys and Zera. They mucked out stalls and fed the horses before joining the rest of the chosen for a run in the outer bailey. After breakfast, they would saddle the horses who were riding out that day. They then made their way to the training grounds where they practiced.

Whenever the horn sounded to announce riders coming, they would drop everything and make their way to the gate. The chosen boys working in the other stables lined up on the right side of the gate and the chosen working the king's stables stood on the left. If the king was riding in, they had to be in full uniform. They all scrambled to get their swords and look presentable before the drawbridge was let down.

Lucas worked hard around the stables and in the training grounds, to get his stamina and fighting skills back up. He learned what it meant to be a chosen one and what was expected of him, but he also did not fail to impress some of the boys with the sword skills he had learned outside of the castle, in his old life.

Bennett, one of the younger boys, was intrigued that Lucas had lived with the warrior monks and wanted to know all about it, so Lucas showed him some different ways of maneuvering the sword during one of their breaks. Bennett picked up on it quickly. Pleased with the progress and eagerness he showed, Lucas smiled and commented that he might even be able to defeat an elite born one day. Bennett immediately paused and looked at him strangely before walking back to the group.

"Did I say something wrong?" Lucas asked when he walked back himself.

"We are not supposed to be better than the elite borns, let alone defeat them. Or even discuss defeating them," explained Davis. "I'm sorry—we should have told you. They tell you this when they brand you with the chosen mark, but I understand you were unconscious when it was done. The only time you are allowed to defeat elites is during the chosen test, but as soon as you are branded, they become your superiors."

"That means we follow their orders," said Warrick, "and aren't supposed to consider ourselves better than them."

"But what if you are?" said Lucas. "I watched your training sessions with them, when I was in the hole. Some of you could have easily beaten them."

"But we didn't, did we?" asked Davis.

"No, because you were holding back!" said Lucas, raising his voice. It was already clear to him that the chosen followed orders without questioning them. "Do we not all serve the king? Should we therefore not all strive to be the best we can be? The elite borns would better themselves if wins were not just handed to them."

None of the chosen answered and he let out a frustrated sigh. "So, when I face Eli again, am I to let him win?" Eli had been riding out with the king a lot, so Lucas had seen little of him, but when he had, Eli looked at him with hatred. Now he knew why. He had done the one thing chosen ones were not supposed to do and made him look bad by defeating him. "What if I don't?" he asked. "What if I can't let him win?"

"Then we'll all get to run a couple of miles in the outer bailey," said Warrick, standing up and putting an arm on his shoulder. "Or face other punishments."

Lucas felt his stomach knot up the day the elite borns started showing up for their single combat training. Since there were more chosen boys than elite borns, only those called by Officer Verron would line up. Lucas was pleased when Eli was not present the first few times. He was able to hold back when fighting other elite borns, even though it did not feel right to him. Then Eli returned and, when Lucas heard his name called, he reluctantly stood up and took his place next to Zera.

"Let it go," whispered Zera. "Don't let him get to you. If you do end up fighting him, remember, you will have to let him win. We already know you can beat him."

Lucas stood silent and did not answer.

The elites were told to choose their opponents after all the chosen boys had lined up and, with their eyes locked on each other, Lucas watched as Eli came straight for him. Lucas was on the far side of the line and before Eli could get to him, Carleton had taken his place in front of him.

Carleton steered Lucas away from Eli, who had to choose Warrick instead. "Follow me," he told Warrick, and Lucas could hear the pleasure Eli found in being the boss. They found a space away from everyone and faced each other to start the practice.

One by one, the chosen were defeated—Carleton and Lucas were the last ones standing. They gave each other a good training, and Lucas's mood changed as he realized the fight was coming to an end. With officers closing in on them and the other boys watching, Lucas knew what was expected of him and he didn't like it. He made one last move and then gave Carleton the upper hand by loosening his grip on his sword and allowing himself to be disarmed.

"You held back during that last move, did you not?" asked Carleton when they shook hands to congratulate each other on a good fight.

"Is that not what I am supposed to do?"

Carleton looked him in the eye and nodded. "As a chosen one, yes, but it's clear you have a hard time with it."

"Did I say that?" asked Lucas, when he let go of Carleton's hand.

Carleton's face softened for a moment. It was a look of sympathy, and it caught Lucas off guard. "Just make sure you are watching your back. Some of us did not look kindly on you defeating Eli a few weeks ago."

He gave Carleton a nod, and when the officers started to call their names, the pair went their separate ways.

Lucas hung a lantern on a hook to give himself some extra light. He was spreading fresh straw out in the stall of the big black horse. The horse was munching on the food he had put in the feeder earlier and turned his head from time to time to see what Lucas was doing, but he had no intention of kicking or biting as he did with everyone else who entered his stable.

"You have a way with horses," Davis told him a few days earlier. "I will be glad to give you the responsibility of Egon's horse."

Lucas had not objected. He liked Egon's horse. He kept his hand on the horse's back while moving the straw around with his foot—the contact always made the horse calm down, and he noticed that it seemed to have a similar effect on himself.

They were working later that night than usual, since some horses had come in late. They were eager to get to their beds and Lucas finished up and was just starting to head out, when he heard one of the big stable doors open and saw Eli enter with three elite borns.

They walked in hesitantly, looking around as if they had lost something.

"What brings you in here?" asked Davis.

Lucas stayed inside the stall, but saw all the other boys standing to attention in the aisle when Eli made his way farther in.

"I thought Lucas was assigned to work here," he heard Eli say.

"He was," answered Davis.

"Then where is he?"

"Somewhere in back," said Davis without moving his head.

Lucas stood perfectly still. He peered out from the shadows at the group that had assembled, watching as Eli made eye contact with Zera, who stood perfectly still as well. An elite whose back was turned to him, and who was mostly obscured by a large beam, called his name.

Lucas took a deep breath and answered casually—as if he did not know who it was or why they had come seeking him out—before opening the half door of the stable and stepping out. He was about to slide the latch across the stable door to lock it when he noticed that Eli was stalking towards him rapidly. He was armed, as the elites always were, not having to abandon their weapons after practice like the chosens did.

For a moment, his hand rested on the latch and he locked eyes with the horse. He then slowly took his hand away and watched the door slightly open, before turning around. Eli closed in on him before he could stand to attention and presented a gloating smile.

"I'm sorry—were you not taught how to properly address a superior?" said Eli.

"I didn't hear you come in," answered Lucas. He found himself stepping across the aisle to stand next to Davis. He wasn't sure if it was because he needed the added security or if he was just tired and preferred for someone else to talk Eli down.

Being this close to Eli for the first time since the fight brought back the last moments of it. He could sense that Eli was remembering as well, and the other boys looked at him in anticipation. Eli's face hardened when he pulled out his dagger to point at Lucas and grabbed a crop from the wall. Zera and Warrick immediately moved to stop him, but were held back by two of the elites, while another blocked the other boys. It looked like Davis was about to knock Eli out of the way when the crashing sound of the stable door flying open stopped them all in their tracks. Eli had to duck when the black horse stormed out and reared up directly behind him. Lucas dashed out of the way, and the horse was suddenly in between them. Eli raised himself up and grunted in anger. He looked for ways to get past the horse, but the horse was snorting and pacing left and right.

"You are in trouble now," hissed Eli. "I'll get you for this."

"Get him for what?" they suddenly heard a stern voice say. All the boys instantly turned around and saw Egon standing at the entrance of the stables, another member of the king's guard beside him. Taking him by the halter, Lucas calmed the horse down and returned him to his stall.

"Get him for what, Eli?" Egon asked again while walking past the other boys, who all stood to attention.

"Sir," started Eli. "It appears that Lucas here does not understand the ranking order we have in place."

"It is not *your* place to make that clear to him," said Egon, stopping next to him and staring at Lucas. He looked at the crop Eli was still holding in his hand. "So, what were you going to do about it?"

"I was going to report him, sir!"

"Oh, really?" asked Egon, glancing over his shoulder to see the other elites all divert their eyes.

"Yes, sir!" continued Eli. "We came here because we saw light coming from underneath the door and since it was late, we thought maybe someone had left a lantern on by accident. Everyone acknowledged us entering and stood to attention, except for Lucas here. He also didn't close the stall door and caused the horse to escape. I was just trying to get him back in," said Eli, indicating the crop.

"And you were just going to report all this?"

"I was, sir!"

"Good, well you have reported it now," responded Egon, signaling to the other king's guard to take the crop from Eli. "You may leave. I will handle it from here."

Eli hesitated, but a dark smile came over his face when he saw Egon had started to unbutton the black jacket he was wearing over his maroon shirt. Lucas caught Zera's stare as the elite borns were leaving the stables, and it was full of worry. He held his breath as Egon continued to unbutton his jacket.

"We have not formally met yet," said Egon, handing the jacket off to the other king's guard. "Do you know who I am?"

"I do, sir," answered Lucas respectfully.

"Good. Then you know you cannot disobey me," said Egon. "Give him your sword," he told the other king's guard.

Lucas took the sword that the guard handed to him and watched as Egon stepped towards the middle of the aisle, stopping just in front of him. "I want to see what you are really made of," he continued, pulling his sword. "I want you to fight me."

At this, Lucas looked at the other chosen for guidance. A few of them nodded encouragingly and gathered closer.

"I am not punishing you," Egon clarified. "I am giving you the benefit of the doubt, as Eli's story doesn't add up. I've been wanting to test you myself for some time now, so tonight seems like the perfect opportunity for it. Now, are you ready?"

Lucas twisted the sword in his hand and nodded. He measured the weight of the weapon in his hand, let his fingers grow accustomed to the grooves of the hilt.

They started to warm up, gently and almost as if they were moving in slow motion, but soon Egon increased his strength and speed.

"Keep up with me, boy!" Egon commanded, between strikes. "Don't hold back!"

Lucas obeyed and gave it his all. He was no match to Egon in strength and had to use every ounce of his skill and agility to stay in the fight. The blows came down hard and he did his best to avoid them, but after some time, he began to retreat, gradually, towards the back of the stable. He was able to push Egon away but, before long, when his back was almost up against the wall, he grew tired and lost his sword when it was knocked out of his hand.

Egon nodded his approval and put his sword back in its scabbard. The other king's guard stepped forward and collected his blade from where it lay in the straw.

"Well done," Egon commended him, putting his jacket back on and tying the buttons. "I have no doubt the outcome may have been in your favor had it been a fight to the death. You possess technique that will get you far, but I have to warn you. Learn your place here," he said more sternly. "If you don't, I will not hesitate to come down hard on you."

Without waiting for Lucas's response, Egon turned to the others. "Finish up here and get yourselves to bed," he told them, before walking through the stable doors and into the night.

CHAPTER 10

As the stable door fell closed behind him, Egon couldn't help but gaze towards the roof of the stables opposite that had once been destroyed. The fire had plagued him in his dreams for many years and had changed his life forever. Even now, he could still hear the popping of the burning wood and the screams of the boys beyond the flames, those who did not make it. He had lost a friend that day and, after he was given the king's mark for his bravery, he had lost even more. He had distanced himself from those he shared a connection with, and it hardened him into the person he had become. What he just did for Lucas, letting him off undisciplined, was something he would have never considered doing for another boy, and he was not sure why. Perhaps because he agreed with the king and sensed that Lucas was different than the other chosen? Or perhaps because Lucas reminded him of the friend he failed to save from the fire?

The horses were taken out of the stables the following morning for a hunt, and Egon stood ready and waiting for his mount to be brought to him. He was just starting to feel the first pangs of restlessness—everyone seemed to take longer than he did, when it came to preparing—when General Finton brought his horse up alongside him.

"Great day for a hunt, wouldn't you say?" said Finton, looking up towards the sky where no cloud was in sight and then down to where Egon was standing.

"I suppose so," answered Egon. He suspected the general was only making small talk because there was something more pressing on his mind that he wanted to discuss. He pretended to be busy, adjusting his belt and scabbard, to show he had little interest in making conversation, but Finton did not move on. Instead, he cleared his throat. "Eli told me he reported the new chosen one to you last night for not knowing his place?"

At that moment, Davis walked Egon's horse up to him, and Egon took the reins. "Yes, he did," he answered and mounted up. "Go on, Davis," he said, turning his horse towards the boy. "We've got it from here. Get to your practice."

The two men sat quietly on their horses, waiting for Davis to leave them. Egon awaited the next nosy question and sighed quietly when it arrived.

"He also said you took it upon yourself to deal with this matter?"

"That's right."

Egon tightened the reins and wriggled in his seat to get comfortable, before turning to the general. "What are you getting at, General?" he asked, though he knew full well that Finton only wanted to know more about the punishment Eli had almost certainly told him Lucas was to receive.

"Nothing." The general shrugged. "I'm just glad someone showed him his place."

"No need to worry, General," said Egon. Other riders, with horses from the stable opposite them, were beginning to join them, and Egon felt himself impatient to get going. "He seems to have enough eyes on him to make sure of that. Unless he is in the wrong group, and we are all wasting our time."

Finton narrowed his eyes. It was obvious that he wasn't quite sure what Egon had meant by that statement, which was mildly satisfying, but the bridge was lowered and, with the hunt on the way, Egon did not have time to give their interactions further thought. He brought his horse to the front and gave him a quick nudge with his heels.

Lucas assumed the officers had all been told about the stable incident, because for weeks they did their best to prevent him and Eli from fighting each other. They moved them as far apart in lineup as possible. Eli, however, could not help himself in his pursuit to get Lucas into hot water, and it soon became clear that he'd started to use other elite borns to do his bidding. Lucas figured out which elite borns were controlled by Eli when he came to fight them. They would give him a hard fight and suddenly drop out by falling down or losing their sword, making it look as if he had defeated them. The chosen boys found themselves running extra miles several times a week because of it.

"Funny how it always happens when an officer is watching," Davis grumbled one day, as they were doing their run.

"But not watching closely enough," panted Zera.

"Yes," Warrick groaned, "I have them to thank for this cramp in my side."

Lucas, feeling guilty about the runs being inflicted on his account, stayed quiet.

The only break they got was when an elite born, like Rhys, who was close to Carleton, chose Lucas in lineup instead, or when Eli was away from the castle and no one felt the need to please him.

When Lucas started to make it obvious to the officers what they were doing, and this particular foul-play scenario had run its course, they changed their tactics and began to hurt or provoke him instead.

He could not help but instinctively defend himself when he received a cut or hard push, inciting more discipline, regardless of the fact that some cuts that he received required a good dose of Garrad's burning cream. Lucas could feel an anger building up inside him that he was only able to control by meditating at every available opportunity, but as time went on it became harder to rein in his feelings. He longed for the moment he would be allowed to go on patrol outside the castle, just to get away for a few days.

One afternoon, after several pointless rounds of practice fights the days before, he'd finally had enough of being in a no-win situation.

"Lucas," shouted Verron, calling out names to line up for practice with the elites.

Lucas raised his head but remained standing where he was. The officer had already called his name twice, and he knew he would have to answer him. "Sir," he said. "I think Tanner should take my place."

"Are you ill?" inquired Verron.

"No, sir," answered Lucas. "I just don't see the purpose of me participating." He could hear the boys around him hold their breath and Davis's whispering voice, telling him to go, but he had made up his mind. "There are others who will benefit from the practice," he continued. "I don't, sir."

"Are you telling me you are refusing to participate?" asked Verron sternly.

"I will only fight those who fight fair. We know who they are."

"You are not the one deciding who fights who," said Verron. "If you don't line up right now, you'll be spending time in the hole."

Lucas didn't comply, and Verron motioned to an officer to get him.

"Lucas, just line up," said Zera, nudging him. "They'll make you, sooner or later."

"Let it be later then," answered Lucas. "It's time they see what's going on here and do something about it."

He stepped forward when the officer told him to follow and allowed himself to be locked up. The hole was as awful as he remembered it, but he didn't care. He sat himself down by the bars of his cell and watched the practice begin without him. Egon and Finton appeared a short time later, convening with Verron by the gates. Seeing them gave Lucas chills and he feared he would have to face them. He sighed with relief when he saw them both nod in agreement to something Verron said.

It would be several days before he was let out of the hole and told he was to participate, or face being locked up again. But Lucas saw this outcome as the better way—a path to avoiding conflict—and he was not fazed by being locked up time after time. After he refused to rise to a fight a sixth time, the officers punished all the chosen. Each time Lucas refused to comply, they lined them all up against a wall and kept them standing there until it was time for them to do their chores. None of them ever complained, since they accepted they were all in this together, but when they found themselves being observed more and more from the wall by Egon or other officers, they became more anxious.

"They're here again," said Zera, looking up at the wall where Verron and Egon stood during one of the chosens' break times.

"Pretty much at any time of the day now," said Warrick, drawing lines in the sand with his foot.

"Guess the wall is their meeting place lately," grumbled Davis.

Lucas was sitting on a barrel, resting his hands on his sword, which he had poked into the ground. He avoided looking up. "I respect Egon," he muttered, "but he gives me the creeps when he looks down on me like that."

"I don't know if it's respect or fear I have for him," commented Warrick.

"You certainly don't want to get on his bad side," said Zera. "With the reputation he has, how he questions prisoners, I'm fairly sure there's not a soldier in this castle who feels any different than we do. I'm just surprised he has not come down here yet to at least talk to you, Lucas."

"He doesn't have to," said Davis. "His presence up there is intimidating enough."

"I'm sorry," said Lucas, sighing deeply. "I don't know what to do. I don't understand why they keep me in training with the elite borns. I've told Verron that taking me out would be the only way to solve anything, and he agreed, but said it's not up to him."

"Maybe you should submit to Eli. Let him know you accept his seniority," suggested Davis. "It might be enough for him to grow bored and leave you alone."

"You really believe that?" asked Zera.

"No," admitted Davis, "but it's worth a try. I fear that if Lucas doesn't act like a chosen soon, Finton will find a way to have him killed."

"He's not the first chosen to defy orders or stand up for what he believes in," said Zera. "You did it."

Lucas lifted his head.

"That was different," sighed Davis. "It was before I came here."

Zera shook her head. "It was already determined you were a chosen and they were coming to collect you. It was no different from what Lucas is doing now."

"What did you do?" asked Lucas, keen to hear more.

"He refused to go," answered Zera, staring into her brother's eyes. "He fought every single person who tried to remove him from our father's house, nearly killing one."

"Because you didn't want to leave your family?" asked Lucas.

"Because I didn't want to leave *Zera* behind," answered Davis. "Our father hit us. Especially Zera. Our mother had died of illness a few years prior."

"Then what happened?"

"The king sent Egon and the king's guard to collect me," answered Davis. "There was no way I could fight them, but Zera did."

Warrick let out a little chuckle. It was clear he knew the story.

Lucas turned to Zera. "You fought the king's guard?" he asked.

"No," answered Zera. "Only Egon." The chosen who had gathered around let out a little laugh and Zera smiled at Lucas. "He was holding Davis," she continued, "and carrying him away screaming. So, I grabbed a broom, snapped the stick off, and charged after them. Egon let go of my brother and turned around with sword drawn. I remember dropping to one knee with the stick in both hands to try and block his sword."

"And did you?" asked Lucas. He knew it was no small feat to stop steel with wood.

"I didn't have to," answered Zera. "Egon had already lowered his sword and grabbed the stick with his hand. When he did, I let go, ducked out of his reach to get away, but another member of the king's guard got a hold of me."

"Is that when Egon decided to take you to the castle as well?"

"I think that's when it may have entered his mind," answered Davis before his sister could, "but I think my father's words, thanking Egon for taking me from his house and mentioning that Zera might finally lose her fighting spirit with me gone, sealed it for him."

"The only good thing our father ever did for us," muttered Zera. "Of course, I had to prove myself—they made me work in the kitchen when I first arrived. I spent some time in the hole myself, for the stink I put up. Let me tell you, there were plenty of things to break down besides brooms!"

Davis laughed, putting a hand on his sister's shoulder and glancing at her with affection. Everyone remained silent after that, until an officer showed up and told them all to get back to work. The chosen got back to it, but Lucas could sense that everyone's energy was low.

He himself stayed put on the barrel a while longer, but after some time, he looked up and caught Egon staring down at him. Verron stood next to him, and the two men occasionally exchanged words. Egon looked far from pleased and disapprovingly shook his head from time to time. Lucas averted his eyes and jumped off the barrel to follow the other boys into training, feeling like any move he made would be the wrong one.

It was only a matter of time before—tired of doing Eli's dirty work— the elite borns began to rebel against his wishes. One day, as they gathered for practice, it became especially clear that Eli's fun was over. Eli's submissive posture and Finton's raised voice told everyone present that Eli was being told off by his father.

"The general's worried Carleton is taking over leadership of the elites," whispered Warrick in Lucas's ear. "I think Eli is being told to leave you alone and concentrate on regaining control again."

"How do you know?"

"Look who's with Carleton right now."

"Milton," said Lucas, glancing up. Milton was Eli's friend, but he was no longer standing with Eli. A few others had also migrated over to Carleton.

"Yep," said Warrick as they took their place in line. "Trouble in paradise."

No one dared look at Eli when he finally made his way over and lined up in front of Bennett. Lucas could tell Eli felt humiliated to have received a lecture in front of everyone, and decided to keep a close eye on Bennett, lest Eli take it out on him. Bennett was half Eli's size, but a fierce little warrior who could stand his ground, and dodge anything that came at him. But Eli was distracted, and Lucas could see that each swing of his blade was sloppier than the one that came before. He watched in horror, when one wrong move caused Eli's sword accidently to slice across Bennett's chest.

With practice having come to an abrupt stop and Verron and one other officer carrying Bennet off to the surgeon's room, the rest of the chosen ones had no choice but to head out to attend to their chores.

"Hurry up," Zera called to Lucas, who had stayed back to pick up Bennett's sword and was putting it in the barrel. He started walking towards the gates at the same time as a group of elite borns, who were busy discussing what had happened. He was so preoccupied he was unaware he was walking among them. When he finally realized his mistake, he tried to slow down and slip to the side but was suddenly pushed hard in the back.

He froze. The other boys stopped and stepped aside, creating a circle around him. Lucas turned around only to come face to face with Eli, who started to taunt him by giving him push after push—harder each time—until Lucas finally pushed back. It was what Eli had wanted him to do and Lucas knew it, but he didn't care anymore.

"I've got you!" sneered Eli. "Where are your security guards to protect you now?"

"You know full well I don't need any, but you clearly do," answered Lucas, gesturing at the elite borns surrounding them. "You had to wait until you had all of yours rounded up, didn't you?"

Eli's face turned red. "Be careful who you're talking to," he shouted. "I can have you disciplined for this."

"Go ahead," said Lucas. "They've already done that. Many times, but you know this won't get resolved until you accept that I beat you. Or when I show you I can do it again."

"You're a chosen one," laughed Eli. "You'll always have to serve under me, and I'm going to make your life miserable until you wished you'd stayed dead the first time."

Lucas could feel the fire burning inside him, but he took a deep breath and stood in front of Eli with all the calmness he could muster. Eli's face had become contorted and his body tense. If Eli decided to fight, Lucas knew he would take him up on it, even though the consequences would be severe.

He contemplated his next move, but before he could do or say anything, Zera and Davis were there, pushing through the circle and grabbing him by his shoulders to pull him away. Eli stepped forward to try and stop them from leaving but was blocked by Carleton, who put a hand on his chest and shook his head. The rest of the elite borns slowly stepped aside and let the three of them pass. Judging by the expressions on their faces and their relaxed posture, Lucas guessed that they were relieved to have the impending mess avoided.

Itan was walking the walls with his senior staff when some trouble in the training grounds caught the group's attention. They had just reached the stairs and were beginning to descend when the altercation between Lucas and Eli enfolded below.

"Do you wish me to intervene, sire?" asked Finton. "This does not appear to be a good situation."

"No," answered the king. "I'd like to see how this is going to play out."

Egon stood directly behind him, but Itan noticed that he did not interject his opinion. When the three chosen boys had made their escape, Finton turned to face him. "I would like to call for immediate and severe discipline for all chosen ones. And, in particular, for Lucas."

"No, you will not," said King Itan before he had made it halfway down the stairs.

"Sire," said Finton firmly. "You saw how he pushed Eli. From where I stood, it looked like the boy was doing a fair bit of talking back as well."

The king sighed and continued to make his way down the stairs. "It did not go unnoticed, General," he replied, "but I am tired of your son provoking that boy. Do not contradict me. I am fully aware of what has been going on between them."

"The boy needs to know his place. He's taunting my son each time we turn our backs. Just take one look at that smug smile of his. He thinks he is better than *all* of us! Time in the hole, running extra miles, withholding food, making him do extra chores . . . these are not the kinds of discipline the boy needs. He's defiant towards authority and needs to be flogged! He's undermined Eli's influence since he arrived here seven months ago. He's making a fool of my son."

Itan stared hard at Finton. "Your son is quite capable of doing that on his own. He was beaten in a fight he should have easily won. Things would have been different if you'd not been so hasty and had the boy branded before any firm decision regarding his future was made. I did not reprimand you for that, as I believed him to be chosen as well, but just because Lucas carries the brand of a chosen, does not make him one."

He stopped and looked for Egon, who had quietly followed. "Egon," Itan said, clearing his throat.

"Yes, sire?"

"Walk with me! We are finished for now, Finton."

The king left Finton standing there and continued to walk on with Egon.

"Have you made progress in tracing his history?" asked the king.

"Well," said Egon. "It checks out that he was raised by warrior monks. We managed to track down the village where he grew up and spoke to the elder. He remembered a young boy, named Lucas, who would wander down into the village from time to time. He lived alone with his father, who arrived in the village with Lucas as a baby and rebuilt the abandoned forgery. He did well for himself and was renowned for the quality weapons he produced. The elder found Lucas to be different from the other village children. He was contemplating putting him forward as a chosen when the boy's father suddenly died, and the boy disappeared. There were rumors in the village that he'd been taken in by the monks, but it was not until a year later that those rumors were substantiated when a young boy in monk's clothing was seen running in the woods. When a circus arrived and left, it was thought that he'd run off with them."

Itan nodded. "I am pleased to hear that Lucas would have been put on the list had he not disappeared. It confirms that it was suspected he was a chosen." He paused in front of the surgeon's room, where both he and Egon peered in. Seeing another physician was already dealing with the injured boy, they continued.

"There is something else," said Egon. "Lucas's father. He did not die from natural causes. It was a single stab wound that killed him, likely from a sword. A robbery gone wrong, perhaps. What's interesting is how Lucas ended up with the warrior monks, who are not known for taking orphans in. Lucas has indicated to Officer Verron that they were already training him before he came to live with them."

"Interesting." Now this was something, thought Itan. "Which makes it more likely they recognized him as chosen and were grooming him to become one of them instead, for reasons unbeknownst to us. But tell me . . . you have been watching Lucas, and you were once a chosen yourself. Do you believe he is just a chosen, or could he be more?"

"There is no doubt in my mind he is a chosen one," answered Egon. "The others would not have accepted him the way they have, or have connected with him, if he did not carry their bloodline. However, his skills are superior to theirs, and he does not think the way the others do. Is that because of his upbringing, what he has endured in his life, or perhaps because he came to us much older? Maybe, but I have also started to wonder if it could be possible that he carries the blood of both. Elite *and* chosen."

Itan looked at him in surprise. "I do not think that has ever happened," he said, "but it would explain quite a bit." He then shook his head, dismissing the idea. "There is no way of substantiating he is both. He will remain chosen, and I think it's time, Egon, that you make sure he takes his place as such. This feud between him and Eli must stop. It's affecting the boys, obviously, but also the rest of the ranks, as well. I don't care what you have to do, but I trust you to take care of this matter."

When Zera, Davis and Lucas walked into the mess hall later that afternoon, Warrick was already seated with his food and looked up when they came and sat opposite him.

"Finally! You're here. Can any of you tell me what happened this afternoon, after we all left the training grounds?" he asked. "And don't say 'nothing,' because all three of your names have been mentioned."

"By who?" asked Davis.

"Elites. I heard them talking amongst themselves about a fight between Eli and Lucas. I was bringing clean bedding to the infirmary and it stopped me in my tracks. You should have heard them!"

"There was no fight," said Zera. "We stopped it."

"But there would have been?"

"Possibly, but nothing happened," Lucas told him.

"Where does Carleton come into this? I heard him and Eli were having words this afternoon as well."

Zera sighed and started to explain what had happened.

"You're lucky the officers were not there to see anything," said Warrick, dipping a large hunk of bread into his stew. "Sounds like it could've been bad for all of us."

Lucas dropped the spoon in his bowl and took a deep breath. "It was seen," he said reluctantly. When all eyes were on him, he continued. "The king, Finton, and Egon. They watched it all. They must have heard about Bennett and were heading our way along the wall. I saw them."

"Did Eli?" asked Zera, shocked.

Lucas shook his head. "No, none of them did, I don't think."

Davis stared at him hard. "But you did . . . and you still continued your standoff? You didn't back down at that point?"

"He kept pushing me," Lucas countered. It was clear that none of them were really going to take his side on this one. He suddenly didn't feel hungry at all.

"Lucas, you talked back to him and *you* pushed him," said Zera. "This is bad."

"I'm surprised we're all still sitting here," said Davis. "They're going to come for us for sure."

Warrick raised his shoulders and put the rest of the bread in his mouth. "Best eat up then," he said with a mouthful. "This may be a long one."

Lucas didn't respond and stood up without touching his food.

"Where are you going?" asked Zera before he got out the door.

"Going to collect my punishment," answered Lucas. "Maybe if I go now, they'll not involve the rest of you."

He left before any of them could say anything and walked outside towards the infirmary to talk to Officer Verron, but he wasn't there, so he assumed they had gone to their mess hall. He asked a guard to send word, as he could not go any farther. He then peeked inside the infirmary and saw Bennett lying on a bed, all bandaged up. His eyes were closed and he lay very still. A nurse was sitting by his bedside, cooling his head with a cloth. Lucas felt a lump rise in his throat when he saw the concern on the nurse's face. Bennett might not make it. He was about to step inside when a voice behind him made him abruptly turn around.

"What is the urgency?" he heard Officer Verron ask. He was marching towards him from across the bailey. From the way he walked, Lucas could tell he was annoyed that he was called away from his dinner.

"I nearly came to fight Eli this afternoon, sir," he explained quickly. "I challenged his authority and put my hands on him, sir. It was entirely my mistake and I am here to take my punishment for it."

Verron stared at him and then scratched his chin. "Yes," he finally answered. "I have already been informed about what happened, but the decision on discipline has not been made yet and will come from higher up. I will tell them that you came to accept punishment and maybe that will soften their considerations. Go finish your food and wait to hear from me soon."

"Yes, sir," answered Lucas. He waited until Verron had turned around to go back to the officers' mess hall before returning himself.

The rest of the evening unfolded as usual, and Lucas was hoping they had forgotten about the incident. He even began to let himself relax a little . . . that was, until they walked out of the stables late that night and he saw Officer Verron waiting for him.

The group stood together when Davis locked the doors and Lucas separated from them when Verron motioned for him to follow.

Lucas thought it strange that he was taking him towards the outer bailey and his heart sank when he saw Egon in the center of it. He had his arms crossed and a stern expression on his face. Lucas knew he was in for trouble, and the forms in which it would come were running through his head.

When he heard a sound behind them and looked over his shoulder, he saw that Eli was heading his way, escorted by an officer. Lucas stood silent when they reached Egon and bowed his head so he did not have to look at him. Egon waited for Eli to get there and then looked down at them.

"Do you know why you are here?" he asked sternly.

Lucas reluctantly answered that he did, but Eli wasn't sure. "The incident with Bennett was an accident, sir," he answered.

"You are not here because of that, Eli," said Egon.

"Oh . . . all right," said Eli, looking relieved. "Of course not." He gave Lucas a sinister smile. "Then I am guessing you have called me to witness Lucas's punishment for defying me?"

Egon took a deep breath in frustration. "Don't worry, you'll be permitted to watch him atone for what happened this afternoon, but you will be right there alongside him, suffering the same fate."

Eli's smile disappeared from his face faster than it had arrived, and he looked up at Egon's somber face.

"If I may ask, sir . . . what did I do wrong? It's Lucas who doesn't know his place."

Egon ignored his plea. "Be honest and tell me, who do you see standing next to you?"

Eli looked at Lucas and shrugged. "Lucas, sir?"

"And what is he to you?"

"A chosen one, sir? An opponent to practice against?"

"Is that all you see?" asked Egon.

Eli glanced at Lucas again. "Yes, that's all. I don't know what else you would mean, sir."

"You do, Eli," corrected Egon. "You're a smart boy. You figured this out from the moment you laid eyes on him." He left it at that and turned to Lucas. "And what do you see?"

Lucas looked at Eli and let their eyes meet. "Someone who makes me angry, sir," he responded. "Someone who's trying to get me in trouble whenever he can and wants to make my life miserable. Someone who hates me and wants me gone from this place."

"And why are you both here, at the castle?"

Eli raised his head and was eager to answer. "To serve the king and protect the realm."

Egon nodded his head. "Yes, but we could take in a thousand boys from villages who would do just the same. What I am asking is, why are the two of you here?"

When neither boy answered, he continued. "You are here," he said firmly, "because of *what* you are, not *who* you are!" He paused and, when neither boy spoke, he took a step back. "Take your uniforms off!" he demanded.

Judging by Egon's tone, Lucas could tell he was not messing with them, and he obediently began to take his shirt off. He then took off his boots and trousers. He stopped when Egon nodded to him, letting him know that it was enough. They waited for Eli to finish.

It was cold, and rain clouds were starting to form overhead when both boys stood in front of Egon in nothing more than their undergarments.

"Now, who do you see, Eli?" asked Egon.

"A chosen one!" answered Eli defiantly.

Egon looked at him. "Really? Is that what you truly see? Because if I did not know you, I would not be able to tell, without the aid of your uniform."

"What makes us different is our blood," said Eli. "My blood is that of an elite born and his is that of a chosen."

"That is true! Your blood is what makes you different and that is the reason why you are both here, but unfortunately a sword on the battlefield will make no distinction between the blood of an elite and that of a chosen. You will both suffer the same fate on the battlefield if you do not have each other's backs." To make his point, he drew his sword and made a cut on Lucas's upper arm. Small droplets of blood flowed down and dropped onto the ground. Then the same was done to Eli.

"You see, my sword could not tell the difference," said Egon. "I managed to cut you both with the same amount of pressure, and both of you are bleeding."

At this, Eli grew furious. He had been reasonably calm, up until that point. "Why am I here?" he said, raising his voice. "I am a distinguished general's son. Does my father even know I'm here?" He looked around wildly to see if his father was coming, but there were only the four officers standing to the side and a king's guard, who was just now bringing Egon's horse to him.

"Who do you think gave the order for this?" Egon said calmly. "You are here at the king's demand and, yes, your father is well aware. I have been given the task to put an end to this little vendetta between the two of you. It is causing a rift in the order and stability of this army." He turned to Lucas as well and, when neither boy replied, he jumped on his horse.

"You will learn to save each other's lives, instead of wanting to take them," he shouted, reaching behind his saddle to unhook a large whip, "and I will wear you down until you do." Egon tipped his face up towards the sky, where clouds were pushing together into one black threatening mass and making his horse dance nervously. Lucas, who had not moved at all, raised his head to look at the horse. It was the same horse that had been out of its stall when he had encountered Eli in the stable months ago. He was a troublesome creature, proud and feisty, but had always been reliable in a chase or on steep terrain, and

Lucas had recognized early on how much Egon loved him. The horse reared up and rolled his eyes back when the first flash of lightning lit up the sky, but then locked eyes with Lucas and settled. Egon regained control of the animal and raised his whip up high.

"It's going to be a long, wet night, but I am committed to see this through, as you will soon discover. You will start running," he shouted down to the boys, "side by side, until I tell you to stop. If one falls behind and the other does not stop to help him up, you will both feel the whip."

Eli looked helplessly to his uniform that was still lying in the sand. Lucas knew better than to acknowledge his own, which he imagined would be soaked before long, even if he did have it on.

"Leave it!" shouted Egon, when he saw Eli reach for the uniform. "No one will be pulling rank here tonight."

Lucas was the first to turn around to start running, but immediately heard the whip slice through the air behind him and land inches from his heels. He paused and looked back to see the whip land a second time close to Eli as well. Egon had meant every word he had spoken, so they quickly met up and started running side by side along the wall.

"I'll hate you even more after this," hissed Eli, looking sideways to Egon, who followed them closely on his horse.

"I would save your breath," replied Lucas. "This isn't going to be a short run."

At that, Eli reached out and shoved Lucas, which made him stumble and fall behind. The whip broke the air a second time and this time hit them both. They continued to run in silence and were doing well until the clouds broke and turned the outer bailey into a muddy pool. Their bare feet kept sinking in the mud, causing them to fall and have the whip find its mark when the other did not stop in time. When they finally felt they had a rhythm going, Eli stumbled again, and Lucas slipped when he tried to stop too fast. He skidded some distance away and struggled to get up. Through the pouring rain and a white flash of lightning, he watched the whip hit Eli on his bare back, making him cry out. He then felt the same done to him. With Eli still struggling, Lucas pushed himself up and ran over as quickly as he could before the whip landed again.

Egon looked like a dark ghost on his horse, with the whip in his hand ready to strike at any moment. He let them run a while longer and then, when neither of them could run anymore, ordered them to come to the center. Lucas could tell, by the expression on Egon's face when the lightning flashed upon it, that he had found no pleasure in this exercise. He was doing it because he had to.

"Eli, look at Lucas and tell me what you see," he demanded.

Eli was out of breath and was leaning over with his hands resting on his knees. He turned his head and looked at Lucas, who was breathing equally hard and gasping for air. They were both soaking wet, caked in mud and shivering from the cold, but he shook his head and refused to answer.

Egon took a deep breath and told them to start running again. Both boys turned and ran before Egon made it back to his horse and whip. Their bare feet splashed through the mud again and their wet hair hung in streaks before their eyes. Every step became harder, and they were on the brink of collapse. Without a word they struggled on, until Lucas noticed Eli's steps becoming uneven.

"I can't run much longer," he heard him say, between labored breaths.

"I hear you," answered Lucas. "But we have to stick together."

"I just want to lie down. I don't care that he whips me—I'll at least get some satisfaction knowing that he will do the same to you."

Lucas did not answer. It was clear now that Eli's hatred ran so deep that, even at his lowest point, he was still thinking of making Lucas's life miserable.

They ran another half a lap until they were at the far corner of the bailey and Eli suddenly stopped. Lucas grabbed him by the shoulders as he sank to the ground. He anxiously watched Egon approach on his horse from a distance and pulled, but he was unable to get him to stand up. He let go of Eli and stepped in front of him to face Egon—there was no point in both feeling the whip, at this point. It would only weaken Eli further, and drag the exercise out for longer.

Breathing hard, Lucas stood up straight and waited for Egon to raise his whip, but he did not. Instead, he halted some distance away, the black horse under him glistening with rain. Lucas waited another moment before looking down at Eli and again grabbed him under the arms. This time he didn't try and pull him up but dragged him to the wall and leaned him up against it. He then stood for a moment with his back against the wall until he slid himself down to sit next to Eli.

The rain kept pouring as they sat there, each of them trying to catch their breath. Eli closed his eyes and Lucas watched Egon back his horse slowly away from them.

They rested for a few minutes, until the sound of the whip hitting the ground startled them. The rain had stopped. Eli was the first to be back on his feet, and he nudged Lucas in an effort to get him to stand up quickly. They approached Egon, who stood in the center.

"Eli?" Egon called out.

"Yes, sir?"

"Who is Lucas to you?"

"Someone who will have my back in battle, sir!"

Egon furrowed his eyebrows and stared at Eli a moment before asking Lucas the same question in reverse. "Lucas. Who is Eli to you?"

"Someone to follow into battle, sir!" answered Lucas, straightening himself up.

Egon observed both boys in front of him. "I'm fairly convinced you are telling me what I wanted to hear. Eli, you are the stubborn one, but I am hoping you give up on this antagonism of late. Lucas . . . I sense a defiance in you. I was surprised to see you step in front of

Eli after he had fallen. Would you have taken all the lashes from the whip yourself?"

Neither boy spoke, but they no longer looked at their feet. Lucas was looking Egon directly in the eye.

"Very well," he finally said. "You both know what is expected of you, so don't make me have to do this again." Without giving them another look, he jumped on his horse and rode off.

Coming to relieve Egon of the boys, Verron had stepped out just in time to see Lucas and Eli sinking to the ground. They were clearly too exhausted to take another step, so Verron called a wagon in to take them back. As they were helped into it, Verron heard Eli whisper to Lucas that he would never forgive him. Verron ignored it, vowing not to tell Egon, as he would get the boys back out there all over again. He felt that, from the moment the king had learned of his existence, Lucas had been suffering at the hands of selfish people who needed to prove a point. Regrettably, he knew he had been one of those people.

He had been present after the chosen test, when a debate was going on between different parties. They were discussing the fight, and Lucas's future. Some senior officers had tried to make a strong case of putting Lucas with the elite borns until his bloodline could be checked out. His degree of strength, skill and willpower was not often seen in chosens, even after years of training. Finton had disagreed, holding Egon's experience up as an example, and staking further evidence in his claim that the chosen had accepted Lucas and had already formed a strong bond. Egon had then urged they wait until Lucas was fully recovered, or more proof of his heritage was found, before making a decision.

The king seemed to be conflicted. The thought of waiting to make a final decision appealed to him most but, considering the bond Lucas already had with the chosen, as well as no knowledge of Lucas's bloodline, he told them all that he had no option but to name him a chosen one for the time being.

Verron had walked with Finton afterwards. They had entered the lush inner courtyard with the loud bubbly fountain, where they stopped. The sound of the water was perfect to keep conversations from being overheard. "I fear the king could still change his mind," Finton had said. "If you don't want to lose Lucas as a chosen, I think you should make arrangements to brand him as soon as possible."

Blinded by his own desire to train him, he had agreed. He and the blacksmith had gone to Garrad's room that same night. Garrad had tried to stop them from coming in. "The boy is far too weak," he had argued, holding the door closed, with his foot up against it. "He will not be able to fight off an infection if one occurs—you may be killing him!"

"You should be willing to help the blacksmith do it then," Verron had replied, "to prevent that from happening." He had pushed the physician out of the way.

When he entered the room and saw Lucas lying on the bed with his eyes closed and barely any color in his face, he was overcome by a strange sensation he could not describe. An inner voice spoke to him and told him not to continue, and he knew what he was about to do was wrong, that they were all wrong. Pushing the thought from his mind, he told the blacksmith to heat the iron, and instructed Garrad to make any preparations necessary to minimize infection.

He'd stayed, observing until it was done. The boy had bucked a little and cried out in his unconscious state, and Verron had kept his eyes fixed upon his pale face. He was still moaning when Verron closed the door behind him. He had then gone to the mess hall and threw himself down on a seat opposite a fellow officer and poured himself a drink.

After watching him throw back two cups of ale, upon which he began pouring another, the officer had laughed. "Are we celebrating something?"

"Not really sure," he had replied, and threw back another cup. It was a question he would have to give more thought to, and he wasn't in the mood for thinking.

CHAPTER 11

Bennett held on to life for several days after the accident, but despite the best possible care, the fever eventually took him. The chosen mourned his loss in silence and carried him to the graveyard on a hill that overlooked the castle. They buried him next to other boys who had succumbed to illness and injuries over the years—a grim reminder of how vulnerable even their lives were.

As weeks turned into months and the months turned into a year, and with Lucas turning thirteen, he felt that his life at the castle had become easier. The elite borns stopped provoking him after they learned about that dreadful night, and Eli was devoting more of his energy into putting Carleton in his place. The officers had stopped disciplining Lucas when he unintentionally did not hold back and took a win from an elite born. They would sometimes yell, "Watch it, Lucas!" or shake their heads in disapproval.

Lucas had just finished his practice with the pell and walked over to the sword barrel to change the wooden sword out for a steel one, when an officer called out to him.

"Lucas! Archery!" he shouted, pointing towards the archery station.

Lucas let out a sigh and dropped the sword into the barrel—archery wasn't something he was particularly good at. He looked over to the other stations, most of which were unoccupied, but saw the officer shake his head.

"You need the practice."

Feeling the officer's eyes on him, he reluctantly walked over the nearly empty training grounds, towards the archery station in the corner. Many of the boys were out. It was tax collecting season and their help was needed to guard the treasury wagons. Every few days, when a new collection caravan was scheduled to go out, the chosen ones were lined up and names were called who was to accompany them. His name had yet to come up, and each day it didn't, he felt something inside him sink. A few times he'd been hopeful, when Officer Verron had glanced in his direction, but he had then called someone else instead. Even the elite borns had been away, with either the king or with patrol troops to guard the border. Sightings of hunters had been more frequent, and they were trying to force them back across the river. Lucas longed to be part of any action beyond the walls of the castle.

"Don't worry," Zera had reassured him. "I'm sure it will happen soon."

Having to choose between the longbow or the crossbow, Lucas picked up the crossbow and loaded it with an arrow. Davis and Zera were talented with the longbow and spent most of their time training with it, but he felt the crossbow was easier to aim, as he didn't have to focus on the additional task of holding the string back with one hand.

He eyed up the target and was about to let the arrow go when the horn sounded from the outer gate, announcing the king's return. Lucas let out a sigh of relief and put the bow and arrow down. All the boys assigned to work with the horses—including himself—dropped what they were doing and ran to get into proper uniform before the king entered the inner bailey.

They took quick turns washing their hands and face in a trough filled with water at the entrance to the weapons room, and then they each grabbed a tunic to put over their shirt. Lucas buckled his belt with scabbard, and put his sword in, before rushing out and lining up on the side near the stables he worked in.

As soon as the king's party rode in, their horses were handed over and taken into the stables. Lucas had to take several since he did not have Davis and Zera there, but the horses knew what he wanted them to do. They followed him right in and walked into their proper stalls. Other boys came in to help him, taking the saddles off and rubbing the horses dry before feeding them.

He worked happily, pleased that he would soon be reunited with Zera and Davis, when they made it back that evening. It was not the same without his friends in the stables and it was eerily quiet during their absence.

His joy to have them back was short-lived, however, when it was announced a few days later that Officer Verron was getting another troop together and they were leaving again. Zera placed a comforting hand on his shoulder when Warrick's and Tanner's names were called out—they would be going with her and Davis. "Be patient," she said. "I'm sure you will be called on soon. I remember how hard it was for me when I had to watch Davis go out, long before I was able to."

Still, he couldn't help but feel sorry for himself as she skipped off to make her preparations.

Officer Verron stopped Lucas when he walked past him to go to the stables.

"I know how much you want to go with them, and I'd take you in a heartbeat, but I've not been granted permission yet."

Lucas tried to put on a brave face. "It's all right," he responded. "Gives me a chance to start beating Davis at archery."

At this, Verron gave him an understanding smile.

Lucas was stepping out of a stall when Tanner walked past him to get a horse to ride out on. There was something a little strange about the slow way in which Tanner was moving, and Lucas stopped what he was doing to observe him. He watched him sway a little and then noticed the droplets of sweat on his face when he leaned against the wall to catch his breath.

"Are you all right?" Lucas asked. "You don't look well."

"I am," answered Tanner. "Just didn't sleep well last night, and I'm tired."

Tanner was tough and not easy to stop when he set his mind on something, so Lucas was not convinced by his statement. He waited a moment, until Tanner pulled himself together, before leading a horse out of the stables.

He was handing the horse over to Officer Verron when Tanner came out of the stables with sweat now visibly running down his face. He had to lean against his horse to steady himself.

"You look sick," Verron said, looking him over with a critical eye.

"I'm just fine, sir," answered Tanner.

Verron shook his head. "I don't think so. I can't take you. You need to have yourself checked out." He looked intently at the convoy for a moment. Lucas could see that it was ready and waiting. The wagon that was used to collect the taxes was surrounded by soldiers, and Warrick and Davis were at the front with a couple of officers. Zera was at the back, where Tanner was supposed to be. Without another person there, the back of the convoy would be more vulnerable.

Lucas was about to take the horse back to the stables for Tanner, when Verron's eyes came to rest on him. His heart started beating faster when he realized Verron may be looking for him to replace Tanner, but then remembered not to get his hopes up.

He was entering the stable when he heard Verron call out to him.

"Sir?" he responded, and stopped to see the officer riding up to him.

"I have an entire convoy waiting and I am one man down," he said. "Get your gear! You're coming with us. And don't make me regret this. I am putting my neck on the line here by taking you."

Only a short time later, when they were crossing the last bridge, did Lucas allow himself to feel the immense sense of freedom. It was really happening! He watched the fields go by where he had camped with the circus. A former life that seemed all but a distant memory. He did sometimes wonder how the circus members were, and especially so when he saw a member of the castle household staff who might remind him of one of them, but he always pushed the memory away as quick as it arrived. He was in the place where he belonged, and he would not want to go back if offered the choice.

"Are you ready for this?" said Zera, smiling as she rode next to him.

"Oh yes," answered Lucas, feeling a big grin spread over his face, as they rode farther and farther away from the castle.

By nightfall, they made camp, and the chosen ones secured all the horses. Lucas worked alongside Warrick, who jokingly kept referring to him as *Tanner*, until he responded by playfully tackling Warrick to the ground, and they were scolded by an officer for fooling around.

"Don't get Lucas into trouble, Warrick," remarked Zera. "Or Verron won't take him along again."

"Sorry," said Warrick, giving Lucas a wink and dusting the dirt off his trousers.

"It's all right," said Lucas, dusting himself off as well. He picked up a bucket and followed Zera to the creek to fetch water for the horses.

"Don't let Warrick drag you into his silly antics," said Zera as she lowered her bucket into the water. "Verron may turn a blind eye to Warrick playing little games from time to time, but he has no tolerance for the rest of us to participate in them."

"How come he lets Warrick?" asked Lucas, as he kneeled by the water and filled his bucket.

"I'm not sure," answered Zera, lifting her bucket out, "but Warrick lived in the town closest to the castle, and he knew Verron before he became a chosen. He was taken in by a muckraker after he became an orphan at a young age and worked for him."

"Muckraker?"

Zera nodded. Realizing Lucas had not lived in a town and therefore may not know, she explained. "A muckraker is someone who cleans the streets at night from excrement. It is filthy work but pays well—not that Warrick would have seen any coin for his work. They are also excellent spies, since they work at night and can get close to people's houses to listen to what is going on inside. The muckraker Warrick worked for also sent him into the streets during the day to follow people suspected of wrongdoing. He told me once that if he was to follow someone and was waiting on them to come back out of whatever building they'd gone into, he would play games to stop himself from falling asleep. He trained himself to remain focused. If he were to lose sight of the person, he knew a beating would await him."

Lucas pulled his bucket from the creek. Some of the water splashed over the rim and soaked his boots. "That explains why Warrick always knows what's going on, even when he seems most distracted," he said as he followed Zera back to camp. "But where does Verron come into this?"

Zera stopped and turned to him. They were close to a group of soldiers sitting around a fire. "Before Verron was appointed as officer for the chosen," she whispered, "he was the one to meet Warrick and the muckraker at night to collect information for the king."

"Ah," said Lucas, now understanding Verron's softer approach with Warrick. "I wonder why Warrick never mentioned this."

"Most of us don't like to remember the life we lived before coming to the castle," answered Zera as she continued to walk on. "Good or bad, it's a life we no longer get to live, so why dwell on it?"

After building the fires and serving food to the officers, Lucas was finally able to sit down and relax before lying down.

After the other three chosen had fallen asleep, Lucas stared at the leaves of the trees, rustling above him in the wind. He had not realized how much he had missed seeing that. He slept peacefully that night, dreaming of flying over a large field. The stone glistened in the sunlight below him, and he could see a group of warriors standing close to it, all looking up at him. Energy flowed through him, and he felt more alive when he woke the next morning. With most of the camp still sleeping, Lucas got up and went to check on the horses. He then took himself off to the side and pulled his sword. He inhaled the fresh morning air into his lungs, and let his body relax, before starting to go through the warrior monks' practice stances.

He was in his own little world, but never lost sight of the camp behind him, and Officer Verron, who stood watching him while sipping something steaming hot from a cup. When he decided it was time to break up camp, he called out to Lucas and told him to get to his chores.

At midday, they came to the first village, where they set up to collect taxes in the square. A table was placed at the back end of the wagon, and a village clerk took a seat behind it. He jotted down the names and payments that he received from the villagers lined up before him. If they paid with coin, it immediately went into a chest that rested on the table. Produce and livestock was loaded up onto the wagon by Zera and Warrick. Soldiers and officers stood close by and kept a watchful eye on all the proceedings, while Davis and Lucas stood guard on opposite corners, at the front of the wagon, farthest from the crowd. With enough soldiers around, it seemed unlikely to Lucas that anyone would dare to cause any trouble.

"It happens," Davis told him that night when he asked. "Some towns and villages feel they don't owe the king anything and resist in paying. We've had to ransack houses to find money owed to the king."

"Really?" asked Lucas. "Isn't that . . . a bit harsh?"

"Well," answered Davis, poking at the fire. "Taxes are paid because the king owns the land they farm, and he provides protection when needed. The people in the east are keener to pay, since we protect them from hunters stealing their livestock. Here in the west, they don't have that problem. Some of them don't think they need to pay for protection."

"Have you ever seen any hunters?"

Davis nodded. "I have! On patrol last year. We saw them and gave chase, but they disappeared before we could engage them in a fight."

"What did they look like?" asked Lucas. "I heard stories in the village where I grew up that they could rip a man's head off with just their bare hands." He chuckled at the mere thought of such a thing now.

Warrick smiled. "I think every kid gets told that story to keep them from wandering too far from home," he said.

"They looked fierce to me," continued Davis. "Like nothing would stop them. They were of large stature, and extremely fast, so I can understand where the stories come from. Their clothes made them blend into the forest and they were hard to spot. We might have been very close to them and yet we did not see them. We lost them."

"Would they not have attacked you? If they were so well hidden?" asked Lucas.

"Hunters have only attacked the king's soldiers when they had the element of surprise. There were too many of us for them to risk it."

Riding into a village the following day, Lucas noticed everyone was more on edge, paying close attention to their surroundings. He suspected they'd encountered problems here before and were expecting problems again, but nothing out of the ordinary happened.

It was at the next village, a few days later, that Lucas's eyes fell on a civilian who walked past him to join the line of people already gathered in front of the clerk's table. The man's stride was resolute, unlike other villagers who were in less of a hurry to part with their possessions, which had also alarmed the soldiers standing nearby and made them step in closer. The man could barely stand still and kept looking around him, drawing attention to himself. Zera and Warrick had noticed him as well and had placed a hand on the hilts of their swords, ready for trouble.

Lucas felt uneasy. Something was not right.

"Where are you going?" whispered Davis as Lucas brushed past him. He had been busy chasing a magpie off a bag of corn. "We can't move away from the wagon."

Lucas shook his head and closed his eyes to let his mind wander above the crowd in front of the clerk. He then came back and continued over the wagon, to the area in front of where Davis and he stood. He saw several men approaching, crouched down in narrow alleyways and armed with swords or daggers.

Lucas drew his sword and, already having Davis's attention, he nodded to the left and right of them. Women and children suddenly screamed in the crowd behind them, when the man jumped the table and held a knife to the clerk's throat.

With the chaos that erupted, Lucas and Davis were the only ones who saw the armed men come out of hiding. They ran towards the assailants to stop them from being able to reach the wagon. By the way the men raised their swords, it was clear they were prepared to kill to get what they had come for. Lucas waited for the attack to begin.

When the first assailant was upon him, he swung his sword from side to side and cut the man's throat in one swift move, then ducked to avoid an attack from a second man and answered it by letting his sword rip through the man's stomach. From his peripheral view, Lucas could see that Davis was able to take his assailants down as well, but with more men coming, they were soon outnumbered. The soldiers were busy dealing with the threat the clerk was facing and could not see what was happening on the other side of the wagon, but Zera and Warrick had, and joined them in the fight.

Lucas watched the man who was holding the clerk hostage glance over his shoulder—it was clear he was looking to see where his friends were. That was the moment Verron had been waiting for. He charged at the man, grabbed the arm that was holding the knife and twisted it, so that it ended up in the man's stomach. The clerk dropped to the ground to get out of the way, but he was no longer in any danger.

Alerted by the sounds of swords clashing, the soldiers rushed to help the chosen, and finished the fighting.

None of the armed men seemed to be from the town, when they looked at their bodies, except for the man responsible for the distraction. A village elder reported that he suspected them to be a group that had been stealing their way through the region and had been wanted for a long time. They had most likely struck a deal with the villager in order to assign him the dangerous task of distraction.

Lucas suddenly felt sick and was walking off into an alley when he heard Officer Verron praise Davis for his alertness. Since he was the most experienced, it was assumed that he was the one who had seen the attack coming.

"It was all Lucas, sir," corrected Davis. "He was the one who saw them approach."

With one hand leaning against a wall, Lucas heaved, and the contents of his stomach came lurching up. He had felt an inner force take over his body, to help him survive the attack. When the fighting was over, and all the energy left him, he felt nauseated. Like he had felt after he was attacked at the inn. He didn't stop until his entire breakfast had made its way to the ground at his feet.

Officer Verron had followed him into the alley and was standing behind him—waiting for him to finish. "Feeling better now?" he asked.

Lucas pushed himself away from the wall and nodded.

"Don't worry," said Verron, who put a hand on his shoulder. "I think we've all done this at some point. It is never easy to take a life." He paused and waited for Lucas to raise himself up before walking him back to the square.

"You did well today. Davis told me that it was you who saw them coming?" Verron asked when they approached the wagon.

"Just happened to turn around at the right time, sir," answered Lucas. He caught Davis's questioning eye, but he did not say anything to contradict his story.

After order was established and the collection of taxes was resumed, Davis walked over to Lucas and stood next to him, his arms folded over his chest.

"You knew they were coming, before anyone could have seen them," he said softly.

Lucas froze, unable to think of what to say. He wanted to be honest with his friend, but it wasn't something he was ready to discuss.

"It's all right—you don't have to explain it. I have suspected you have a *seeing mind* for a while now and so have they," he said, directing his gaze towards Zera and Warrick.

"You know about it?" asked Lucas, his heart beating a little faster at the thought.

"We are chosen ones, Lucas," said Davis, slapping him gently on the back before walking away. "We don't have to know about it. We just have to protect the one who has it."

Verron dismounted quickly after arriving back at the castle. He knew the king had been informed about the incident in the village, and he would be expected to give a full report without delay. He'd been on the road for days and stopped at the washroom to rinse the dirt and sweat off his face. The rest of him would have to wait.

"What do you think? Presentable enough?" he said, smiling, when he saw Egon standing in the doorway.

"Well, if you don't account for the bloodstains on your vest or the broken belt buckle or the layer of dust," Egon said, "then yes."

Verron laughed, drying his hands on the cloth that hung from a brass hook next to the wash bucket. He was about to leave when he noticed Egon's uneasy stare. "What's wrong? You look like you accidently ate my dinner or something."

Egon released himself from the doorway post. "Before you go to the Hall," he said, "there is something you should know."

"What is it?" asked Verron. The look on Egon's face told him it wasn't anything good. "Did something happen? Are all the boys all right?"

"Yes, the boys are fine."

"Then what is it?"

"The king released you of your command over the chosen ones, and I placed another officer in charge," answered Egon after a moment's pause. "I'm sorry."

Verron stared at him for a moment. Then it dawned on him. "Because I took Lucas," he said understandingly.

"Yes," answered Egon. "The king was not pleased when he discovered that was the case, and Finton—"

Verron stopped him from saying anything else. "It's all right," he said, putting his hand on Egon's shoulder on his way out. "I was aware of the risk when I took him without the king's consent."

He stopped to take a deep breath before entering the Great Hall—he would have to stay calm and keep his temper under control. He could tell, by the atmosphere in the room, that this meeting would revolve around his insubordination. He was glad his fellow comrade had warned him, so he was prepared, and ready to take a stand.

"Sire," said Verron after he had approached the throne and given a deep bow. "I hope the news of our achievement reached you well?"

"It did," answered the king while looking him over. "I am pleased you were successful in preventing a potential disaster and I will see to it that you and your men are rewarded accordingly."

Verron nodded and could tell that the king felt troubled in breaking the news to him, so he did something he had never dared before.

"If I may be so bold, sire, as to speak before my turn?" he started, and he made sure to continue without giving anyone a chance to stop him. "You have praised me for my command and leadership on more than one occasion, for which I am grateful. Yet, I have just been made aware that I have been reprimanded for a decision that led to the success of this command."

The people in the room remained silent and waited for the king's reaction to Verron's bold statement.

"I do not believe I follow, Verron," said the king, looking puzzled. "You have been reprimanded for going against the order not to take Lucas with you. Not for the handling of the incident at the village. You will still have full command over patrols, just not the chosen ones."

"If I may be so frank as to help clarify this for Officer Verron, sire?" Finton interrupted. He waited for the king to raise his hand to allow him, before continuing. "It is our belief that your affection for the boy drove you to disregard orders and it is therefore in the best interest of your career to remove you from the temptation to do so again."

Verron took a deep breath and tried to compose himself. "It is true I hold some affection for the boy, but I would never allow that to get in the way of any military decisions I am appointed to make. If it is the king's wish to remove me from the chosen ones, then so be it," he said. "I just want to make you aware that not taking Lucas on future missions will prove to be a huge mistake. For it was him who foresaw the attack and took down the first man."

News that Officer Verron had been stripped from his command over the chosen ones came to Lucas as soon as they returned. He knew the reason and he felt somewhat responsible. If he had not made his discontentment known to Verron, he may not have felt so inclined to disobey an order and taken another chosen to fill in for Tanner.

"Verron knew what he was doing," Zera tried to tell him. They were all sitting down in the mess hall to eat. "It'll work itself out."

"I'm sure he's fine," Warrick added.

"I heard that he had taken leave," Lucas said. "I haven't seen him in two days."

"Yes, that's right," said Warrick. "He went to see his ailing mother, apparently."

Zera looked surprised. "Verron has never taken leave in all the years that we have been here. I didn't even know he *had* a mother!"

"I'm just reporting what I heard a couple of officers say," said Warrick, taking a mouthful of food.

"You hear anything else?" asked Lucas, who had the feeling Warrick was holding something back.

Warrick shrugged. "Just that the king has reinstated his command."

The three of them gasped.

Zera was first to speak. "How can you continue stuffing your face like that, as if you haven't just told us something of utmost importance?"

"And why are you only telling us this now?" asked Davis.

"I was hungry. I'm telling you now, aren't I?"

"Well," said Davis, "I'm glad your belly means more to you than sharing important news with your friends." He pushed Warrick's plate to the side. "He'll be back then?"

"Yes, in a few weeks," said Warrick with a cheeky grin, and just barely avoided a playful slap from Zera.

When the next tax collection was scheduled to go out, the chosen ones lined up to hear the names called for those who would participate in protecting the caravan. Lucas looked eagerly towards the gates, in case Verron had come back for it.

When he didn't, and they were told another officer would take command, Lucas held no hope his name would be among those to be called. He barely paid attention to the officer's voice and the names he called out. He watched Davis step out of the line when his name was called and expected Zera to go next. It therefore did not register with

Lucas nodded. "Yes. Verron thought it was because of the sight of the killings."

"But it's not?"

"No," answered Lucas, climbing back on his horse. "I get a surge of energy flow through my body when something is wrong." He settled back in the saddle and gripped the reins. Father Ansan had told him he was to accept the gifts given to him by the stone and he wondered if foreseeing danger was an ability he had not been aware of and had yet to accept. But why did he have all these abilities? What made him so different from anyone else? Aware Zera was still staring at him, he continued. "I must get quicker in responding to it and trust what I feel. I'm fine now."

"You are special," said Zera as they rode towards the road. "Whatever it is that's warning you of danger, it is telling the rest of us to follow you! We are all feeling the connection with you getting stronger and clearer. Especially my brother."

Lucas looked sideways over his shoulder to Zera. "He told you this?" he asked. Davis was the last chosen he expected to follow him without question. Since the last incident with Eli, Davis had kept an even more watchful eye for him, but he now realized that had been to protect him.

"He doesn't have to," answered Zera, turning to him with a smile. "We're twins, remember? We just know these things."

Egon walked down the steps of the castle into the bailey and was surprised when he saw prisoners being marched towards the dungeon. Several wounded soldiers were being led into the infirmary.

"What happened?" he asked Verron, who was dismounting.

"We fell into a trap. It could have been really bad, but . . ." He nodded towards Lucas, who was walking his horse into the stables.

Verron handed his horse off to Tanner and began to explain. "We were ambushed when passing through a forested area, but Lucas sensed danger and was able to get behind the assailants and attack before we were overwhelmed by their numbers. A few managed to reach us on the road, but it was nothing we couldn't handle, at that point. I keep telling myself it is the training he received at the monastery that makes him more advanced than the others, but I feel I have been lying to myself for far too long. He is not a chosen, and I don't think he is an elite born either. It's something else, something bigger."

"What are you implying?"

Officer Verron shook his head. "There's no way Lucas could have seen that log from where he was, let alone the two men that were holding the release rope. They never even got a chance to cry out—he was that fast," answered Verron. "And Zera, Davis and Warrick? They have started to follow him, as if he is leading them. Chosen ones don't have leaders. We all know that."

Egon placed his hand on Verron's back and led him towards a recessed wall away from where anyone might be passing by. "I suggest you play this event down. It was Zera who saw movement on the hills and Lucas saw nothing until he got to the front, at which point, you had noticed the log as well and were already stopping."

"May I ask why?" asked Verron.

Egon took a deep breath. "It makes no difference whether he is chosen or elite. Unless you prefer to have him removed from under your leadership?"

"No, sir," answered Officer Verron.

"I didn't think you would . . . so change the story."

"I can do that," Verron called after Egon, who was starting to walk away. "But the rest of my men will have their own opinions and versions of the story to tell. Especially since they have not called him a chosen one for some time now."

"What do they call him?" asked Egon quietly. He had paused but kept his back to Verron.

"They call him 'the King's Chosen.'"

Egon smiled and continued to walk away.

CHAPTER 12

Different versions of what happened in the woods emerged in the days following, and in the end, it was put down as a lucky escape. Egon had made sure that the prisoners were dealt with before they could get their story out and so the saving of the treasury was recognized as a lucky coincidence.

Eli had shown a renewed interest in Lucas after the attack on the treasury, even though he was not mentioned as the one foreseeing it. Lucas's new nickname added fuel to the fire already burning inside Eli. Lucas did his best to avoid him and to ignore the taunting when he was close. They were still not allowed to fight each other in practice, but it came to no surprise to Lucas that Eli took his chance one afternoon and sought him out. As soon as the signal was given for the elite borns to pick an opponent, Eli appeared in front of Lucas.

"Finally," he said. "I hope you remember what the rules are?"

"I'm not allowed to fight you, nor do I want to," said Lucas and looked for the officers to intervene, but they were conversing with each other and not paying attention.

"They clearly don't mind anymore," said Eli who had followed his gaze towards the officers. "So, now I have picked you and you can't refuse."

"I am *not* fighting you," said Lucas, more resolutely this time.

Not all the elite borns were finished choosing an opponent yet and some of the chosen ones were still free. They became aware of Eli and Lucas's standoff, and by the look in their eyes, Lucas could tell all of them wanted to prevent it from escalating.

Warrick stood right next to Lucas and suddenly dropped to the ground to tie his boots, forcing Lucas to take a step back. Archer then closed the gap, so Lucas had to move two spaces over. Eli grunted when he was faced with Warrick in front of him instead and pushed two other elite borns out of his way to catch up with Lucas.

It was clear to him that Eli would do anything to make him fight him. Without a word, he turned his back to Eli and walked away.

"I want to fight you!" snarled Eli and walked across the line to go after him, but several chosen ones stepped in, and blocked his way. In response, elite borns grouped behind Eli and the two groups faced each other.

Finally becoming aware of the issue, the officers shouted at the boys, urging them to get back in line. When the boys did not respond, guards were called in to split the two groups up. The elite borns were sent back to their own training grounds and the chosens found themselves pushed up against the wall and lined up in the baking sun.

"I'm sorry," said Lucas quietly to Davis, who stood next to him.

Davis subtly shook his head. He was careful not to attract attention from the officers watching them. "Don't be," he answered. "I think Eli might have tried to kill you if you had fought him, and we both know that would not have ended well for either of you."

They were made to stand for the rest of the afternoon without being allowed to move a muscle, until the sun went down. Before they were finally released to do their chores, Egon walked into the training grounds and spoke with Verron. They were too far from the group for Lucas to hear what they were saying, but it didn't look good. All the chosen were dismissed, except for Lucas, who found himself taken away to the dungeon.

"This is probably for the best," said Verron, as they waited for a guard to unlock one of the cell doors. "I have been told that General Finton wants to see you flogged for turning your back to a superior. And for inciting a riot against the elite borns."

"I was trying to avoid having to fight Eli," said Lucas, "and the others were only blocking him from going after me, but I wish you would let me fight him, now."

Verron gave Lucas a little nudge to move when the door opened. "That is exactly why Egon thinks it best that you are locked up for some time. By keeping you out of sight, he hopes it will give Finton some time to settle down . . . that he will forget about flogging you."

Lucas looked around when he stepped inside the cell and waited for the door to close behind him. When he heard Verron leave, he sat down on a pile of straw in one of the corners. He was surrounded by darkness, and the musty smell reminded him of the prison he had once been locked up in. The memory sent shivers down his spine, and he quickly shook it off. At least he did not have to hear the screams of other prisoners and there was no odor of feces in the air. He took a deep breath and decided that spending time in the dungeon was a good alternative to being flogged.

Five days later, Officer Verron came for him, unlocking the cell door to let him out. "Don't assume you got off lightly with this," he said, holding the door open. "General Finton rode out this morning with the king, which will give you a few days, but he still wants your flogging to be carried out, as soon as he gets back."

"I only tried to avoid fighting Eli," said Lucas sullenly.

"I am aware of that, but that is not why you are being punished. They feel you set the other boys up to be defiant. They want to make sure you will not attempt this again."

"They were only doing what they felt was right. I did not tell them to back me up."

"You didn't have to," said Verron. "The other chosen ones are rallying behind you and have done so for a while. I have seen it—others have seen it—and you must be aware of this as well. They are likely to defend you at any cost. So, every time you decide to stand up against a superior, for whatever reason you may have, there is a chance they will too. And that—we cannot allow to happen. The success of this army depends on everyone adhering to their rank. Do you understand?"

"Yes, sir," answered Lucas as he followed Verron outside.

Lucas went through his chores and practices, and tried to put the upcoming punishment that would follow with the king's return out of his mind. When that day came, he was getting sympathetic looks from the other boys and, when the horn sounded, some of them slapped him on the back for support as they ran past to meet the king by the gate. Lucas took his time and was the last one to take his place by the gatehouse, where the portcullis was already hauled up and the drawbridge lowered. He sighed and tried to relax. He looked along the line of boys. They were all standing still, facing forward. Their swords hung by their sides, and they held their arms behind their backs.

He looked down at his own sword and briefly touched the hilt, before looking up to the top of the gatehouse. A magpie sat perched on the wall, looking down at him. Their eyes met and suddenly Lucas understood. Every time he had ever seen a magpie, something bad was about to happen. The first time he remembered seeing one was on the night his father was killed. If a magpie had not flown into him and had stopped him from bursting through the door, he too could have been killed that night. The second time was at the inn. There had been a magpie on top of the woodshed only minutes before he was attacked inside. The third time—he had seen Davis trying to chase one off the treasury wagon. If a single magpie was the omen for death, then why was it here now? Flogging meant pain, not death, and there was nothing he could do to stop it.

The bird hopped from one end to the other and started to chatter, just as the ground started to tremble from the approaching horses. Lucas was straightening himself up to be in line with the other boys when, over the din of the horses, he heard an alarming sound behind him. He turned his head to look at the mechanism that was holding the portcullis up. The faintest movement could be seen in the lever that was holding the gears in place, and he knew full well that it shouldn't be doing that. To his horror, he realized the lever wasn't locked in!

Lucas saw the first horses coming across the outer bailey. They would be riding over the bridge and underneath the gate in a matter of seconds now. The movement of the lever, as it wanted to slip off the gear, sounded as loud to him as the ringing of a bell next to his ear. No one else seemed to notice what was happening and were oblivious of the danger.

Without waiting another second, Lucas spun around, pulled his sword and ran. The first horses were coming across the bridge and the trembling moved the lever further off the gears. With a thundering sound, the portcullis dropped a foot, when the lever slipped past the first tooth of the gear. Realizing what was happening, panic set in, causing horses to suddenly stop. Lucas slid across the ground, just as the king's horse was underneath and lunged his sword in between the two gears. The gears twisted and grinded in response, but he had stopped the portcullis from coming down further. Lucas was holding on to the sword, as best as he could, to keep it in place until help arrived, but it was getting harder and harder. He looked behind him and saw that the king was pulled clear, but General Finton's horse had panicked and was rearing up just underneath, blocking other horses from coming through.

For a split second, Lucas knew he could make one person who made his life here harder simply go away, if he just let go of his sword. The general was struggling to get his horse under control and looked desperately around him to see what was happening. Their eyes met, and Finton knew at that moment that his life was in Lucas's hands. Lucas diverted his gaze back to the mechanism in front of him and stared at his hands on the hilt of his sword. He took a deep breath, before stepping closer to push the sword deeper between the gears with the weight of his body. With guards rushing over to help, he tried to hold on, but they stopped and backed up when they realized his sword was about to snap under the strain. Sweat was pouring from his face and the pain in his arms became almost unbearable, but he held on until Finton and the horses that had been held up behind him were all clear from the gates. Then the sword snapped, and Lucas was thrown backwards by the force. The portcullis came crashing down, a big cloud of dust rising when it hit the ground.

Lucas rolled over to his side and put his head down on his arm to let the feeling of sickness pass through him. He then stood up and brushed the dust off his trousers. The bailey had filled with chaos, as all the boys struggled to calm the panicking horses. He knew he could help with that but felt he had done enough and let it be.

"Are you hurt?" he heard someone say.

"No, sir! I'm fine," he answered, somewhat surprised to see Egon come to his side. Egon had not spoken a word to him for months and Lucas did not think he gave a hoot about his well-being.

"You could have let go," Egon said, his voice low. "It would have been seen as an accident."

"Yes, I could have," Lucas answered.

"But you didn't."

"No."

"Why not?"

"Because *I* would have known it was not an accident."

Egon stood quiet for a moment and nodded understandingly. He then patted Lucas gently on his back, before rushing over to the king, who was trying to make his way through the chaos.

Officer Verron told Lucas to take the rest of the afternoon off, as he was clearly distracted and making mistakes. Lucas could not keep his mind off the impending punishment he was supposed to receive now that Finton was back, even though Verron told him that was not likely to happen now. Sitting down off to the side to watch the training, Lucas saw Verron being called away by Egon and caught his troubled look as he was leaving.

"Don't worry," said Zera, coming over to him. "I'm sure Verron will put a good word in for you."

"I don't know if his word will be of any use against Finton's," remarked Davis, who had walked over as well. "But there's no point worrying about it. Come on—let's take your mind off it. See if you can beat me."

Lucas nodded eagerly, and Davis extended a hand to pull him off the ground.

It wasn't until evening when Verron finally returned and told Lucas that Finton, although reluctantly, had agreed that flogging him, after Lucas had just saved his life, would not be the most reasonable thing to do. The king had agreed, however, that Lucas was responsible for influencing the chosen ones to step out of line and so, for the time being, he would not be allowed to train with the elite borns. He was to leave the training grounds as soon as they came in and be put to work instead.

At first, Lucas saw this new development as a punishment, which was not helped by Eli's remarks or looks every time he passed him on his way out.

"Go on, errand boy—out you go!" Eli would say, and his two closest companions, Milton and Baldric, would sneer and add their own comments.

Lucas tried to ignore it, but the insults hit him like rocks and he felt a hot rage inside him that he was not proud of.

Carleton, surprisingly, stepped away from the elites one afternoon to stop him at the gates when he was making his daily departure.

"Don't let it get to you," he said, putting a hand on Lucas's shoulder. "It's only temporary and probably best Eli can't get to you right now. His father wasn't too happy you went unpunished for going against us."

"I never intended to go against you," said Lucas. "Couldn't you see that?"

Carleton looked him in the eye. "Well," he said. "Maybe not intentionally, but it *did* happen."

Mulling over Carleton's words, Lucas acknowledged his role in what happened and even though he felt it wasn't entirely his fault, it was best for himself and his friends that he was not there. He began looking forward to the extra chores he had to do. It gave him a chance to be in places where he normally would not be allowed to go, and he got to see castle life from a different angle. At first, he had little interaction with the castle staff and was treated with indifference or apprehension. The staff didn't talk to him, and he had been instructed not to talk to them, but cold stares and blank looks turned into occasional nods and smiles over time, as he showed himself to be helpful and eager to please.

It became Lucas's job to unload the wagon of goods into the storage room in the afternoons. The person who usually completed this task had become ill. Lucas had to walk down several steps into the dark room, which only had a few tiny windows just above ground level, for light. On the opposite side of the room were three steps leading to a platform and more stairs around the corner leading into the main castle. He felt tempted to go up them every time he was setting the crates and barrels down in the storage room, and had to resist the urge.

On one such occasion, when he was lifting a crate up to place on top of another, Lucas heard a little bumping noise coming from the stairs behind him. He glanced over his shoulder and saw a small ball bouncing down the steps and, as it reached the floor, it rolled towards him. He stopped it with his foot and bent down to pick it up. It fit in the palm of his hand and was made of pieces of neatly stitched leather. He could tell that it was finely crafted and surmised that it was not a toy that would belong to just any child. He rolled it around in his hand and played with it for a moment, before looking up to see why it had rolled down. He immediately kneeled and bowed his head when he saw the princess standing on the bottom steps. She looked at him and smiled warmly.

This was the closest he had ever been to her. Apart from her birthday celebration, he had only seen her a couple of times, and from a distance—he could not help but notice she had grown taller and lankier, and that she had a radiant face. He guessed that she must be around the age of ten. She was wearing a forest-green velvet dress with a white ribbon tied around her waist, and the hem of the gown trailed along the ground. Her curly brown hair was partly tied back into a braid. She stared at him with a cheeky smile and her lively blue eyes showed her excitement when she saw he was holding her ball out to her.

"I know you," she said happily. "I watched you fight once."

Lucas didn't answer. He didn't know what to do. If he wasn't allowed to interact with the staff, he most certainly wasn't allowed to interact with the princess.

"I'm Amalia," she said, jumping off the steps and darting across to him.

Lucas nodded, but avoided eye contact and extended his hand to return the ball. She took it, but to his surprise, she didn't run off and instead remained standing in front of him.

"You can get up now," she said nicely. When he remained on his knees, she continued. "It's all right. I have told you to get up. What is your name?"

"My name is Lucas, my lady," he answered as he rose.

Amalia's eyes lit up. "Then you are the one they talk about so often!" she said. "And you saved my father." The princess held the ball up to him. "Will you play with me?"

"I . . ." stammered Lucas. "I don't think I'm allowed, my lady. I don't think I'm even supposed to be here with you."

Amalia looked past him to the door and then shrugged her shoulders. "There's no one else here. They won't know and I won't tell. Please?"

"Only a few minutes then," he said, and took the ball back from her.

Amalia skipped to the other side of the room and happily held her hands out for him to throw it to her.

They played catch for a little while and then Lucas told her it was best if he continued to unload the wagon. Amalia agreed but waited and, in between each load, she passed the ball back to him. It became a little game between them for him to catch it quickly, before it dropped to the ground. Amalia was visibly disappointed when she heard her name being called and had to run back to the stairs. "Goodbye, then, Lucas," she said, and waved before turning the corner and disappearing.

"Goodbye, my lady," answered Lucas and waved back at her.

He assumed that would be the last he saw of her, but she showed up a few days later and then again and again. Each time, she brought her little ball, and they would play just long enough so as not to arouse anyone's suspicion. Lucas certainly did not tell any of the other chosen boys about his encounters with Amalia. Sometimes she simply followed him around the room and they talked while he sorted crates out. Other times, she insisted on helping, even though he reminded her she was a princess and probably not supposed to.

"My father likes you," Amalia said one day.

Lucas lifted a crate up from the floor and stacked it high. He didn't answer, but he was listening. The news was a revelation to him, since the king barely gave him the time of day and had not even thanked him for saving his life.

"So does Officer Verron," she continued. "But not General Finton. He doesn't talk nicely about you."

"I'm not surprised at all to hear that Finton doesn't care for me, but what makes you say your father likes me?" he asked, without interrupting his work. He was more at ease in talking to Amalia nowadays. He still respected her as the princess, even though she had stopped him from calling her "my lady" early on, and she acted more like a little sister. "Does he talk to you about these things?"

"No," she answered. "But I can hear them. My father wants me to learn to read, so sometimes I have to sit in the library, which is next to the Great Hall," she explained. "I get tired of all that reading— especially the histories!—so I go and listen by the door instead, when I hear them raise their voices. My father never used to discuss any issues about chosen ones or elites before. He let his senior staff and Egon handle all that, but now he says he wants to stay informed about you. He tells everyone to bring him any news, no matter how small. It's a bit odd."

Lucas went to get another crate and Amalia waited patiently for his return.

"They were talking about you, you know, before you saved my father at the gatehouse," Amalia continued. "I was afraid for you."

"Hmm, yes," said Lucas. "I got into a bit of trouble."

"With Eli!"

Lucas paused and looked at the little princess. "You seem to know a great deal about what's happening."

"My father says I will make a great queen one day. That is why he wants me to learn to read, so I don't have to rely on an advisor to read things to me and lie to me."

Lucas smiled. "*That* is the reason he gives you for learning to read?"

"Yes," responded Amalia.

"Well, that is one good reason," he said.

"My mother and my lady-in-waiting say that princesses don't have to read, so they don't make me."

"But your father does?" asked Lucas while continuing to stack crates.

"Yes, he insists, but it is so very boring."

"I was made to read when I was younger. I hated it at first as well, but then I discovered some books that had great stories in them. I would stay up late reading them, until my eyes were closing on their own. You just have to find the right book."

Amalia's eyes lit up in amazement. "You can read? I did not think soldiers could read."

"Well, like you, I had someone who felt it was important for me to learn. He taught me to write as well." He lifted the last crate up and smiled at the princess. He enjoyed their conversations, as brief as they were.

Amalia took the ball out of her dress pocket. "Can you write my name on my ball if I bring you ink?" she asked.

"I can do better than that, and carve the letters into the leather so it will not rub off," he answered, "but I will need something sharp to do that."

Amalia thought for a moment and then pulled a pin out of her hair. "Will this do?"

Lucas nodded and took the ball and pin from her. They sat on the bottom steps while he slowly started to carve the first letter of her name. He paid close attention to the curves and made beautiful lines. It took him longer than he thought, because he wanted it to be perfect, and working the leather was hard. When he finished the *A* and the *M,* he handed the ball back to her. It was getting late, and they both needed to go before someone missed them.

Amalia looked at the letters on her ball and beamed with happiness.

"Will you finish it tomorrow?" she asked with pleading eyes.

"I can try," he said. He didn't think anyone knew he could write, so unless she told anyone, they would not suspect him and find out about their meetings. He had grown fond of the princess and loved to see her happy. In a small way, she reminded him of Ana, Nadia's daughter, of what Ana might have been like, if he had had the opportunity to watch her grow up.

They both stood and said their goodbyes before going their separate ways.

Lucas walked back to the training grounds, as practice with the elites would have finished and he could still get some practice in by himself before evening chores. He stopped by the water barrel inside the gate and drank water from the ladle, before glancing over at the group of chosens in the far corner. He immediately noticed that none of them were practicing. Instead, they stood gathered in a circle, with some boys lying on the ground and others being held up to stay upright. He dropped the ladle back in the barrel and quickly walked over. Zera turned when she saw him coming and looked extremely worried.

"What's going on?" asked Lucas as he got nearer.

"We don't know," answered Zera. "They suddenly became sick."

The group of boys parted to let him through, and Lucas saw two of the youngest lying on the ground. They were clutching their stomachs and wriggling in pain. Both of them had thrown up.

"Did someone go and get Verron?" Lucas asked.

"Archer went," answered Davis, who didn't look very well himself.

Lucas looked at the other boys who were being supported. Gradually, they gave up and sat down on the ground. "What's wrong with you?"

"Not feeling good," said Peyton. "My stomach hurts and I have a funny tingling in my legs."

"Anyone else?" asked Lucas.

"I don't think any of us are feeling good right now," answered Zera, sitting down next to him.

Just then Officer Verron arrived. He surveyed the situation and quickly ordered everyone still standing to help bring the sick boys inside and to have pails placed by each bed, when more boys suddenly started to vomit.

Once inside, Lucas helped Zera to lie down on her bed, her face pale and clammy.

"What is going on?" asked Zera. "I have never felt so sick in my life."

"I don't know," answered Lucas. He grabbed a pail and slid it across the floor, as she was about to throw up. "Feeling better?" asked Lucas, when she was finished.

Zera nodded and put her head back down on the pillow. "A little bit. Just really tired now," she said, closing her eyes. "Strange thing is the feeling in my legs."

"What kind of feeling?"

"No feeling at all," Zera answered softly, before drifting off to sleep.

Lucas made his way over to Davis's bed near the door, where Warrick was helping him. Like Zera, Davis had vomited also and now lay asleep.

Warrick and Tanner were the only ones still standing and set about scrubbing the floor of the vomit that had not made it in the pails, when Egon entered the room, followed by the officers. He set about to check a few of the boys and listened to the symptoms that were described to him.

"Seeing that nearly all of them have succumbed to the same illness in a short amount of time," Egon told Verron, "I suspect it may have been something they ate."

"Food poisoning?" said Verron, frowning. "Shouldn't other staff be sick then? They all eat the same food."

Egon raised his shoulders. "I am only informing you of my suspicions. Give them plenty of rest and they should be up on their feet again in a day or so."

With everyone else out, Lucas set about doing the evening chores with only Warrick and Tanner by his side, until halfway through feeding the horses, they too became ill.

"Egon must be right," said Tanner. "It must have been something we all ate, but I don't understand how you are not sick then."

"I don't know?" answered Lucas. "Maybe just lucky?"

"Or a stronger stomach," said Warrick, as he doubled over with cramps.

"Go on," said Lucas when he saw them in pain and clutching their stomachs. "You go and I will finish." Their faces were ghostly pale and drawn, and he did not want to keep them from their beds a moment longer.

"Are you sure?" asked Warrick, even though he was already halfway out the door, and Tanner was already on the other side. Lucas watched them close the doors behind them and continued feeding the horses where they had left off.

It was late when he finally raked the aisles between the stalls, and he was almost finished when he felt danger nearby. He paused what he was doing and, focusing, allowed his mind to venture outside. He was expecting to see Eli coming, since word would have probably gone around the castle by now that most of the chosens had fallen ill, but outside, all was quiet. With the bailey empty, the only people he could see were the few guards up on the gatehouse, and they showed no signs of anything being amiss.

Lucas placed the rake against the wall and decided to see for himself what it was that he had sensed. The feeling had not left him—if anything, it had only grown more intense. He was about to put his hand on the door to push it open, when he was overcome with a cramp in his stomach, and despite his desire to stay aware and focused, he doubled over in pain. An exploding headache pushed everything out of his mind, and, like Peyton, he felt a tingling in his body that made him unsteady on his legs.

Knowing he was now sick as well, and with his feelings of vulnerability heightened, he quickly left the stables. He did not make it far before he retched in a gully next to the stables. Sweat started dripping down his face and he felt himself becoming weaker with every passing second. He looked around for help, but when there was none, he staggered along the wall to the barracks and up the stairs to the dorm room. Like Zera, he just wanted to sleep and saw that all the chosen were doing just that when he made his way past them, to his own bed.

He felt too weak to undress or even remove his boots, and was barely able to crawl on top of his bed. His stomach had settled after the vomiting, but his head still felt heavy and the rafters above him soon started to spin. The room was dark, and he barely noticed the door to the dorm room opening, and the four figures that entered. He could hear their cautious footsteps on the floorboards and watched as they carefully examined each boy. He assumed it must be Egon, or another physician with nurses, who he imagined would be coming to check on them, but wondered why they were dressed in black, with hoods casting shadow over their faces.

Thinking his mind must be playing tricks on him, Lucas turned his head away, until a dark figure showed up at the foot of his bed and three more gathered around. Before he realized what was happening, one of them lunged forward and gagged him. It was the largest man who put a rag in his mouth to stop him from calling out, while two others held him down. The fourth then put a sack over his head, blocking out the little vision he had left. Helplessness overwhelmed him—he could not fight them. His body felt paralyzed, but he was aware that his hands and feet were being tied, and that he was lifted from his bed.

The floorboards creaked with the weight they were carrying, and Lucas could hear Davis's voice. "What is going on?" Davis asked, but his voice was weak. He heard what sounded like someone falling out of bed, and then the closing of the door and the dropping of the heavy latch that would barricade the chosen ones in the room.

Lucas vaguely heard the banging that followed from multiple fists, but he was swiftly carried outside, and the sound disappeared. His mind was too foggy to focus, and he had no idea who had taken him from his bed or where they could be going with him. He was carried only a short distance and then put down onto the ground. A rope was wrapped around his waist and he heard an iron hatch being opened. He was lifted again, and the rope tightened around him. The hands that had held him disappeared and he knew he was being lowered down, like a puppet on a string.

He went down a long way, before shouts could be heard and a horn blasted an alarm. For a moment, Lucas felt himself hanging, suspended in midair, before being lowered faster and then—there no longer was any tightness from the rope around his midsection. Air rushed past him as he fell into nothingness. His head hit something on the way down and it pulled the bag off his face. He tumbled lower still, and then hit the ground hard, with the sound of bones snapping in different parts of his body. He heard his own screams inside his head, but not one of them could be heard in the outside world.

He saw the grid pattern of the hatch that had been closed above him and knew exactly where he was.

Not in a million years could he ever have imagined lying at the bottom of the old well. It used to be connected to an underground river, but when the water level dropped, a new well was dug and this one was sealed up with an iron hatch. He had walked past the alcove in the wall where it was located many times in the last few weeks on his way to the storage room.

He groaned when he lifted his head to look at what he already knew. His legs were badly broken. Blood trickled into a pool underneath his thigh where his trousers were ripped, and more warm liquid ran past the side of his face. The slightest movement caused him immense pain, and he could only imagine what his legs would feel like if they hadn't been numbed by whatever poison had been slipped to him. He wondered who could be behind it all and what had he done to deserve this. The people who took him had something familiar about them, but it had not been enough to recognize them.

Lucas put his head back and lay still. The noise in the castle intensified and he could see faint shadows of light being cast on the walls above. He knew they were looking for him and hoped he would be found soon.

He blacked out for a little while and, when he came around again, his mind was clear enough to focus on what was happening aboveground by using his seeing mind. He saw the king's guard shouting orders at different groups of guards and soldiers frantically searching the grounds and buildings, blazing torches in their hands. He saw that his friends, who no longer appeared to be sick, were being corralled into the training grounds, and that officers were shutting the gate to lock them in. They looked enraged and had to be pushed back by soldiers. Several elites, including Carleton, had joined search parties, but he did not see Eli or any of his friends. Torches were lit up all over the castle, shining light on every inch of it. Except for the old well—which had long been forgotten.

The king stood motionless on the wall, with Finton, and observed the frantic search that was going on around them.

Lucas realized that if they couldn't find him, this was the place where he was going to die, unless he could get himself out. He heard water dripping in a small cave to his right and he could smell the dampness that filled the air. If only he could untie his hands and drag himself to the underground river, then he might be able to float himself out. He tried to move, but a pain shooting through his entire body told him his injuries were greater than he had hoped, and he didn't try to move again. He closed his eyes and, when he opened them again, he could see it was light outside. There were no more shouts, no more feet running aboveground. All was quiet, but Lucas was in too much pain to care. He wanted it to be over and knew it would be soon. He was losing blood and felt extremely cold.

He allowed himself to drift to the field with the stone, with its soft, long grass, and he started walking down the hill towards the warriors. He no longer felt any pain and—eager to get to them—he increased the length of his stride. He ran then, but instead of getting closer, they continued to be the same distance away. Lucas stopped and looked at the warriors, who stood with their arms folded across their chests and their swords by their sides. The warrior who had once held his sword out to him stepped forward and slowly shook his head.

A sound coming from above made Lucas lift his head slightly and open his eyes to see the hatch being opened. Calls of his name echoed off the walls and he could see several faces looking down at him. He recognized Egon, who asked if he could move, but all he could do was close his eyes again. They had found him, but he feared it was too late. He was vaguely aware that Egon was being lowered down the well, and when he reached the bottom, he kneeled beside him in the dim light. He took the gag out of his mouth, touched his forehead and felt his chest.

"How is he?" shouted someone down from above.

"Not good," answered Egon, "but he is still alive."

"Can he be lifted up?"

"I will need a second person down here and a ladder to strap him down on. He is losing blood and I don't think he has much longer."

There was the sudden scuffling of feet, as people began running off to obey the order and Lucas heard Egon take off his belt. "Hang in there, boy," Egon said as he lifted Lucas's thigh up. "We'll try and get you out of here."

Lucas writhed in pain when the belt was tightened just above the cut in his thigh to stem the bleeding, and he felt Egon's hands on his shoulders, in an attempt to calm him. "I have to do this," he said. "I'm sorry."

A ladder was lowered down, followed by Verron, who could not help but throw out a few inappropriate words when he reached the bottom.

"Whoever is responsible is going to pay," he said. "I don't care who it is."

"And I am sure they will," answered Egon, positioning the ladder next to Lucas. "But for now, we need to get him out of here as fast as possible, if we are not already too late."

With haste, but great care, they pushed the ladder under Lucas and strapped him down on it. They paused when he let out a soft groan, but then continued and worked faster. Ropes were attached to either end of the ladder and then a sign was given to the people above to start hauling him up. Verron stayed down, while Egon was hauled up at the same time to keep the ladder from hitting the walls. When they reached the surface, Lucas was unstrapped and heaved onto a proper stretcher. He gave no sign of life until they untied his hands and feet and he cried out in pain. For a second, he found the strength to open his eyes to see the magpie perched on the edge of the wall above him. It flapped its wings and flew away as soon as his stretcher was lifted, and they rushed him away.

CHAPTER 13

The sound of whispering voices pulled Lucas from the darkness he was in. He tried to open his eyes, but the light was too much for the pain in his head. His moaning alerted someone who came to his side and tried to give him some water, but he could barely swallow.

"Lucas," he heard an unfamiliar voice say. "Can you hear me? It is important for you to tell us who did this. Did you see your attackers?"

He tried to listen to the voice and recognize it, but he could not, and he didn't understand the question he was asked. The last thing he remembered was getting sick and lying down on his bed. After that, his memory was vague and the bits that he did remember seemed like a nightmare that he desperately wanted to forget. He let himself drop back into the darkness, like a turtle hiding in his shell.

An indeterminate amount of time later—it may have been minutes, or days—hands were placed on his shoulders to hold him down and a stick was placed between his teeth. He tried to resist. He heard someone hush him as he let out an ear-piercing scream. They were trying to set his legs. A tear dropped down his cheek and he squirmed to get away, causing himself more pain. More hands grabbed hold of his body to keep him still, and they pulled on his legs again. He heard

Verron's voice this time, trying to calm him down, but the pain was unbearable. When it was finally over, he felt the stick being removed from his mouth and they let go of him.

"This is the best I can do," he heard Garrad say. "I am afraid that, even if he does pull through, he will never walk again."

There was silence in the room when Lucas opened his eyes to look up at Verron. "Kill me," he whispered. "You have to kill me."

And then everything was black again.

Egon stood by the window, looking outside. Life below him continued, as if nothing terrible had happened. He had just heard Lucas plead with Officer Verron to end his life. It struck him hard. More than once in his employment he had to do just that—end someone's life to stop their suffering. And though he had done so without as much as blinking an eye, this was different.

Verron joined him by the window, and he could hear his deep sigh.

"You know I am going to have to do what he asked," Verron said reluctantly. "I owe it to him. We all owe it to him. We need to let him die as a soldier, rather than allowing him to suffer the hardship that comes with not being able to walk for the rest of his life."

Egon nodded. He agreed, but he couldn't help but feeling that there was a reason they had been able to find him in time and he had not died at the bottom of the old well. Surely the gods did not intend to have him suffer like this, only to have him killed in the end. He turned to Garrad, who was still in the room, tending to Lucas's wounds and adjusting the splint. "Are you sure you have done all that you can do?" he asked.

Garrad hung his head and stared down at Lucas's legs. "I'm afraid so. His legs are badly broken, especially his left one, and I suspect he has more injuries in his upper body that I cannot detect or do anything about."

"What about those books you read?" asked Egon, not willing to give up so easily. "Is there nothing in them that can help?"

"Yes, the books. I have already gone through all of them. That is how I came up with these splints for his legs."

"So, he has no hope of a full recovery?" interrupted Officer Verron.

"No," said Garrad. "Unless . . ." He then shook his head.

"What were you trying to say?" asked Egon, agitated when he didn't continue.

"Come on, Garrad," urged Verron. "If there is anything at all . . ."

"It's a long shot," said Garrad reluctantly. "But the people most advanced in understanding and healing the human body are monks."

"Then we will take him to them," said Egon resolutely. "I will go and start the preparations immediately."

"There are several monasteries, and even if you find the right one, you may go there for nothing," Garrad responded before Egon had made it out the door. "There is only a slim chance they will be able or even willing to help, and the boy may not survive the journey."

"It is worth a try," answered Egon. "And it is all we've got."

Lucas was aware of the people who were coming into the room to try and take care of him and to make him as comfortable as possible. He mostly slept and only woke when they tried to give him water, which he took in small sips. He did not speak and barely opened his eyes, but when he did, he just stared at the ceiling. His mind was mostly blank.

"How long has he been like this?" he heard the king ask from the doorway, before making his way over to his side.

"You mean staring up like that?" asked Verron. "Two days."

The king lifted the fur blanket and the worrisome look on his face, as he stared down at Lucas's splinted legs, told him enough. He wanted to die right there and then. He did not want to live if he could never walk again. The king would no longer have any use for him and if he allowed him to stay, it would only be out of pity. He would not be able to face the chosens, let alone the officers.

Lucas closed his eyes. He felt the king's fingers brush a lock of hair away that had been covering his face and felt his hand rest on his head. The gesture reminded Lucas of a time when he had been sick with the fever, and his father had to close the forgery so he could sit with him. Every time he had woken, he had felt his father's hand on his forehead and listened to his words of encouragement—that he would be better soon, and that he had to be strong. Words that he could do with hearing now, but by the somber expression he had seen on the king's face, he knew they would not be spoken.

"Why have we not found who is responsible yet?" he heard the king say.

"We searched the entire castle, sire," sighed Verron, "and the king's guard questioned everyone, but we have yet to come up with anything substantial. The chosen ones hold the elite borns responsible, but there is no proof of this. And now that we know that the water in the drink barrel was poisoned, it is even less likely. It was a heinous crime and well planned, but I am afraid that, at this point, only Lucas might be able to tell us who it was."

"He has still not spoken?"

The shuffling of feet indicated Verron had moved closer and was now standing next to the king. Lucas could almost feel their eyes penetrating through him, as they continued their conversation. Thinking he was asleep and could not hear them.

"No, not since he asked me to end his life if he is to never walk again."

"Which we will honor," said the king. "If Egon is not successful."

"Most believe that what happened was either a prank gone horribly wrong or someone disliked him enough to see him killed," continued Verron. "But there may be another reason why someone might want to harm him. There were rumors about him, even before he saved your life."

"I have heard them," interrupted the king, an edge of frustration in his voice. "But you know full well that I don't run my kingdom on rumors and legends. Unlike my brother, I don't wholeheartedly believe in Toroun's prophecy that the gods would send another to decide the true and only king. I will not allow it to cloud my mind. I don't foresee a battle between King Boran and myself to happen anytime soon. There has been no indication Boran has made a move or is even considering laying claim on lands that once belonged to his ancestors." There was a pause when neither of them said anything, and the king turned to leave. "Find me the persons responsible for this," he said from the doorway. "Or get the boy conscious enough to tell us."

Exhausted and confused by the conversation he had overheard, Lucas fell into a deep sleep. When he awoke, he could tell it was morning by the sun shining on his face. People were talking and moving about the room. He was lifted from the bed and strapped down on a stretcher again. The pressure of the straps across his body caused him more pain and he started to sweat profusely. Lucas heard Egon clearing his throat to speak. "He is distressed. See how he struggles to breathe? Everyone, step back for just a moment. Give him space and let him settle down."

Lucas took deep breaths and turned his head to the side to look past the crowd of people that stood whispering and waiting for further instructions. A little body had appeared in the doorway that now wiggled her way through and continued to slip past to get closer to him. For a moment, Lucas saw things clearly. Egon was pulling Amalia away, back towards the door, but suddenly stopped. "Amalia," he said, "why are there tears on your cheek?" When she didn't answer and began to struggle against him, he let her go, and she came to stand just inches from Lucas.

"You still have to finish this," she whispered softly in his ear, and slipped her hand underneath the fur cover. Lucas felt a round object being pressed into the palm of his hand and his fingers closed around it. "Promise me," she whispered again. "That you will get better and finish it?"

Lucas wanted to answer, but a shooting pain tensed up his body and Egon pulled her gently back. He turned the princess around and kneeled in front of her. "What is he to you?" he asked quietly.

"A friend," Amalia said softly. "He plays catch with me."

"What?" asked Egon. "Is this true?"

"He is my friend," Amalia said again, as if Egon had not heard her the first time. "I play with him when he works in the storage room."

Lucas saw more tears rolling down her cheeks, and he watched her pull herself free from Egon to run out of the room.

To absorb the bouncing of the wagon, they had it laden with layers of fur on which they placed the stretcher. Egon checked to make sure he was secure, before giving the king's guard the order to mount and ride out.

They rode slowly and carefully, only stopping to check on Lucas or to rest a few hours during the darkest part of the night. They passed the remnants of an old forge the following afternoon and followed the road upwards to a large, whitewashed stone building with a red roof.

Egon dismounted and knocked on the double wooden doors that marked the entrance. When his knocking was not answered, he started to pace up and down, until finally a little hatch opened and the face of a monk appeared to ask what he was there for.

"I apologize for the intrusion," said Egon politely. He could tell that the monk had noticed the king's insignia on his clothing by the look of surprise on his face. "The king requires a healer specializing in broken bones for one of his soldiers," he continued, "a chosen boy of almost fourteen who had a bad fall. I was told you may have such a healer here."

"You have brought this boy here?" asked the monk, straining his neck to see past Egon.

"We have," he answered and stepped aside so the monk could see the wagon. "The boy's injuries surpass the expertise of even the king's physician, and he fears he may never walk again unless something else can be done." He stopped and noticed the monk's reluctance when he saw the king's guard next to the wagon. "Look," Egon added quickly. "All I ask is for someone to take a look at him and help if they can."

"Very well," said the monk. "I will have a look." He closed the little hatch and Egon could hear the turning of a key. A moment later the monk stepped out and followed him to the wagon where the fur blankets were removed from Lucas's body. He climbed in and checked Lucas over from head to toe, who flinched when different parts of his body were touched. The monk shook his head when he finished doing his examinations and climbed out of the wagon. "I am sorry," he said, "but this boy is in bad shape."

"Are you telling me you cannot heal him?" asked Egon.

The monk looked back at Lucas, who had the fur put back over him and shook his head again. "We are a monastery, not a hospital, and we do not have the resources it would take to heal these kinds of injuries."

"But, you could do it?"

"Possibly," the monk said thoughtfully, "but his injuries would require invasive procedures and weeks of severe pain for the boy, with no guaranteed outcome of success. If you care about this boy, and I assume you do, as you made the trip all the way out here, you should let him go peacefully. We can certainly help with that, if you so wish. I am sure the king has plenty of other boys to replace him with." The monk then started walking back to the monastery, as casually as if he had just declined to purchase a basket of apples.

Egon was dumbfounded. They had come so far, only to be brushed off. "Would you do it for one of your own?" Egon called after him. "I believe he may have lived here as a young boy and was trained by members of your order."

"We do not raise children in monasteries, sir!" answered the monk, without stopping. "Whoever told you that has told you a lie."

Egon ran both hands through his hair and took a deep breath. This couldn't be it. Lucas would most likely not survive the trip back to the castle and coming here had been his only hope, his only chance. He quickly stepped onto the wagon and shook Lucas gently by the shoulders in an attempt to wake him.

"I need the names of the monks who taught you how to fight," he said.

When Lucas groaned in pain, Egon repeated the question and waited for him to answer. When he still didn't, he reached for a flask and rubbed water over his face until Lucas finally opened his eyes and drank some of the water. He asked the question again and leaned closer to hear Lucas croak an answer.

"Father Ansan!" shouted Egon towards the monk, who was about to step back inside. He got off the wagon and took big strides towards the monastery. "He says his teacher's name was Father Ansan!"

The monk stood frozen in the threshold. Without turning around, he asked, "What is the boy's name?"

"His name is Lucas," replied Egon. He watched the monk immediately react to the name by quickly looking over his shoulder towards the wagon. He then told him to wait and hastily disappeared inside. Egon waited with anticipation and paced back and forth until the monk reappeared and, without flourish or emotion, looked Egon square in the face and matter-of-factly instructed him. "You can bring the boy in now. Watch the step here, the one that sticks out more than the others."

As the king's guard followed the monk down the hallway, Egon saw a different kind of monk approach from the opposite direction. His head was shaved, and he was dressed in a red satin robe with gold trim. "Are you Father Ansan?" Egon asked, noticing the look of great concern on the monk's face.

"I am," answered Father Ansan. He had stopped to let them pass and started walking alongside the stretcher Lucas was on. "How did this happen?" he asked.

"He fell down the shaft of an abandoned well," answered Egon.

"Have you caught those responsible?"

"Not yet," answered Egon, surprised by the question. They had reached a room where a healer was waiting with several monks. He followed but stayed by the door to keep out of the way. Father Ansan did the same. Egon watched closely as Lucas was moved from the stretcher onto a table with devices and clamps. "Why would you not assume it to be an accident?" he asked quietly.

Father Ansan gave him a sideways glance. "Only once have I ever seen him come close to losing his balance. The boy is sure-footed. He used to scale the walls and climb to the roof here all the time."

"Hmm," mumbled Egon and sighed. Under normal situations, he would have smiled, but the image of Lucas climbing only reminded him of the dire situation he was in now.

"What will you have to do?" he asked the healer after he had checked Lucas over.

"We will have to straighten his legs and immobilize his entire body," answered the healer. "The bones are already setting, but not in the proper way and his wounds are not healing. It is going to be a long and painful process." He looked to both Egon and Father Ansan. "Are you sure you want him to go through this? He is not going to thank any of us for it."

Egon looked hesitantly towards the table where Lucas had started to resist what they were doing to him. If he still had fight left in him, then Egon did not feel it was up to him to end it. He looked to Father Ansan, who gave him a subtle nod. "Yes," he answered. "It needs to be done."

"Very well," said the healer. "Then we will start right away." He gave a sign to a monk who made Lucas drink a liquid that would keep him from resisting. Within seconds, when his body went limp, Egon noticed Lucas's hand letting go of something he had been holding on to. The object dropped to the floor. Egon bent down as it rolled towards him, and he recognized Amalia's ball. She must have put it in his hand just before they left. Egon was surprised Lucas had been able to hold on to it all this time without anyone noticing. He rolled the ball around in his hand until he felt Father Ansan's hand on his shoulder.

It was time for him to leave, to return to the castle, so they could do their work. Egon walked over to a niche in the wall where he placed the ball next to a burning candle and left the room.

Lucas opened his eyes when he no longer felt the sharp sunlight blinding his eyes. He could smell incense burning, and the echo of footsteps on a stone floor reminded him of a distant place in his memory. He watched a vaulted ceiling pass overhead and thought he was dreaming when he heard a familiar voice close by. But if he was dreaming, why did he still feel pain? He closed his eyes to go back to a place of no pain until he was moved onto a table. He resisted the many hands grabbing hold of him and once again opened his eyes. In the corner of the room, Egon stood next to the man who used to be his teacher. For a moment, Lucas forgot the pain he was in. Father Ansan would make the pain go away. He would help him. He always had.

He heard the words of the healer asking permission to proceed and saw both Egon and Father Ansan give their approval. He then felt a liquid being poured down his throat and his eyes were forced to close. He fought against it. He wanted to see Father Ansan. He wanted to talk to him. For a few seconds, he won the fight and watched Father Ansan turn his back and walk out of the room with Egon. Lucas saw a movement from the corner of his eye and watched Amalia's ball fall out of a niche in the wall and drop to the floor. He watched it slowly roll across the floor and disappear from his sight.

When Lucas awoke several hours later, he found his entire body locked into a device that would allow for no movement. He had clamps attached to several areas of his legs that caused a crushing pain. He stared at the vaulted ceiling above him and remembered where he was. It had not been a dream.

Father Ansan appeared by his side and looked down at him. "I am so sorry," he said with sorrow in his eyes. "I wish we could have met again under better circumstances." He paused and gently took his hand in his own. "Egon told me what happened to you. They want to find who is responsible and urged me to ask you as soon as you woke up."

Lucas stared up at him. He felt so tired. He wanted to embrace his old teacher, but he couldn't move. He felt trapped in a body that was unable to function and he had no idea what had happened to him. All he remembered was getting sick and waking up inside the castle with people pulling on his legs. He knew he was missing a part of his memory, but when he tried to retrieve it, that part of his mind was like a blank slate. When he didn't answer, another monk appeared by his side. It was Father John, the monk who used to care for him when he was a younger boy. The monk who would shave his head, who made sure he looked presentable and carried him off to his bed on nights when he had fallen asleep on his desk while studying.

Father John leaned over and gave him more liquid to drink, which made him sleep again.

For several weeks, he was kept in the body device. They drugged him whenever it was time to tighten the clamps that helped straighten up his legs, or when they worked on other parts of his body. A few times, he saw Father Ansan by his side, but he still couldn't say anything and dealt with the pain alone. Slowly, his body started to heal, and parts of the device were removed until only the leg brace on his left leg remained.

When they eventually stopped drugging him, he felt an unreasonable amount of pain. He could not bring himself to move properly. He spent his days staring up at the ceiling, hitting the bed beneath him with his hands, counting stones or listening to the church bell announcing the time of day. Who cared what time it was? The hours ran together. They tried to have him sit up, but he refused to cooperate. What was the point? He did not want to spend his life not being able to walk the way he was used to. Why had he not died? He missed his life at the castle, the routine, the practices, but most of all, the other chosen ones. He missed his friends terribly and feared he would never be with them again.

He heard familiar voices outside his room and pretended to be asleep when the door opened and Egon walked in with Officer Verron.

"He still has a brace on his leg?" he heard Egon ask. "I thought you said his legs had healed well."

"Yes," Father Ansan answered. "His right leg is healed for the most part, but his left still needs more support."

"But he can move his legs?"

Father Ansan scraped his throat and answered reluctantly. "We think he can."

"What does that mean?" demanded Egon. Lucas had often seen him become impatient when he didn't get an answer he was expecting.

Father Ansan did not seem to be affected by Egon's change of tone. Lucas was not surprised, as he also never seemed to be affected when Lucas refused to cooperate.

"I have seen movement in his right leg," answered Father Ansan calmly. "But he has not moved his left at all. It is hard to tell if he has no feeling in it or if he just refuses. He will not talk to me."

"Why does he not talk to you?" asked Egon. "I thought you were his teacher."

"I was," answered Father Ansan, "but he is not in his right frame of mind, and I am unable to get through to him."

"Can we take him?" asked Verron, whose presence Lucas felt kneeled next to him, "and have him heal further under the care of the king's physician?"

"I do not think that wise under the circumstances," answered Father Ansan. "I am afraid that if you take him now, our work here will have been for nothing. His body may be healing, but his soul is not. He is in a dark place from which he has not returned yet. That is why he cannot remember what happened to him. He will need more time."

"How much longer?" asked Egon. "It has been four months and

since it has become clear he will survive—the king has given orders to bring him back."

"Lucas," said Verron softly. "I need you to keep fighting. I have never known you to surrender. Your fellow comrades are all waiting for your return."

Lucas listened to the words but gave Verron no indication he had heard him. Turning off his emotions had become second nature to him, so Verron's little speech meant nothing to him.

"He is like this most of the time," said Father Ansan, when Lucas gave no response.

Verron stood up and prepared to leave. "We need to give him more time," he said, and left.

"See what you can do, Father," Egon said at the door, "but next time I come, I plan to take him."

Father Ansan waited for Egon and Verron to leave the room, before he spoke quietly. "I have been able to hold them off for now, but you heard what was said. Next time, they will just take you. You can leave the same way you came, in the back of a wagon, or you can choose to ride out on the back of a horse. That is a decision you will have to make yourself."

Lucas had opened his eyes and was staring at the ceiling but said nothing. When the door closed, he turned his head towards the wall.

The next morning, he woke up to see a set of wooden crutches next to his bed. They appeared to be made for his size, and would fit under the armpits. He had seen people use them and knew exactly what they were for. At first, he ignored them, then just stared at them for a long time and then . . . rage, total rage. Everything he had bottled up for weeks came out all at once. Like a dead animal that had finally exploded after it had bloated in the sun, and now spilled its guts out, for all to see. He screamed with all the power in his lungs, grabbed one of the crutches and swung it wildly over the side table next to his bed, sending an earthen plate with untouched food and a mug of water flying. Both shattered into pieces when they hit the ground.

Father John appeared in the doorway and disappeared quickly when he saw Lucas was not finished destroying things. In his rage, he had sat up and his right leg had swung over the side of the bed. His left leg was motionless.

When Father John came back, he wanted to clean up the broken pieces of pottery and food, but Father Ansan, who had followed him in, interfered.

"Let him clean it up," he said firmly. "He made the mess, so he will do the cleaning. And don't give him any more food or water until he has done so."

Father John backed hastily out of the room when he saw Lucas's angry face and Father Ansan followed, closing the door behind him.

Lucas grunted and laid back down. The rage had cost him all the energy that remained inside him, and it had worn him out. He lay breathing hard for a while and then rolled over to his side. He stared at the crutch that had fallen next to his bed and picked it up. He held it out, to try to pull the broken plate towards him, but it was just out of his reach. He leaned further to try and get it but reached too far and he fell forward out of his bed. His chest hit the ground, but his legs were still on the bed, so he rolled over and let his legs slide off. His leg brace made a loud noise when it hit the stone floor and he waited for someone to come, but when no one did, he pulled himself back towards the bed, dragging his legs behind him. He picked up the shards of broken dishes as he moved along the floor.

His muscles were weak from lying in bed all those months and he had to stop to regain his strength several times. When he laid his head down on the cold floor to rest again, he spotted something in the far corner, underneath his bed. Curious, he reached for the crutch and pushed it into the corner. To his surprise, the object rolled towards him, and he grabbed it.

When Father Ansan came to check a few hours later, he found Lucas asleep on the floor. The broken plate and mug pieces were neatly stacked on the side table and both crutches were on the floor by his side. A few monks lifted him up and put him back in bed, and Father Ansan noticed the ball Lucas was holding tight to his chest. He took it out of his hands and placed it on the side table. Then he smiled and blew the candle out for the night.

Lucas woke up when the bells were ringing to announce the morning prayer. He expected to hear the shuffling feet of Father John, who would come to bring his food soon after, but after all remained silent outside his door, he wondered if maybe he had already been, and looked towards his bedside table, but it was empty. No mug, no plate, just the candleholder and Amalia's ball. The crutches were standing against the wall next to his bed and he averted his eyes. He lay waiting for some time before he finally heard the shuffling feet and Father John entered his room. He came empty-handed and walked straight up to the bed to collect the chamber pot. Lucas watched him bend down to pick it up.

"Is there no food this morning?" asked Lucas. It wasn't that he was very hungry, but he could definitely do with a drink.

"In the kitchen," answered Father John, without looking at him.

"Will someone else bring it?"

"No."

"Then . . . how do I get it?" asked Lucas. He wasn't expecting a full conversation since he had brushed away any attempt of a chat himself before now, but he did want to know what his next step should be.

"Father Ansan feels that it is time for you to get up," answered Father John. "You are to get your own food from now on."

"What . . . how?"

It was at that point that he saw Father John motion to the crutches.

"I can't use those."

"Cannot or will not?"

Lucas stared at Father John who was already backing out the door. "Where is Father Ansan?" he asked. "I want to talk to him."

"I am sorry," said Father John before closing the door, "but he is not here. He will be back in a few weeks. Father Ansan has left strict instructions on how to care for you in his absence. The decision to stop bringing food stands firm, though I and the other monks responsible for your care are sympathetic to your pain."

Lucas tried to walk with his crutches, but the first few attempts were pitiful, and he barely made it to the door. His left leg felt like a dead weight and his right leg didn't have enough strength to support him. He had to stop often and, out of sheer frustration, had let himself drop to the floor several times. It took him the entire morning to get out the door and reach the kitchen.

Following Father Ansan's directive, Father John made sure there would be no one around he could ask for help or shout at whenever he ventured out of his room. Left on his own to struggle, Lucas gained more strength over time, and moving around became easier. He avoided the courtyard where the warrior monks trained and instead went to the one that had a garden with paths between flower beds and a neatly manicured lawn in between. At the center of the courtyard stood a cherry tree. As a child, he had rarely made it there. It had been too quiet and uninteresting for him then, but now he welcomed the peace and tranquility of it.

With spring in full bloom and the sun making everything look brighter outside, he sat on a bench by the tree every day after breakfast. He would sleep or watch a little bird build a nest in the cherry blossom tree for hours, or read a book he'd found in the small library until it was dinnertime. He kept to himself.

He saved some of his bread at breakfast and broke little crumbs off for the little bird. She had grown accustomed to him being there and happily picked up the food he dropped for her on the ground. When she had enough and flew back to her nest, he picked up his crutches and hobbled to a small wall fountain at the back of the courtyard. He stared at the water as it cascaded from a spout into a stone basin below and then leaned forward to quench his thirst.

"It is good to see you up and about," he heard a calm voice say behind him.

Lucas lifted his head and closed his eyes, but his gift of seeing had left him some time ago. His mind was blank, and he was feeling empty inside. He slowly turned around.

"You left," he said bitterly, even though his heart leapt with joy that his teacher had returned, and he wanted nothing more than to throw himself into his arms and sob his heart out. He longed to be comforted, to be that little boy he once was, but he couldn't. Instead, he lowered his head and returned to watching the water drop from the spout. "Did you leave because you could no longer bear to watch what I have become?"

"No," said Father Ansan. "I had some business to attend to that I put off when you arrived. I didn't want to leave you. I rushed back when I received the news you were up and about."

"You shouldn't have."

"And why is that?"

"Because I am no longer the boy you once knew," he said.

"What makes you think you are not?"

Lucas gave a hard sigh of frustration. "I am sure you see the brace still on my leg and the crutches I need for walking."

"From what I have been told," answered Father Ansan, "your legs are now completely healed. It is simply a matter of getting your strength back . . . and your desire to live."

"Well, you've been told wrong. I have tried, but it's no use."

"We will see," said Father Ansan.

After a moment of silence, Lucas turned around, only to see Father Ansan already disappearing around the corner of the cloister.

He waited in the garden the following day, but Father Ansan did not appear. When he wasn't there again the day after that, Lucas's heart sank with the thought that his old teacher had heeded his advice and had left the monastery again. Then someone walked up to him and gave him a note. He opened it and saw it was Father Ansan's writing, with instructions to come to the pool. He shook his head and crumpled up the piece of paper. He stayed seated on the bench for a few minutes longer before picking up his crutches and making his way down the hallway to the underground pool.

He took a moment before going down the steps. He recalled Father Ansan taking him to the pool for the very first time—to teach him how to swim. To get over his fear of water and to stop the nightmares that plagued him at night. How he wished he could have the nightmares back, instead of the emptiness when he closed his eyes at night now. He longed to dream again, to feel anything. He took a deep breath and carefully hobbled down the steps. He opened the small wooden door and took in the ambiance of the underground pool as he remembered it. The soft dripping of water from the damp moss-covered walls and the light that came through openings in the vaulted ceiling and sparkled on the water.

Father Ansan stood at the top end of the long pool with his arms folded behind his back.

"You took your time!" he said sternly.

"Yes, well, I don't move very quickly these days," he replied. "Why am I here?"

"I think you already know the answer to that question," said Father Ansan, and he held his hand out towards the pool.

Lucas's mouth dropped open. "I can barely walk!" he said, raising his voice more than he would have liked to. "You can't expect me to go swimming now!"

"Swimming requires different muscles. You can even swim without your legs, but I think you will find that moving your legs through the water will make them stronger."

"I am not going swimming."

"Suit yourself then," said Father Ansan and started walking away again.

"Wait!" said Lucas before he made it out the door. "What is the real reason you brought me here?"

Father Ansan stopped and turned around to face him. "They mended your legs," he said. "Now we need to heal your soul."

"And you can do that?"

"No, only you can do that, but I can help you. If you let me."

"With swimming?"

Father Ansan smiled. "No, you can do that yourself as well. I am just here to make sure you work hard. Your lazy days are over, Lucas, though I won't say you haven't earned them. It is time to get you back in the saddle."

Lucas looked at Father Ansan, and it was as if a light came on in his head. He knew his teacher's words had been meant as a figure of speech, but he suddenly realized how much he had missed riding a horse. If he was to get back in the saddle, he would have to push himself harder. Make his legs work again.

Lucas slowly made his way over to the water's edge. He sat down and took his shirt and leg brace off. Then, without a word, he dropped into the water. It felt refreshing when he let himself sink under and used his arms to go forward. His legs felt heavy, but they were moving a little, with the rhythm of the stroke, and it didn't feel as bad as he had expected. He swam up and down for a while, until he got tired and Father Ansan told him it was enough. "Rest today," he said before leaving the pool. "Because tomorrow we are starting the real work."

True to his word, Father Ansan got him in the pool every morning from then on, and he followed Lucas's swim session up with meditation and physical exercises. He helped Lucas with his stretches, and was careful and gentle when doing so. Slowly, Lucas gained enough strength to put some weight on his left leg.

"I have decided it is time for you to try and walk without the brace," he told Lucas one morning, after they had finished with swimming.

His leg was stiff and didn't feel like his own when he made his first steps towards the wall fountain, but it didn't crumple underneath him as he had expected. When he made it to the fountain and back and put himself down next to Father Ansan on the bench, Lucas smiled. It was the first time he had done so, since the accident. Together, they watched the little bird feed her young, which had hatched only a few days before.

"It is interesting, you know," said Father Ansan. "That little bird returns every year to the same tree, to the very same nest, and every time she returns, she finds the nest destroyed by the wind. She doesn't complain, but just picks up new nest material and rebuilds. Then she lays her eggs and waits patiently for them to hatch. When they do, she works hard to bring them up until they are big enough to fly out themselves. Only to do it all over again next spring. You can learn from her."

"Learn what?" asked Lucas. "I am not a bird."

"No, but you have to rebuild your life, as mother bird has to do every year."

"She rebuilds the same life every time," said Lucas glumly. "I can't put mine back together. Not the way it was."

"And why is that?"

"Where should I begin? For one, I can't focus on anything. Finishing a meal feels like a chore. I feel empty inside. I don't feel motivated. I don't even know why I am letting you push me to learn to walk without the brace. With the way that my legs have healed—the way they feel—I will never be able to fight. Not that I even have any desire to. I'm done. Finished."

"Now, that," remarked Father Ansan, "is not the boy I remember. The boy I remember was angry when I didn't teach him to fight the very first time I met him."

"I'm not that little boy anymore."

"Hmm," mumbled Father Ansan. "You have just lost your way. Come," he said. "Sit here, on the grass. I want to show you something."

Lucas did what he was told, suppressing the urge to grumble.

"Remember I told you, a long time ago, that we all have to follow our path in life? Our paths crossed when you were younger and then our paths parted when you continued to follow yours." Father Ansan used twigs to outline both their paths. Lucas's twigs curved away to show his path going in a different direction when he met the circus and again at other points in his life. Both paths twisted and turned. Then, when Lucas's path finally went straight, Father Ansan placed a rock that broke the twig. At that point, his own path turned and met up with Lucas's.

"What does that mean?" asked Lucas when he saw the rock crushing his twig.

"That's where you are on your path now and this is mine. My path met up with yours again."

"So, we meet up again," said Lucas.

He was losing interest.

"Look at your path," said Father Ansan. "What do you see?"

"It has a big stone on it, and it is broken!"

"Exactly," said Father Ansan excitedly. "But your path still continues after that. You see, you were on the right path and in the right place. You were going in the right direction, but something unexpected broke your path. Whatever happened to you was not supposed to happen. It was not written on your path. That's why you have lost your way, and why your soul is searching."

"How can I remain on the path as a chosen one if I am not able to serve the king?"

"Are you a chosen one?"

Lucas shrugged. "It is what they say I am, and it is what I feel."

"Do you?"

"Yes."

"Do you follow orders like a chosen one?" asked Father Ansan.

"Most of the time."

"But not all of the time?"

"No," Lucas admitted.

"Why not?"

"I don't know. Because it doesn't feel right at times?"

"Do the other chosen ever disobey an order? Do they ever initiate something on their own?"

Lucas sighed with frustration. "Where are you going with this?"

"I don't know enough about chosen ones to determine who is one and who is not, but I can tell that you have had doubts. You feel you are a chosen one, yet you feel different?"

Lucas reluctantly answered. "Yes."

"And the rest of the chosen ones, they know that and accept it?"

Lucas nodded.

"Then you need to accept it too," said Father Ansan. "It is important that you stop fighting who you really are so you can find your way."

"And how do I do that?"

Father Ansan smiled and pointed to his twigs. "That is why my path meets back up with yours. You must remove the obstacle that is on your path or find a way around it. You will not be able to heal unless you can remember what happened."

"I don't think I want to remember being dropped down the old well shaft," said Lucas, shaking his head. "I only know that is what happened because they told me, but it is not something I want to relive."

"And that is why you cannot remember. You erased that part from your memory in order to survive, but with that, you accidently also erased the reason the gods want you to live."

Lucas kept staring at the twigs. Deep down he did want to know what happened. He wanted to know who was responsible and why, but most importantly, he wanted to be himself again.

"Come," said Father Ansan and motioned for Lucas to lie down on the grass in front of him, and Lucas did not resist. "Just as the stone unlocked your gifts," he continued, "it has given me a gift, as well. I can remove the darkness and give you the light to show the way, but only when you are ready to receive it." He folded his legs and placed his hands on Lucas's head. "Are you ready?" he asked.

"I think so," answered Lucas.

"Then close your eyes."

Lucas obeyed and soon felt himself drift off into a deep sleep. He started to dream of riding a horse, a black horse with a shiny black mane that was glistening in the sun. He felt the wind through his hair as they galloped over an open field. He heard thundering hooves from the horses and riders that were following him, kicking up dust into a huge cloud as they rode. His horse ran with its neck outstretched and breathed hard. He rode over the crest of a hill and slowed down to see two large armies standing face to face in the field in front of him. He looked to his left and saw hundreds of warriors riding down the hill towards them. Lucas gave his horse a hard kick and spurred him forward as fast as he could.

At that pivotal moment, Lucas awoke. Father Ansan was removing his hands from Lucas's head. "And? What did you see?"

"I had a dream of riding a horse."

Father Ansan looked down at him. "Then you will."

Lucas pulled himself up onto his elbows. "Is that it? A dream? I thought you could give me my memory back?"

Father Ansan stood up. "For now, a dream is enough. Same time at the pool tomorrow," he said and walked away. Lucas folded his arms underneath his head and laid back down in the grass, thinking about all that Father Ansan had told him and the dream of riding a horse again. A flock of geese flew in formation overhead. He followed them until they disappeared from sight and then got up. He made his way along the cloister, past the warrior monk training courtyard to a hallway he had avoided up until now. He looked over his shoulder to see if anyone was watching and then continued.

The stone was exactly how he remembered it, black as if it had just fallen from the sky. Slightly smaller, now that he was not staring at it through the eyes of a young boy, but still impressive in size. He walked closer and stood at the edge of the water surrounding the stone. The plank used to get to the island was already in place. He hobbled over to it, realizing it would be tricky to navigate with his crutches and put them down on the ground.

The plank wobbled briefly when he put his right foot on it to test its stability. He stretched his arms out to keep his balance and put his left foot in front of his right. He carefully started to make his way across and was dripping with perspiration from the effort it cost him. When he reached the island, he gazed at the stone, allowing himself to catch his breath and to let his heart rate slow down. He didn't know if the stone would speak to him without a ceremony or the presence of the other monks, but he needed to try. He needed to know, and he wanted the stone to show him what he could not remember himself. He needed to see.

Lucas moved his hand towards the stone and let his fingertips touch it. He felt a jolt, a tingling sensation, and pulled his hand back. He looked at his hand and felt his fingertips, but they were fine. He hesitated for a moment, then closed his eyes and placed his whole hand flat onto the surface of the stone. The strong tingling sensation entered his hand, but he resisted the urge to pull back. It traveled up his arm and through his body until it touched every fiber of his being. Lucas then placed his other hand onto the stone and let the darkness surround him as he connected. There was silence at first but then . . . a giggle—the faintest giggle of a young girl—and a curtain opened before his eyes to show Amalia playing. She was happy and he was happy for her but, when she turned to him, she was no longer smiling. A tear rolled down her cheek as she held her hand out to him. He looked and saw the ball with two carved letters on it. He stepped forward, and she placed the ball in his hand.

Then he was suddenly somewhere else. He was . . . there, back at the castle. The king was standing over him, his brow furrowed with concern. Then he was being held down while Garrad tried to set his legs. There was pain, so much pain, his screaming filling the space, filling his own head, and there were worried faces everywhere, all around him.

He began to feel faint and, slipping out of the vision for a moment, had to steady himself on the stone.

The magpie was flying away. Egon was by his side. He lay broken at the bottom of the shaft. The water dripping in the cave . . . the sound it made, the darkness . . . the hatch closing above him. He felt the tightness of the rope around his body disappear, and the wind, as it rushed past him. The panic, when he knew there would be an end. Then he was being taken from his bed and the four dark figures that had come into the room.

He remembered everything as it came back to him in reverse order and finally, he could take no more. He felt himself starting to black out and collapsed on the ground in front of the stone.

CHAPTER 14

Lucas opened his eyes to see Father Ansan looking down at him, concern in his eyes. It took him a moment to realize that he was lying on the ground at the base of the stone. He had a pounding headache but felt more alive than he had in months.

Father Ansan kneeled next to him and gently held him down when he tried to get up.

"Hold on, Lucas. Take it easy," he said. "That was quite a fall you took there. What happened? Why did you come here?"

"I wanted to remember," said Lucas, "and was hoping the stone could help with that."

"And?" asked Father Ansan, anticipation in his voice. "It would be unusual for the stone to work its magic without a ceremony."

"It did," said Lucas, smiling. "It opened up my mind. I remember everything. The only thing I did not see was who the four dark figures were, but I'm ready to get back in the saddle to find that out. I'll need a sword and a carving knife for leather. I made someone a promise I intend to keep."

With Father Ansan's guidance, Lucas went back to practicing the ancient ways of the warrior monks and joined them in training. He regained his strength and focus and was determined to put the last few dark months of his life behind him. Every morning, he rose before dawn to swim, then worked all day and didn't return to his room until after dark. His left leg continued to cause him grief until he was willing to accept help and let Father John swaddle it twice a day in hot rags to get the circulation going. Soon, a slight limp was all that remained from the trauma that he'd suffered, and even that, he was told, would disappear over time. His gift of seeing had come back the day his memory returned and was more profound than ever before. He could turn it on and switch it off with little concentration and was delighted in the control he now had, in his ability to easily focus on whatever it was he wanted to.

"Well done," said Father Ansan, when Lucas disarmed him during practice, the sword falling to the ground with a clank. "You have been working hard, my son. You have become more powerful than even I have ever been."

"That is because you've taught me well, Father," answered Lucas, wiping the sweat from his face with his sleeve.

"Hmm . . . yes," replied Father Ansan. "The day the student defeats the teacher is the day the teacher knows his work is done. That student now becomes the teacher." He looked at Lucas with a grave expression. "Do you think you are ready?"

"I do," answered Lucas in earnest. Father Ansan gave him a nod of approval and then left him to finish up the practice on his own, as he did every day. It was a bright, clear afternoon, and Lucas enjoyed having the sun on his skin. When he became too hot, he sought the shade of the cherry tree that had replaced its blooms with lush green leaves. He was aware of approaching footsteps in the hallway, loud and determined, and not the kind made by monk's sandals. Soldier's boots. He had expected this day to come and knew he had no choice but to return to the king. With his back turned towards the cloister, he listened for the footsteps to come to a halt and heard Father Ansan's voice telling him that he had visitors. Lucas nodded but did not turn around. "I see," he answered and continued to finish his practice.

Father Ansan turned to the group of men who had followed him. "He will be finished shortly."

"We can wait," said Egon, who looked pleased by what he saw.

Lucas finished and acknowledged the officers as he walked towards them. He saw that Egon was eyeing him up from head to toe and knew he had probably noticed the slight limp he still carried in his stride.

"You look well," Egon said, "for which I am glad, as the king has requested your return."

"I'm ready," Lucas answered, before making his way over to Father Ansan to hand him the sword. "Though I am sad to have to leave my teacher behind again," he told him.

"But excited to soon be reunited with your friends?" Father Ansan asked, a smile crossing his face. "It will be good for you." He gracefully took the sword from him, and they bowed out of respect for each other. Lucas then took the new uniform Verron had handed him and went to change.

Lucas closed the door and looked around the room where he had spent so much time contemplating the meaning of his life, the place where he had searched for a reason to continue. He had been disappointed when his memory returned and he did not get the answer as to why he had been dropped in the well, or by whom, but Father Ansan had reminded him it did not matter. What mattered was how he got through it, how he had survived and how it could make him stronger. He changed into his new uniform and picked up Amalia's ball from the bedside table. He stuck it in his pocket, before giving the room one last look.

Father Ansan and Father John were waiting by the door when Lucas stopped to thank them for everything they had done for him.

"Do not forget what you have learned here," said Father Ansan as he held Lucas by his shoulders and looked him in the eye. "Embrace the gifts inside of you—they have been given to you for a reason. Follow your intuition and your heart, and never doubt them."

"I will, Father," said Lucas with a heavy heart, and then stepped over the threshold to join the mounted soldiers. He walked to the horse they were holding ready for him and stroked its soft neck. He inhaled a deep breath and took in the horse's aroma, a scent he had missed. He then put his foot in the stirrup and pulled himself up in the saddle. Egon had been watching him closely and Lucas assumed it was to see if he could mount up on his own. He gave Lucas a satisfied nod when he did.

Father Ansan stepped outside and pointed to the sky. Lucas looked up and saw a magpie flying high above. He nodded to Father Ansan and grabbed the reins of his horse.

They rode hard throughout the night and, at first light, the castle came into view. They passed through the first gate, where the chosen ones were exercising in the outer bailey, and Lucas smiled when he saw them. The boys came running when the horses slowed to a walk and passed through the second gate. They surrounded him when he dismounted and bombarded him with questions, but Egon told them there would be plenty of time for talk later and they were to get to work. "Except for you, Lucas," said Officer Verron. "You can go and settle in. I'll see you on the training grounds in an hour."

"Yes, sir," answered Lucas, and handed the reins of his horse to Zera.

"I missed you," said Zera. "We've all been really worried. They wouldn't tell us much, but Verron was not hopeful when he saw you last."

"I'm good now, and happy to be back," Lucas answered. He was looking over his shoulder and saw that Egon was about to walk away.

"Sir?" he called and rushed over when he saw Egon turn around, stop, and wait.

Standing in front of this tall, earnest-looking king's guard, Lucas hesitated for a moment, but then plucked up the courage and reached inside his pocket. "Sir, I am supposed to give this back, but I do not know how."

Egon's piercing eyes stared at him and then looked down at his hand, in which he was holding Amalia's ball, now beautifully carved with her name. Lucas had wondered how to get it back to her once it was finished, but then he remembered that Egon was in the room when Amalia had come in, which would make explaining how he got the ball easier.

"You did this?" asked Egon with admiration when he took the ball from him.

"Yes, sir," acknowledged Lucas. "It's the princess's ball. She wanted me to carve her name on it. She gave it to me when—"

"I know," interrupted Egon. "I picked it up when it dropped out of your hand at the monastery."

"It was never my intention to interact with the princess," Lucas began to apologize, but stopped when Egon raised his hand to silence him.

"No one knows about this," he said sternly. "Only you, the princess and myself, and I suggest we keep it that way."

Lucas waited anxiously while Egon turned the ball around in his hand, to admire it one more time, and then watched him put it in his pocket.

"I will find a way to get it back to her," Egon said, "but you know full well that you are not permitted to have any contact with her, so don't let it happen again."

Lucas nodded and watched Egon walk away. He was left standing alone and soon became aware he was being watched. He slowly turned towards the elite training grounds and saw Eli smirk at him from the gates. He had a large group of boys around him. Eli had noticed the slight limp in Lucas's leg and was making fun of him by imitating an exaggerated version of his stride in front of the group. Lucas had not been back for more than half an hour and already Eli was antagonizing him. The other elites laughed in response, but Lucas could tell that some boys only did so to please Eli. Something was amiss with that picture. He ignored them and walked away.

"Good to have you back," said Davis, the last one to embrace Lucas after he joined them on the training grounds. Zera stood at his side.

"Why is that?" said Lucas with a smile as he took a practice sword from the barrel. "Have you worked so hard in my absence that you think you can beat me now?"

"I'm always willing to give it a try. Should be better than fighting this lot the whole time. It was getting a bit boring," joked Davis, gesturing to the other boys.

"Elite borns haven't been giving you a hard enough time, then?"

"They have not allowed us to practice with them," commented Warrick.

"Since when?"

"Since the night we were all poisoned and you got hurt."

Lucas tested the weight of the sword and looked at the boys standing around him. "That's a long time."

"Yes. But they still don't know who was responsible," said Zera. "We are hoping you can tell us."

"Eli has been telling tales amongst the elite that he did it," said Davis, before Lucas could answer Zera. "He denied it, obviously, when he was questioned officially. There was no proof, and the king had to lct it go. Now, Eli boasts about the fact that he got away with it and threatens that he can do anything to any of us, at any time. Even the elite borns have started to fear him. More so than before."

"That explains why I saw him surrounded by a large group."

"Yes," said Warrick. "Eli has established control over the elite group."

"What about Carleton?"

"He still has his own entourage behind him," said Davis, "but many have abandoned him."

Lucas picked up a different sword and tested the weight of that one. "Having Eli in charge like that is not good for us in the long run," muttered Lucas, more to himself than to anyone else.

"Did he do it?" asked Zera.

Lucas stepped away from the barrel when he found the right sword and looked at the faces around him. They desperately wanted the answer he had pined for as well and were looking for him to give it to them. "No," he said, shaking his head. "I don't know who was responsible, but I do know it was not Eli."

"It wasn't?" asked Davis. "Have you told Egon this?"

"No."

"Why not?"

Lucas let out a deep sigh. "Egon is only interested in knowing who did it. Knowing it is not Eli will not change anything."

"It will stop Eli from boasting about it," commented Davis.

"I'll have to tell him to stop that, myself," said Lucas resolutely, walking over to the pell. The officers were coming in.

"You just got back, Lucas," said Zera. "Why not take it easy before getting into trouble again?"

"I'll take it easy when I have dealt with the trouble," Lucas answered. He looked at the wall and counted the number of soldiers on it. "I take it that the king is not here?"

"No," answered Zera. "He'll be back tomorrow, as will Finton."

"Then it will have to be tonight," said Lucas. "Warrick and Tanner, you two still work in the stables, when the elite borns come and get their horses in the afternoons?"

"We do," confirmed Warrick.

"Perfect, then you can get a message to Carleton for me!"

"What makes you think he will not betray you?" whispered Davis. They were waiting inside the stables and had just finished their evening duties. They were ready to lock up.

"I don't know," answered Lucas, "but he has as much to gain from this as we do."

Zera had the door slightly open and watched for a sign from the opposite side. "They should be finished soon," she said. "Get ready!"

They had to wait a moment longer before Zera opened the door wide and they started talking and walking out of the stables. The door of the stables on the opposite side had opened as well, and Warrick, Tanner and Archer started filing out from there. They were laughing and fooling around when they closed their stable doors, drawing attention to themselves from the guards on top of the gate house.

"Now go," said Davis quickly, when they saw the guards were focused on the other group, and Lucas slipped away.

Lucas stayed in the shadows and moved along slowly, until he got close enough to the elite borns' barracks. There he hid and waited behind a wagon, until every single elite born had returned from the officer's mess hall, where they had the privilege of taking their dinner every night. He took a deep breath to prepare himself, and then boldly walked straight into their dorm room. The elites were all getting ready for the night and were listening to Eli rambling on about something at the back of the room. Lucas looked around when none of the boys noticed him coming in. Their dorm room was as large as the chosen ones', but there were fewer beds with more space in between each one. Tall oak wardrobes stood against the wall in between the beds, unlike the trunk he had under his bed. The room was better lit, with two chandeliers hanging from an elaborate ceiling. The large windows along the top of the wall no doubt provided plenty of light during the day.

It was Eli who stopped mid-sentence when he spotted Lucas, his mouth dropping open in disbelief. The other boys followed his gaze and froze and looked to Eli.

"Go and get an officer," Eli said hastily to a boy closest to the door, but before he even took a step, Carleton had closed the door and blocked the way. Several other boys stood near him, to make sure no one came in or out.

Eli stepped away from his bed. He crossed his arms in front of him and tried to compose himself. "You have guts, Lucas—I must give you that. You just got back, and already you're looking to start something? Surely you're not here to take revenge for what I did to you?"

Lucas looked him straight in the eye. "You and I both know you had nothing to do with that!"

"Ha," responded Eli. "How can you be so sure, when they tell us you had a sack over your head and saw nothing? You don't think I am capable of it?" He laughed and looked around the room. Some of the boys had straightened up and were paying close attention.

"Oh, I know you are quite capable," continued Lucas. "There's just one problem."

"What is that?"

"It was four people that attacked me."

Eli looked puzzled. He wasn't sure where Lucas was going with this. "So?" he said. "What's your point?"

Lucas shrugged. "Well, that's the problem. Who could the other three be? Baldric? Andrew and Milton? They would be the ones you would recruit, but I do not believe they would be capable of such a cowardly act. I only know one coward, not four! Besides, the ones who took me were men, not boys."

Eli's face grew red with anger. He looked at his three friends, but they were clearly not going along with claiming they were responsible.

Eli still couldn't let it go. "I had outside help," he stammered.

The elite boys were clearly not buying it any longer and shook their heads in disbelief. Some even laughed.

"It's a shame it wasn't you, though," continued Lucas. "It would have saved me from having to come in here tonight to straighten things out—I would have just killed you the minute I set foot inside those gates this morning."

He had said the last words with such fury that all the elite borns looked at him, stunned. Without waiting for Eli's response, Lucas turned around and headed for the door.

Lucas expected to be questioned over the nightly visit to the elite's dorm and feared the moment had arrived when some officers walked onto their training grounds and talked with Verron the next day. They were all looking his way while they talked, but then Verron shook his head and both officers left again. Later that afternoon, Tanner reported that the elite borns had not come to get their horses and another chosen said that he had heard no sounds coming from their training grounds all day either.

When the king rode in that evening and Lucas stood in line to receive the horses, he saw Finton being approached by one of the officers who had talked to Verron that morning. They spoke briefly and he saw the general nod before walking away towards the elite dormitory.

Lucas startled when suddenly the king patted him on the back. "Good to see you again," he said, and handed Lucas the reins to his horse.

"Thank you, sire," Lucas responded quickly.

The king followed it up with a friendly nod before walking on. Lucas heard Amalia's voice and saw her dart off the big steps of the castle and run towards her father. He put an arm around her when she hugged him and gave her a tender kiss on her cheek. It was a moment of happiness Lucas didn't often get to see and it softened his heart. He saw that the king noticed her holding the ball and asked to see it. She gave it to him and while her father looked at it, Amalia found Lucas in the crowd. He was afraid she might tell her father that he was the one who had carved it, so he quickly looked away and distanced himself, walking the king's horse into the stables.

News of what happened to the elite borns after Lucas had visited them in their dorm room came to the chosens a few days later. As soon as Carleton had stepped back into the room after aiding Lucas in his escape, he had been confronted by Eli and a fight had broken out involving several elites. Guards, alerted by the noise, came and broke it up. When asked to explain themselves, Carleton had responded by saying that it was just a fight long overdue, but Eli jumped in, admitting it was because Carleton had allowed Lucas to confront him in their dorm room. That explained why the two officers had come to talk to Verron that following morning, but Verron had responded by calling the allegation ridiculous.

Even Egon had not wanted to hear any of it and claimed that Eli's story was too far-fetched, that Lucas had only returned hours before and was not in a state to challenge anyone. No chosen one had ever dared to even get close to the elites' dorm room. Eli's story was not supported by any of the other elite borns either, and so was quickly dismissed. By the time the general was informed about his son's fight, Eli had changed his story to match that of Carleton's. They had both been locked up in the dungeon for a few days, while the rest of the elite borns had been confined to their barracks.

Lucas made sure to keep his head down after that night. He was happy to be back and worked hard to settle into the routine again. He trained, did his stable work, obeyed every order and went out on patrols. Eventually, the elite borns came back to training with them, and it became clear that Carleton was the go-to person now among the elites. Eli kept to himself, clinging to his little group of followers and avoiding contact with Lucas.

In the weeks following his return to the castle, Lucas was just coming back from a patrol trip when he noticed a young, scrawny-looking boy by the gates. He was saying goodbye to his parents. His mother hugged and kissed him, while his father patted him on the head and put up a brave face. The boy's eyes were teary when the two soldiers pried him away from his mother, just when Lucas passed by on his horse. It was the first time he had gotten to see a boy being brought to the gates, and he felt sorry for him.

"A new chosen one," he heard Zera say.

Lucas looked back over his shoulder and saw the boy being led through the gates, his eyes downcast. As the gate closed, he watched the father place his arm over the mother's shoulders. Lucas glanced over to Zera, who had her eyes rigidly fixed forward. He knew she had no happy memories of her own parents and was avoiding looking at the couple by the gates, who clearly loved their little boy.

Lucas caught the boy's eye when they were dismounting, and he was walking past. He wanted to say something to him but knew no contact was allowed until he came out of the hole and was put through the chosens' test.

"Don't worry," he heard Zera say when they were leading the horses into the stable. "That boy will be fine once he settles in. We all were."

He couldn't give the new boy much thought, as, that same day, the castle was in the midst of preparing to receive three lords, all from different parts of the country. Every five years, they would come to sign a new alliance treaty with the king. The chosen ones were busy building stands in their training grounds and the outer bailey. The lords, as well as small delegations of their armies, would be staying for a few days, and the king had given orders to organize tournaments of single-combat sword fighting and jousting, for entertainment.

"Why an alliance treaty?" Lucas asked Davis when they were carrying more planks for the stands. "Are they not supposed to support the king regardless?"

"It dates back to when King Itan's grandfather, Linus, first became king," answered Davis. "To guarantee the support from the other lords, he had them all sign an alliance. They fought with Linus in the great battle against King Rodin and after that the alliance was renewed every five years."

"Why?"

"Linus was a lord at first, and only became king because the people wanted him to become one. Some of the other lords had more land, bigger armies, and Linus feared they could, one day, try and make claim to the throne."

"So, the treaty guarantees that they don't."

"Exactly. If one breaks the treaty, the others remain united," continued Davis. "Having the lords allied with King Itan also means more protection against the king across the river border."

"King Boran."

"Yes."

They worked hard the rest of the afternoon and the following day to set up for the tournaments, only to discover that they would not be allowed to participate. Only a handful of the elite borns and soldiers selected from different units would be put forward to represent the king.

"At least we get to watch some of it," said Davis, somewhat moodily. It was the night before the lords were due to arrive, and they were sitting on their beds in the dorm room, not one of them able to sleep because of the excitement in the air.

"Only when you have a job at the event," said Warrick. "You were lucky enough to see Lucas that time at the princess's birthday celebration. I was stuck inside."

"You saw me?" asked Lucas.

Davis nodded. "Yes, from the wall, though," he said. "A group of us were on watch."

"Yes, I remember that. You were good then, too," said Tanner.

"I remember seeing some of you that morning," said Lucas, "but I was too busy that afternoon to look up." Lucas was quiet for a moment when he reflected on that day, which now seemed so long ago.

"Well," said Tanner, clearing his throat. "I heard from some elite borns that Eli will get his moment to shine again. He's to fight the new boy in the chosen test, and all the lords are going to be present to watch. The test will kick off the entertainment."

"Poor kid. He's not going to stand a chance," replied Warrick. "Eli will be sure to make a show out of it."

"Yes, especially since they are changing the rules," Zera said in a hushed voice, shaking her head. "To pass the test, the new boy has to last at least twenty minutes. Better for the entertainment apparently."

The poor boy, thought Lucas. Eli was sure to enjoy every minute of it.

CHAPTER 15

The following day, the chosen made all the preparations assigned to them, and just in time for the lords' arrival that afternoon. The first lord who rode through the gates did so with such confidence, as if he was coming home. He shouted orders out straightaway and jumped off his horse without waiting for the king to arrive. Lucas felt he had an arrogance about him that he did not like.

"Lord Killeand," whispered Warrick next to him.

"Have you met the lords before?" Lucas whispered back.

"Yes. I had only just arrived, but I remember this one very well. Very loud fellow and with his blond locks, he reminded me of Eli. Thought at the time he could be a cousin or something."

"Are they related?"

"Not that I know of, but the king and Killeand are distant cousins, I believe."

Lucas could see a resemblance, in their hair and fair skin. He also seemed to like attention and didn't look like he would easily accept *no* for an answer. He watched the lord dismount and walk up to the king with open arms. The king, who was usually reserved in his mannerisms, returned the gesture, and they embraced each other like old friends. They then slapped each other on the back and walked towards the castle.

The next two lords were different. Lord Hammond was much older, with gray hair and a long beard. He took his time getting off his horse but refused help from anyone trying to offer it. Lucas was to take his horse and stood waiting patiently. When Lord Hammond stepped onto the ground, he leaned on Lucas's shoulder for support. They briefly looked each other in the eye and Lord Hammond gave him a friendly nod before patting him on the head and walking off.

Lord Aron was the last to arrive. His red hair and beard made him stand out as he rode through the gates. He was very direct in his orders to his men and Lucas could tell he was greatly respected by the way they responded to him. He seemed like someone who was firm in his decisions, but fair. He carried himself with the elegance of nobility but did not seem to look down onto others. Lucas decided he liked him the most.

They all worked late into that night to get their chores done and, when they were finally ready for bed, it was still noisy outside from the visiting soldiers. Lucas could hear their boisterous laughter and the clinking of their cups. They were all camped in the outer bailey, but the inner gate was left open, so there was a great deal of shuffling back and forth. Lucas lay on his bed and tried to fall asleep, but even though he was exhausted, sleep did not come to him. Every time he tried to close his eyes, he felt his chest tighten up and felt he could not breathe. Every noise outside startled him, and he found himself staring at the door. After a while he got up and went to sit on the top step of the stairs. Zera soon joined him.

"Can't sleep?" she asked.

"No," answered Lucas with a sigh.

"It's all right," said Zera. "I understand. You know, we pushed our beds in front of the door to block anyone from coming in for weeks after the attack on you. But you didn't seem to have a problem before. Is it all coming back to you, because of all the new people in the castle?"

"I guess so." Lucas turned to Zera and looked her in the eye. "I don't think the people that took me were from this castle."

Zera stared at him, looking confused at first and then shook her head. "Lucas, they had to have been," she said. "No one can approach this castle unseen, let alone enter. And even if someone could, why would they?"

"I don't know," answered Lucas softly, trying not to wake anyone. "But the two men I killed, at the inn . . . they were part of a group of six. All of them dressed in black, much like the people who entered our dorm room that night. And the men who caused my father to kill himself . . ."

Zera took a deep breath. "Mercenary soldiers dress without color, so they can be hired by anyone, but who would have hired them to kill you? And why go through all that trouble to drop you down the well?"

"Because they were not supposed to kill him," they heard Davis say. He had crept up behind them and joined them on the stairs. "Right, Lucas?"

"No, I don't think they were," confirmed Lucas. "I was lowered down. If they had wanted to kill me, they would have just dropped me. I was supposed to be taken, by the water."

"Through the underground river," muttered Davis. "That makes sense now."

"But the river moved its course and that well has been dry for a long time," said Zera, shaking her head.

"Yes," answered Lucas. "Which means they were going off old information."

"Which means they could not have been working for anyone living inside the castle walls," Davis said, an edge of excitement to his voice.

They continued to talk for a little while longer. With no answer to their questions, Zera had insisted on informing Verron or even Egon, but both Davis and Lucas were against it. They felt it was best to keep quiet, at least for now, until the alliance was signed, and the lords had left, since there was a possibility that one of them could have been involved.

Standing in line with the other chosen ones in the training grounds, Lucas rubbed his eyes and struggled to stay awake. They had formed a semicircle with the elite borns in front of the stand that had been erected for the king and his guests. Unlike Zera and Davis, he had stayed up all night and the lack of sleep was starting to affect him as they waited for the start of the chosen test. Warrick nudged him when the king and his entourage finally made their appearance, and he stood to attention. Lucas watched as the lords took their seats next to the king and were told what was about to happen. Lord Hammond and Lord Aron nodded understandingly, but Killeand asked several questions. When the king nodded to give the start signal, Eli stepped proudly into the middle.

Lucas heard the door to the hole open and took a deep breath. He did not want to be there. It did not feel right, to make a spectacle of something that had nothing to do with outsiders. He already knew this boy was a chosen, and he felt the need to protect him. With the added fear that Eli would go beyond the rules of the fight to put on a show, all of the chosen had agreed that they would not raise their heads until the last few minutes. They hoped that Eli would be easier on the boy if he believed he was not fighting a chosen one, and that this might give the boy a chance to last the full twenty minutes in the fight.

With their hands behind their back, the chosen ones waited until the new boy was close enough, and then stepped aside to let him through into the circle. The boy was visibly trembling when he was handed a sword, and Lucas could see it was difficult for him to focus on listening to the rules. He was small for his age and the lack of food and water had affected his body greatly. He looked pale and was unsteady on his feet when Eli approached him. The boy instinctively stepped back to get out of his way, and a booing could be heard coming from the stands. It was Killeand, who was standing up, and clearly wanted to see action. Eli paused and looked towards the stand but continued when he was urged forward by the king. Lucas saw the boy was able to block the first few blows and dash out of the way on others.

"Not bad," whispered Zera next to him. "Feisty little fellow."

"Eli's on a mission, though, in spite of most of us still having our heads down," said Warrick quietly. "He just loves an audience."

Lucas said nothing. He was watching the fight with great interest and studied every move. The boy was fast and had potential, but he was tiring too quickly. Eli was coming down on him hard and the boy had already tripped several times, falling at their feet.

"He's not going to make it," said Zera, when the boy fell again. "He's not going to last another ten minutes."

Lucas thought for a minute. Father Ansan had told him to trust the inner voice that was deep inside him. It was telling him that he could not lose a chosen one, and he had to do something about it. He had been counting Eli's steps and knew he would be able to help the boy, if he could get near him. Lucas took one last look to make sure the officers close to him had their eyes on the fight, and then stepped back. "Cover me," he said to Zera and Warrick, who immediately closed the gap he left. Quickly, but discreetly, he moved behind the line of chosen, until he felt he was in the right spot and squeezed in between Tanner and Archer. He watched and waited until the boy was pushed hard by Eli and fell on the ground right in front of him. Lucas kneeled to whisper quick instructions in the boy's ear, while helping him back on his feet. The boy nodded that he understood and let himself be gently pushed back into the circle. Lucas watched as the boy waited for Eli to come at him again and instead of ducking, blocking or stepping away, he did what Lucas had told him, and moved in closer. Every time Eli came again, he did the same thing, changing his direction each time. Eli needed to have space to swing his sword, but when the boy no longer gave that to him, Eli was forced to move around more and used up time by doing so.

On the stand, Killeand had been watching the fight with great interest and had also been paying attention to the chosen boys standing around. He was intrigued when he noticed one of the boys get out of line and move to the spot where the little boy fell.

Killeand leaned back in his seat towards Verron, who was seated behind him. "Was he just told something by one of the chosen ones?" he asked, without taking his eyes off the fight.

"It appears that way," answered Verron. "I am really sorry, but that was not supposed to happen and is not allowed."

"No need to apologize," said Killeand. "I quite enjoyed that. It was an interesting move and whatever instructions were given—it seems to be working in the little one's favor. One of your better fighters, I take it, if he can predict the course of a fight like that?"

Verron nodded. "Lucas is the most gifted chosen one we have right now."

Killeand watched the last few minutes of the fight with less interest and kept an eye on Lucas. When time was called and the fight ended, Killeand turned to the king. "Thank you for allowing us to be witness to this," he said. "That was entertaining . . . and impressive. I can't wait to see that boy fight in the tournament."

Finton overheard the comment and gleamed with pride. "That was my boy, Eli," he said proudly.

Killeand raised his eyebrow and stared at Finton. He had known the general for a long time and wondered why he would think he would not be referring to Eli by name, if he had been the one who had caught his eye. "I know your son, General," he said. "But I wasn't referring to him. I meant the chosen boy who changed positions so he could give the young one instruction to stay in the fight."

Finton's expression changed. "Well," he said, trying to hide his embarrassment. "I am afraid we will have to disappoint you. The chosen ones will not participate in the tournament."

"That's a shame," said Killeand, as they stood up and started exiting the stand.

"I agree," said Lord Hammond, carefully making his way down the steps. "Especially if what Officer Verron said is true and he is the best chosen one there is."

"Itan!" Killeand said loudly, after hearing that Hammond shared his opinion. "Are you truly going to deny us some good fighting here? Any reason you are holding that chosen one back?"

Even Lord Aron was nodding his head in agreement and, from Egon's expression, Killeand could tell he was willing to let the boy fight. He watched as Itan contemplated his question and thought for sure that he would come up with a reason why chosen ones were not allowed to participate, so he was surprised to hear otherwise.

"You're right, my good man," said Itan. "I promised you all some good fighting and Lucas will certainly provide that. He is, however, recovering from a bad leg injury, so no promises. I will allow him to fight, but only if his officers tell me he is fit to do so."

Lucas was told by Verron that he was to participate in the single combat tournament and was given little time to get ready. He was sent to the outer bailey where all fighters had congregated and saw they were all given protective armory to wear. Lucas chose leather arm chaps and chest armor but declined the chain mail and helmet. He relied on speed and agility in his fights, and both would be a hinderance. He saw Eli, Carleton and Baldric standing off to the side, swinging their swords, and he went to sit on a barrel away from them, to strap on his gear.

Seeing the king cross the bridge with his entourage and the lords in tow reminded Lucas of the time when he had stood waiting with Sable, Everett and Rowan. The setup with the stands was near enough the same, except the fighting arena was smaller. He had been anxious then, as he was now, but for different reasons. Back then he had wanted to impress the king with a circus act, to fulfill a childhood dream of joining his army. Lucas smiled inwardly at the thought. If he had only known then, that he would now be fighting in earnest, against the best.

Lucas watched the lords stop near some of the fighters to have a chat and to wish them luck. He was putting his foot up onto the barrel to tie his boots when he caught Killeand's eye. Killeand excused himself from the other lords and walked over.

"I am glad to see that they are allowing you to participate," he said with a smile and motioned for Lucas to remain seated. "I noticed how you helped that young boy this morning," he continued. "He is a true chosen one then, is he?"

"Yes, sir," answered Lucas. "He is."

"Like you?"

"Yes, sir."

"Can you tell me why I have heard some people call you the King's Chosen?"

"They call him that," interrupted General Finton, coming up behind Killeand, "because the king was the one who put him on the list, instead of a village official. He was a circus performer, acting out the great Toroun, and impressed the king enough that he wanted him, no matter what," said Finton, glaring at Lucas with great animosity.

Lucas pretended not to notice, as he understood that it must have infuriated Finton to see Killeand showing interest in him, while he had walked straight past Eli. If Finton had meant for his words to discredit Lucas, it seemed to have the opposite effect. Killeand's eyes had lit up upon hearing he had worked in a circus.

"Really?" said Lord Killeand. "I do love the circus. Never miss a performance when they come into town. What did you do in your act?"

"I showed my sword skills, mostly," answered Lucas. "Nothing special."

Killeand eyed him up from head to toe, and grinned. "You are modest, and I like that," he said. "I wish you luck in the games, and I can't wait to see what you can do."

Lucas jumped off the barrel when the first two fighters were called into the arena, as he was eager to watch them. A circle had been painted onto the ground with lime and each fighter took his place in the center, facing the other. Although it was full-contact sword fighting and it was possible to get hurt, the main purpose of the fight was to knock your opponent out of the circle. As soon as a fighter crossed the line with any part of his body, the fight was over and the next two opponents were called.

Lucas was able to watch the first few fights to size up the competition and to see how they were fought. Sometimes swords were abandoned and a wrestling match unfolded to push an opponent over the line, causing the crowd to boo and cheer. He learned quickly that the games were as much for entertainment for the soldiers as they were to determine who had the best fighters. Each fighter wore the colors of their employer on their shield, and these were easily recognizable for the crowd.

When it was Lucas's turn to fight, he stepped into the arena with apprehension, but then the crowd's energy reached him and a thirst to entertain overtook him, as it had done when he was with the circus. Lucas walked up to the centerline and faced a fighter from Lord Hammond. He was big and strong, but slow and clumsy. It did not take Lucas long to outsmart him. He used skill and technique rather than brute force and was able to win his first few fights that way. Carleton and Eli were able to do the same, but Baldric was taken out after the second round. Lucas was waiting to go in for his third round when Baldric walked past him as he exited.

"What are you staring at?" asked Baldric, giving Lucas a mean look.

"Nothing," answered Lucas. "I think you fought well."

"Don't assume you can do better," said Baldric, looking over his shoulder to the soldier Lucas was about to fight. "It'll be your turn next to face defeat."

Lucas saw that the soldier was one from his own castle. He had seen him a few times, mostly with a group of soldiers who accompanied Finton on personal business. The soldier stepped into the arena and Lucas could tell he was eager to prove himself. Bets were waged among the soldiers, and Lucas hoped the odds were in his favor. The soldier barely waited for the start sign before he attacked. Lucas planted one foot firmly on the ground and blocked. The soldier leaned in hard to push him to the ground, but Lucas swung his other foot back and stepped to the side, making the soldier lose his balance and stumble towards the circle's outer perimeter. He managed to stay in and composed himself to do it again. Lucas watched the soldier look over his shoulder towards the crowd. He followed his gaze and saw Finton with his head slightly down, giving the soldier a subtle nod.

Lucas knew then that this fight was going to be different from all the others he had fought that afternoon.

The attacks came swiftly and were aimed at unprotected parts of his body. Lucas had to duck and dart out of the way to prevent a blow to the head. He tried to fight a clean fight, but it became increasingly difficult to do so.

Very briefly, he glanced over to the stand where the king and the lords sat watching. The king was leaning forward, and his expression looked grave. Amalia sat next to him, her hands covering her face.

The soldier circled Lucas again and took instructions from Finton again. Lucas picked up on them this time and was ready when the soldier came running towards him, dropped to the ground and slid towards him with his leg outstretched to try and kick Lucas's left leg from underneath him. At the right moment, Lucas leaped up into the air and landed behind the soldier. His eyes met the king's, who gave him a gentle nod of approval. When the soldier stood up and turned around, Lucas jumped up and kicked him hard in the chest. The soldier flailed as he stumbled backwards, trying to regain his balance, but it was too late and he stepped outside the circle.

Lucas touched his leg, which was sore from landing on the ground. When he was given the win, he watched Lord Killeand rise from his seat to give him a standing ovation. Lucas bowed to the king and saw Amalia giving him a little wave. He gave her a discreet bow as well, before limping out of the arena.

He had just made it to a bench when Officer Verron rushed over to him.

"How hurt are you?" he asked, touching Lucas's leg.

Lucas had his left leg outstretched and was leaning back on his elbows. "It will be all right," he answered.

"Can you continue?"

"Yes. It's stiff, but it'll be fine."

With eight fighters remaining to go into the final rounds, Eli, Lucas and one other soldier were the only ones representing the king after Carleton lost his fight.

The crowd roared when Lucas stepped back out. They were rooting for him to win again. He tried to walk normally, to hide his weak spot, and he fought again with all that he had. With the crowd now clearly on his side, he put on a good show and did not let them down.

He had some time before the next fight and was stretching his leg when Carleton walked over. "They have you fighting Eli," he said, sounding somewhat alarmed.

"Really?" asked Lucas.

"Yes, just saw it on the board," answered Carleton. "He's not going to make it easy for you. Do you think you will be all right?"

"I'll have to be."

"You could just say you are injured," said Carleton, motioning to his left leg. "Opt out. Nobody will question it. We have all seen how you keep limping out of the arena."

Lucas shook his head. "I'll fight him if that's what they want me to do."

"No, you won't," said Officer Verron coming up from behind Carleton. "You have been pulled from the tournament."

"Where does this come from?" asked Carleton. "Eli or General Finton?"

"Neither. This order came directly from the king," answered Officer Verron and then proceeded to point to Lucas's leg. "Go and have your leg checked out."

Somewhat disappointed, but also relieved, Lucas abandoned the tournament grounds. Now that he could let his guard down, the awareness of the pain in his leg flooded his senses. He would have fought Eli, but Carleton had been right in wondering if he was up to it. Having been pulled from the tournament was the best thing for him. When he walked into the infirmary, he could see physicians and nurses all busy at work, dealing with injured fighters. Most had cuts from swords, and one looked to have a broken nose, but all would live to fight another day.

"Find yourself a bed," said one of the nurses when he walked in. "We'll attend to you as soon as we have time."

Lucas walked towards the back of the infirmary, where it seemed quieter, and saw the new chosen boy lying on a bed. He saw a bed right next to him and sat on it.

"How are you feeling?" asked Lucas, seeing the boy was awake. "Are you keeping fluids and food in?"

"Yes," the boy replied, turning his head to answer.

"I'm Lucas." He held his hand out to the boy. "I am a chosen one, like you."

"Ando," said the boy, and extended his hand. "My name is Ando."

"Nice to meet you, Ando," said Lucas, lifting his sore leg onto the bed so that he could lie down.

"You're the one that helped me stay in the fight," said Ando. "What happened to your leg?"

Lucas saw him look at his leg with a worried expression on his face. "Old injury," he explained. "Just need to rest it and it'll be fine."

It was dark outside when Lucas was finally cleared to leave the infirmary. He was told to take Ando with him and to bring him to the tailor's to collect his uniform before taking him to the dormitory. Leaving Ando with the tailor, Lucas decided to wait outside to get some fresh air. As soon as he stepped out, he bumped into someone who was rushing past the doorway in a great hurry. He apologized and the man muttered a quick apology back, without stopping. Lucas wasn't familiar with everyone who worked in the castle, but something about this man told him he was one of the lords', and not one of the king's. He had acted suspiciously, shielding his face right after they bumped into each other. Lucas used his mind to see where the man was going, as something didn't feel right.

The man kept to the shadows and seemed nervous. Lucas followed the stranger until he stopped, and another figure stepped in front of him. Their faces were hidden by the shadows, but he saw a small parcel being exchanged between the two men. He tried to get closer, to see who the other man was, but Ando had come out of the tailor's room and broke his concentration.

"Are you all right?" Ando asked.

Lucas looked at the younger boy next to him. "Look at you," he said. "A proper chosen one now."

Ando smiled proudly at his uniform and happily followed Lucas to go and meet the other chosen.

Restless and not wanting to sleep in his own bed that night, Lucas decided to stay in the stables instead. It was the only place he felt somewhat comfortable. Zera had wanted to stay with him, but Lucas refused her offer. He had already kept Zera up most of the previous night and, after what he had seen tonight, he felt he would probably be up all night again.

"Nobody should come in here this late," Lucas said, as they wrapped up their work. "And if they do, I'll just tell them that I am keeping watch on a horse showing signs of sickness."

"Are you sure?"

"Yes," said Lucas. "Ando will need you, since it's his first night as a chosen." Zera reluctantly agreed, as Lucas knew she would, since she was the one who felt most responsible for new arrivals. He waited for Zera to leave before heading to the tack room at the back of the stables. If he was to stay awake, he might as well make himself useful and clean some tack to pass the time.

He had cleaned several bridles when he heard the door to the stables opening, and quickly hid himself behind two barrels of oats. His first thought was that Zera or Davis had come to check on him, but then he heard soft talking. Finton had walked in with Lord Killeand.

Finton began shining his light in every stall and eventually made his way to the tack room The barrels prevented the light from shining on Lucas.

"All clear," said Finton when he turned away from the tack room.

"You were very thorough," said Killeand. "Would it not have been obvious someone was here, the minute we walked in?"

"Probably, but I cannot take the risk of one of them seeing us together. The chosen ones have changed these last few months. They don't seem to be as complacent as they have been in the past and . . . I think someone in my inner circle is betraying me. I think they are reporting to someone higher up, who in return is using the chosen ones to do his bidding. There is no way they could have known about the ambush on the treasury otherwise."

"Do you suspect anyone in particular?"

"I think it can only be Verron at this point. He has always been Lucas's biggest advocate and that boy has been involved in stopping everything."

"Well, that is your problem to sort out," responded Killeand, "but I am getting the last of my people into place. If you want to secure your future, you need to make sure you do your part. Your attempts so far have failed miserably. Itan still has too much power."

"I will apply better efforts," reassured Finton. "It was unfortunate that the heist on the treasury failed, but it was never suspected to be an inside job, so I can try again."

Killeand shook his head. "It would be too soon and too risky. We have a better chance if we can stop the new alliance from being signed."

The men moved away from the tack room and continued to talk in hushed voices, and Lucas could no longer hear them. They left the stables shortly after and Lucas had no idea what to do with the information. He couldn't tell anyone. They would not believe the word of a chosen against that of a general, and if Finton discovered he knew, he would have him killed before the day was out.

"Lucas!" shouted Verron, and he pulled himself to attention, straightening his achy back. It had been a long night. The older chosen boys had been gathered at the training grounds and stood in line to receive instructions for the banquet that was being held that night in the Great Hall. All the lords, as well as their officers and soldiers who participated in the tournament, had been invited.

Both the sword fighting and jousting competition had been won by members of the king's army. Eli had lost his round after Lucas had left and the final had been fought between one of Lord Hammond's and the king's men. The jousting had been won by the only member of the king's guard who had entered. The rest of the king's guard had been busy all day setting up extra security around the castle, and Lucas had noticed how stressed Egon had looked when giving orders. It was therefore no surprise to him that the chosen ones had been called in to provide extra security during the banquet. They were dressed in their finest uniforms, bearing the king's colors, and had their swords at their sides.

All night, Lucas had pondered the conversation he had heard, and he had not slept at all. It was the second night without sleep, and he was exhausted. He also thought about the two men he had seen meet in secret and wondered if there was a connection.

"Lucas!" shouted Verron again.

"Yes, sir!" answered Lucas as he straightened up again. He could tell Verron was losing his patience.

"Do I have your full attention, or do I have to take you off duty tonight?"

"Sorry, sir. You have my attention, sir!" he answered quickly.

Verron stared at him for a moment more before continuing his instructions. "There will be six of you inside the Great Hall," he continued, keeping an eye on Lucas. "You will report to the king's guard and take your instructions from them. The rest of you will be stationed in the corridor outside the Great Hall and the entrance to the castle. You are our eyes and ears tonight. You see or hear anything suspicious, you report it to a senior member, preferably the king's guard."

"Are we expecting an attack on the king, sir?" asked Davis.

"Whenever there are people within these castle walls other than our own, we have to be mindful of the fact that the king is vulnerable," answered Verron. "So, if you hear your name," continued Verron, "you will go to the Great Hall straightaway. Zera! Davis! Archer! Warrick! Tanner! And Lucas!"

As soon as the chosen heard their names, they moved out of the line. Lucas was the last to leave and Verron stopped him briefly before letting him follow the others.

"You were specifically requested tonight," he said in a firm tone. "Otherwise, you would not be on my list. You look like you have not slept in days. If you are not fit for duty, you need to tell me now."

"I am fine, sir," said Lucas, trying to sound more alert than he was. He had so much on his mind, but knew he had to be there. He waited patiently for Verron to look him over more closely and, when he finally waved him on, Lucas ran to catch up with his friends and followed them towards the castle.

They walked past the storeroom, where people were busy taking baskets and crates out to bring to the kitchen. Lucas looked into the kitchen and saw one staff member from each of the lords going in. He knew them to be their tasters by the black vests they were wearing over their white kitchen clothes. The king always had someone taste his food before it was given to him, to make sure it wasn't spoiled and tasted as it should.

Zera and the boys continued up the steps and into the main corridor that led towards the Great Hall. Lucas had never been there and was fascinated by what he saw. The floor in the corridor was made of black stone and the ceiling was high and arched. Old weapons hung on the walls as decorative pieces and their footsteps sounded hollow as they echoed off the walls. Two double doors at the end of the corridor were guarded by soldiers, who opened them simultaneously to let them through. The Great Hall was even bigger than Lucas had imagined. The ceiling reached beyond the second floor of the castle and huge candlelit chandeliers hung down on chains over the long tables that had been placed inside for the banquet. They walked up to the raised platform where the king's table sat and where the king's guard stood grouped together. Lucas was still looking around when Egon finished talking with them and came over.

"You have all been told what we expect from you?" he asked when he stood before the chosen. "If you see or hear anything suspicious, you find a way to let one of the king's guard know. I don't want heroics. No jumping to conclusions and no one will draw their sword unless they have been instructed to. With all the extra security we have in place, we hope no one will try anything foolish, but tempers can flare, and arguments can get out of hand. The king desires a peaceful banquet, and we are going to make sure he gets it. I need Zera and Davis on either side of the king's table. Lucas and Warrick, you will position yourself on opposite sides of the guests' tables, with Tanner and Archer at the ends. The elite borns have a table at the back and will assist if anything goes down. Any questions?" He looked each one of them in the eye to make sure they understood and stopped at Lucas. "You look preoccupied. Is there anything you don't understand?"

"No, sir," answered Lucas. He had become increasingly uncomfortable with the burden of the knowledge he was carrying. Several times that day, he had contemplated telling his friends but had decided against it. Davis had his eyes on him now as well and, like Egon, he knew something was troubling him.

Egon stared down at him hard. "I have seen that look before," he said firmly. "So, what is it?"

Lucas hesitated a moment before answering. "It may be nothing sir, but . . . I bumped into someone last night, outside the tailor's room and—"

Egon held up his hand, stopping him for a moment. He then waved several of the king's guard over. When they stood ready to listen, he asked that Lucas continue.

"The man was in a hurry, staying in the shadows, like he didn't want to be seen. He jolted when he bumped into me but hurried on. I followed him." Lucas didn't tell them how, but they did not seem interested in that anyway. "He met an officer who had been waiting for him and they talked briefly, and a parcel was exchanged."

"A parcel?"

"I think so. It was small but wrapped up."

"And an officer handed him this, you say?"

"Yes. I could tell by the clothing, but he was not one of the king's."

"Colors?"

"Too dark, sir," answered Lucas apologetically. "I could barely see them."

"It's all right," said Egon. "Would you recognize the man you bumped into?"

"I don't know, maybe. I have been looking at everyone all day and trying to remember all the little details."

"Very well," said Egon. "If you see him here tonight, let one of us know so we can keep an extra eye on him. If you don't, we will talk more about this tomorrow."

Egon dismissed the king's guard and the rest of the chosen ones to their positions and was ready to leave, when Lucas cleared his throat. "Is there something else?" asked Egon.

Lucas wanted to tell him about the conversation he had heard, but he suddenly didn't know if he should, or if Egon was even the right person to tell. How would he be able to explain that he always seemed to be at the right place, at the right time, when something went down? It might also make him less believable in Egon's eyes. If the king was under any kind of threat tonight, they would have to prevent that first, before anyone would believe Finton or Killeand could be involved.

Egon gave him a penetrating stare and seemed to want to say something, but the doors opened, and the first guests started walking in.

Lucas took up his position, marveling at the clothing the lords and senior officers were wearing. None of it was fit for battle. It was all to impress, and to show their wealth. Even the king showed up in extravagant garments Lucas had not seen him wear before. For a moment, he forgot what he was there to do, until he felt eyes on him and saw

Egon watching him intently from his seat at the end of the king's table. He began to focus, and looked at every face, at those already seated at the tables and at each individual entering. He tried to go back in his memory to think of something that would help him recognize the officer he had bumped into. Not everyone in the hall wore their colors, and there were no designated tables for each group to sit at. Even if it had been one of Killeand's officers, there was no way to guarantee he could identify who they were.

Then, he considered another option. If the two men had met to plan something, they would most likely not sit together, but might seek each other out discreetly at some point.

Instead of desperately trying to remember a face, he started observing everyone's behavior. Soon, the food started to arrive from a side door of the Great Hall, and big platters were put on the tables for people to help themselves. At the king's table, where the lords were also sitting, everyone received individual plates of food. Each plate was carried in by a member of the kitchen staff in order of the people seated at the table. Lucas watched every person walking in, and it was then that he noticed it—someone else was doing the same thing. It was only a slight look over his shoulder, but he was the only one at his table, or any table to do so. Everyone else was busy eating, or deep in conversation. As soon as the man could see that only fruit was served on the plates, he immediately lost interest. Why? Why had he been interested in the food that had come out on the individual plates? No one else had cared. Lucas couldn't be sure if he was one of the men he had seen, but his mind was racing back to the moment he had walked past the kitchens and had seen the tasters go inside. Suddenly realizing what could have been in the parcel, Lucas took a step backwards and caught the attention of a king's guard.

CHAPTER 16

Egon had taken his seat at the king's table after the lords arrived in their flamboyant outfits. Their political talk was already boring him. The last twenty-four hours had been extremely tiring, and even more so after an informant had revealed to the king that he could be in danger. No other information was given, and they had nothing else to go on, but Egon had stepped up security, nonetheless. He had advised the king to cancel the banquet, but the king had insisted on keeping everything as normal as possible. If only he had heard Lucas's story sooner, then the king might have taken the threat more seriously. The story had certainly sounded plausible. He just hoped the boy would stay alert, since he looked as tired as Egon felt.

Egon took another sip from his drink when he noticed Lucas had taken a step backwards and one of his king's guard was walking over to him.

"Excuse me," Egon said to his table companions, but they paid him no mind and continued to eat and laugh and argue. One of the lords spilled a goblet of wine, and there was a hustle and bustle to clean it. Egon took the opportunity to rise from the table, and made his way over to Lucas, who was already talking to the king's guard.

"The boy thinks he recognized one of the men going into the kitchen," said the king's guard in a hushed voice.

"The kitchen?" asked Egon.

"Yes, sir," answered Lucas softly. "I believe him to be one of the tasters."

Egon turned to the king's guard as soon as he realized what this could mean and spoke hastily. "I need you to go to the kitchen. Take Lucas with you and secure the tasters," he said. "It needs to be done quickly, but discreetly. I don't want anyone to know that we are on to them. I will be there shortly."

"Everything all right?" asked Finton, when Egon returned to the table. Egon sighed when he sat back down and picked up his cup again. "Yes," he answered. "I don't know why Officer Verron put Lucas on duty. He cannot stand still on that leg for very long, so I had him taken out."

"It's a shame that he is injured," Lord Hammond commented. "He's a good fighter. I enjoyed watching him yesterday. If you ever decide to let him go, Itan, I will surely take him from you. Even with a bad leg, he will be of some use."

"I doubt that will ever happen, Lord Hammond," interjected Finton. "You saw how he was pulled from the tournament when it became obvious that his leg was ailing him. We sacrifice soldiers every day, except for that one."

The king remained quiet but gave Finton a disapproving glance.

"Well," said Lord Aron. "I would probably have made the same decision. Too much potential there to be wasted on entertainment."

As soon as the doors closed behind them, the king's guard increased his pace towards the kitchen. Lucas followed him through narrow passageways, up and down steps, until they came into a hallway over-looking the kitchen. They both leaned over the balustrade and looked down to see where the tasters were. The kitchen was in full swing, with people rushing around and orders being shouted out. Lucas spotted a table near one of the doors with individual plates of food. The plates had been lined up with their designated tasters behind them. It looked as if they had already done their job and were waiting until it was time to take the plates into the Hall.

"I only see three tasters," said the king's guard, alarmed. "There should be four, one for each of the three lords and the king. Where is the fourth?" Without waiting for a response, he backed away from the balustrade and bolted for a stairway leading into the back of the kitchen, leaving Lucas staring after him. Lucas watched him talk to the main cook and then called guards in, who started searching the kitchen and the adjacent rooms. Lucas's eyes went back to the plates that were now being guarded, and knew whose taster was missing. He also knew which plate had been poisoned, and it wasn't the king's. It was Hammond's.

Lucas made his way down the stairs and went to stand in a quiet corner, out of the way of kitchen staff, who continued to do their work as if nothing was happening. It wasn't long before the guards found Hammond's taster sick, and doubled over in the privy. Lucas saw the man's eyes to be full of fear as he was helped through the kitchen and escorted out by two soldiers holding him by the armpits.

Egon arrived in the kitchen a short time later, having made another excuse to leave the table. He ordered new plates to be sent out to the king's table. He then looked around and found Lucas standing in a corner, staring at seemingly nothing. He quickly walked up to him and grabbed him by the shoulder to shake him out of his trance. "Do you know who poisoned Hammond's plate?" he asked.

Lucas looked up at him and nodded. "Lord Aron's taster," he answered. "He is the one I saw last night."

"Where is he?" asked Egon, looking around frantically.

"He snuck out when they started to search the kitchen," answered Lucas. "He's up on the second floor. Guest quarters. He will be trying to jump out of a window into the moat to get away."

For a moment, Egon stared at Lucas, before letting go of his shoulder. He had no idea how he could know this, but there was no time to waste, so he told Lucas not to move and ran up the stairs with three soldiers. He found Aron's man, just like Lucas had described, trying to open a window in one of the guest quarters.

The man, surprised he had been found so quickly, put up little resistance when they grabbed him before he could make the jump.

"Take him to the prison cells," Egon instructed. "But don't let anyone see you."

He waited until the soldiers left before looking down to the water below and closing the window. When he made his way back to the kitchen, he was told that Hammond's man had died. They removed his body from the privy without the kitchen staff ever knowing what had taken place, and no one was the wiser.

Lucas had remained in the same corner Egon had found him in and avoided eye contact with the kitchen staff. He was sure that they found his presence there to be strange. When Egon finally made it back into the kitchen, he motioned for Lucas to follow him, and they made their way into the king's guard quarters through a hallway not far from the kitchen. Egon then walked him into a small empty room and shut the door. "I need to know how you knew exactly what we were looking for," he said sternly. "Your story is too convenient." He was pacing up and down and appeared stressed.

"What I told you is the truth," answered Lucas. "I bumped into Lord Aron's taster, followed him, saw he met someone in secret, who gave him a parcel. It was only tonight that it occurred to me that it could have been poison and then I recognized him in the kitchen."

"But you didn't see the other person?"

"No!"

"You didn't recognize anyone at the banquet?"

Lucas shook his head. He suspected that the man whose intent observations had alerted him to the food might be the one, but he could not be sure. They had Aron's man now and he was sure they would try and get that information out of him. "I may still be wrong about Aron's man," said Lucas.

Egon rubbed his hands through his hair. "I don't think you are. You don't try and jump out of a window if you are innocent. What I want to know is how did you know he was going to do that?"

Lucas stood silent.

When he did not answer, Egon shook his head in frustration. "Fine, don't tell me. I'm starting to get the feeling it is best you don't," he said and tried to collect himself. "I need you to stay here. Out of sight. I have no idea how the king is going to want to handle this, but I will come back for you."

Lucas watched Egon leave and heard him lock the door behind him with a key. He looked around the empty room and went to sit in a corner with his arms around his knees. It was several hours later before he heard the turning of the key again and Egon entered. "Come. Follow me," were the only words he spoke. The castle was quiet, and Lucas took it to be after midnight. He followed Egon into what he assumed was his private bedroom and watched him slide a wooden panel aside, revealing a secret passageway between the inner walls of the castle. The light of the torch Egon was holding cast long shadows on the walls as they moved along. They made several turns and passed an occasional door that could be locked from the passageway.

They finally stopped by a door and Egon knocked. He waited until he heard a voice on the other side answer, and then he opened it and stepped through. Lucas followed and saw that the door looked exactly like the wood paneling all around the room. With the door closed, one would probably not be able to see it at all. He immediately noticed the large four-poster bed resting on a woven carpet, and the tapestries covering all the walls. He looked up at the painted ceiling above, and an uneasy feeling overcame him when he realized he was somewhere not many people would ever go. His unease was confirmed when Egon stepped to the side and Lucas saw the king standing by the window. He immediately dropped his knee to the ground and bowed his head when the king turned around. Egon tapped him on the shoulder and motioned that he could rise.

The king eyed him gravely. "I hear you were instrumental in preventing a disaster tonight?" he asked. Lucas looked up at Egon, who urged him to respond.

"I just did what I was told to do, sire," he answered, bowing his head so he would not look the king in the eye.

"You did more than that," replied the king. "Do you realize what impact it would have had if Lord Hammond had died here tonight?"

Lucas slowly shook his head. He didn't know any of the politics between the lords and the king.

"Hmm, of course you don't," answered the king. "The reason why you are here is because nobody is to know what transpired this evening. Egon believes you can be trusted, but I think it carries more weight when I am the one telling you, that you are not to speak to anyone."

"What about Aron's man, sire?" He wasn't sure if he could ask the king questions, but he had blurted it out before realizing he may be crossing a line. He saw Egon stare at him, but the king did not seem to mind.

"He is still being heard," he answered sternly. "But that, however, is none of your concern. Do you understand that I need your complete cooperation in remaining silent?"

"Yes, sire," answered Lucas.

"Good," said the king, relaxing his shoulders and taking a step closer to Lucas. "Everyone at the banquet was told you were taken out because your leg ailed you, so that is how we are going to play this. You will be taken to the infirmary, and we will keep you there for as long as we think it is necessary for people to truly believe that was the reason you left your post at the banquet. Only when Egon tells you to get up will you do so. I don't care how you must play this, but you will not take orders or listen to anyone other than him. Do you understand?"

"Yes, sire," answered Lucas again, bowing when Egon gave him a sign that it was time to go. They left the king's private room the same way they had come in, through the secret passageway and the king's guard quarters. When he arrived at the infirmary, Lucas realized that there were other people who knew what was happening but were also sworn to secrecy and played their part. Garrad was already waiting and wasted no time in strapping his leg into a leather splint and immobilized him without asking any questions, and a guard walked in from time to time to make sure no one was talking to him and that he was left alone. He picked up, from the castle's gossip, that one of Aron's men had gotten drunk the night of the banquet and fallen out of a window. They had recovered his body from the moat the following morning. Another death was reported of one of Hammond's men. He apparently had suffered a heart attack and died in his sleep.

The fact that both men had been tasters during the banquet was not mentioned and was questioned by no one. Lucas did his best to keep himself occupied with what was happening outside, but he was bored out of his mind and had a hard time lying still when nothing was wrong with him. Only when Lord Killeand was suddenly heading to the infirmary to check on one of his wounded jousters, did he lay still and pretend to be asleep. Killeand walked up to his soldier and bent down to speak to him, but his eyes were scanning all the beds and he clearly had another reason to be there. He rose back up when he saw Lucas and slowly started to walk towards him. A nurse, who was coming from the back, carrying new blankets, stopped him before he got too far.

"Can I help, my lord?' she asked politely, but Lucas could sense a defensiveness in her tone.

Lord Killeand pointed to Lucas. "Can you tell me how long he has been here?"

The nurse looked over her shoulder. "The young chosen one?" she asked. "I believe he came here after the tournament."

"The night of the banquet?"

"Yes. I did not attend to patients that night, but he was here when I arrived the following morning. He has been here a few times recently."

"Leg issues?" asked Killeand. When the nurse nodded, he apologized for keeping her from her work and gave Lucas one last look before he left.

Egon stood on the wall with the king when the last lord rode out of the castle. He felt relieved to see the gates finally closing, and the drawbridges being pulled up. The king was staring hard into the distance, his mind seemingly troubled and somewhere else altogether.

"You look worried, sire," said Egon, when the sound of the last bridge being pulled up reached him.

"Yes," answered the king. "You know how important it is to have the alliance signed every five years."

"But they signed, did they not?"

"They did, but we would not have a new treaty if Hammond had been murdered here. Too many Hammonds are against the treaty as it is and would have had a good excuse not to sign again. Without their support, my days as king would have been numbered." The king paused a moment before continuing. "I don't believe Lord Aron was behind this, even if it was one of his men who was involved. He has always been my most loyal ally. Any idea who the second man Lucas saw belonged to?"

"There was someone at the banquet who Lucas suspected," started Egon. "He told me this morning when I released him from the infirmary. He did not want to point him out at the time, since he could not be certain, but if he was involved—he was Killeand's."

The king nodded. "That does not surprise me. I have long suspected I can no longer trust Killeand. The boy did good. I trust he has not said anything to anyone?"

"No, he has not."

The king sighed, and Egon looked out over the road that wound away from the castle. The dust was settling over it, as the last soldier had disappeared into the forest.

"Times are changing, Egon," he said. "And I think I may need to make some changes myself." He turned around, forced a stiff smile, and tapped Egon affectionately on the shoulder before heading down the stairs.

CHAPTER 17

The echo of loud steps came thundering up the stairs to the dormitory. Lucas, who had been sleeping, jolted up just as the door slammed open and Verron, accompanied by another officer, entered in a hurry.

"Up! Up, up!" they shouted as they made their way in, banging poles against beds to wake sleepy occupants. Judging by the amount of moonlight that was still shining through the rafters, Lucas determined it couldn't be more than two hours after midnight. His first thought was that they were being punished, but he could not think of anything that had gone wrong in the two weeks since the lords left. No horns were being blown from the walls, so no emergency either. When all the chosen had swung their legs over the edge of their beds and were rubbing their eyes and yawning, Verron stopped in the middle of the room. "I need everyone dressed and in the king's stables in ten minutes to get horses ready," he shouted. "The king is embarking on a hunt, and he wants to depart before daylight."

Lucas watched as he paused for a moment, clearly to see if any of the boys was going to complain, but they were all too sleepy to even consider objecting, and Verron left the room, looking satisfied that his order was going to be followed. Rubbing sleep from their eyes, the chosen got dressed quickly and were piling down the stairs towards the stables. Soldiers were busy loading wagons in the bailey with supplies for a hunt, which could sometimes last several days.

"This is crazy," muttered Warrick, when they were filling the horses' feeders with fresh hay. "Why were we not notified about this last night?"

"Doesn't look like anyone else knew about it either, judging by the way they are all rushing around outside," said Zera. "Looks disorganized to me."

"Well, then let's hope they'll allow us all to go back to bed when the hunting party has departed."

"Good luck with that," said Davis. "You know that never happens."

"I can still dream about it, can't I? No harm in wishful thinking!"

After feeding and watering all the horses, they groomed them and were saddling them up when Officer Verron entered. "Lucas, Zera, Davis, Warrick!" he called out.

"Yes, sir?" all four answered in unison.

"It's your lucky day," shouted Verron. "There has been a last-minute request. You four are to accompany them, so prepare your own gear and horses as well."

"We are to ride with the king, sir?" asked Warrick, stepping out of a stall with an expression of wonder on his face.

"Yes, Warrick, those are the orders I was just given," said Verron, who appeared just as surprised. No chosen ever had, to Lucas's knowledge, and he was overjoyed with the new development.

Their own horses were the last ones to be led out of the stables, and they quickly joined the procession at the rear as they were directed to do. Egon briefly turned in his saddle and caught Lucas's eye when he mounted up. It was the first time he had acknowledged him since his release from the infirmary. Even the king had avoided looking at him and did so yet again when he walked past him on his way to the front. No word had been spoken about what nearly happened at the banquet, and there was no indication to Lucas that Finton, Verron or any of the officers were aware of the events. Lucas had watched himself around Finton for a while, but Finton seemed to treat him with no more animosity than he always had.

Riding with the king turned out to be not so different than the regular patrols. They were still the ones tending to all the horses and doing chores when camped, even though the king had brought his own personal staff with him. Unsure of the role they were supposed to fulfill and for what purpose the king had requested them, they were treated apprehensively by most of the staff. The boys and Zera stayed out of the way and kept to themselves as much as possible but were content when they sat by a fire late at night and enjoyed their share of the hunted meat, while the king and the rest of his senior staff slept in tents close by.

"I still think the best part of all this," said Davis, while he chewed on the bone he was holding, "is seeing Eli's shocked face when he came out of the stables and was told he was not invited. Priceless, to see him turn his horse around and go back."

"Because of Lucas, I'm sure," said Zera. "Eli and Lucas don't go together. The king must have realized that some time ago."

"Probably, and that's all right with me," said Davis.

"For me, the best thing is the food," said Warrick. "When was the last time we ate venison?"

"Enjoy it—it may be the only time we get to go out with the king like this," said Zera, who turned to look at Lucas. "What do you think? You've been quiet."

Lucas was poking the fire with a stick, making sparks come off the logs and stepping on them with his foot when they jumped too far out of the pit. "I don't think this will be the last time," he finally said. "I believe the king is finally starting to see us for what we are. He's realizing we're much stronger and more valuable to him if he loosens the reins on us."

All three of his friends looked at him.

"You think?" asked Davis.

He nodded, before throwing the stick into the fire and moving away to go and lie down. It'd been a long day, so he folded his arms behind his head and closed his eyes. The sounds of his friends talking gave him a bit of peace, and he slowly felt himself drift into sleep.

Lucas was right that it would not be the last time they were told to ride out with the king, and every time they did so Eli was left behind and Carleton led the elite borns.

The king had just mounted his horse when Lucas watched Finton walk towards the king with big purposeful strides. Lucas, at the back of the line of riders, was far enough away that they would assume he could not hear them, and at this moment, he truly appreciated his ability to listen.

It was Finton who spoke first, and he did not bother with formalities or greetings of any sort. "You are yet again bringing the chosen along and leaving Eli behind," he said flatly.

"I am indeed," answered the king.

"Why bring them, over your most loyal soldiers? What has changed, that has made you feel them to be more important? To be given . . . priority?"

"What has changed is that I've come to realize who my most loyal subjects are."

"Are you implying that Eli is not loyal?" asked Finton.

The king barely looked at him when he answered. "You assume that I should automatically believe your son is loyal to me, because he is an elite born. For far too long, I did just that, but actions speak louder than words. Lucas has proven himself to be loyal on several occasions and, you must agree, that I cannot take both him and your son along. That is why Eli is staying behind."

Lucas dropped his head when he saw Finton turn towards him to give him an evil stare. He wished he could go up to the king, to ask if he would be allowed to stay behind. He knew that the sudden change in status of the chosen ones would backfire on them sooner or later, and the responsibility of that prospect weighed heavily on his shoulders. He had stayed out of trouble as much as possible, but he was growing and changing and, along with him, the rest of the chosen ones were as well. They followed his lead and started working harder when he did. To make matters even more complicated, the entire group had now picked up on his different gifts through the connection they shared. He finally told them about the black stone at the monastery, when they were getting ready for bed one night.

"So, it chose you?" asked Tanner when he was rolling out his blanket. "And gave you the seeing mind and the control over horses?"

"I guess so, and yes, it did," answered Lucas. In the past, he had only been able to connect with a horse while riding, or by standing near it, as he had in the stable with the black horse, but lately he had discovered he could control multiple horses if he was near them. On some evenings, the boys from the other stables would come over and they would lock the main stable doors, sit on the hay bales and watch him. He would open all the stall doors and have the horses step out simultaneously, turn and walk back in. The boys laughed and the younger ones would request that he do it again, their faces glowing with wonder. It was a welcome distraction in the midst of their hard-working lives.

"I was young," Lucas continued, putting his boots under his bed. "As young as you all were when you were brought to the castle gates."

"Is that why you are different?" asked Ando. "Because it was the stone that chose you to be a chosen one, and not the people?"

Lucas looked at Ando, who was standing in the middle of the aisle, and so did several of the other boys. Ando had a way of making others think with the questions he asked. He was the youngest, smallest in stature, affectionate and with freckles on his face. He was the one they all mothered over, even though he was tough as nails in a fight.

Before Lucas could answer, Davis came over and ushered Ando towards his bed. "You know what we are, Ando," he said somewhat sternly. "We are born this way. We were not chosen by people."

After leaving Ando on his bed, Davis walked back to his own and Lucas caught his stare. There were things Davis was not willing to discuss, and he had told Lucas, some time ago, that they should let things unfold as they were meant to happen. "You are not the only one," he had said, "that feels the change, and you are not the only one who feels different from the other boys. Even my bond with Zera has changed. I used to imagine we were attached by an imaginary rope, but that rope unraveled when you came and tied us both to you. I don't have the answers yet and neither do you."

With the third summer passing and Lucas turning fifteen, reports of hunters crossing the river border in large numbers made their way to the king. Patrols were always sent out to deter any crossings, but this time there seemed to be more reports and from a diverse range of areas. When a messenger arrived from Lord Aron claiming that hunters were targeting his area for game, that several civilian deaths had occurred at farms, and that Aron did not have enough men to stop it, the king made a drastic decision. He mobilized his entire army, including any chosen ones aged twelve and over. They set up a large base camp close to Lord Aron's castle, from which they ran daily patrols. Day in and day out, and even at night, troops were sent out in different directions. Some stayed away for several days at a time to cover farther afield.

Lucas was sent out with different troops every time, as were the rest of the chosen ones. They were in the saddle for hours, finding plenty of evidence of animals being killed by hunters or storage rooms raided, but no one ever got any sightings of them. They were well camouflaged to hide within the forest, and they were long gone before any soldier could get close. After a week of no sightings, Lucas was sent with Officer Verron's troop to go farther south. Zera was riding with him, and he was happy to finally have someone he could talk to along the way. The scenery changed as they moved farther south. More brush covered the hills around them, making it hard to see any-thing, and they were all exhausted when Verron finally decided to make camp at the end of a long day.

When they were finished settling in, Zera took her bow from her saddle. "I'm going to ask Verron if I can go hunting," she said. "It would be nice to eat some meat tonight."

"Do you think you'll be able to find any game? Here?" asked Lucas. He was doubtful it was the right area for hunting. They had made camp on the banks of a small stream, with a high hill on the other side, and he could barely make out the ridge, as it was covered with dense vegetation.

"There may be no deer," answered Zera, "but there should be plenty of rabbits hiding under that brush."

Lucas stood up and watched Zera walk over to Verron. It couldn't be long until sundown, and he wondered how she was going to spot even the smallest animal in the dense foliage. But he was pleased that Zera had found something she was passionate about. As chosen ones, they had been given more freedom recently, and Zera had seized every opportunity to go hunting whenever she got the chance. She had perfected her aim and skill, but more importantly to Lucas, she was happy. Lucas looked at the trees above him. The evening sun was shining on the leaves, making them like little stars shimmering in the forest. It was quiet, but then, they had already made enough noise making camp to scare any birds away. The muscles in his body were tense, a sensation he had felt frequently lately, riding so close to the river border. He tried to ignore it.

"Don't go too far, and take Lucas with you," he heard Verron tell Zera.

"I won't," answered Zera and walked towards Lucas. "Come on," she said. "Verron wants you to come with me."

"I'll be there to help keep you safe," Lucas replied, "but I'm no hunter."

"Doesn't matter. You can be my eyes and ears."

"Unless the extra noise I make scares everything off." Lucas laughed, reluctantly grabbing his sword and following Zera to the stream. They stopped and drank some of the cool refreshing water before wading across. The vegetation was even denser than it had appeared from the other side, and Lucas was even more certain they were going to be wasting their time. For some reason, he couldn't just relax and enjoy the time wandering around with his friend, regardless of whether they caught sight of a rabbit or not. Something nagged at him. "I know you are a good shot," he said, "but I think this is asking too much. Why not wait until dusk and see if any deer come out to the lower fields we passed earlier?"

"Maybe it will be less dense on the other side of this hill," said Zera. They were already climbing up and she was hurrying ahead. There was no stopping her. "If it isn't, we'll go back."

When they were halfway up the hill, Lucas looked back down and felt a strange energy take over his body, one that he had felt before when things were about to go very wrong. His heart rate increased, causing him to feel every muscle in his body, and his senses heightened. He saw and heard the slightest movement around him and felt time had slowed down. He could still see the camp, but they were too far away to hear, and no one was watching them. The soil underneath their feet was soft now and was slowing their progress. No birds were around them, no magpie in the tree, and yet Lucas felt something was different. Before they made it to the top, he grabbed Zera by the arm and stopped her.

"What is it? A rabbit? A badger?" Zera asked and put an arrow on her bow to be ready.

Lucas put a finger to his mouth and Zera froze. "I don't see anything," she whispered, but Lucas motioned to her that they were surrounded and needed to head back down the hill, quickly. Zera nodded and started backing up, but they were not going fast enough. In one swift motion, Lucas pushed Zera to the side when an axe flew through the air, barely missing both of them and landing in the tree behind him. The hunter who had thrown it rose from where he had been hiding underneath the vegetation and three more hunters followed suit. Within moments, they were charging towards Lucas and Zera.

"Get to camp," shouted Lucas, pulling his sword from its scabbard.

Zera shook her head, aiming her bow and letting the arrow loose, taking out one of the hunters close to Lucas. She took a second arrow and was ready to take out another, when they saw more hunters heading down the hillside towards the camp. She let the arrow fly, but only grazed her next victim on the side of his neck, which did not even slow him down.

"There are too many," Lucas shouted. "You have to warn them!"

Verron was taking his bedroll off his saddle when he heard shouting behind him. He turned to see where it was coming from and saw Zera half sliding, half running down the hill, shouting something he could make no sense of. She kept waving towards her right, and Verron followed the direction.

"Shield!" he shouted, when he saw what Zera was trying to warn him about. A line of soldiers immediately formed, holding shields out in front of them. A line of archers directly behind them began shooting off arrows, aiming towards the hunters who were streaming over and down the hillside.

Zera made it across the stream and behind the defense line and Verron grabbed her by the arm. "Where is Lucas?" he shouted.

"Up on the hill," said Zera out of breath. "He engaged them, to slow them down, so that I could warn you."

"How many?"

"Hard to tell, sir. They came out of nowhere and kept coming."

Knowing there was not much he could do for the moment, Verron continued giving orders to his men. The hunters stayed on the other side of the stream and slowly started backing up.

"They want us to fight them on their grounds, sir," one of his junior officers commented.

"I know, but I need you to stay here and keep defending," said Verron, calling for three soldiers to get on their horses.

"Where are you going, sir?" asked the officer, but Verron did not reply. He was already on his horse and jumping the creek to charge up the hill.

He could hear the clattering of metal upon metal up ahead, which meant Lucas was still in the fight and he was not yet lost, but the horses were straining themselves on the steep hill. When they got halfway, the sound suddenly stopped, and he feared the worst.

Lucas had no time to worry over whether Zera was making it down the hill all right. The first hunters were on him before he could even contemplate what was happening. They were nothing like the soldiers or warrior monks he had fought before. They reminded him of his father and of Bernt, of men who could lift logs and toss them over their shoulders as if it was nothing. The hunters' rugged appearance made them look wild and fearless, and they fought with a variety of weapons. Some had swords, but others had axes, spears and knives.

He could barely see where they were coming from and he had to use all his senses to stay alive in this fight, but he was calm, fast and precise in his defense. He blocked out any thoughts or feelings that would hinder him and fought as he had been taught to from a young age. He refused to look at the carnage he was creating around him, but the hunters did, and they looked shocked and enraged. Lucas could only assume that their rage came from the fact that they were not able to take him down.

He had no idea how long the fight lasted, or why it suddenly stopped, but the last hunters in front of him were backing away. Lucas watched them disappear over the ridge and then noticed the biggest one of them, a man with dark curly hair and a full beard that hid any facial expression he might have, staring down at him. From everywhere, hunters were slowly backing up the hill and disappearing over the ridge, until only their leader still stood at the top. Lucas lowered his sword and they stared at each other for some time. The hunters' leader then slowly raised his hand and gave a nod, before disappearing over the ridge himself.

Lucas could hear the labored breath of horses coming up the hill behind him, but he kept staring at the spot where the leader had stood. He had felt a familiarity and a strong urge to follow him and probably would have, if Verron had not jumped off his horse and grabbed him by the shoulders.

"Are you injured?" Verron asked and gently shook him when Lucas did not reply. Verron looked at the dead hunters all around him and started checking Lucas for any injuries. There was blood all over him, splattered on his torso and down his arms and legs, covering his boots, but it wasn't his own. "Are you hurt?" he asked again. This time Lucas shook his head. "No, I am not," he answered softly, in a trancelike state. "They chose to let me live."

"What do you mean?"

"They chose to let me live," Lucas said again, and then turned to walk back down the hill.

As he kneeled by the creek to clean up, Lucas could feel the eyes of the other men, watching him. He took off his clothes and laid them out over the flat boulders near the water's edge. The water was cold, and he tried to ignore the slight shiver he felt, as he worked to wash the blood from his clothes. Zera walked over to him and put her hand on his bare shoulder for a moment, before heading out to help set up defenses for the night. Lucas welcomed the gesture, though he still felt a residual numbness, an inability to really feel much of anything. They had a few wounded who needed to be cared for, but could not ride, so a messenger was sent back to the main camp to report on what had happened and request for aid.

Lucas's mind remained occupied, even as he sat warming himself by the fire, staring into its innermost flames, where the coals burned hot and red. He couldn't bring himself to say anything when, one by one, the soldiers came over that evening, patting him on the back and congratulating him on a fight well fought. The hunters' bodies had been brought down and laid out for burial the next day. They all knew, if it had not been for Lucas and Zera, the outcome of the evening would have been different, and that many lives would have been lost. Some of those soldiers had been with Lucas when he stopped the attacks on the treasury years before, and those tales were told again that night, the fire dancing in the eyes of the storytellers.

When he couldn't take any more of it, Lucas took himself off and went to lie some distance from the fires. He saw Zera move to follow him, but she was stopped by Verron. "Leave him," he heard Verron say. "I think he needs time alone."

The image of the hunter's leader at the top of the ridge would not leave Lucas's mind and, when he finally fell asleep, he began to dream. In his dream, he was stopping his horse in front of the river that had plagued him in nightmares as a young boy—in which he had feared to drown and had been watched by five dark figures on horseback from the forest's edge on the other side. He looked across to the dark forest now but saw no one. He could hear his name being called through the wind, the voice beckoning him to make the crossing. Lucas stared at the raging river, until he controlled it, and the water calmed down enough for his horse to wade through. The calling of his name was louder and clearer now, and he pushed his horse to walk past the first trees.

He rode until he came to a clearing and stopped in the middle of it. The sun was warming his skin and it was a welcome feeling, after the cold, dark forest. His horse snorted and pawed its hoof restlessly over the ground while Lucas waited. The first hunter, who stepped into the clearing and stood before Lucas, was their leader. After him, other hunters emerged from the tree line, until they had formed a complete circle. They all stood and stared at him, waiting for something. Lucas had his hand on the hilt of his sword and slowly pulled it out . . .

Lucas woke to the rustling of the leaves in the wind above him. The fires were down to embers, and everyone was asleep around him. He lay still and tried to ignore the urge to get up but couldn't. He knew that what he was about to do could get him into a lot of trouble, but he had to see for himself. He looked for Zera and spotted her, fast asleep, not far away. Lucas pulled the blanket off himself and slowly made his way to the horses. He managed to slip past the two soldiers posted nearby, until he mounted his horse and the other horses all moved out of his way. Noticing the movements the animals were making, the soldiers called out and asked where he was going, but Lucas took off at a full canter before they could stop him. He made the rest of the horses rear up, tossing their heads, and they refused to let anyone mount them.

He rode hard and let his horse find the way towards the river. The sun was just rising when he heard the rushing of the water and broke clear from the tree line. Lucas walked his horse along the river's edge until he found what he thought might be a passable spot. He let his horse step into the water and stopped to look across to the other side. The same dark forest he had seen in his dream. He still felt the strong desire to go there, but why?

He hesitated and looked back to where he had come from. He knew that Verron was not far behind him, with soldiers along to bring him back. Again, he looked across the river and fought the urge to spur his horse forward. He should not have left, but it was too late to turn around now and pretend it had not happened. He stared at the water rushing around his horse's hooves and thought for a moment that the intensity of the current had diminished, that it would be possible for him to cross, but then something else caught his abrupt attention. He was not alone. He was being watched. Instinctively, Lucas jerked on his horse's reins to pull him back, when he felt something hit the side of his neck. He pulled the dart out and held it in his hands, before dropping it in the water. The world around him began to swirl and dim, until it went black.

Dastan lowered the dart pipe and watched as Lucas slumped forward on his horse on the other side of the river. He took a deep breath and briefly glanced over to the large hunter standing next to him.

"Why did you not let him come?" asked Orson.

"Because it is not the right time," answered Dastan. "He is not ready."

Orson shook his head in disagreement. "It is becoming too dangerous to have him stay there," he said. "If you tell me that The Dark Order almost had him twice already, then they will not wait long before they will try again. Him showing up to the river must be a sign, and he needs to be informed."

Dastan did not disagree, but he still felt it was too soon to bring the boy over. They needed more time, but him running into Orson the day before was not something any of them had foreseen, and now he had gotten himself into trouble by coming to the river. Why? What had made him come?

Dastan watched as soldiers appeared by the river just when Lucas started to slip from his horse. The leading officer reached him just in time and dragged him onto the shore. Dastan backed up into the woods and walked to his horse. He put the dart pipe in his saddlebag and again looked towards the water.

"You are going back across," said Orson, who had followed him.

Dastan looked at him and nodded. "Yes," he answered. "For I believe you are right. It is time he learns who he is."

ACKNOWLEDGMENTS

When you read this page, it means that this story made it to print, and all the blood, sweat, and tears that went into it were well worth it. Of course, I am only joking. There were no actual tears, or any sweat or blood. However, what did transpire was the outpouring of support I received from many people around me while writing book one of *The King's Chosen* series, for which I am incredibly grateful. I am sure you know who you are, but a few of those I want to acknowledge. First, I would like to thank my husband, James, for always being there and bearing with me. I know he had hoped that after I wrote a few hundred pages, he would see the end of me staying up throughout the night, but little did he know that *Blood Ties* was only the beginning. Second, my children, Maxwell, Matthew, and Madison, showed patience and understanding—sounding out the word *mom* did not always receive an immediate response when I had other words occupying my mind. Next, I want to thank my editor Ava Justine for all the encouraging words, guidance, and patience that kept me focused and made this journey fun. And Carrie-Sue Kay, whose artistic talent captured my vision of the map and brought the king's shield to life on the cover of this book.

ABOUT THE AUTHOR

Blood Ties is Leonie Waithman's debut novel. She lives in Texas with her husband and three children. When not writing, she volunteers her time to archeology and the education of students about the Texas Revolution of 1836.